HOPE
ON
HATTERASK

MICHAEL

GRAYHAWK

PARSONS

In Memory of
Ralph H. Steele, PhD
East Carolina University

For Matthew and Allison

FOREWORD

Most of us would probably agree that our lives today are infinitely easier than that of our early nineteenth century ancestors. In contrast to their time almost all of us are blessed to have the essentials of life abundantly available. We are also fortunate to enjoy basic human rights in an imperfect but functional system that provides among other things protection and justice. And most of us are blessed with the love and security of family, friends, and those whom we may identify with ethnically and/or culturally. So even with the inequities that exist in a flawed society... we still have it pretty good.

But what if we lived in conditions that were dramatically worse? That severely tested our will to survive and robbed us of virtually everything but hope. Could we survive? Would we even *want* to survive? This was the case for many of our own ancestors. Surely there are life lessons hidden within the stories of each of our ancestors that could be relevant in our lives today. Perhaps some elements of these will emerge as you read this story of two of my respected ancestors and their loyal and beloved friend.

☙ ☙ ☙

Imagine the despair of a young Scotch Irish boy, a hated minority in Northern Ireland, who is essentially without family; has virtually nothing but the clothes on his back; and who faces the constant threat of harm and sustained hunger each day. Or ponder the profound pain and suffering of a proud West African warrior who is abducted, transported to a strange land,

and enslaved in a life of dehumanizing brutality and terror. Or consider the loss and degradation in a young Native American girl, who as part of a demonized culture, cannot safely venture outside the immediate borders of her village. A village located on a continent which only two centuries before her birth was occupied exclusively by her own indigenous people.

Imagine the incredible strength and courage necessary for any one of these three to survive within such hostile environments. And even though each of their stories is uniquely their own, it is reasonable to assume that they also represent many others whose similar stories may never be told. In a broader perspective they also represent the three groups of people that played the most significant role in American history since the first recorded contact between indigenous North Americans and English speaking Europeans. They are representatives of the European, African, and Native American Diasporas.

In this book you will meet a diverse mix of colorful characters and each are important in the totality of the story. But the focus is on the three primary characters identified in the previous paragraph. Their lives essentially parallel each other in time and then intersect in a most profound way. Each was born on a different continent and spent their childhood and at least a part of their teen years on that continent. Emerging from different backgrounds they also differ in their individual expression of spirituality. But they do share a common belief as regards the recognition of a supreme being.

All three individuals generally represent their respective groups of origin for the period in which they lived. Two of the three are the same age being born in 1815 and one is a few years older. By virtually any historical standard they lived during a time of social ignorance which was replete with racial, ethnic, religious and socioeconomic bias. The prejudice they encountered was often the basis for acts of suppression, abuse and violence. Many times these were carried out by the most powerful members of the dominant culture in which they lived. And yet there *were* exceptions, even amongst the dominant, who courageously offered a helping hand along the way.

In youth, their cultural value systems were the product of trial and error over many past generations and instilled in them by elders within their own families and communities. These elders lived as models of what they espoused to be right. And our three main characters, the elders' respective descendents, were watching, listening and learning as they experienced first hand what right, wrong, and personal responsibility looked and sounded like. They incorporated these ethics into their own everyday lives as they grew to understand the concomitant benefits for both their community and for themselves.

Consequently, the critical life altering decisions that each would make came from a place within themselves that was capable of ultimately looking beyond superficial differences. Their *initial* mutual respect and empathy may have been due in part to their recognition of each other's deprivation and suffering at the hands of oppression. But their cohesion was solidified by the unselfish actions of yet another elder, a model of responsibility and wisdom within his own culture. Their relationship existed in contrast to a world where mainstream thinking was filled with suspicion, intolerance and exclusion to anything different than one's own perception of self and immediate community. In that regard these three have indeed become models for us all.

I believe that you will connect in some way with one or perhaps all of the three main characters in the story. And maybe in doing so, this may chronicle in some way your own ancestors' story. Surely some of *them* were challenged in many of the same ways as those in my story. And like my own, some of them obviously persevered and survived. And they no doubt left their own trail of wisdom for you to discover and to live by. If so, I hope that you will ponder the following questions: Do we live in a time of enlightenment, tolerance, and advanced humanitarianism as compared to when they lived? How would we have reacted had we been in their situation then? Or perhaps more importantly, how would we react if faced with similar challenges today?

Since early adulthood I fantasized that I would one day write this story as a complete factual history. So I took a year off from work and quickly achieved first name status with the staff of my local bookstore, library, and with several museum curators. And that effort did empower me with a great deal more historical and cultural background information on the three main characters than I had previously acquired. But in the final analysis it was the time spent conducting formal interviews and participating in informal discussions with family elders and cohorts that provided most of the basis for the story. And of course, adhering to my original goal, I engaged in the tedium and due diligence of perusing census records, courthouse documents, old newspapers, etc. It was an attempt to gather as much information as possible on all three main characters, but in particular on the lives of the two that I am personally related to. And certainly the experience was productive and often even personally gratifying for me. But it fell way short of providing enough substantiated data to write a complete factual accounting of even just *their* lives.......let alone that of the character that I share no blood relationship with. However, on the positive side, the information gathered from different sources did provide support to the validity of several critical elements of the story. And although not by design, the process also uncovered details that in the end I believe will significantly enrich perspective into the minds and souls of these three people.

Still, much of this story had to be fictionalized in order for it to be told in its entirety. There was simply too much information missing during significant periods of time. I have, however, made reasonable effort to describe the basic aspects of life in their time and place as accurately as possible. And although the dialogue is contrived, it falls well within the range of possibilities given what I know to be true. The event which culminates in the intersection of the lives of the three main characters is fundamentally true but there is obvious dramatization of the specific actions. Some other events and relationships are factual as well but I dare not speak of them here for fear of interrupting too much of the context and flow necessary to the essence of the story itself.

Perhaps you will find the story of the early lives of my maternal great, great grandparents, Elijah Sermons and Eliza Harva Hudson Sermons, and of their friend, whom I call Embato Ngawai, entertaining, informative, and perhaps even a source of inspiration. I hope that in particular you will gain new insight into the three cultures from *their* perspective. I will humbly ask your indulgence as a reader in doing so however. In order to provide the depth and authenticity of their character it was necessary to provide some of the key elements that defined their respective cultures. It was the only way that *they* could truly speak to you.....from *their* cultural point of view. I believe your patience will be rewarded and particularly so in Part III. It is in this detailed and admittedly sometimes tedious discussion that I reveal for the first time a previously unidentified mechanism of cultural preservation utilized by some Eastern Native Americans. My own maternal grandfather still utilized this subtle method as late as the decade of the seventies in the twentieth century.

I believe a brief comment on Native linguistics is necessary. Most of the words quoted from Native language in this work come from the Algonquin Coastal dialect. This was used by many of Native descent in Eastern North Carolina even though they themselves saw their identity as both Skura:re (Tuscarora) and Algonquin Coastal Natives.

Each reader will comprehend the meaning of this story through his/her own prism of life's experience. But as for me, it is above all else a testimonial to the value of the incredible power of hope. May you and those you care for never lose hope.

Michael GrayHawk Parsons

CONTENTS

PART I

THE SCOTCH IRISH

ELIJAH

THE SCOTCH IRISH HYBRID

"The Scots-Irish had a system of religious faith and worship which has ever borne an inflexible front to illusion and mendacity, and has preferred rather to be ground to powder like flint than to bend before violence or melt under enervating temptation".
J.A. Froude, 19th century historian

It seems that whenever a specific population is oppressed and impoverished they will eventually either revolt against their oppressors or seek a better life elsewhere. The timing of the latter is most often dictated by both opportunity and the pathway of least resistance. The eventual migration to Northern Ireland of a significant number of those residing in the Lowlands of Scotland during the seventeenth and eighteenth centuries is a good example of this.

For centuries the Scotch Lowlanders were oppressed and abused by the Crown of England and had suffered a higher frequency of violent acts at the hands of English tyranny than did their northern brethren in the Scottish Highlands. This was primarily a consequence of proximity and accessibility as the Lowlands, the southern one third of Scotland's land mass, shared a common border with England. In addition to religious and economic oppression from the English there were other conditions which contributed to the subsequent exodus of many of the Lowland Scots. Among those were the long standing repressive social class system but also a climate and soil that were less than ideal for agriculture, and the perception of opportunity elsewhere.

Scotland's population had historically operated in a feudal system that was very clannish and tribal in nature. It was essentially an established pecking order of several well defined levels whose membership was established primarily through birthright. The Lords, also the landowners, occupied the top of the power and wealth pyramid. Next in line were the Lairds or Gentry who were somewhat akin to a middle class. The remaining levels were in descending order of prominence; tenants, sub-tenants and their agricultural workers.

Many of the Scots at the lower end of the scale accepted their lot in life from one generation to the next largely because it had simply been that way for so long. However, there were occasional exceptions of individuals who elevated their status either through marriage or a rare meritorious appointment. But the vast majority of the population suffered from the absence of any control over positive change in their lives. So why then did it take so long for those with seemingly so little to lose, to finally act? And what was the impetus for that action?

Even though the living conditions for most Lowland Scots were of abject poverty, the feudal system provided those on the lower levels with a misguided sense of security. They felt it was the responsibility of the Lords and Chieftains to protect and feed them. Given this kind of thinking perhaps it was the element of only an exceptional period of *enduring* hunger that had fertilized the seeds of change for the Lowland Scots. The ultimate motivation however came from an unlikely source, the English. They offered an opportunity that held the hope of improved living conditions for even the poorest of the Lowland Scots, and in a land that lay just a few miles across the water from where many of them already lived.

When the English moved to colonize Ireland they benefitted greatly from a competent agricultural work force of Scottish Lowlanders who were willing to go. Whatever lay in wait for them in the English planta-tion system of Northern Ireland could hardly be worse than the bare existence they had known in the Scottish Lowlands. Thus there was little to lose for most and the hope of a better life to be gained. Additionally the English provided incentives for common workers to move up to the level of sub-tenants and for sub-tenants to move up to tenants and so on. In some cases this was a guarantee but conditioned of course upon making the physical relocation.

Those Lowland Scots who chose to relocate to Northern Ireland were promised that they would be allowed to continue practicing their Presbyterian denomination of Protestant Christianity. They believed in this promise even though there was constant propagandizing from the English of the virtues of the monarchy's established Anglican Church. Many were unable to foresee, however, the unique troubles coming their way simply by virtue of being a religious minority in Ireland. They would be caught in the power struggle between the indigenous Irish Catholics and the transplanted plantation Lords of the Anglican Church of England. The Lowland Scots had traded their only element of status, their position as a member of the Presbyterian majority in Scotland, for the potential of better living conditions in a country that was almost uniformly Catholic.

With the exception of their commonality in religious identity the transi-tion from Lowland Scot to Scotch Irish had begun. Presbyterianism was the primary remaining connection to Scotland that would survive after their succeeding generations would become more and more Irish and less and less Scottish Lowlander. After only a few generations in Belfast-Northern Ireland they had become the truly distinctive hybrid culture known as the Scotch Irish or as some prefer Scots Irish. They would never again be simply Scotch. But could they ever become truly Irish?

In the view of the indigenous Irish one could be Irish only if one were Catholic. So the Scotch Irish of Belfast quickly became a persecuted religious and cultural minority......again! They were ridiculed, scorned and sometimes the objects of violence. Their situation was worsened as the English fanned the flames of anger and resentment among the Irish Catholic majority with their repeated acts of aggression against them. Forcing the indigenous Irish into political and religious capitulation was indicative of the arrogance in the Crown's colonial mindset.

This just made matters worse for the Presbyterian Scotch Irish. In this case the old adage of "the enemy of my enemy is my friend" did not seem to apply. Although the Scotch Irish and the Irish Catholics both detested the English, they still for the most part could not seem to find common ground with each other. The indigenous Irish Catholic population saw the Scotch Irish immigrants as puppets of the English and as unwanted intruders. And even after a century of generations the Irish Catholic attitude toward the Scotch Irish Presbyterians remained largely unchanged.

Although living conditions had improved slightly for some of the new Scotch Irish in Belfast it had not reached a level of comfort adequate to override the pain of religious bigotry and persecution. Their roots had not taken hold to the extent necessary to engender a sense of national pride and loyalty to their new homeland. They were clearly no longer Scotch but once again neither were they Irish. They were still fighting both the oppression of the English and the increasing resentment of the Irish Catholics. And as a general rule they were still hungry and impoverished and marginalized from mainstream Irish society. So by the early eighteenth century many of the Scotch Irish were on the move once again. Once more they sought a better life, a life that would be absent of servitude, religious persecution and poverty. Many would move west again but this time across a much larger body of water than before and several thousand miles from their origin. They would cross the Atlantic to a land that was aggressively promoted as one of almost unlimited opportunity....... America.

There were several periods of significant immigration to America during the eighteenth century which coincided with economic hard times in Northern Ireland. The last one took place in the decade of the seventeen seventies during the period of infancy of the newly formed

United States of America. And by the early nineteenth century fifteen to twenty percent of the American population was made up of those claiming Scotch Irish ancestry. Reports of a better life continued to reach those Scotch Irish still living in Northern Ireland. But the message of new opportunity fell on deaf ears for many who intermarried with indigenous Irish Catholics or had otherwise improved their condition. For many who had seen little or no improvement in their lives, however, there seemed little to lose and much to gain by immigrating to America. The only remaining barrier for most was simply the cost of the voyage itself.

Those with no other means chose to fund their transport and food costs to America by signing articles of indenture for either four or seven year terms. For some who chose indentured service in the agricultural fields the deal included the incentive of a parcel of land and tools upon fulfillment of their term. There were others whose dream, however, did not include work in the fertile fields of their new homeland. This group had a more adventurous *maritime* spirit and they would opt for a term of servitude at sea instead of on land. Elijah Sermons was a member of this group.

HUNGER, HOOLIGANS, AND... HOPE

He knew better than to be out by himself in the dock area after sundown. But the powerful attraction from the smell of freshly baked breads and mutton stew drifting from Barney's Pub had nestled comfortably in his mind. After eating nothing for two full days he found the aroma intoxicating and it left him singularly focused on its origin. He was creeping quietly toward the rear door of Barney's when his focus was suddenly disturbed by the foul odor of urine. He had just passed the firewood pile. For years it had provided some cover as the most favored spot of relief for many of Barney's drunken patrons. The unpleasant odor was a blessing in disguise however. It caused him to once again be acutely aware of his physical surroundings and of the inherent danger that he had exposed himself to that evening.

Strangely enough he had little memory of leaving the relative safety of the tiny attic space he called home, nor of even moving along the dark alleyway toward Barney's. The brief two minute walk to Barney's under a moonless sky now seemed surreal to him. Nevertheless he had indeed left the security of home, such as it was. And he was only steps from Barney's kitchen.......but exposed. He must act decisively and quickly but also with great care. If caught trying to steal food he would surely face a serious arse whoopin at best. And at worse he could be tossed into the freezing waters of Mist Harbor, a virtual certain death that time of year in Northern Ireland. Crouching down next to the rear exit he quickly peaked through the keyhole of the old heavy door to see if the cook was about. His confidence grew as there was no sign of anyone standing between him and the big crusty chunk of golden brown bread that had immediately caught his eye.

His mouth watered and he could almost taste it as a full belly was but an arm's length from where he stood. He gently pushed against the door. And then a wide grin spread across his pale weathered cheeks. The door was not only unlocked. It wasn't even latched! As he slowly nudged the door it moved open just enough so that he could see the entire brown oak breadboard only a few feet away. The sight and smell of that unguarded prize immediately erased all but the last bit of his discipline and patience. He pushed against the heavy door but with greater effort than before. It made a heavy cracking sound that in Elijah's frightened state of mind sounded as loud as thunder. And in all likelihood it would have announced his intrusion had Barney's patrons been a more docile and sober crowd. But thankfully for the hungry young lad it was absorbed into the mosaic of raucous sounds emanating from the drunken crowd.

Their miserable attempt at song was truly offensive to the ear but not nearly as much as the pathetic whine of Jim O'Donnell's fiddle. Nevertheless Elijah was sure that the sound of the door had been heard by someone in Barney's. His hand began shaking and his heart pounded harder and faster. But then his breathing came to a sudden halt as he forced his right arm and shoulder in between the door's edge and the interior stone wall of the pub's kitchen. He could now hear the laughter and conversations of the drunken sailors in the pub so clearly it seemed as if he were in their midst. The saliva in his mouth stimulated earlier by the aroma of the bread had all but disappeared. It had succumbed both to fear and to the odor of stale pungent beer that over the years had become as much a part of Barney's floor as its solid oak planks.

He was terrified by the thought that someone would spot him. *Real* hunger, however, at some point ultimately overcomes fear. Just as his forefinger felt the warmth of the outer crust he heard someone stumbling down the wooden steps leading to the kitchen from the guest rooms above. He was momentarily paralyzed with fear. But then pulled his arm back away from the bread and for the first time was sure he would be caught in the act. The footsteps came closer. Panic stricken and without forethought he thrust his arm back through the narrow opening and bumped the oak panel with his shoulder. It forced the door open further and it creaked even louder than before. He grabbed the entire chunk of bread and quickly squeezed it through the opening. His whole body began to tremble uncontrollably but somehow he had the presence of mind to pull the heavy door partially shut behind him. Ravenously hungry he tore off a piece of the large chunk of warm bread and quickly stuffed it into his dry mouth. Offering a brief silent prayer of thanks to his Great God Almighty, he turned back and began to reverse the steps he had taken only minutes before.

His indulgence in the taste and texture of that warm bread temporarily obscured his awareness of the danger that may be lurking about. But respites from deprivation were rare instances in his life to be sure. And at that moment he held in his possession manna from heaven, a chunk of warm and tasty happiness. It was an instant mood changer. But after only a few more steps he once again became aware of the potential danger that seemed to be a constant in his life. Looking up into the night sky he noticed that the moon had moved just enough from behind a cloud that there was sufficient light to see to the end of the alley. He then quickly broke into a slow trot for home. He was less than a hundred paces from safety and with enough bread in his possession to last for a good two days or more. He once again gave thanks to his Great God Almighty above and for a moment felt something akin to what happiness must be like. If only his true friend Harold were with him, then it would have truly been cause for celebration.

He was nearing the end of the alley and was almost home. And he was already indulging in the fantasy of a feast of fresh warm bread followed by a rare but good night's sleep on a full belly. But then suddenly he heard voices coming from just around the corner very near the steps leading to his room. He immediately recognized the ominous sound. It was the unmistakable voice of Shane McVeigh., the meanest, and unfortunately for Elijah, one of the biggest bullies in the dock area. This was real danger for him and quite possibly the life threatening kind. He began to feel that he made a big mistake and wished that he had stayed home and just gone to bed hungry. Instantly his possession of the delicious warm bread became secondary to flight and survival.

During the light of day and in public view Shane was necessarily more restrained to a modicum of civility. But out of view of officials, and particularly at night, he was a blatant terror to all who crossed his path and particularly to those whom were smaller or weaker than he. On occasion he could be bribed if sober. But by nightfall he was often drunk and looking for someone to hurt. Jealous of Elijah's good looks, Shane truly hated him and saw him as easy prey...... unless Harold was about.

"Damn ye Harold", Elijah mumbled quietly to himself, "ye should have stayed in Mist Harbor for the raid on Barney's and I wouldn't be in this fix".

There was little time for strategy. His initial reaction was based purely on survival instinct. The only option was to run like the wind back toward Barney's and away from certain physical harm. Still clutching the prized chunk of warm bread, Elijah spun in the opposite direction and sprinted up the alley with all the speed he could summon from his short but muscular legs. McVeigh and two of his buddies heard the footsteps echoing on the cobblestone. As they turned the corner they saw Elijah hightailing it.

McVeigh screamed "Sermons! Ye sorry little bastard. I'm gonna kill ye this time!"

All three hooligans immediately ran in Elijah's direction. And although momentarily shocked at the sudden appearance of his nemesis, Elijah clearly recognized his predicament and the need for decisive action. He rarely ventured outside the relative safety of his place at night and never before without his formidable defender, Harold. By his third stride, however, Elijah was at full speed and thankfully still with a sizeable margin of distance between him and his would be attackers. But given the unfortunate three to one odds in the hooligans' favor, he still sought help from above and began to pray to his precious Lord Jesus........... and to any other spirits that may be in the vicinity.

"Please, Lord Jesus......me God..... if ye'll jes git me home I'll ner steal as much as a crumb agin".

As he once again approached the woodpile behind Barney's he noticed the back door was still slightly ajar. Fearing the evil Shane McVeigh more than punishment from Barney he quickly shoved the door with his right hand without breaking stride. It flew wide open and slammed against the hard stone wall creating a very loud sound that echoed down the alley. At this point Shane and his hooligan buddies, although clumsier and slower than Elijah, were no more than forty paces behind him. Elijah knew that he had to keep the distance gap close enough for them to think that they could catch him. He had slowed a bit on purpose. He was hoping their drunken state had also altered their ability to think clearly. If they were sober and smart, and in most cases they were neither, they would have split up and sent one hooligan back in the opposite direction just in case Elijah were to circle back around in the direction of home. As Elijah slowed even more to make the turn onto West Way he glanced over his right shoulder and saw three bodies rumbling toward him. At least no one had turned back to cut him off on Water street, where he lived. Just as he turned the corner he heard Barney's voice thundering with anger.

"Ye fatherless heathans! Steal me bread will ye! I'll kick all yer arses ye worthless thievin peterheads!"

In just seconds the Great God Almighty had divinely intervened and answered Elijah's prayers. Not only were the hooligans slow and cumbersome but they were dumb and drunk to boot. They were so determined to get Elijah that they completely ignored Barney and just kept running. But fortunately for Elijah, Barney did not ignore them. As Elijah slowed to make another right turn onto Water Street he once again glanced back and saw one of the hooligans, Tim McCain, just turning onto West Way with one other person next to him.

Surmising the situation he became amused and uttered aloud, "That big dumb drunken bastard Shane must'a stumbled and fell down."

Elijah pictured his enemy falling in his mind and almost laughed out loud. Now he was on a dead straightaway gallop to safety which was only two blocks away. As he passed the front door of Barney's he heard a loud commotion of footsteps and several adult male voices. Now approaching Rose Bay Lane, the last cross street before his home block, he was confident of survival. He glanced back and saw big Barney and friends storming out the front door of the pub just as hooligan Tim and his buddy had made the turn onto Water Street. It was poetic justice. The hooligans could not stop in time. They ran straight into Barney bouncing off his huge barrel chest and down onto the stone street. Barney and his drunken patrons began to exact justice upon the thieves with neither hesitation nor mercy.

Crossing Rose Bay Lane, Elijah was less than twenty paces from home. Although maintaining his fast pace toward safety he began to once again think of the chunk of freshly baked bread which he clutched tightly in his left hand. It was still warm. He was tempted to tear off another mouthful but wisely resisted. He would wait until he got inside where he could have water along with it as a good meal. Approaching the outside staircase in the rear of 14 Water Street he slowed his pace and turned to go up the stone steps to the door. He breathed a sigh of relief. He could see his breath in the bright light of the now full harvest moon. The clouds had moved westward revealing thousands of tiny pin points of light in the contrasting black bowl of sky above.

"It Puts me in mind of me grandma," he whispered.

Moving up the steps he slowed his pace and was about to indulge in a good bite of bread when he heard a shuffling noise behind him. Just as he turned to look he felt a tug on his pant leg and heard the voice of evil from just below him on the bottom step.

"Now I've got yer sissy lil arse ye lil bastard ".

It was the bully himself, Shane McVeigh! Elijah was momentarily in shock and simply couldn't imagine how it could be. Surely Shane fell behind Barney's or at least got caught by his patrons. Then his mind's eye instantly replayed the events of the last two minutes as he recalled seeing the hooligan Tim McCain and his buddy turn both corners. And he remembered his delight in what had apparently been nothing but fantasy of Shane falling or being captured by Barney. He had clearly underestimated the cunning mind and physical speed of his adversary. The bully must have turned and run in the opposite direction when Barney stormed out the back door of his pub.

McVeigh had a strong grip on Elijah's left ankle and the initial force was so powerful that it had spun Elijah around and off his feet, landing him backside down on the hard stone steps. Although terrorized Elijah quickly came to terms with the reality of the situation. And as his heart pounded his mind was racing through various options. His first thought was, that short of some divine intervention, he might be deader than Hector.

McVeigh, in his drunkenness struggled to get up the steps to Elijah. Still breathing heavily due to the long sprint from Barney's he growled in a low guttural tone with every movement. Fortunately for Elijah his adversary was near physical exhaustion from the whole effort. He could see McVeigh's breath mist as they began to struggle. They were eye to eye and so close that the mist fanned out all over Elijah's face. He could even smell the putrid blend of alcohol and rancid fish that McVeigh had consumed earlier. Still gripping the chunk of bread in his left hand Elijah chose to use his right hand and right leg in whatever defensive options he may have. But before he could act, McVeigh gripped Elijah's left ankle with his right hand then lunged forward swinging his left arm and fist in an upward motion. It caught Elijah on the upper right cheek with a glancing blow. Elijah was so filled with adrenalin, however, that he hardly felt it. The lunge caused McVeigh to lose footing and he slid backward down several steps but still maintained his grip on Elijah's leg.

McVeigh regained his footing and began moving back up the steps intending to finish Elijah off. The bully was maneuvering to grab his diminutive prey by the throat with both hands but had to release Elijah's left ankle in order to free them. Elijah anticipated McVeigh's move and knew he had one chance to act or his life was probably over. With his left foot free Elijah came straight up with all his might and planted the toe of his old worn boot square in the crotch of McVeigh. As McVeigh leaned forward and grabbed his painful crotch Elijah quickly recoiled his short leg and with full force continued the upward motion of the heel of his right boot. In a move that surprised even him Elijah caught McVeigh square on the nose. Elijah heard a sickening crunching sound just before McVeigh tumbled backward down the steps. Landing on his backside in the mud, the drunken hooligan was immobilized in pain for a few seconds. He was also shocked that Elijah had actually made any effort to defend himself.

As Elijah struggled to regain his footing he put both hands on the steps to push himself up. Unfortunately in doing so a large chunk of bread tore off and fell to the ground. Turning to run up the steps Elijah glanced down and saw a dark stream of blood flowing from McVeigh's flaring nostrils. It poured down over his lips and dripped off his chin as the drunken bully struggled to stand up. Elijah was shaking and trembling from head to toe. Yet he somehow fished the long metal key from his pocket and finally got it in the keyhole and successfully turned the lock. Just as he opened the door he heard McVeigh running up the steps after him.

"Ye broke me nose ye lucky lil bastard. Now I'm gonna break ye damn neck right thar where ye stand!"

Elijah managed to get inside the tiny attic space above Robert's Pub when McVeigh reached the top step. As McVeigh lunged for the door Elijah slammed it shut and dropped the latch to keep it from opening. He was still shaking as he jammed the key into the lock and turned it twice clockwise. It was locked tight and secure! Finally, he knew he was safe..... at least for the night. The pub's attic storage area was old and deteriorating but the door was solid oak and very heavy. It provided a physical barrier that was literally the difference between life and death for Elijah at that moment. He was truly thankful and very relieved.

McVeigh cursed and beat on the door for what seemed like several minutes. After awhile however he stopped but Elijah could still hear McVeigh snorting and moving around below the steps. After a minute or two Elijah began to hear other voices outside. He recognized Barney's voice over the others.

He heard Barney scream at McVeigh, "Ye thieving bastard, yer goin to the stocks".

Barney found his bread half eaten and the remainder in the clutch of Shane McVeigh and as far as he was concerned he had found his thief. Somehow.......and in a very convoluted journey of logic…....it seemed as though justice had indeed prevailed in Mist harbor on that cold damp night.

After everyone left the area, Elijah realized he still held a small round compressed ball of bread in his left hand. He realized it had separated from the main chunk during the struggle. He first gave thanks and then held it up to his nose and savored its aroma one last time. He then placed it on his tongue and began to chew it very slowly. It was still warm and he could taste the separate ingredient flavors of butter, salt, milk, and oats. He finally swallowed the last bite but still relished its remnants which lingered along the edges and back of his tongue.

He was saddened by the loss of the big warm chunk of bread and the happiness baked inside it's golden brown crust. But no matter the circumstance, he was always appreciative to his Great God Almighty above for what he *did* have. Once again he would wake up with an empty paunch in the morning like most every other day in his life. And his survival would continue to be a struggle. But he *would* survive, because in spite of all the deprivation and danger surrounding him, he somehow still held on to the one intangible value that was requisite to the perpetuation of his meager life ....hope.

ELIJAH

"Hope is both the earliest and the most indispensable
virtue inherent in the state of being alive. If life is
to be sustained hope must remain, even where
confidence is wounded, trust impaired."
Erik H. Erikson

A strong gust of wind rattled the loose window frame next to his head causing him to stir from a deep sleep. The morning light joined forces with the wind and blocked his escape back into the fantasy of his dream. It would require him to once again embrace the reality of his squalid surroundings as it slowly transformed dark grays into muted browns. He tugged on the tattered edges of his wool blanket first covering his cold ears and eventually his whole head. It was the first move in the dilemma he faced each day. He could choose the relative security of home, such as it was....and endure hunger. Or he could choose to venture outside into a hostile environment in search of food.

His life was blessed in simplicity but also cursed with deprivation and loneliness. At the age of fourteen he already personified the human will to survive. There were others of his kind that had not survived at all. Would he choose warmth and safety that morning and endure the pain of an empty belly? Or would he choose cold and risk, but draw strength from the hope of satiating his hunger? Hope rarely loses the struggle when one is but a lad.......and still eager for life's adventures.

And those last few moments of twilight sleep were oh so good. Maybe he would be able to withstand the hunger and just sleep......and dream. But then he heard the high pitched shrieks of Mist Harbor's seagulls. They seemed louder and more excited than usual. Elijah understood the value of listening to the signs and warnings offered by the natural world. Living a life that was close to the earth had proven to be a key element of his survival thus far. So when the gulls spoke, he listened.

In his first fully conscious thought of the morning he knew the most likely source of the gulls' active behavior was the arrival of the schooner, the *Virginia Gray*. She was due the day before so he assumed she had anchored in the lee of Rathlin Isle during last night's blow. Elijah knew the potential consequences of navigating the submerged boulders and exposed rock of the Antrim Coast during a gale. He had heard tragic stories regarding those who challenged the sea off the coast of Northern Ireland in unfavorable conditions. He surmised however, that Cap'n Jonathan T.Borden, of the *Gray*, was too cautious for such ill advised action.

For some of the merchants in Elijah's community, the contents of the *Virginia Gray's* inbound cargo was of the utmost importance. However, Elijah and other impoverished wharf boys could care less *what* her barrels contained. It was simply her presence alone that was of such magnitude. For them she represented hope. For adolescent boys like Elijah Sermons, the *Gray* brought the prospect of work and the possibility of a full belly. If one was extremely fortunate he might even sign on as part of the crew, but most likely as a lowly cabin boy.

If none of the regular cargo work aboard ship was available then there was always a pence or two to be made by a young boy who could offer up the intimate services of his "sister." After several weeks or months at sea many members of the all male crew would gladly pay for the momentary intimacy of a fine woman. In fact Elijah owed his very existence to sailor whoring, as did many children living in the slums of Northern Ireland ports. Being the bastard child of a visiting seaman was quite normal in Ulster in 1815, the year of Elijah's birth. In fact most of the cabin boys from Mist Harbor were fatherless and many were orphaned.

Elijah had dreamed of being a cabin boy but was aware that many of the captains saw these children as easy prey for whatever abuses they might dole out. Having no parents to deal with, the captains were rarely if ever held accountable for any mistreatment or even the child's death. The children were simply expendable. There were reports of fatherless boys going to sea against their will never to return. In the view of some captains a cabin boy occupied a status barely above that of the African slaves such as those Elijah had once encountered on the *Sea Runner* when he was helping to unload sugar.

REVELATIONS

Elijah remembered the *Sea Runner* and its illegal slave captives too well. He discovered the hidden slaves in the ship's hold by mistake when he was helping to unload cargo. From the very beginning of the work day that morning he and the other boys from Mist Harbor became suspicious when they were told that they were not allowed below deck under any circumstances. Usually the dock workers were *expected* to go below and help move the cargo from the hold to the deck and down to the dock.

About mid morning Elijah walked over to get a drink from a water barrel that was next to the entrance to the cargo hold. As he bent over to drink from the ladle he was startled to see movement below. As his vision began to adjust from the bright daylight to the surrounding area of the hold he was able to see the upper torso of a young African man. As the man's head moved up toward Elijah the morning sun washed over him revealing his black skin and highlighting the stubble of his coarse black beard. Elijah could then see the man's dry chapped lips and surmised that he might be thirsty. He filled the ladle with cool water and extended it down toward the African. As he lifted his cupped hands in an effort to first catch and then guide the precious fluid to his parched tongue the iron chains that bound them together made a loud rattling sound. The metal glared brightly in the light of day and revealed the horrid secret of the *Sea Runner's* hidden cargo.

The first few drops of cool refreshing water soothed the African's sore throat and for an instant possibly even lifted his crushed spirit. Although shocked by the reality of what he had discovered, Elijah forced a reassuring smile toward the pathetic man and reached over to fill the ladle once again for him. He lifted the ladle from the barrel and once again moved it in the direction of the African below. But before the African could extend his hands up, the ladle was slapped violently out of Elijah's hands by First Mate Jeremiah Johnson

Johnson was furious and seized Elijah by the worn collar of his wool jacket and slammed him up against one of the smaller masts. He gripped the terrified young man's throat tightly in his powerful left hand and pushed the butt end of his cat o nine tails between both eyes. He then delivered a harsh cursing and threatened to lash Elijah for his actions. But fearing attention to the situation the captain quickly ordered Johnson to stand down and off load the cargo so they could shove off as soon as possible. Johnson glared at Elijah for another few seconds but obeyed the captain's orders. He stepped down partially into the entrance below but quickly scanned the immediate area to make sure that no one but Elijah was watching. He then turned his fury toward the unfortunate African man.

Elijah was shocked and confused by the First Mate's reaction and violent outburst toward him. But powerless to question authority he had allowed rationalization to take over. In his typical survivalist approach he began to see the entire incident through a prism of denial and simplicity. He knew there was plenty of water aboard and everyone else had helped themselves once their work was finished. Thus he saw no harm in offering the water. He just wanted his day's pay and some leftover sea rations. Elijah was thinking only of what was best for him and the African. He never even considered the consequence of the discovery for the *Sea Runner*. But the slaver captain surely did. His quick intervention had averted what otherwise may have been a legal disaster for him and the ship. He cared little or nothing for his human cargo. He was intent on breaking both the law of the Almighty and of government.

The slave trade had been outlawed in England and its colonies for more than two decades but there were still some captains and ship owners who defied the laws and continued smuggling African slaves by ship. The *Sea Runner* was one of them. And Elijah had unintentionally revealed their participation as an offender of British law by simply offering a thirsty man a drink of water. But from the perspective of the *Sea Runner's* first mate and observant captain, the young lad had opened a doorway for trouble.

Elijah's continuing moral conflict with the incident was reflected in his discussion with his best friend, Harold. "Maybe the first mate knew sumpum 'bout that water that I didn't. Maybe 'twas tainted. Maybe it would make that Afreekan sick."

Deep down in his soul, however, he knew that was not really the case. Somehow the truth seemed to always find Elijah's conscience. He had recently developed an awareness of that trait in himself and theorized that it was the presence of God in his heart. His grandma always said he had a good heart. In any case, however, he dared not argue with the first mate for fear of being passed over for work or being barred from ever becoming a cabin boy.

Still, Elijah couldn't erase his visual recollection of the event. The look of disappointment and despair in the African man's eyes etched a permanent place in Elijah's memory. After slapping the water ladle out of Elijah's hand Johnson had given the African two hard lashings across his exposed back. As the slave crouched and screamed in agony a slow but steady trickle of blood ran from his right shoulder blade diagonally toward his left ribcage. The man's flesh had immediately torn into two separate but parallel gashes of about seven inches each. Pretending to proceed with unloading the sugar, Elijah abruptly turned away. Just as he turned, however, his keen eye caught a glimpse of bright white framed in crimson flesh and shiny black skin. He had never seen exposed bone in a living human being before but he knew that had to be it. He felt sick to his stomach but held it in. For once he was truly thankful for an empty paunch.

On the exterior Elijah maintained a tough, insensitive image like most of the boys of the rough dock area. He knew this façade to be necessary for his very survival. But he had begun to understand that this was not really who he was. In fact he was quite sensitive to the world around him and especially to all living things. And he was very uncomfortable with violence excepting of course that which was necessary in the defense of one's own person or a loved one. But he had to suppress the expression of his sensitivity. He simply could not afford to be viewed by most of those in his world as anything but selfish and uncaring. Otherwise he would become more of an object of ridicule and violence himself.

There were incidents recently in which he found it almost impossible to suppress his feelings. The incident on the *Sea Runner* touched him in a profound way. After the initial shock of the event had worn off there was still something about the unnecessary brutality that left him with an overwhelming feeling of sadness. What concerned him the most, however, was that no one else seemed to have the same reaction, or at least displaying outward signs of it. He realized that he would not be able to maintain the facade much longer. He would eventually react without forethought and control and thus become vulnerable to what he knew to be a very hardened and insensitive population of young thugs. The incident on the *Sea Runner* was a clear warning. He was now at risk. He had to get out of Mist Harbor..........and soon. But he just couldn't put the incident on the *Sea Runner* behind him yet. It was forcing him to face himself and the world around him as they both really were.

He began to see a profound difference between himself and the African. Although Elijah had endured a life riddled with disappointment and pain, he could visualize his future. He still had hope. In stark contrast there was nothing in the African man's eyes or behavior that suggested the slightest hint of any hope. For the first time in his life Elijah realized that there was another human being who had it worse than he did. He didn't quite understand why, but for some reason it made him feel better to have pity for someone other than himself. And that feeling began to evolve into a driving force that would dictate much of his behavior for the rest of his life. He had a burning desire to help anyone who was being mistreated by someone who was more powerful. He vowed that if he ever became a captain, he would make water available to everyone when ever they wanted it. And he wouldn't allow anyone bound in chains, "less a course they mutinied or murdered". But in order to help he would have to get himself in a position to do so. So first things first, he still had to get hired on as a cabin boy.

CABIN BOY FEVER

Signing on a ship as its cabin boy would only be the first step. Successfully discharging the duties of the position would require at minimum an understanding of the consequence of one's place in the pecking order of the crew. And Elijah was well aware that a cabin boy could become the entire crew's whipping post if he fell into the slightest disfavor of the captain. He already knew how to avoid this dilemma however. He would simply do more than asked in every situation, all the time.

He knew others that wanted to hire on as a cabin boy but some of them had a fear of the sea itself. Not so for Elijah. He surely was no landlubber. In fact his greatest fear was being stuck forever in Mist Harbor in a life of despair facing hunger, poverty and danger on a daily basis. He could not imagine that life at sea would bring worse conditions than he was already experiencing. At least at sea he was guaranteed food and water daily.

And he would happily take his chances with the *Virginia Gray* and Cap'n Borden over having to see the violent beatings his mother endured from her men "visitors". He also would be free of his occassional arse whooping from the village bully, the bastard Shane McVeigh. The sea might be the unknown, but the unknown had to be better than the life he lived for his first fourteen years. Yes, he would he happy to sit on the stern of any seaworthy vessel and watch Mist Harbor gradually disappear in the distance.

The type or size of ship that he would sail on mattered little to Elijah. He didn't care about her cargo, or length of time out. And although he had heard tales of far away ports of call, he really didn't care where his first ship was headed. He just wanted to get started. And his grandma had told him long ago that beggars cannot be choosers. He would start out as a cabin boy. This would be his first step to becoming an ordinary seaman, then an able seaman, then a first mate, or maybe even a captain someday.

Seamanship was his destiny. He came by it naturally. In fact the only thing he knew for sure of his biological father was that of his life as a seaman. Life at sea was evident from his mother's lineage as well. He was told that his maternal grandfather had spent several years before the mast along side Elijah's great uncle Cleeland. Elijah's first cousin Bonner, also a brave sailor, sadly lost his life at sea just the year before. And most of his clan that he knew of had been seaman at one time or another as well. There was simply no choice to be made. His path in life was predetermined. It was clear to Elijah that "God Almighty had already done the choosin" for him.

He figured that God created some folks for potato farming and some for sea going. He had no disrespect toward potato farmers and in fact appreciated their skill and the product of their hard work. Being a perpetually hungry boy he would gladly chow down a helping of taters and buttermilk, a local favored dish. But given a choice, Elijah would much rather have a mess of oysters or clams. And he knew for sure that he'd rather be "catchin fish than growin taters".

Several years before he was of an age to be considered for cabin boy, he began to listen carefully to the visiting captains and crews in their discussions of seamanship. There were few accounts of kindness on the high seas and no shortage of those detailing horrific abuses. On some of the ships even the paying passengers were mistreated. So what then could a lowly cabin boy, an apprentice, expect? Nevertheless he learned a great deal about the ships and also formed a mental list of which captains might be more tolerable than others. Cap'n Borden and the *Virginia Gray* were near the top.

He was confident that if he got on with the *Gray* and did all that was asked of him, that Cap'n Borden would not punish him harshly. Elijah had a reputation as a reliable, hard working dock hand unlike some others in Mist Harbor. And he knew some that were intimidated by the *Gray's* captain and still others that were afraid to go to sea. Thus many would have already eliminated them selves from consideration. So when the *Gray* sailed into Mist Harbor that chilly morning Elijah was already aware that it may represent his most optimum opportunity thus far. And the time to leverage his reputation and knowledge may be drawing near.

Perhaps that reality rose from his sub conscience and motivated him to face the new day. Pushing the woolen cover down from over his ears he heard the gulls' message even clearer now. His grandma told him that there was a time when animals and humans spoke the same language. Maybe the gulls *were* speaking to him.

In his mind he heard them saying, "Get up Elijah! Now! Your ship of hope has arrived!"

Suddenly warmth, sleep, and even his hunger pains were secondary to the hope of a new life. Perhaps today would be the start of his life at sea. As his feet slid from under the warm cover and onto the cold rotting plank floor he could already smell the coffee and fried pork from Robert's Pub just below. He had grown to hate the smells. It seemed to make his paunch emptier and the hunger pains worse. But he tried to forget the brief fantasy of food as he shuffled toward the window to view the harbor. But a beam of bright sunlight diverted his gaze toward a rusting basin filled with water where his reflection stared back at him. It revealed a few whiskers of no particular color and a healthy but unkept head of shoulder length brown hair with random hints of auburn. His hair color was one of several inherited characteristics he shared with his mother. For an instant he thought of her and for the first time he wondered if he might actually miss her.

"Course not", he muttered to himself. "How can a body miss anotherun what taint ner 'bout no way".

His tough talk however only masked his true pain from the irreparable damage that the absence of a mother's love can cause. Perhaps it was the fantasy of having a real mother who loved and cared for him that Elijah might miss. Other than her occasional need of his quarters for her men friends he saw her only about four times per year. He was concerned for her well being but at some point he just gave up trying to gain her love as his mother. The experience left him confused about love and emotions in general.

LOVE... AND IN LOVE

Elijah's buddy, Harold, offered his advice in the matter. "God Almighty made that love stuff mostly fer girls and sissy boys, not fer grown men like you and me."

He agreed with Harold on almost everything but he knew for sure that he *had felt* something for at least two folks. His maternal grandmother, Sarah Cutler, was first and foremost in his life. She had become Elijah's functioning mother for as long as he could remember and he felt some sense of security and happiness while in her care. Although he didn't know what love was supposed to feel like, he was pretty sure that she had loved him, and he her. He was blessed to have her for the first ten years of his life before she passed over from the fever in 1825.

He thought at the time of his grandma's death that he wanted to go to heaven with her for he had never felt so completely alone. She was the only consistent source of stability and affection he had ever known.

The day she was buried in a pauper's grave Elijah went under the covers where he stayed for a solid three days with no food or water. What time he wasn't crying his eyes out he was praying for her return. On the fourth day, however, he reasoned that God decided to keep his grandma in heaven and that she would have wanted him to live. It was at that moment that he was sure that she loved him. He began to think that Harold may have been wrong, at least where his grandma Sarah was concerned......and perhaps on account of one other person as well.

Whatever Elijah felt for Becky Bradshaw was real to. It was very different than the safety and security he enjoyed in the dependent relationship he had with his grandma however. Whenever Becky would walk past the docks he got nervous as a cat. If her deep blue eyes happen to meet his, "the jeebies got holt to him". Once at the foot of the dock and once on the backsteps of the First Presbyterian Church he and Becky had actually sat and talked. During their first encounter at the dock he felt the flush of warm blood rising rapidly upward into his face and ears. He first feared the presence of a daylight haint having never experienced blushing before.

Later on, however, Harold had explained that the strange feeling of sudden warmth was most likely just the devil trying to get hold of his pure thoughts of Becky. Elijah considered himself fortunate to have a wise and learned friend like Harold. But later he gained a more learned perspective himself. And a portion of that was the realization that Harold sometimes left out critical details in his pearls of wisdom. Such was the case during a subsequent encounter between Elijah and Becky.

The infatuated pair enjoyed each other's company during a second meeting on the church steps. This time sweet little Becky held Elijah's hand in hers. And for a few moments Elijah was in pure heaven. Once again, however, he felt that devilish flush. But on that particular occasion the warm blood shifted due south and seemed to settle in what his grandpa use to call his body's main mast. As Becky got up to leave, Elijah at first refused to stand. But Becky became impatient and said she was late to meet her father and that he would be angry if she did not return right away. Facing embarrassment, Elijah was left with no choice. But as he started to stand he yelled out and grabbed his left ankle with both hands and as he told Harold later, "commenced to rubbing it to beat hell."

In order not to seem rude and ungentlemanly Elijah had to fake that his foot had gone to sleep. While rubbing his foot vigorously and sneaking a peak up at Becky out of the corner of his right eye he prayed silently and with great fervor that God would quickly move the excess warmth back where it came from. He asked God to save the stiffness down below for later when he was old enough to properly use it as a whoring sailor.

Just seconds later Elijah's faith in the Almighty was once again confirmed. He stood partially upright and with a slight limp began to slowly move. He then proudly walked the beautiful Rebecca Bradshaw down the narrow cobblestone alley known as Water Street. As they reached her father's fish house Becky without warning turned and kissed the shocked youngster on the lips. Sensing an eminent southerly shift in his nature he quickly whirled away from Becky, and miraculously limp free, broke into an all out run toward his place. He stumbled on the uneven stones and in an instant was air born and head fomus for Old Man O'Neil's milk wagon. Luck was on his side however, as he righted his short frame just in time to avoid falling under the left rear wheel. Adeptly bouncing off the wagon's heavy oak panel he looked over his right shoulder and saw Becky grinning like a possum eating briers. Without question his heart skipped a beat and for a moment he could have affirmed to God above that his feet were no longer in contact with the good green earth beneath him. He knew one thing for sure about feelings being for sissy boys only. He was no sissy boy, and furthermore......... Harold was dead wrong on that advice.

Elijah would surely miss the angel like smile of Becky Bradshaw once he went to sea. He was confident he would see her again though. Once he made ordinary seaman and worked hard for a year or so he would eventually find a good ship headed in the direction of his former homeland. He could sign on and work his way back to Mist Harbor. In his mind's eye he saw himself leaping from the starboard rail onto the crowded dock and into the open arms of pretty little Becky. He figured that Harold would be a bit jealous but nevertheless happy to see him. Next he would stick out his chest and walk straight into Finney's Dry Goods and buy a brand new wool sweater for his Becky. He would ask for blue, to match the ocean that lived in Becky's eyes. Then he would seek the services of Big Timothy Scot. He would enter a gentleman's agreement to pay Big Timothy a full pence in exchange for publicly dousing the bastard bully Shane McVeigh with the full contents of the Captain's swill bucket.

Elijah dreamed big for a poor orphan boy of Mist Harbor. But his dreams were supported with preparation, a well thought out plan, and hope. All he needed was opportunity. And maybe today would be the day that those dreams would take a major step forward. He dipped his fingers into the cold water and splashed the sleep from his crusty eyelids. With growing optimism for the day he approached the tiny window in the attic above Robert's Pub. Emitting a low grunt he opened the heavy wooden shutters and suddenly the room flooded with sunshine. Slowly his eyes began to adjust as he focused on the harbor area. And sure enough it was just as the gulls had told him. Gazing out over the dock area of Mist Harbor he saw the tops of three large masts passing just behind one of the local warehouses. And only seconds later her prominent shiny bow came into view. The schooner in all her majestic splendor was slowly gliding its way across a slick cam harbor.

He excitedly proclaimed "Hits gotta be the *Gray!*"

He realized he must quickly dress and get down to the dock for this was sure to be an eventful day. Moving away from the window he reached for his worn out boots and soiled wool leggings. Just as he pulled and tied off the top lace of his faded brown jacket he heard the clanging sound of hope. Two bells proclaimed the approach and eminent docking of the *Virginia Gray.*

He said "Grandma Sarah was right. The seagulls *can* speak the same language as humans. A feller just has to be listnin right."

Moving toward the door he saw a tiny gray mouse scurry from behind the coal bucket next to the crumbling stone hearth. Over time Elijah had grown tolerant of the little critter and of late had actually tried befriending him. He stepped toward him and the mouse ran back and hid behind the bucket. Elijah smiled and stepped back.

"She's all yerin fer the day. After I've had me slarce of the *Gray's* leftover rations I'll bring ye a crumb or two."

As he closed and latched the creaking door behind him he realized that he had forgotten the lucky stone that Becky had given him as a token of their special friendship. He left it on a rotting lateral support beam next to his bed. He turned to go back in for it, but was deterred by the shrieking of the gulls. He abruptly reversed himself and headed lickety split for the dock. He didn't want to miss the chance to fill his paunch… and more. And on *this* day he had to be first in line for work on the *Gray*. He promised himself that he would make it up to Becky by sleeping with the stone next to his heart all night long. And Elijah always kept his promise…….at least up to that point in his life.

Bounding down the steps he turned toward the dock and began to run. Glancing back toward his attic room something out of the ordinary caught his eye. It was in the same window that he had seen the *Virginia Gray* from only minutes before. It appeared to be the image of an older woman. There was something atop her head that put him in mind of the light blue bonnet his Grandma Sarah wore almost every day. He slowed his walk and then came to an abrupt stop. He stared for a moment thinking that perhaps his imagination was playing tricks on him. Moving forward once again he thought the image might disappear. But the figure seemed to be holding her left hand near her heart. Her right arm was extended toward Elijah with an open hand. Then it began to fade away.

Perhaps it had just been a shadow or an unusual reflection. Or perhaps it had been more than that. Elijah tucked it away in his memory and began running toward the dock and the *Gray*. As he turned to look at the window once more he noticed that the old weathered structure was now awash in bright morning sun. Elijah had no recollection of ever having seen the place in such fine detail before. The gray stonework appeared almost white. He could even see the tiny flecks of black that was common in the indigenous rock of the Northern Ireland coastline. His mind's eye would replay this scene many times over throughout his life; for it was the last that he would ever see of his childhood home........... or of his beautiful Becky.

THE VIRGINIA GRAY

By the time Elijah reached Water Street the *Virginia Gray* was just nestling up to the dock. Several able seamen were securing her to the posts when Elijah saw the great anchor drop from her stern. It was always exciting for him to see the splash and to hear the chains rolling untill it hit bottom. There was still a bit of chill in the air but the bright morning sun was providing some welcome warmth on his bare face as he slowed his pace and turned onto the cobblestone dock. Sure enough, he was the first to show up for work. He quickly surveyed the situation including a count of the number of crew members. There were seven seamen not including the first or second mates, the carpenter and seamstress, and of course Cap'n Borden.

A wide grin gradually spread across his boyish face. If there *had* been a cabin boy aboard then he would have been visible on deck and assisting in the docking; the preparation for unloading cargo; and in the acquisition of personal supplies for the captain and/or first mate. All such tasks were ones that needed to be accomplished in rapid succession once a ship was in port thus it was a time for *all* hands on deck. The *Gray* was in need of a cabin boy!

Elijah had committed to memory virtually every aspect of a ship's operation from the moment a vessel enetered Mist Harbor until she pulled up anchor and departed. Finally his opportunity to apply that knowledge and leverage it to his benefit appeared to be at hand. The seagulls were right. This surely must be his ship of hope. And Elijah wasted no time in making himself available to help.

He addressed the first mate in a confident voice saying "Top of the morn to ye sir. Me name's Elijah and I'm in dire need of work. What can I do fer ye and ye Cap'n sir?"

The first mate paid him no attention at first and continued giving orders to his crew. The man's cheeks were chapped and rosey but his chin and throat were protected by a tangled gray beard. His left eye was slightly offset and appeared to focus in a different direction than his right. And Elijah had neither seen, nor smelled worse of a living breathing human being before. But he wasn't looking for a best friend. He was there to work, eat, and God willing, sign on as cabin boy. Refocusing on his goals, he was anxious to speak again for fear that some of the other locals would show up soon and try to bully him to the back of the line. But then his memory replayed a scene that had taken place just a year earlier between him and the same first mate.

He had spoken *too* soon in his previous conversation which resulted in a severe scolding by the first mate. And as if the verbal abuse hadn't sufficiently gotten his point across, the first mate also forced Elijah to go to the back of the line where he stayed for the remainder of the day with no work or food. But this time Elijah disciplined himself to stay quiet. After a couple of minutes of silence the first mate abruptly turned and stared at him for an uncomfortable period. But then Elijah's patience paid off.

He snarled "Well, what ye waitin fer boy.....hell to freeze over! Least ways now I know ye can listen *and learn* and maybe follow orders. Ain't ye that lil fart that couldn't keep his mouth shut las time we was in port? Yeah.......ye are! Me eyes is good and me memory as well. Now git yer scrawny arse oer here and hep the crew coil her lashings and unload."

Elijah's confidence had waned a bit while waiting for a response from the gruff old salt dawg. And although he expected to get work on the

Gray that day, the sudden reality of it left him a bit shocked. So he didn't move right away which apparently angered the ill tempered first mate.

"Damn ye boy……… Now! Get hoppin or take ye arse back to ye whoring mama's sweet tits."

The first mate took pride in his ability to verbally abuse those of less status than himself. It gave him a sense of strength and importance in his tiny part of the world. Feeling his oats a bit he let out with a whining high pitch laugh that seemed incongruent with his attempt at intimidation and humiliation. It had such a feminine sound that it evoked an immediate giggle response in Elijah. Always thinking, however, the young boy quickly covered his mouth with his hand and transformed the involuntary action into a coughing spell. The first mate ceased his laughter immediately and glared straight into Elijah's eyes with an intensity that got his message across loud and clear. He intended to put the fear of God into Elijah. And while still fighting back the giggles, Elijah played along with the fright scenario. He sprang up on to the plank and walked briskly up the incline while all the while continuing to fake the cough. He had no other recourse. Otherwise he would have given in to an uncontrollable guffaw of laughter that couldn't have possibly resulted in any favorable outcome for him. In dire need of work and food, he smartly suppressed his response………at least for the moment.

Elijah finally eeked out "Yessir first mate……..uh…..uh…"

The first mate glared at him and finally growled "It's Connors ye dumb lil bastard. And don't ye fergit it."

"Yessir……". And while still struggling to stop the giggle from taking over his entire countenance, he forced out "Yes…sir… First Mate Connors……and thank ye….. fer the work sir!"

Elijah turned and moved quickly toward the *Gray's* stern to get as far away from Connors as possible. He was howling with suppressed laughter on the inside. The more he thought about the incident the funnier it seemed. His shoulders were shaking and saliva began running down his chin. Elijah knew he could no longer control himself. By the time he reached a double stacked hogshead tall enough to hide behind he was already bent over and losing his breath. He began to laugh so hard that he fell to just his knees and let it all out. He indulged fully in reliving the experience of that absurd sound of the girly laugh coming out of Connors.

He was thankful that almost all the activity was focused in the bow and amid ship so that no one was about. And he was thankful to be alone because he sorely needed the work and the rewards that came with it. And if his buddy Harold had been with him they would have both lost complete control right there on the dock...... and all the day's work and rations along with it. Harold's absence that morning had proven to be a blessing in disguise for Elijah.

Elijah quickly got busy moving boxes, crates and barrels onto the deck from the hold and subsequently onto the wagons that were already lined up on Water Street. He was happy to be busy and loved the energy surrounding the arrival of a visiting ship. Whenever a ship visited Mist Harbor it always provided a boost to the local economy with an immediate surge of activity and commerce in the dock area. The surge rippled through the community at large as goods and services were being exchanged, bartered or sold. The cycle started with the dock workers like Elijah who were offered the opportunity to work and even included the ship's crew. Many spend a good portion of their pay on food, drink, and sometimes ladies of the evening. The activity lasted sometimes for up to four days and then tapered off until the next ship would arrive and initiate the cycle again.

The *Gray* was rarely in port for more than two days however. Cap'n Borden preferred the larger ports of call where there was greater anonymity. That seemed to lower any risk associated with any indiscretions with the ladies. He was a married man and intolerant of inquiries into his personal life. So from the moment the *Gray* docked in Mist Harbor he prevailed harshly on First Mate Connors and the crew to be expeditious in their business. He issued strict orders to pull up anchor and depart for the next port as soon as possible. And that day was no exception. His outbound cargo destined for the merchants of Mist Harbor was lighter than usual. And he had only one inbound load of Irish whisky to receive before departure. It was his intention to sail back out to the Irish Sea once it was secured.

Elijah had been working hard for about a half hour in the hold when he heard a familiar voice. As the voice became louder and more defined he recognized it. It was his best friend Harold. Elijah looked up toward the deck and saw Harold peeping down the stairway into the hold.

"Elijah....ye about anywheres are ye?" Harold yelled.

"Yesiree.......I'm in the hold. It smells worse than hell down here but me work's almost done. I'll be up in two shakes of a goat's tail Harold. Hey. Gimme a hand here and I'll finish quicker".

He rapidly moved the three remaining crates up the ladder in succession and handed them off to Harold who in turn handed them off to another crew member. Elijah grabbed Harold by the arm and looked him straight in the eye.

"Harold ye just ain't goin believe what I've got to tell ye bout last evening. Ye know Barney's....".

But before Elijah could finish his sentence Harold burst out laughing and said "Yep. I already hearn bout it Elijah! I saw Shane McVeigh comin out the jailhouse on me way to see bout work on the *Gray*." Still laughing loudly Harold continued. "Now ain't that a helluva note! Lil Elijah Sermons....... broke that..... ugly bastard's nose! That's the funniest thing I've ever hearn in me whole damn life. I'm proud of ye lil buddy. And now that I'm back ye got no worries me friend. I'll stand up to that drunken coward any day and he damn well knows it. But by his look this morn..." breaking into laughter once again "he ain't a lookin fer no more trouble. Looks like somebody else got holt to him after ye did yer damage to his nose last eve. He looks....like a damn owl.....with two black eyes....a bloody crooked nose... a swoll up right cheek...and a nasty cut that goes clear cross both lips."

At this point both Harold *and* Elijah were roaring with laughter. Elijah didn't usually take enjoyment in someone else's pain but in McVeigh's case he made a justifiable exception. But their laughter was suddenly interrupted by the voice of First Mate Connors.

"Sermons! Elijah Sermons. Git your arse to the Capn's quarters straight-away boy! And send ye big ugly arse friend back oer here so he can git these damn crates off loaded now. Cap'n wants to shove off by midday!"

All Elijah heard was the command to go to the Captain's quarters. Everything after that was a blur. But Harold heard the whole statement clearly. He moved quickly to comply so as to make sure he got his pay and rations. He duly noted, however, that Elijah was being summoned to the Captains quarters and surprisingly that the ship was sailing very soon. As he was walking toward the wagons with a crate on each shoulder it hit him. Cap'n Borden must be talking to Elijah about being a cabin boy. Why else would the captain of a fine ship such as the *Gray* summon a lowly dock worker to his quarters? Harold had always said that Elijah would get on as a cabin boy before most of the others simply because he was so much smarter about the ships and the sea and also because he was the hardest worker on the docks. And since a cabin boy's areas of duty and living quarters were so cramped Elijah's small stature figured positively into the equation as well. Harold was eager to hear the whole story. He thought to himself that he would be proud of his friend if he went to sea on the *Gray* but he would surely miss him. He and Elijah had been best friends for seven years. That was half or more of their whole lives. That sudden realization caused Harold to reevaluate the whole idea.

All of a sudden Elijah's departure to sea maybe wasn't such a great idea to Harold. He kept looking back up to the hatch on deck which led down to Cap'n Borden's quarters below. He finished loading the last crates on the delivery wagons which were headed to Larson's Dry Goods Store a few blocks away. Still Elijah had not emerged from below. Harold was beginning to grasp the reality that this cabin boy idea may really happen for his friend. He was really starting to worry about his loss when the sound of wagon wheels striking the cobblestones interrupted his thoughts.

The wagon stopped right behind Harold. It was carrying the four hogsheads bound for America that were labeled O'Sheas Old Irish whisky. Even before Connors could bark out the orders Harold was on it. He and another dock worker already started to unload the heavy barrels off the wagon and onto the ramp leading up to the ship's deck. Harold positioned himself on the lower end of the ramp where most of the brute force was needed in order to move the barrel upward. The other smaller worker pulled it up toward the ship but was mainly there for balance and guidance. Harold heaved and pushed untill he finally got the barrel to the deck. They righted it and then turned it over to the crew to secure the lines. After three of the four barrels were loaded and secured on the *Gray*, Harold leaned against the rail for support. Moving the heavy barrels up the incline was very hard work and he needed a breather. He also was using the moment to stall for time while hoping Elijah would emerge from below. His ploy worked. Elijah came walking up the steps from below just as Connors growled at Harold to get moving again.

Harold turned and said "What in hell's a goin on? Naw! Are ye goin be the cabin boy on the *Gray*?"

Elijah just grinned. Harold became annoyed and using a harsh tone said "What's goin to happen now Elijah?"

After a few moments of tense silence Elijah said "Ima cabin boy on the *Virginia Gray* Harold! I knew today might be the day. I just felt it….and the seagulls told me…" Elijah stopped short as he knew that Harold did not believe that animals and humans could actually communicate.

Harold started grinning and said "Well I'll be damned and hell faar. Elijah Sermons is a goin to sea!"

Just then Connors screamed "Now I've had me fill of ye mouf there bigun. Ye and Sermons git down here and git this last barrel a whisky on board now if'n ye want ye pay and rations!"

Connors had done well in maintaining a burly sort of outburst until the last few words of the phrase. It went into that uncontrolled high pitch tone that had set Elijah off earlier into belly busting laughter. And it was at an even higher pitch than before. The whole crew turned and stared at Connors. Connors turned beet red and stormed up the incline cursing a blue streak. By this time almost everyone on the crew and the dock workers were starting to giggle. In his fit of rage Connors grabbed one of the smaller dock workers and slammed him up against the rail and threatened to throw him overboard. The crusty old sailor then turned and glared at Harold who was shaking with stifled laughter.

Connors growled "Ye think sompm's funny do ye? Well after I whoop ye fat arse with me cat a nine tails ye shan't be laughin!"

Cap'n Borden emerged from his quarters just as Connors turned to head down the steps below. The *Virginia Gray's* captain was tall but slight of build and had a close cropped dark brown goatee with a waxed handlebar mustache that curled at each end. He spoke methodically and enunciated each syllable of his proper King's English as if delivering a Shakespearian soliloquy on stage. He made no attempt to disguise his true attitude toward the *Gray's* crew and his behavior had earned his reputation of arrogance.

"What's all the fuss and commotion Connors? Ye should have had the hogsheads of Irish whisky loaded on deck and secured by now!" Pointing to Harold he said "Sermons, you and your ratha large friend thaah get that last whisky loaded on deck now! The rest of you dock worker boys depart the vessel. Pay the urchins their rations and wages Connors, and prepare the ship to cast off."

He then abruptly turned toward the bow sprit and strutted a few steps forward. He paused for a moment and then pulled an emerald green silk scarf out from under his bright red vest. He shook it and then ever so softly wiped it across across the shiny oak grain of the ship's wheel several times. He mumbled something under his breath and then sneered at Connors and the crew just before disappearing below.

Elijah and Harold immediately ran down the incline and both were now laughing out loud about the Connors outburst *and* Cap'n Borden's dramatic behavior. Elijah had smartly suppressed his laughter on deck. He knew that inside of an hour he would be on the Irish Sea and heading for the North Atlantic with no place to hide. He would be at the mercy of First mate Connors for months to come, so it was best to stay on his good side. After a good laugh together Harold asked about the details of his friend's new situation.

Elijah began to explain the deal that Cap'n Borden had offered him. It was the apprenticeship of cabin boy on the *Gray* in exchange for food, water, lodging, and transportation to America. In America Elijah would continue working aboard the *Gray* for another six months as it ran up and down the American East Coast during the colder months. At the end of that time period he had the option of signing papers once more for the *Gray* as it sailed for European ports during the milder weather. Otherwise he could seek work either on another ship or in some land based business in America.

It was an easy decision for Elijah. And although he had dreamed of this very moment for years, he was a bit nervous that the ship's departure was imminent. He suddenly realized he would not have time to retrieve the lucky stone Becky had given him, or even say goodby to her! So he gave Harold his key and requested he take the stone and keep it safe until he came back to Mist Harbor in a year or so.

After the two best friends got the final whisky barrel loaded Elijah walked back down with Harold onto the dock. First mate Connors had given the order to prepare to cast off and the stand by order to raise the foresail.

This was the moment Elijah had waited practically all his life for but as the reality set in so did a certain level of trepidation and melancholy. He looked into the eyes of his longtime friend and saw that Harold was tearing up.... as was he. He quickly grabbed Harold's big right hand in both of his and shook it firmly.

"I'm goin miss ye a lot Harold. Take care of ye self and don't git caught at night by yeself if McVeigh's drunk and got his buddies with him. I know ye can whoop McVeigh and maybe one of his buddies with him, but I don't know bout a gang of em. And one more thing Harold, please tell Becky I'll miss her and......and....I...I....I...love her."

Elijah abruptly turned and ran lickety split up the ramp and onto the deck. He looked back at his best friend Harold and saw a tear rolling down his plump cheek. It touched his heart but he could not dare show it. Just as he was fighting back the tears he heard Connors barking orders and sure enough the last few words went into that feminine girly high pitch once again. He couldn't help it this time. He laughed out loud and so did Harold. With nothing left to fear from old salt Connors, Harold quickly doubled over with laughter as the *Gray* began moving away from the dock and toward the harbor's channel. The last image Elijah had of his best friend in the world was one of a smiling happy face. It made him feel a bit better.

Elijah tried to look busy on deck so as to delay going below. Every minute or so he stole a glance back at Mist Harbor as it seemed to be rapidly diminishing from his view. He was excited to begin living out his boyhood dream but at the same time he felt a strange sense of loss. As he finished coiling one of the hemp lines he looked up to get one last glance of the only home he had ever known. But it had disappeared below the horizon and in its place was a vast expanse of sea. For a moment he felt a wave of panic but he courageously fought it back. Signs of weakness could bring ridicule or even physical abuse from Connors and disrespect from the rest of the hardened crew. It was at that moment that the irony occurred to him.

One of the main reasons he felt pressure to leave Mist Harbor quickly was because he had found it increasingly difficult to hide his sensitivity and concern for others. Yet the *Gray* was surely no safe haven for one who would express such emotions. That realization was a turning point in the development of his growth and maturation of emotional control. It wasn't a conscious choice driven out of courage by any means. It was simply because he had no other choice........and no where to run and hide. He was at sea.

GOOD AND BAD MATES

By the time the *Gray* was in sight of Rathlin Isle the sun was already slipping below the surface of the dark green water off their port bow. And the seas were growing steadily higher and further apart as they reached the area at which the Northern Irish Sea gave way to the great North Atlantic. Just an hour or so earlier Elijah's eye was drawn to the view of a beautiful stretch of land off the *Gray's* starboard. It appeared to be a rocky shoreline with rolling hills in the background. The foreground gradually flattened out as it merged with the murky waters of the Irish Sea. He was mesmerized by the sight and crouched between the rail and a hogshead to hide from Connors in order to watch it. It seemed familiar, almost as if he had visited it before. Then it came to him.

Elijah realized the stretch of land had to be part of the Scottish Lowlands that his grandma had told him about. It looked exactly as his mind's eye had pictured it based on her description. She had explained that it was where his ancestors from just a few generations back lived before immigrating to Northern Ireland. The recounting of her family's history there had been interesting, but not very meaningful for Elijah until he laid eyes on those Scottish Lowlands. But actually seeing the land, even from a distance, had bridged the gap between fantasy and reality.

A small part of Elijah's fragmented family history, and thus who he was, had suddenly been authenticated for him. He finally felt connected to something beyond the poverty, hunger and loneliness he experienced for most of his life. It was only the first step toward a positive self awareness that he would struggle with for years yet to come. But it was indeed a beginning. It would be one of several turning points after leaving Northern Ireland that indicated he was something other than just another pathetic member of an oppressed population; a population that had been transplanted into a country that never wanted his kind in the first place. The whole notion was just sinking into his consciousness when reality literally kicked him in the backside.

"Sermons! Ye good fer nothit lil wharf bastard! Ye've yet to complete as much as half a ye first dog shift and ye're already slackin in ye duties....... jes like ye filthy whoring mama taught ye no doubt!"

First Mate Connors had not only literally kicked Elijah's buttocks with the full strength of his right boot but the words cut through him like a knife. Elijah's mother had never been a devoted one, but she had given him life through her own pain and on occasion expressed concern for him. Elijah was hurt but he was also very angry at Connors. That was twice in one day that Connors had unjustifiably insulted his mother. He replied with a defiant tone that even surprised him as the words rolled off his tongue.

"Sorry First Mate Connors... but ye have no jes cause to talk that way bout me own mother. Me mama tis a good woman and...."

Before Elijah could finish his defense of his mother's reputation Connors interrupted. "I'll teach ye yer place on the *Gray* right heah and now ye ungrateful lil heathan. Ye are worthless as tits on a bull. Ye'll be singin another tune fer me and Cap'n Borden once ye take yer whoopin from me cat a ninetails."

Connors reached under his shirttail and pulled and drew the weapon back all in one motion. His face reddened and the veins bulged in his neck and forehead. "Take yer whoopin boy...or jump to ye cold dark death. I'll break ye childish no good arse from slackin on me watch. I'll....."

Just as Connors came forward with the whip a tall black skinned man stepped between him and Elijah. The man slapped Elijah across the forehead and scalp with his large opened palm but barely grazed him. He repeated the slap from both back and forehand several times in succession. His frame blocked the view of Connors from seeing the actual contact with Elijah's face. Thus Connors was unaware that the slaps were minimal in their damage and pain. The black man spoke to Elijah in a slow steady but stern voice.

"Boy Sermons! Ya mean nuntin to nobody here. Now shut your mouth boy and get up and come with me. You'll scrape the rust off the anchor chain until daybreak. Your fingers and thumb will be so sore and bloody that the next time your childish temper flares up you will remember the punishment that's to come behind your insulting mouth."

The man paused and glared down at Elijah. Elijah covered his head with his arms and curled up in a fetal position on the deck as his entire body began to tremble. The man then grabbed Elijah by the coat collar and lifted him up with one arm.

Turning to Connors the African said, "I am sorry First Mate Connors. It will not happen again or he'll be swimming in the deep with the likes of Davey Jones."

He turned to Elijah and said, "Boy, you gots to learn the hard way don't ya? Aboard the *Gray* I am responsible for the conduct and work of the cabin boy. I, Owahou Seymour, am the ship's Second Mate. And you have shamed me on ya furs day as cabin boy. You heah me boy?"

Elijah was in fear for his life but was able to nod his head up and down and in a shaky voice answered "Yes…Yessir."

Owahou then pushed Elijah along and they disappeared behind the entrance to the hold below as Connors could only watch. He was still a bit shocked at the sudden and unexpected turn of events. Connors technically was the African man's superior in the ship's chain of command but the *Gray* actually operated somewhat outside the norm compared to most other ocean going vessels.

There were a few black sailors here and there on the high seas but in the early nineteenth century it was the exception rather than the norm. And having a *second mate* who was of African ancestry was extremely rare. But Owahou Seymour had a superb command of the English language and had a vast array of experiences in sailing. Even Connors would have admitted his inferior intelligence to that of Owahou. Owahou, like any African of his time, would have had to be over qualified to obtain any position of authority over white men aboard ship or for that matter in any line of work. And Owahou certainly was. He could have very easily captained the *Gray* if necessary. In fact he was often consulted (in secrecy) by Cap'n Borden during a critical situation that might arise from time to time while on the high seas.

First Mate Connors was well aware of the status that Owahou enjoyed with the captain and the ship's owners as well, so he rarely pulled rank on the African. Connors only did so when he felt it necessary to save face in front of the crew. And Owahou was smart enough to allow it when necessary. It kept peace and everyone was content. Owahou had become very adept at feigning different emotions over the years as Elijah was about to learn.

The off duty crew were gathered in the galley for the early evening meal when Elijah and Owahou arrived below. They were engaged in loud conversation and barely noticed when the two passed by them.

When Owahou was confident that he and Elijah were alone and could not be overheard he said to Elijah "I am sorry for what happened up on the deck just now boy. I had to strike you in order to make Connors think that I was very angry with you and would indeed carry out your punishment. If I had not intervened when I did he would have beaten you to a bloody stump. You are most fortunate that I was not sleeping and was able to hear Connors yelling at you. I tried not to strike your head and face with full force. Are you hurt?"

Elijah was stunned for a moment and did not speak. He was confused at the whole experience. He had been on board ship for less than a day and had already experienced a variety of extreme emotions. First he was offered what seemed the opportunity of a lifetime by a captain he knew to be tough but fair. Then he hurt from leaving the only home, family and friends he ever knew. He had just seen his ancestral homeland for the first time in his life and watched his first magnificent sunset at sea. And moments later he was threatened with a brutal beating by a superior he was obligated to serve for the entire voyage. And finally he had apparently been saved by another superior who initially pretended to be as mean and threatening as Connors. Elijah was still scared and confused and decided there was nothing to be gained from speaking.... at least at that point.

Owahou could sense Elijah's fear and confusion and knew it to be justified under the circumstances so he decided to give Elijah a chance to relax and gather his emotions.

After a moment he said "Elijah, I must go up on the deck and get a tool that I left there before it is lost or stolen by one of the sea vermin that Connors and Cap'n Borden believe to be able seamen. I will be back in just a short while. Have a drink of water. It is next to you there on the shelf."

The African disappeared up the ladder and onto the deck. Elijah drank the water and began to realize he had no reason to mistrust Owahou. The slaps across his face and head were deliberately delivered so as to only appear damaging but had barely even stung. And he concluded that Owahou was right about Connors intent to severely beat him. He had seen the wild look in Connors eyes and was convinced the old sea dawg had lost part of his mind over the years. And Owahou conveyed a sincerity through both his voice and in his eyes that somehow put Elijah at ease. The frightened young lad prayed to God Almighty and to his grandma's beloved Jesus for some help and guidance just to make sure however. Elijah began to feel right about trusting the African. He decided to talk openly when Owahou returned.

Before Owahou returned, one of the younger ordinary seamen came out of the galley and saw Elijah sitting down in the mate's quarters. The short stout white man poked his chest out a bit and looked directly into Elijah's eyes. "Why ya sittin in me mate's quarters on ye arse when there's work fer ye ta be doin all about ye? Did ye think ye was a passenger on the *Gray* did ye? Maybe ye'd like a frothy mug of ale while ye're a sittin......huh boy?"

Before he could go further with his sarcastic spewing he heard footsteps behind him and turned to see Owahou coming down the ladder. He quickly moved back toward the galley after nodding his head to Owahou in a gesture intended simply to acknowledge his presence. It was not meant to convey submission or respect. Just after Owahou passed him he raised his fist toward the Second Mate's back and shook it in a threatening gesture. Owahou quickly glanced back over his right shoulder and caught a glimpse of it as the man abruptly dropped it to his side. The sailor was clearly embarrassed as he turned immediately beet red in the face before ducking back into the galley. Owahou smiled as he turned back toward Elijah. Elijah smiled back as he saw the humor in the situation as well.

Having loosened up a bit Elijah said to Owahou "Sir, do ye have eyes in the back of ye head..... as well as in the front?"

Although a bit surprised at the quick turnaround in his young cabin boy's confidence, Owhaou understood the attempt at humor. He was relieved that Elijah had calmed down a bit and felt more comfortable around him. He laughed out loud.

"No Elijah, I saw the intensity of your stare and that it was still focused on something or someone behind me even though it was *I* that was approaching you. Your eyes told me that something was out of the ordinary. And I know how most of the crew feel about me anyway. It is not surprising that any of them may make a gesture behind my back. I would be more surprised if they would speak their real minds to me or make a gesture in front of me. There is a lot of jealousy about my position and especially because I am not a white man. But even if I were white like them there would still be some level of jealousy and resentment simply because a second mate gets paid about twice the wages of an ordinary or able seaman. Unfortunately I also have to work twice as hard in many instances."

Owahou paused for a moment to let Elijah's young mind absorb some of what he had said. Continuing he said "Observing and adjusting the behavior of the cabin boy is only one of many responsibilities I have as the second mate. I have responsibilities on the *Gray* that most second mates on other ships do not. I am the one who is expected to go aloft and reef and furl the sails more so than any other. And that is at any time of day or night and in all weather. I am responsible for the daily mainte-nance of the ship including all the cleaning, swabbing, scraping and just about anything else that needs to be done. The captain makes the big decisions about where and when we sail and of course about our cargo. The First mate carries out the captain's orders and issues the commands to the crew. He is also responsible for administering any punishment to the crew if they do not carry out their duties and commands properly. Pretty damn near everything else is left up to me…except the cooking. My job on the *Gray* is an all the time responsibility. I don't necessarily have to do every single task alone but I have to see that it is done right."

Elijah never took his eyes off Owahou the whole time he spoke. Owahou took note of this. He had learned over the years that steady eye contact usually was accompanied by truth and good intent. Owahou continued. "But with this crew of lazy no gooders I am often alone in doing the tasks at hand. That is where you come in Elijah. I need a reliable ambitious helper that I can trust and depend on to do what is expected of him. A cabin boy is responsible to the officers. And you know of course that the captain's needs always come before anyone else. Usually next in line is the first mate, then the second mate, and perhaps the navigator or quar-termaster on a larger ship. But on the *Gray* I am your immediate supe-rior officer. In most cases the majority of your work will be directed by me. Cap'n Borden will sometimes intervene which is his right. And even though First Mate Connors has the choice by superior command to do the same, he most likely will not. He generally leaves the cabin boy up to me. It's just the way things are done on the *Gray*. And in your case it is in your best personal interest that it remains this way. After what you were about to experience at the hand of the first mate I think perhaps you might be agreeable...yes Elijah?"

This time Elijah did not hesitate. "Yep....I mean yessir Second Mate Seymour."

"Don't call me by my last name. Its better if you address me by my first name."

Elijah was getting a real education about life on board the *Gray* even before his first sunrise at sea. He began to think that God had delivered a guardian angel to him in the form of a good African man named Owahou. He whispered a small prayer of thanks to the Great God Almighty for his relative good fortune.

Laughing politely once again Owahou said "Who you talking to boy? You got a make believe friend?"

Elijah thought for a moment and then decided that he could trust Owahou enough to simply tell him the truth. "No sir. I ain't got no maginary friend er nuthin...Sir. I was just thanking me God Almighty fer me chance to be a cabin boy on such a fine vessel as the *Gray*........and to learn the ways of the high seas........proper ways I mean sir."

Owahou smiled. He understood. "Yes, boy, it is good to talk with your God. You will do it many times no doubt before we reach the port of New York."

Elijah had heard of New York before. But he had no idea where it was in relation to Mist Harbor or even the North Atlantic. He was already confident however that Owahou would get the *Gray* and its crew there safely. Het felt that Owahou was probably a very learned man......way more than even his best friend Harold. He also figured that he would need to trust *someone* on the *Gray*; and based on what he had seen thus far from Connors and the sailor from the galley, Owahou was clearly the best choice. Owahou had demonstrated in both words and actions that he was worthy of the young boy's trust.

Breaking into Elijah's thoughts Owahou said in a serious tone "I have to go aloft and adjust some of the rigging. It will take a couple of hours as long as the crew is alert and helpful. Elijah it will be cold tonight as we are about to enter the waters of the North Atlantic now. So boy, you must listen to everything I tell you carefully and do exactly as I say no matter what anyone else says to you. Now button your coat and pull the collar up around your ears. And grease your hands and face up with some of this whale oil soap right now. It will protect your exposed skin from the wind and salt spray. Take this scraper and spend a few minutes scraping some of the rust off the anchor chain like I told Connors that I would have you do. I'll yell down to you when its time to sleep. By the way, your hammock is the one closest to the entrance to the crew's quarters. That's so if Cap'n Borden or I need you during the night we can get you without waking the others unnecessarily. Now lets go up and get to work Cabin Boy Sermons."

Elijah liked the sound of his name attached to his new title. Hearing the words spoken by a superior in command actually helped frame the experience as reality for him. Up to that point the whole day had seemed almost surreal. Although still harboring fear of the unknown, he was beginning to feel a bit more optimistic. He was confident that he had the protection of an experienced sailor who was a fair man in his dealings with folks and one that would teach him well. And he still had the ear of the Great God Almighty. Once again the young man from the ghettoes of coastal Northern Ireland was filled with hope.

THE TORY ISLAND TACK

Elijah's first night on the *Gray* was very uncomfortable. He was unable to adjust to sleeping in a hammock that swayed back and forth with the movement of the ship. He was also bothered by the stifling odor of mildew in an area with no movement of air whatsoever. At one point during the ordeal he felt seasick but bravely fought it off. For the first time he was beginning to have doubts as to his fitness for seamanship. At least the worn out old bedding at his dilapidated place in Mist Harbor didn't move around throughout the night. So even though he was very tired from a lack of sleep it was a relief to hear Owahou's voice the next morning. At least he would be on deck for part of the day where there was plenty of fresh air and maybe some sunshine.

Elijah was wide awake when Owahou stuck his head into the sleeping quarters of the crew and said "Get up boy and get to work! Cap'n Borden will be wondering why his slop bucket hasn't been emptied and his grub delivered to his quarters. Move it you little bastard!"

Before Owahou's last words were even spoken Elijah was up and standing next to his new boss. He was a bit surprised at Owahou's harsh greeting. As they both walked toward the ladder to the deck Owahou addressed him in a tone barely above a whisper.

"Elijah, there will often be times when it sounds as if I am angry with you but I am not. I must pretend to be stern with you in front of the crew so that no one thinks that I am treating you on the same level as an ordinary seaman. Then there would be jealousy and it would only result in worse treatment for you by the others. Do you understand?"

Elijah quickly replied "Yessir."

Owahou had been honest with Elijah, but he did hold a secret that he had not revealed to the youngster. He had observed Elijah's behavior while in port at Mist harbor on one other occasion without the ladd's awareness. He had recommended Elijah to Cap'n Borden. And he had read Elijah's personality like an open book. He surmised that the boy had a very sensitive side and thus would be vulnerable to having his feelings hurt easily. And he was right. Elijah would have been hurt by the unnecessary rough words had Owahou not taken the time to explain the situation to him. Owahou however wanted to make sure that Elijah was alright before heading to the captain's quarters so he asked again.

"Are you sure you understand?"

Elijah smiled and nodded his head several times up and down in the affirmative. Satisfied with the exchange, Owahou went his way and Elijah quickly got to work.

After Elijah performed his menial morning tasks according to plan, he joined Owahou on deck for some initial orientation and training. The sky was feathered in layers of gray and the air was cold and damp. And within an hour of being topside Elijah's boots and pants legs were soaked from the near constant spray of cold salty sea water. Nevertheless he quickly learned some commands, a few new terms, and the beginning fundamentals of line and rigging work.

Owahou knew that Elijah would learn and retain some things from actually listening. But he would occasionally let nature take its course with the young boy and watch him grow on his own. Elijah seemed to be paying attention and repeated accurately most of what Owahou had explained to him. But the second mate thought it best for his new apprentice to learn some things the hard way. He knew that once Elijah felt the discomfort of a constant cold North Atlantic wind against a soaked body that he would seek a better way to protect himself from the elements at sea. And unfortunately for Elijah, the North Atlantic seas were particularly rough that morning as they broke against the bow with a jarring thud.

There was a sudden but apparently anticipated wind shift and Elijah heard First Mate Connors yell "Starboard tack."

A flurry of activity occurred on deck immediately following the command. The *Gray's* crew was forced to utilize the tack maneuver while sailing into a strong head wind as they entered the waters of the

North Atlantic in a southwesterly direction. And after almost a full day of sail they were still within sight of Tory Island. Elijah asked Owahou why the *Gray* would first move away from Tory Island and then back in the opposite direction toward it. Owahou explained that when facing a head wind the ship had to turn at an angle in order for the sail to catch the wind at all. And that would move the ship mostly laterally but slightly forward as well. At a certain point then the ship would turn in the opposite angle relative to the headwind and once again move primarily laterally but with some slight forward progress.

Elijah was having trouble grasping the concept. Owahou withdrew his knife from its leather holder and scratched a zigzag pattern on the top of a hogshead in order to diagram the sail pattern of the tack for Elijah. Once Elijah saw the sketch he was able to understand what the *Gray* was doing and why. Elijah was an inquisitive young man and he asked for further explanation. Although Owahou understood the physics involved in the forward propulsion resulting from the tack, he felt it unnecessary to explain.

"Elijah, while on the sea it is always very important for a man to know *what* to do in a challenging situation. Sometimes knowing what works can save a man's life. But it is not always necessary for him to understand *why*. This rule applies on land as well. Life is less complicated that way. A simple life has brought less trouble my way."

Elijah said nothing. He was still pondering the last part of Owahou's words. After a moment he thanked the wise African for explaining everything to him. The young aspiring sailor now understood why Tory Island was still in sight. He had also learned the basics of his first complex sailing maneuver, the tack. The part about a simple life seemed to make some sense as well. But it would be awhile yet before he would fully understand the value of that.

Owahou purposefully limited the interaction between the crew and Elijah on the first day. He wanted the new cabin boy to feel at least some modest comfort level with the fundamentals of routine aboard ship before the crew seized an opportunity to destroy any confidence the boy had. He had witnessed how nasty and degrading the crew could be to each other and in particular to a lowly cabin boy. So he kept Elijah busy all day scrubbing, scraping, emptying and running back and forth between the captain's quarters and the deck. By sundown Elijah was completely exhausted from all the long day's work and also from a lack of rest from the previous night. So Owahou sent him to bed just after their evening meal together in the galley.

Just before he turned in for the night however Elijah wanted one quick breath of fresh sea air. He quickly walked up the ladder to the deck and looked briefly out over the horizon. Much of the overcast sky had broken up and it was beginning to fill in with bright stars. Off to the west he spotted a thin sliver of bright orange and red sky still clinging to the surface of the North Atlantic waters. Owahou was standing only a few feet away.

Owahou said "Red sky at night, sailor's delight. Red sky at morning, sailor's warning."

Elijah turned and confidently replied "So we'll have us a good day fer sailin tomorrow right sir?"

Owahou was a bit surprised at Elijah's quick and accurate response. A wide smile broke out on his face. "Now get to bed boy......and yes we will have good weather for sailing tomorrow."

"Good evening sir" replied Elijah.

The *Gray's* new cabin boy descended the ladder and turned into his sleeping quarters. He collapsed into his hammock and was already asleep before Owahou had even taken his boots off.

THE NORTH ATLANTIC DRIFT

After several days of on and off tacking with very minimal progress westward, the *Gray* encountered a weather anomaly of essentially no sailable winds at all. They were still only about one hundred and seventy miles off the northwest coast of Ireland when they entered the North Atlantic Drift. The North Atlantic Drift is a slow but steady current of warmer waters that drifts northward. It exists between the fifty degree North and the sixty four degree North latitudes. The original course for the *Gray* was set for the vessel to cross through the lower one third of the Drift area. Based on an average sail the vessel would have been in the Drift area anywhere from ten to fourteen days. But with the very unusual condition of little or no winds the time spent in the Drift area would be extended.

Cap'n Borden allowed the *Gray* to follow the northerly drift for the better part of a day. After drifting uncontrollably off course for about seventy miles however he gave the order to drop anchor in an attempt to create drag and slow the northward movement. Since the depth of water greatly exceeded the length of chain the anchor was never even close to bottom. Therefore the maneuver was of minimal effect and after a couple of hours it resulted in an excessive level of stress on the anchor chain and the *Gray's* stern. Owahou and Connors were becoming very concerned about the situation while Cap'n Borden was napping below in his quarters.

When questioned earlier by Connors about pulling the anchor back up, the captain seemed uncharacteristically aloof to the whole situation. He told Connors to just wait for a bit. Connors backed down and retreated to the deck. Elijah pretended to be engrossed in scouring the port decking as Connors emerged from below. The young cabin boy had, however, paid close attention to the commands and exchanges amongst the officers for several hours. He could sense there was something wrong. For the entire afternoon there had been very little conversation amongst the crew and most had adopted a somber demeanor. He remembered what Owahou had said several days earlier about knowing *what* to do in a threatening situation. He was confident that his new mentor would handle the situation the right way.

Owahou and Connors moved to the bow where they initiated a private conversation in which Owahou spoke and the first mate just listened.

Connors made no attempt to hide his apparent respect for Owahou's comments as he nodded affirmatively to the tall African's every word. Owahou abruptly turned and walked back toward amid ship and then disappeared down the ladder. In less than a minute he reappeared and nodded to Connors. Connors immediately barked out the command to lift anchor.

"Lift the anchor and with haste" he screamed.

Just as the crew began to pull the chain up the whole ship began to shake fore and aft and the bow lifted several degrees and almost out of the water completely. Connors had the look of fear in his eyes and apparently was panic stricken. He simply could not speak. Owahou recognized Connors inability to act right away. He immediately called out the command.

"Lift the anchor!"

The crew looked at Connors for confirmation. There was no response.

Owahou screamed "Now you fools or she's going to crack her keel!"

A well built red haired able seaman turned toward Owahou and said "Hell no, ye black heathen. Ye ain't our captain. Hell, ye ain't even the first mate. We're a waitin for Cap'n Borden's orders."

Owahou acted without hesitation. He walked straight up to the sailor as the *Gray* began to make an even louder creaking sound and continued to shake violently. The sailor dropped the lines he was holding and raised both fists up as Owahou approached. Owahou spoke in a calm but serious tone.

"Seaman Hurley, drop your fists now and follow the command to lift anchor or face the consequences of insubordination."

Hurley glanced quickly to his left and gave a nod to a dark bearded seaman who had been crouched near the wench. Without hesitation the smaller seaman then lunged at Owahou's lower body as Hurley drew his big right fist back to strike the African. In one fluid motion Owahou lifted his left arm and came down full force with his fist on the back of the neck of the smaller seaman. Without changing position he raised the same arm and deflected the intended blow from Hurley's right fist. As Hurley's momentum carried him forward Owahou then came upward with his right fist catching the seaman under his chin with full force. Hurley's head and neck snapped back violently as his knees buckled beneath him, and he went down face first on the deck. Both seamen were out cold. From first contact to finish the entire encounter consumed less than seven seconds. The speed, accuracy and extreme force with which Owahou had dispatched his insubordinate adversaries was shocking to all who witnessed the bizarre event. It even startled Connors back into action. He barked the orders loudly.

"Ye worthless varmints heard the order now get to it! Lift the anchor!"

The creaking and violent trembling continued while the crew worked feverishly to pull the anchor up. And within a couple of minutes it was secured aboard ship once again. Almost as quickly as the threat to their safety came about, it was over. There was an eerie silence as everyone was relieved at the cessation of violent shaking and the ominous sounds, and thus the remediation of a possible life threatening situation. A couple of the able seamen even complimented Owahou on his recognition of the danger and his quick decisive action. Connors broke the silence as he ordered two of the ordinary seamen to tie the two insubordinates' hands behind them and drag them down into the hold with the cargo.

He then turned to Owahou with a wide grin and said "Ye did good Second Mate Owahou. Yer a helluva man. And Cap'n Borden will no doubt have them two charged with mutiny."

Elijah watched as Owahou simply smiled and went on about his daily routine as if nothing out of the ordinary had occurred at all. The frightened cabin boy had observed the entire ordeal from amid ship. He hadn't moved an inch since Owahou confronted Hurley. His emotions had run the gamete from fear, to shock, to awe and finally relief. He was still somewhat dazed til he felt Owahou's large hand tap him on the shoulder. Owahou knelt beside his frightened new cabin boy and waved his hand in front of Elijah's face.

"Are you alright there cabin boy Sermons?" he said.

Elijah was still holding on tight to the scrub mop with both hands. He looked up at Owahou and after a moment said "Uh...Yessir.... Second mate Owahou."

There was a pause. Owahou could tell that the whole scene had frightened Elijah quite a bit. He knew that the boy had survived the tough dock environment of Mist Harbor. But still, Elijah was only a kid who had most likely never witnessed such danger and upheaval so close before. And even though it had only been days since his life threatening encounter with the bully Shane McVeigh, danger on the high seas was different than danger on land. There was no safe refuge in the great blue water.

He said to Elijah "Are you sure you are OK there boy?"

This time Elijah reacted better even though Owahou could tell that it was a poor façade of bravery. Elijah replied in a slightly shaky voice. "I'm right as rain sir."

"Good. Then get down to the captain's quarters. He's not feeling well and needs some attending to."

"Yessir." He quickly turned to head for the ladder when suddenly the winds came up. "First Mate Owahou sir. Looks like we got our winds we been lookin fer sir."

Owahou turned and walked away and said "Yes cabinboy Sermons. We'll be on a dead run for awhile now until we take a port tack and make up some of the lost time from the Drift. All's well that ends well. That god you've been praying to must be listening."

As Owahou walked slowly toward the foredeck of the *Gray* it seemed to Elijah that the crew was looking at the African with a different expression than they had just minutes earlier. It was with a look of real respect; the kind that surpasses that given by necessity to a superior officer within the prescribed chain of command. It was the kind that is earned through actions that are consistent with the fundamental goodness that exists somewhere within all of humanity, but yet rarely seems to surface in most. Elijah was confident that the entire crew had gained an even deeper respect for Owahou than before the day's dramatic events had unfolded. He felt that it would be an enduring one.......at least for the duration of the voyage to America.

The next morning brought clear skies and more importantly a brisk, steady wind off the *Gray's* stern. By day's end they would make up the distance lost during the Drift and be back on course for the port of New York once again. The *Gray* had survived the ordeal with no damage and so had the crew with the exception of Hurley and his buddy. They were charged with insubordination and mutiny by Cap'n Borden and lashed to the keel of the ship below. There was some discussion of turning back to one of the ports on the West coast of Ireland and dropping them with the authorities but the captain did not want to lose any more time. He ordered them secured and restricted to bread and water rations only. They would be dealt with in the maritime legal system in the port of New York immediately upon arrival.

The captain pulled Elijah aside and warned him to stay clear of Hurley and the other insubordinate seaman for the remainder of the voyage. Elijah understood and assured the captain that he would follow orders. To avoid any confusion later however, Owahou advised him of the peculiar circumstances of the situation. He explained that normal protocol on the high seas designated the cabin boy to be responsible for delivering food and water to anyone either ill or under arrest aboard ship. But due to Elijah's inexperience their bread and water was to be delivered only by Connors or Owahou. Even the crew was excluded just in case some members might be sympathetic to their cause and be tempted to help them gain their freedom. Once charged with criminal conduct on the high seas, insubordinate crew members had little left to lose. Thus they became even more of a potential threat to the safety of the ship and crew than before if not properly constrained.

As the *Gray* sped along course on a straight dead run Elijah stayed busy running back and forth between the captain's quarters and the deck. His first priority was always cap'n Borden's needs but once those were met, he was eager to be back under the tutelage of Owahou. His trust and respect for Owahou grew daily as he learned more and more about sailing and adjusting to different situations that would arise unexpectedly. He had learned a lot about weather, fishing and agriculture from his relatives while on land but everything was different at sea.

On the high seas one was required to anticipate dramatic and sudden change in conditions and more importantly to adjust in order to survive. Elijah learned what a squall line was and how those low dark horizon to horizon clouds associated with it could travel very rapidly and bring on very dangerous gale force winds. Owahou had pointed one out to Elijah a day or two earlier and he warned his new cabin boy that the winds would be upon them in just a matter of a few minutes. Elijah was doubtful at first as the clouds seemed much further away to him. Owahou had acted immediately upon seeing the squall line rather than wait to see if it might curve around them. And sure enough Owahou was right once again.

Elijah was shocked at the powerful winds and how quickly they reached gale force. Had action not been taken immediately upon sighting the line, surely some of the sails would have been damaged or perhaps completely destroyed. The experience served as yet another important lesson in safety and preparedness for young Elijah. Even though there were many fearful moments on the voyage just in the first few days, Elijah felt safe as long as Owahou was around and in control. And already his confidence in his own seamanship skills had grown.

Fortunately for Elijah, Owahou had reduced the need for routine contact with Connors. Connors still barked at the young cabin boy occasionally and even reached that comical but annoying shrill high pitch tone of voice every now and then. Elijah would see the other crew members snickering but he had learned to control some of his emotions back on land and continued doing so on sea as well. He even caught Owahou himself giggling once at Connors silly outburst. He simply smiled in Owahou's direction as acknowledgement but was careful not to laugh out loud however. He knew Owahou would not allow his cabin boy to disrespect the first mate openly no matter what he really thought of Connors as a man.

Elijah had learned that the sailing life required discipline and absolute adherence to hierarchy and command. Otherwise there would be confusion and ineptness that could ultimately lead to trouble at best and disaster at worse. He was learning both the substance and content of sailing on the high seas but also the more virtuous characteristics of behavior necessary for a young man to properly mature and to move forward in life. He was indeed blessed to have such a strong *and* righteous mentor as Owahou. Perhaps it was a sort of balancing out of some of the difficult challenges that Elijah had already faced so early in life.

The winds of optimism, both literally and figuratively, seemed to surround the *Gray* for the remainder of the voyage to America. She enjoyed a very unusual period of steady strong tail winds which cut their travel time dramatically. It would eventually allow them to actually meet the original schedule for arrival in New York Harbor. After the difficulties between Owahou and the two insubordinate crew members were resolved there existed a more positive attitude in terms of a cooperative effort amongst the crew. And Elijah emerged as an integral part of that effort. He had continued learning and following his daily regimen and fulfilling his duties beyond expectation.

In the brief 14 weeks that Elijah had served aboard the *Gray* he had demonstrated his strong work ethic, his humility and sincerity to learn, and his competence as a cabin boy and seaman apprentice. During the last couple of weeks of the voyage some of the ordinary seamen had even begun to acknowledge him when on deck and occasionally included him in their casual conversations below. Several of them even wished him well on his 15th birthday. Elijah was on his way to living his dream of becoming an ordinary seaman. He had noticed seagulls near them the day before and so surmised that the *Gray* must be near land and perhaps only a day or two out from port.

Sure enough by midday one of the ordinary seamen excitedly yelled "Land ahoy! Off the starboard bow!"

Excitement filled Elijah's soul. Finally, he was going to see America!

NEW YORK

Once land was sighted Elijah thought that it would be a matter of only a couple of hours before the *Gray* docked in New York Harbor. He eagerly awaited the order for the crew to gather their personal belongings and make ready for departure from ship. But as the sun began to set in the western skies the *Gray* was still heading straight into what seemed to be open water. There *was* land to their starboard but it appeared to be uninhabited. And after several hours it seemed to have no end. The young boy was very impressed with its beauty as the bright afternoon sun displayed the land's white sandy beaches bordered by a dense green forest in the background. He continued his gaze even as the sun light yielded way for the night sky. His moment of tranquility came to an abrupt end however when the order came to turn in for the night. Owahou joined him for a moment as all the night crew made their way to the sleeping quarters below.

"It is called The Long Island by the Americans. The name seems to fit doesn't it boy?" said Owahou.

"Ohhhhhhh…….its really an island sir? I never knowed an island could be so big. It sure looks like a nice un sir."

After a few moments of silence Owahou said "We should be docking just after sun up in the morning so you should get to sleep now Elijah."

Elijah responded "Yessir".

Without hesitation he turned and headed toward the entrance to the hold. Just as he placed his boot on the first step to go below he heard Owahou clear his throat loudly. Elijah glanced back over his left shoulder in his superior's direction. Owahou was smiling at him.

"Elijah. You did good. You did real good. Your folks would be proud of you. You're on your way to becoming a fine sailor one day. You just continue doin right boy. Now git below and get your shuteye. You will need it in the morning."

Somewhat shocked at what he had just heard Elijah still managed to acknowledge Owahou's gesture with a verbal response and a polite nod. "Thank ye sir. Thank ye much."

After hearing Owahou's kind words he was filled with pride and optimism as it boosted his confidence. Perhaps it was the embryonic stages of self worth being born within him. Just moments earlier his mind was racing with visions filled with colorful imagery of what New York Harbor would be like. But in spite of all the exhilaration caused by the anticipation of what was surely to come in the morning, he somehow found himself very relaxed.

The *Gray* rolled gently back and forth with the ever softening waves off the waters of the great long island that led to New York Harbor. Elijah over time had grown accustomed to the steady rocking of the ship in the night. The motion had become a source of security for him and at some point during the voyage it began to serve as an effective sleep inducer. As he replayed Owahou's words in his mind he quickly fell off into a deep slumber.

The high pitched call of the seagulls awoke the *Gray's* seasoned cabin boy as a glimmer of light entered the sleeping quarters from the entry way. Just moments later the order came for all hands on deck. Even half asleep Elijah couldn't help but notice the similarity in pitch of Connor's voice and that of the gulls. Resisting the temptation to indulge in a moment of laughter at the old salt dawg's expense, Elijah quickly slipped his boots and coat on and was up the steps and on deck within seconds of the order.

"Yessir Mr. Connors. Cabin Boy Sermons at your service sir."

Connors was surprised by both the content and confident tone of the lowly cabin boy. But the first mate made no mention of it as the *Gray* was entering the protective waters of New York Harbor. There was no time for small talk. The order of the morning was for speed, accuracy and efficiency in every movement as the *Gray* needed to look her best when she entered the busy harbor. A coaster's clean, neat appearance often sent a positive message to prospective shippers about how securely their cargo may be handled and transported. And while in New York Cap'n Borden would be searching for high profit clients in need of the *Gray's* services.

The local harbor pilot guided the sleek vessel into port and adjacent the dock. The *Gray* nestled up dockside with only a very slight trimmer as she made contact. Even Elijah could appreciate the skill of the pilot and his own crew as the *Gray* came to rest after a docking that was as smooth as any he had ever witnessed.

Within moments a whole crowd of young boys had gathered on the dock next to the *Gray*. They were already pushing and shoving each other in order to gain the best position to get work from the new ship. Elijah realized for the first time that he was now the envy of the young boys waiting in line for work and rations. He stuck his chest out while skillfully tying several knots, and responded to Connors' commands in a loud, confident tone.

Connors smiled in Owahou's direction and the second mate was grinning almost to the point of laughter. But he held it in as he understood what a proud moment it was for Elijah. He did not want to diminish the boy's fragile self confidence. But still Owahou recognized that Elijah was a different person than the diminutive Northern Ireland lad that had gone to sea for the first time just months earlier. During the voyage on the *Virginia Gray* its cabin boy had suffered, endured and learned. And the experience had strengthened him in his growth as a young man.

AMERICA

Elijah spent only one night in the port of New York. He would depart the very next morning on an American coaster headed for Philadelphia, Pennsylvania before sailing on further South. His papers of indenture had been traded by the *Virginia Gray's* owners despite the objections of both Cap'n Borden and Connors. They both were surprised when Owahou stayed quiet on the matter.

Elijah was told that his debt had been transferred to the owners of the *Blue Ruby*. The *Ruby* was a commercial coaster that sailed up and down the East Coast of America delivering a variety of items from one port to another. Coasters generally were not engaged in Trans Atlantic trade. And like most, the *Ruby* was not as large as most sea going vessels such as the *Gray,* and thus operated with a smaller more flexible crew. On the *Ruby,* Elijah would be filling the multiple roles of seaman, cabin boy, and cook as needed.

Elijah felt a bit more at ease once he met his new crew. It was a relatively youthful group excepting the captain and first mate. And during the introductions he learned that none of them had experience in the open seas. Some even seemed envious of his experience on the transatlantic voyage. Elijah felt much less intimidated than when he had joined the crew of the *Virginia Gray* in Mist Harbor.

Elijah began to understand just how fortunate he had been to have learned under such veteran sailors as Owahou, Connors and the rest of the *Gray's* men. And he immediately understood that his relative value upon the *Ruby* was far greater than his value had been upon the *Gray*. This bolstered his self confidence and would also contribute to his immediate acceptance amongst most of the *Ruby's* crew. It also gave him a different perspective on a somewhat distressing conversation that he had earlier in the day.

Just before departing the *Gray* he had a brief but emotional farewell with Owahou. The tall African grasped Elijah's right hand in his and placed his left hand on the boy's right shoulder. He paused for a moment and looked intently into Elijah's eyes. He then delivered a brief farewell to his former cabin boy with great sincerity in his voice.

"Elijah, you are a good young man. You listened well and have learned more than even *you* realize. You will be of great value on the *Ruby*. Be respectful and of course obedient but always stand your ground when you know in your heart that you are right. Soon you will be asked to do things that will require your fundamental knowledge of right from wrong. If ever in doubt of what to do, just pause and pray to your god and you will have your true answer. Once you know what is right, you must then choose that path and remain steadfast. Following through with the right actions will require great courage. When that time comes you *will* do the right thing. I know this because I have seen who you are. I am proud of you my young friend. May our paths cross again."

The harsh reality that he may never see Owahou again began to settle on the young man. Owahou had become a surrogate for the strong caring father figure that he never had while growing up in Mist Harbor. Tears welled up in Elijah's eyes but with great discipline he held them back. He tried to focus on the positive compliments he had just received. But while Owahou's words bolstered Elijah's self esteem they also raised his curiosity. He wanted to inquire but Owahou had already anticipated Elijah's response. He interrupted Elijah's thoughts and in a very curse manner, delivered his final words to the young man.

"It is better for you to go now Elijah."

Elijah tried to speak but it seemed to anger Owahou. He interrupted Elijah and spoke in a very stern voice. "Your preparation here is done. Just trust me! Now go and report to the captain of the *Blue Ruby*. I have no more time for this! Go boy! Now!"

Caught off guard from Owahou's harsh tone, Elijah stood speechless. In hopes that he misunderstood Owahou's intent, Elijah searched for any sign in his mentor's expression that might provide a counter balance to the harshness of the sudden outburst. But there was nothing but a cold stare. For a moment he pondered the meaning of Owahou's last few words. He simply could not imagine any justification for the abrupt parting. But like other times in his life he had to once again absorb disappointment without expressing his true feelings. He forced the pain into a place deep inside himself that was a kind of holding area. The coping mechanism afforded him an opportunity to temporarily ignore the hurt and routinely move on about his business as if the disturbing event had never taken place at all. He would indeed have to deal with his pain at some future point. But standing in the midst of New York's dock ruffians was not the time or place to show any expression of emotion that may convey weakness. So in survival mode once again, he somehow found the self discipline to do as he was told.

Elijah looked coldly into Owahou's eyes and in a businesslike tone said "Thank you sir.......for everything. May the Great God Almighty be with Ye. Good by Sir".

Elijah made his way off the *Gray* and down onto the dock. When only a few steps from the *Blue Ruby* he heard Owahou's booming voice. "Until we meet again….. Seaman Sermons".

Still stinging from Owahou's insensitive tone, Elijah never acknowledged his former mate's final salutation. It only left the young man even more confused. But he did notice that Owahou had said it loud enough that even the crew on the *Ruby* heard it. Owahou was generally reserved. So any overt action on his part had purpose and meaning and those words were no exception. They were meant to both bolster

Elijah's self confidence and to create a level of respect for him amongst his new peer group on the *Ruby*. Owahou knew that Elijah would need both in order to begin preparation for the task that eventually would be thrust upon him. He had struggled with whether or not to reveal more details to Elijah as to what lay in his path. But he had wisely decided that the mission would have to remain a secret for the time being........even to Elijah.

PHILADELPHIA

When the *Ruby* arrived in the port of Philadelphia Elijah was summoned to the captain's quarters. To his surprise the captain told the young seaman that his papers had been traded once again from the *Ruby's* owners to a prominent local family. Elijah was in disbelief and very concerned, but contained his emotions and simply said a silent prayer for strength. The captain then went on to explain that the family had agreed to allow him to utilize Elijah's services as a seaman for the *Ruby's* voyage southward down the Atlantic Coast and back to Philadelphia. He was told that upon his return to Philadelphia he would then be housed in the family's home and work off his debt in their watchmaker and repair business. And from time to time Elijah might be loaned back to the *Ruby* for seaman duty on the coaster. The captain gave him a piece of paper with the name and the address of the watchmaker's location and instructed him to immediately go there to meet with the owner.

The captain said to Elijah "You will stay the evening with the family but report back here for duty at sunrise tomorrow. We depart for a southern port one hour later. Did you hear me Sermons?"

Elijah nodded in agreement and walked out of the captain's quarters and up on deck where the gray skies seemed a bit darker than just minutes before he went below. As he made his way down onto the dock he was somewhat dazed. Everything seemed to be happening to him very quickly and he realized that he had absolutely no control in any of it. His confidence began to wane a bit.

But Elijah began to remember Owahou's parting words to him: "Trust me son. You will be fine".

The emotional impact of Owahou's harsh tone had diminished somewhat since their farewell in New York Harbor. It was the content and meaning of his words that had remained in Elijah's memory. He still trusted Owahou implicitly.

Elijah decided that he would do as Owahou had said. He had little or no choice in the matter anyway. As he began to walk down the cobblestone streets he realized that he hadn't even checked the paper for the address. He was already several blocks away from the dock area and in what appeared to be a busy commercial section of the city with many fine stores. He quickly opened the folded paper and read it.

In a whisper he read: "Sol Berman, Owner, Berman's Watchmakers and Repair, 114 South Street, Philadelphia."

Elijah politely approached several well dressed men on the street in an attempt to get directions. Each one however just ignored him. He finally got the attention of a very attractive shapely dark haired woman who pointed him in the direction of the watchmaker's place. As she spoke to him she smiled flirtatiously revealing a small space between her two front teeth. Elijah marveled at her rosy cheeks and ruby red lips. They appeared to be painted on as they stood out in deep contrast to the rest of her very pale white face. For a moment he was unable to pay attention to her words as he became lost in the beauty of her emerald green eyes. Finally regaining his composure he thanked her for helping him and he watched intently as she turned and slowly sauntered down the street. She had only taken a few steps when she abruptly turned and looked back over her right shoulder in Elijah's direction and smiled once again. She knew that her beauty would capture the eye of any young man. Her full length bright red dress was adorned with white lace around the cuffs, bottom and neck. It was form fitting and it accentuated her small waistline and curved hips as she moved.

Elijah, pleasantly surprised at being the object of a smile from a beautiful woman, stood motionless as he watched the pretty woman move farther and farther down the street. She seemed to look directly in the eye of every man she passed and each acknowledged her politely with a smile, a word and/or a tip of the hat. The women she passed, however, seemed to go out of their way to make it obvious that they were ignoring her. As one middle aged couple passed her the man began to remove his shiny black top hat. This seemed to anger his gray haired wife as she began to verbally scold him. He stopped the gesture and placed his hat back upon his head and quickly refocused his gaze away from the young woman. Just as she was about to disappear from Elijah's view he noticed that she turned and walked into a tavern that he had passed on his way from the dock area. He pondered what he had just witnessed for a few moments and then a grin began to raise the usually downturned corners of his mouth. He never saw a real lady enter a tavern alone back in Mist Harbor. He naturally assumed that the rules of etiquette to be the same elsewhere including Philadelphia. He thought to himself how much prettier the harlots of Philadelphia were compared to those of Northern Ireland. Still smiling inside, he turned in the direction that the pretty woman had advised him to go.

After walking for several blocks he saw the sign for South Street. As luck would have it number 114 was just across from where he had stopped on the opposite corner. He crossed the busy street dodging in and out of the way of several horse drawn carts and buggies and stopped at the door before entering. As he peered at his reflection in the glass window his eyes began to gradually refocus on the myriad of sparkling gadgets inside. His curiosity was growing.

As Elijah walked into the store he was enamored by all the different styles of clocks on the walls. He simply could not have imagined such a sight. There were pocket watches the size of a silver dollar and clocks the size of a full grown man and everything in between. He began to hear ticks and tocks, gongs and bells, whistles and even the tweeting of a small bird. He counted himself fortunate to have seen such a place. He was duly impressed with America thus far. His mind began to wander with fantasy about the future in his new country when his thoughts were interrupted by a low guttural sound. He recognized it to be someone clearing their throat.

When Elijah looked up he noticed an older man and a middle aged man standing behind the counter. Both wore spectacles and had full length beards. And they were dressed exactly alike. Each wore a white long sleeve shirt with a collar and dark leather coverings from elbow to wrist. Their black bowties matched perfectly with their pants and skull caps. They had curious white strings hanging down the sides of their pants from the side of their waist. The younger of the two men seemed preoccupied as he was bent over close to the counter holding a watch in his left hand and a small metal tool in his right. He paid no attention to Elijah whatsoever. The older man however turned toward Elijah and smiled.

"Good day my young man. How can I help you?"

Elijah grinned back and said "Afternoon Sir. I'm here to see Mr. Sol Berman. I was sent here by the captain of the coaster.......uh, the *Blue Ruby* sir".

After an awkward moment of silence the older man slowly removed his spectacles and walked out from behind the counter steadily looking Elijah up and down as if studying the lad's pant and jacket size for a fitting of a fine suit. He looked the young boy in the eye and after a moment let out with a long sigh shaking his head slightly from side to side. He then turned toward the younger man and laughed out loud.

"Oi vey eshmere! It seems the captain has sent us a young man without a name!"

Turning back quickly before Elijah could say a word he laughed loudly and said "But if you had a name I bête a penny that it would be........... Elijah! A handsome lad such as your self surely would have a proper biblical name now would he not?"

Laughing loudly and turning once again toward the younger man he said "What do you think Samuel? He looks like an Elijah to me! Ehh Samuel"

Without ever looking up from his work the younger man uttered in a monotone "Yes Pop. Of course. You are right." He then continued his work.

By now Elijah began to understand that the whole conversation was playful and so he went along with it. "I am indeed Elijah. Elijah Sermons at your service. Would either of Ye gentlemen be Mr. Berman?"

With a smile that seemed to stretch from ear to ear the old man chuckled which caused his large round pot belly to bounce. His grin exposed a yellowish discoloration on several of his front teeth and the spread of his lips seemed to thin the hair in his graying mustache. He extended his right hand toward Elijah.

"Yes son. We are both Mr. Berman. But I am Sol Berman, master watch and clock maker and repairman. I am pleased to meet you. And this is Samuel Berman. He is my only son. Would you care for a drink of water or perhaps some matzo.......uh, uh, crackers son?"

Elijah had no idea what the strange word "matzo" meant but he clearly understood the words "water" and "crackers". Without hesitation he replied "Yessir Mr. Berman...sir."

"Samuel, please get some matzo and water for our young friend and bring a knife and that jar of grape preserves that your Bubby made."

Samuel never even looked up but turned and disappeared into a back room and within seconds returned with the items the elder Mr. Berman had asked for. He placed them on the shiny solid oak counter in front of Elijah. Elijah hesitated for a moment but then took the plate and cup of water and thanked Samuel and his father. Elijah was not accustomed to being treated so well but nevertheless took full advantage of the offering of kindness. He quickly devoured the treats while Sol provided a brief history of how his family came to live in Philadelphia and how his business got started. Elijah listened with modest interest but made no comments. He would ask questions later. He did not want to seem uneducated.

After the afternoon snack Sol explained the general responsibilities of Elijah's new job while in the store. They seemed very reasonable to Elijah.

"Fair enough my boy?" he said to Elijah.

"Yessirree Mr. Sol Berman. And thank Ye agin sir fer the crackers and sweets."

Sol then said to Samuel "Elijah is staying with us tonight. So he and I are going to leave now and meet your mother at home. Please close up in another hour and I will see you in the morning. Give my grandchildren a big hug and kiss for me please Samuel."

The old man waddled over to his son and kissed him on the forehead and hugged him. Samuel in turn kissed his father on the cheek and hugged him also. Elijah was surprised at such expression of affection between two adult males. He was not accustomed to that behavior. But there was something about it that seemed right to him in that particular situation.

As the elderly watchmaker and Elijah walked the mile and a half to the Berman home, Sol encouraged the young man to talk freely. By the time they reached the two story brick front house Sol knew Elijah's brief life history. He was not shocked but still empathetic for his new helper. During his 70 years Sol had grown very wise and had become a very good judge of character in a man. He quickly determined that Elijah was most likely the right man for the mission that he had in mind. He surmised that Elijah had a good heart. He understood now why the young cabin boy had been chosen for such an important task. In his mind he began to formulate how best to explain the entire situation to the young man. Their time together would be very brief. He would have to find a way to make Elijah trust him implicitly. He concluded that it would require blunt honesty and perhaps some help from his God above whom he called Adonai in his Heberew language. The old man's lifetime of experience had taught him that divine intervention was always helpful but rarely occurred in the absence of much sincere prayer.

As they approached the front door Sol said "Elijah, I am going to ask that you spend a few moments talking to my wife while I do my evening prayers alone. Please tell her everything about yourself that you told me today. It is very important that both she and I get to know you and that in turn you get to know us......and right away. We *have* to be able to trust each other my boy."

Elijah was again puzzled at Sol's words but out of proper respect did not question. He just submissively accepted Sol's direction for the moment. The elder gentleman seemed very sincere and had thus far treated him in an extraordinarily kind manner. So whatever was brewing must be right with the Great God Almighty.

Sol disappeared into his study after a brief introduction between Elijah and Mrs. Ruth Berman. As Sol had requested Elijah began telling Mrs. Berman the fundamentals of his life's story. When he concluded she complimented him on his faith in God and on his courage in making the voyage to America at such a young age. She then began to talk about her and her husband's own faith and tried to explain the shared common ground between Elijah's Christian religion and Judaism. Elijah had heard mention of Jews from his grandma before but only in Biblical stories. To his knowledge he had never met a living Jew.....until Mrs. Berman identified herself as one.

Concluding her brief but adequate explanation she then referred to the Old Testament of the Holy Bible. She explained to Elijah that what he knew as the Old Testament was known to her people as the Talmud. She then went on to quote several passages of scripture describing the plight of the Jews while in slavery. Sensing that Elijah agreed with her view that the concept of slavery was indeed unjust and a very bad sin she paused for a moment. She moved closer to Elijah and held both his hands in hers. She closed her dark brown eyes and lifted her head upward and prayed in a soft voice.

"Baruch Ata Adonai. Blessed be thou oh Lord our God, Ruler of the universe. Hear our prayers oh Lord. Give us strength in our righteous endeavors. Give us courage in all our efforts to right the wrongs of mankind. Amen."

Just as Ruth concluded her prayer Sol reentered the living room where Elijah and she were sitting. "Come. Lets eat. The sun is setting and we must offer our Sabbath prayers."

Turning to Elijah he said "It is Friday you know. Friday evenings and Saturdays are our Shabbat or as you, a Christian, would say, our Sabbath. It is like your Sunday. Please have a seat at our Shabbat dinner table."

Once all three were seated, Ruth then rose and lit the Shabbat candles and once again prayed in Hebrew followed by the English translation, "Baruch Ata Adonai. Allahenou Malech Alom. Asher Kiddishanu bomitzvotav vitzivanu lahad lachner shal Shabbat. Blessed be Thou oh Lord our God. Ruler of the Universe who by thy commandment has sanctified us to kindle the Sabbath lights."

She then turned to Sol and said "Dear, please do the prayer over the bread."

Sol picked up the roll of baked bread and broke it in half. Looking upward and holding the bread in both hands he began to pray aloud.

"Baruch Ata Adonai. Allohenu Melech Alom. Hamotzi lechem min ha auritz. Amen."

Sol then turned to Elijah and said "It is our family custom to have our guest say the prayer over the wine in Hebrew. Elijah would you please honor us by repeating these words after me. Baruch Ata Adonai. Allohenu Melach Alom. Bare Paree Haguffen."

Elijah had mixed emotions about saying words from another language and religion that was not his own. He secretly and silently asked for forgiveness from his God Almighty if he was doing wrong. He then complied as best he could with Sol's request. With a shaky voice he nervously repeated Sol's words in his Northern Ireland Scotch Irish accent. After a little help from both Ruth and Sol he was able to say his first Hebrew prayer. At the end he smiled triumphantly and sat a bit taller in his seat. After all, the Old Testament was part of his upbringing as a good Christian. He concluded that God would approve. He was proud.

After filling his belly with what was undoubtedly the best meal of his life, he offered to help clean the table but Ruth politely refused. She suggested instead that he and Sol move to the study and talk further. In an almost somber tone Ruth began to convey the seriousness of their meeting.

"We have very little time and there is much left to discuss and to plan. You and Sol must begin to talk. I will join you in a few minutes."

Sol motioned for Elijah to follow him into his study. As they entered the small oak paneled room Elijah was amazed to see nothing but books from wall to wall. Elijah had never read a book and was quite intimidated by the surroundings.

"Have you read some of these here books Mr. Berman?"

Sol laughed loudly and replied "Yes Elijah. All of them. And some twice! It is very important for a Jew to read and be as educated as possible. It is a very strong part of our history as a people. It starts with the religious readings of the Talmud, the Old Testament in your Holy Bible. As a good Jew, and I might add as a good humanitarian as well, I believe that knowledge is necessary as a pathway to truth.....And then truth is a pathway to Righteousness. Righteousness is then a pathway to God. And Elijah, isn't knowing and feeling the presence of God the true meaning of life? Isn't that what your beloved grandma tried to teach you son? Isn't that our final goal in life?"

Elijah took a minute to digest what Sol had said. He couldn't say that he understood all of Sol's words but most of his message sounded good and it did also sound familiar. And he believed that Sol and his own grandma were both good people.

"Yessir. I believe that you are right sir".

As Sol bent forward moving closer to Elijah, Ruth entered the room and sat next to him. Sol said "Please lets all join hands and pray now."

The three joined hands as the elder prayed with very emphatic tones: "Dear God, Ruler of the Universe, Our father, our Creator. Please hear our prayers. Open this young man's eyes, his soul and his heart to our words and your commandments oh Lord! Surround him with your power and your protection. Strengthen him so that he might do your will and successfully carry out this righteous task oh Lord. Amen."

There was an extended and almost uncomfortable period of silence. Both Ruth and Sol sat completely still as they stared intently into Elijah's boyish face. The serious nature of all the conversations and prayers of the last two days was beginning to settle upon him. Owahou's final words; the sudden change in debt papers ownership twice in one day; And the whole experience with the Berman's. It was all leading up to something. Elijah now knew that indeed some unusual task was planned for him and that he was about to find out what his role would be. Finally, feeling that the Berman's extended absence of communication was an invitation for him to speak, Elijah broke the silence.

"Well…..well. What is it sir? What is it that you want a feller such as meself to do? I mean…. it must be righteous with the prayin and all. Ye both are good people and ye've treated me kindly. So lets have it."

The young man felt that he had little to lose in getting right to the point. And the elderly couple respected his attitude and boldness. Sol and Ruth both spoke at the same time. Sol in his kind gentlemanly way yielded to his loving wife. Ruth smiled respectfully at her husband and then turned her attention to Elijah.

"Remember our discussion earlier about the enslavement of the Jews as told in the Old Testament of your Holy Bible Elijah?"

"Yes maam. I do. And I remembered that we both agreed that slavery is a very bad thing...for anybody" he confidently stated.

Sol's and Ruth's eyes lit up as they both smiled. It was as if the pressure had been lifted off their shoulders. It was all falling into place just as Adonai had willed it. Elijah was expressing the right values. His words were confirmation that their comrade, Owahou, was right about the young man. He was indeed the right person to implement their plan. Sol patted Elijah on the right shoulder and ended the gesture with a strong grip upon it as he smiled. Ruth once again held the young man's hand in hers and smiled in unison with Sol. Sol then reared back in his chair and turned toward his beloved Ruth.

"Well now Ruth I think we have our man. Don't you sweetheart?"

"Yes Sol……..without question dear."

In a voice just above a whisper Sol said "Elijah. There isn't much time left for explanation so please listen carefully. A while back in your Northern Ireland home town you were observed as you unloaded goods off a ship docked in your harbor. There was an incident involving a young African slave and a white sailor in which the slave was severely beaten. Your attempt to provide water to the slave was noted for exactly what it was…..a pure act of kindness. The entire incident was being observed from another ship docked just in front of your own by your friend Owahou who happened to be in port at the time. You were most likely unaware of Owahou's presence nearby and no doubt thought that you had hidden your true feelings when you witnessed the brutality of the attack. But Owahou saw you turn your eyes away. He is a very good judge of character in a man. Still, it was necessary for Owahou to get to know you over a period of time in order to confirm for sure that your heart was indeed in the right place and on the side of righteousness."

Pausing for a moment Sol continued. "Elijah, my wife and I are part of a very secret organization of good and righteous people who are dedicated to the abolition of human slavery. We assist others in their efforts to create means of escape from slavery in the southern United States of America. We purchased your debt papers so that we could place you in a position to help in this righteous battle. Once you have served as a coasting sailor for another year or two you will be perfect for the missions that await you. Once you have performed your assigned tasks then you will be declared debt free by us, your debt paper owners. This is our gift to you in exchange for your courage and righteous acts in assisting these poor enslaved people."

"So you see son. You have an opportunity to act upon your true feelings and also to personally benefit at the same time. You must, however, also understand that there is risk and danger involved. If you are caught by those who are sympathetic to slavery then you could be severely punished. We know where your heart resides on this issue son. What we are simply asking at this moment is: Elijah, do you want to do this? Do you have the courage to place your own life at some risk in order to save that of another fellow human being?"

Sol's and Ruth's smiles had faded to looks of total solemnity as they paused and gave Elijah ample time to think the proposition over. They understood how overwhelming and scary this whole experience must be for the poor young man. It was at that moment that they both began to view Elijah almost as their own son. They both began to experience emotional conflict within themselves about asking this very descent and naïve young man to place his own life in jeopardy. They both understood that his life had been for the most part very difficult and basically a sad one up to this point. He had just begun to emerge into a life of some promise. And now they were asking him to be incredibly unselfish and to potentially sacrifice what little happiness he had finally acquired.

Sol would have readily exchanged places with the young man if it were possible. He had been blessed for most of his adult life after fleeing the persecution his people had historically suffered in Europe. In America he had lived a long and good life. He knew what loneliness and suffering could do to a young man however. When he was Elijah's age he had experienced some of the same heartache.

Perhaps it was that very moment of empathy that caused Sol's momentary consideration of termination of the plan involving Elijah. He swore to himself at that moment that if Elijah survived the risk placed before him, he would do everything in his power to ensure a good life for the deserving lad. He would adopt the young man as his own son. His thoughts were interrupted when Elijah spoke.

"I will do it. It must be the Great God Almighty's will fer me. Me conscience is heavy with what I saw on that slave ship back in Mist Harbor. It was wrong and I knew it then but I could not do anything bout it Mr. Berman. But maybe I can now. If Owahou has chosen me for the job then I must be the right man."

As the word "man" rolled off his lips he suddenly realized that he had never before used that word in identifying himself. But in this instance it felt right. He thought to himself that maybe boys become men at different ages. And that it must all be on account of different situations in one's own life. He thought a bit more about it and decided that maybe no one would ever become a man unless they were forced into it by circumstances beyond their own control.

By the time Elijah had concluded his statement of acceptance both Ruth and Sol were in tears. Sobbing like a baby, Sol motioned for the three to stand and embrace. And they did. After the emotionally charged moment Ruth then disappeared into the kitchen and Sol settled down and began to explain the plan to Elijah.

The two men spoke for about another hour in increasingly greater detail. Then Ruth brought out a colorful variety of sweet deserts including

Hamentashen and Mandel bread along with hot tea. After their snack Elijah repeated the plan and his responsibilities back to Sol one more time. Satisfied that they both understood Elijah's role, they decided to turn in for the night.

Sol told Elijah that he would see him in the morning and that they would walk together back to the store before Elijah went back to the *Ruby*. Elijah asserted himself however and said that it would be best if they were not seen together. Swollen eyes from tears during an emotional goodbye would not project an image of masculinity amongst his new peer group. Sol was pleasantly surprised at the young man's keen sense of situational adjustment to survival. It increased his confidence in Elijah's ability to survive whatever obstacles he may encounter. He agreed with Elijah's decision. So they embraced each other one final time and said good night *and* their goodbyes.

Ruth gave Elijah a bag of fresh baked sweets to take along for the voyage to the southern ports. She then showed him to his room. Assured that her overnight guest's comfort was properly secured she then kissed him on the cheek and wished him a good night and a safe journey. Elijah was tired by the time he hit the soft warm feather bed that Ruth had prepared for him. His mind was racing with the myriad of possibilities that lay in his future. But he had fallen off into a shallow sleep about half way through one of his favored nightly prayers, the 23rd Psalm.

It seemed as if he had been asleep for only a few minutes when the high pitched shrieking of the gulls awakened him. For an instant he wasn't sure if he was in Mist Harbor or New York or in Philadelphia. But as his eyes adjusted to the morning light he recognized the embroidered six pointed star framed in oak that hung from the wall next to the bedroom door. Ruth had explained to him how it had been handed down from generation to generation in her family. It was the Mogan David, the Star of David.

As the cobwebs of sleep disappeared he began to recall the details of his conversations with the Bermans from the previous evening. He quickly refocused on where he was going that day and what he was charged with doing over the next few months. He was filled with excitement at the prospects of the adventure that was soon to unfold......and with some trepidation as well regarding the accompanying risk. Perhaps the gulls were once again notifying him that his ship of destiny had arrived yet for a second time. But this time he was more learned and less naïve than just a few months before in Mist Harbor. This time his boyish exuberance was tempered with the solemnity of his transition to manhood and the responsibility that came with it.

Unlike that chilly morning in Mist Harbor Elijah was now on a different continent and in a very large American city, the name of which he could hardly pronounce. He was totally surrounded by strangers with no family or friends to call upon. He was about to sail under a new captain and crew that he knew very little about. And yet in the midst of all these threatening conditions that would surely have induced boyish insecurities in most...... he had summoned the courage to accept a challenge that would place him in great jeopardy. But nevertheless, just like when he sensed the unique opportunity in Mist Harbor he was bursting with optimism about his future. He was moving bravely forward with his life that day in Philadelphia. He was on a new path of positive direction which was founded in his devout belief in God.....and fueled with hope.

COASTING ON THE BLUE RUBY

As the coaster departed Philadelphia Harbor it sailed directly into a brilliant stream of bright Sun that had just risen above the unusually serene waters of the Atlantic. The *Blue Ruby's* shiny sky blue bow cut through the shimmering green waves with ease. There was a good breeze and it was blowing out of the northwest so their forward progress was steady.

The shape of the *Blue Ruby's* hull was unusually sleek for a coaster. Her beam had been narrowed by a foot and a half from the average coaster width. This design diminished her overall cargo capacity in the hold slightly but it also diminished her resistance in the water. This gave her greater speed and maneuverability. Her owners had the vessel constructed with this in mind. She was well known on the East Coast of North America for meeting her appointed schedule in port. This gave her owners an edge when negotiating cargo fees. This edge translated into a higher profit which meant financial stability for the crew. It also provided a perpetual fund set aside for her maintenance. Thus she was always amongst the finest looking coasters in the East.

The *Ruby's* newest crew member was busy that morning lashing the lines and trimming the mainsail as the captain observed him from his vantage point near the bow. Elijah pretended to be unaware but it was always smart to know the whereabouts of one's captain. And the young seaman had learned to be aware of all his surroundings as a young boy. His survival in the tough dock area of Mist harbor had depended upon it. So he was not at all surprised when the captain tapped him on the right shoulder. He had seen him peripherally as the middle aged man moved toward him from the bow. The captain chuckled as he addressed Elijah.

"Mornin Seaman Sermons. Luck seems to be with ye today ladd. It's always a blessing to have fair weather on yer first day upon board a new vessel, heh boy."

Continuing tying off a neat bowline he looked up and smiled at the captain as he replied "Mornin Cap'n. Yessir. It's a fine day sir. And I'm surely thankful for it."

The two remained silent for a long period as the captain continued observing Elijah perform his assigned tasks. The young seaman was confident in his work as he adeptly completed task after task. He was comfortable staying busy. He was not so eager to engage in conversation with anyone as he wanted to stay focused on the challenge that had been given him the previous day by the Bermans.

Without experience or skills during his first voyage on the *Gray*, he was eager to reach out and seek advice and acceptance. Not so upon the *Ruby* however. He knew that he had to be careful forming any long term serious friendships. For the next 1-2 years he would essentially have to be a loner or otherwise risk exposing himself to danger. He was carrying a secret agenda on board. And there was simply nothing to be gained by having any in depth conversations that may inadvertently expose any of it.......and there was a lot to lose.

After several more minutes of observation the captain began walking away but turned and said "I can see with me own eyes now that ye are satisfactory at the skills necessary that ye be charged with. Carry on Seaman Sermons."

Elijah in his typical mannerly fashion would have thanked the captain for his compliment. But the bowlegged captain had disappeared toward his quarters before Elijah could even respond. He sensed that it would have been unnecessary anyway. The captain was polite enough but seemed to be all business and did not seem to need friendship or even the extension of common courtesy. And that was perfect for Elijah in this instance. He just wanted to do his job and get farther south to his ultimate destinations as soon as possible without interruption or trouble. In fact if it had been within his power to do so he would have headed the *Ruby* straight for the southern coast immediately and passed over the ports of Baltimore, Maryland and Norfolk, Virginia. But he was not in charge, so he would have to be patient for at least a few more weeks if not months.

By the end of his day Elijah was exhausted. He had worked very hard for almost 14 hours with only a midday meal break. He would have worked through the evening meal as well in order to avoid idle interaction with the off duty crew but was fearful that it might raise suspicion. So he entered the galley and without a word to anyone quickly slurped down his hot broth and hard bread soaked in lukewarm gravy. No one spoke during the short time Elijah was in their midst. This added to the already discernible air of discomfort in the room. He could not wait to finish his rations and leave. And with his mouth half full of bread he abruptly stood up and turned to head to his sleeping quarters. He was relieved to depart the galley. The relief was premature however as one of the crew spoke up loudly and directed his words to Elijah. He was a well built white man, a seasoned coaster crew member in his mid twenties.

"Yer a strange one ain't ye Sermons. Ain't nobody here goin bite ye. What's the resh boy? There ain't a fine whore awaitin fer ye in yer hammock now……. is thar?"

The blonde haired young man who had spoken laughed loudly, and he was joined by the others as the tension seemed to be broken by the humor. Elijah stopped and turned back toward the group. There was an uncomfortable silence for a few moments after the laughter died down. But then the corners of Elijah's mouth gradually turned upward. He began to chuckle as a full grin broke out. He was aware that no response at all would have been taken as an insult and may eventually result in trouble down the line. Only a few weeks earlier the former cabin boy of the *Virginia Gray* would have been intimidated by those words coming from an experienced and respected seaman. There may have even been a trembling in his voice during a forced response. But not at *that* time on the *Ruby* with *that* crew. So with confidence he said what he felt was only necessary and proper to diffuse any animosity that his self imposed isolation may have created.

"I meant no harm fellers. I'm jes slam tuckered out after me first day here on the fine *Blue Ruby*. And seein as I didn't ketch much shut eye last eve I'm jes in need of some good rest now. So I'll bid ye all a good eve and The Great God Almighty willin, I'll break fast with ye in the morn."

The blonde man speaking for the group replied "Well…. I spose thats good nough fer me……what say ye fellers?"

In unison and to a man they uttered their approval in agreement with their self appointed spokesman. Elijah concluded that this man must be the defacto leader of the crew. Relieved at the positive response, he turned away once again and headed for his sleeping quarters. The weariness in his body caused his boots to drag along the freshly painted oak planking. By the time he reached the sleeping quarters he could have collapsed and fallen asleep on the damp hardwood floor. Physical and emotional exhaustion had found a temporary home in the young man and was demanding that his body have immediate rest after a very busy and eventful two days.

Elijah quickly slipped his boots and jacket off and quietly climbed into his hammock so as not to awaken the other off duty crew members who were already sleeping and snoring away. A familiar sensation of the steady swaying of the ship dancing in unison with the gentle rolling seas made him feel almost at home. The elements on that night were the friend of the *Blue Ruby* as she steadily made her way southward on a rare dead run toward the port of Baltimore. Elijah began thanking the Creator for all his blessings and prayed harder than usual for the additional strength and endurance that he was sure to need soon. He concluded by whispering his favored prayer but before he even reached the middle verses he fell off into a deep slumber.

BALTIMORE

The voyage from Philadelphia harbor to the port of Baltimore was uneventful and in typical fashion the *Blue Ruby* made excellent time. Depending on weather and wind conditions the average time would have ranged from about 3-7 days. But she was unexpectedly held up at the confluence of the Chesapeake Bay and the Patapsco River just outside Baltimore Harbor waiting for a local harbor pilot. Had the *Ruby* not been delayed almost a half day waiting there, she would have made port easily before noon of day three. This dilemma infuriated the captain and first mate but not the crew. Their vested interests diverged at this point.

The captain was solely focused on efficiency of operation and financial gain for both the owners and himself. And a significant portion of the captain's compensation was based on the profit of the *Ruby's* overall operation. The less time the crew spent aboard ship the lower their cost to the owner(s). And the quicker the vessel made the journey the sooner it could set sail on another. This was more money in the owner's pocket and more in the captain's. But in most cases the crew was not compensated in the same way. So their interests lie elsewhere.

Arriving early in the day would have afforded the crew no opportunity to spend the evening sloshing down beer and flirting with the "ladies" of Fells Point in the dock area of Baltimore. Had the *Ruby* arrived in port before noon the captain would have demanded that she be unloaded upon arrival. His goal would be immediate departure for their next destination the same day. That of course would also be contingent upon the local harbor pilot's willingness to cooperate. But due to the delay she docked in port late in the afternoon on day 4 only a few minutes before sundown. Too late for unloading the full bill of goods designated for Baltimore that evening. Thus the cargo offloading would be delayed until sunrise the next morning. The crew was delighted. This meant a full evening of fun and frolic in one of their favorite port cities. And for a lucky few the frolic might include the brief but nevertheless physically intimate companionship of a fine woman. So given the time of day, the harbor pilot's delayed arrival was welcomed news to the crew......... excepting one, Elijah.

Elijah noticed the subtle smiles and frequent snickers between the crew as the afternoon wore on. But he was unable to make the connection as to why. He had learned much about life in the open sea but coasting was new to him. He was curious but he knew that time would eventually tell all. As the day passed on however the crew seemed a bit nervous as several kept looking toward the harbor area. Elijah, finally giving in to his curiosity, began running through the various what if scenarios in his mind. The first mate interrupted his thoughts however.

"Well. Thars the worthless thief. That'd be the fat bastard in that rowboat off the port bow sir. Roderick G. Smith hee self. Crooked as a black snake he be. The worse harbor pilot in all the ports any coaster has seen. Captain, sir, let me give it to eeem good. He'll no doubt be demandin way more than we should pay. If'n he does sir.... then what? *I* can take her into port sir. There ain't no danger here abouts in these waters.

88

Nothing but lots a big fish, blue crabs and fat oysters in the narrows of the Chesapeake and the Patapsco River Sir. I'm goin cuss him a blue streak. Then I'm goin knock his rotten yaller teeth clean out a his head!"

The captain had heard enough. "Allright Donehue. Ye said yer piece. Yes he is indeed a scallywag and no different than a thief in the night. But we are better off now haggling with him. We have the upper hand today. Its far too late for that bucket a blubber to row all the way back to the docks from out here by himself. And even though we would be required by law to furnish the thief with a dingy he would be too afraid to try it. There's no hurry now anyways. As soon as he boards we'll shake his grimy hand and smile and begin the talk about his fee with the promise of a bottle of rum from me cupboard below. But nare drop a rum shall touch his filthy tongue til after the docking of the *Ruby*. I don't want that drunkard touchin the vessel's wheel ifn there's even just a *smell* of liquor on eem."

The local harbor pilot finally boarded the *Ruby* several hours after they had anchored at the mouth of the Patapsco River. But before guiding her into the Baltimore dock area he was obliged to negotiatie his fee with the captain. Once the bottle of rum was raised, the captain was able to talk the harbor pilot into releasing the oarsman that had transported him out to the *Ruby*. This shortsighted decision by the pilot gave the captain the upper hand. Just as he had predicted the pilot was indeed too afraid to row back to port by himself. He had many enemies lying in wait in the dock area and did not want to be out after dark alone. So the captain was successful in getting a lower than normal fee. But the pilot emphatically conditioned his agreement of the lower fee on two points. First, he required someone from the crew escort him safely back to his room upon docking. The pilot stayed above "The Horse That You Came In On" saloon. The popular pub was only two blocks from the dock, which could be a dangerous place at night. His secondary condition, as the captain had anticipated, was the bottle of rum.

Thinking ahead, the captain had the bottle of rum available and had already designated just the right man to escort the pilot back to his room. It was the one least likely to be drinking and whoaring that evening. It was the one that was sure to return safe and sober and ready to sail bright and early the next morning. It was his *newest* crew member; the one that seemed so focused on doing the job the right way; the one least likely to stir up trouble.

The captain identified the same good qualities of dependability and character in Elijah that both Owahou and the Bermans had seen. And Elijah did not disappoint him. Within a quarter hour of docking the *Blue Ruby* the old pilot was safe in his tiny room with his beloved rum. Within another quarter hour Elijah was back on board the *Blue Ruby* in his quarters and heading for dreamland. Elijah's interest had peaked earlier after hearing a few tales of Fells Point in the great city of Baltimore. And for a brief instant he was tempted to visit the famed saloon just under the pilot's room. But he remained steadfast in his commitment to Mr. and Mrs. Berman. He was singularly focused on the preparations for the righteous task that was growing closer to a reality.

FROM THE LABRADOR TO THE GULF

The final port of call for the *Blue Ruby* before sailing back up the Atlantic Coast to its homeport in the Northeast was Charleston, South Carolina. Elijah had learned earlier that the *Ruby* would bypass one of her frequent stopovers, the busy port of Norfolk, Virginia. The primary remaining challenge for the *Ruby*, barring any extreme bad weather, would be avoiding the perilous shoal area off the coast of North Carolina. The thin strip of islands off the coast of North Carolina forms a barrier that separates the Atlantic Ocean from the Pamptico Sound. About midway along the ocean side of these barrier islands is where the warm waters of the northerly flowing Gulf Stream current collide with the cooler waters of the southerly flowing Labrador Current.

Both of these major ocean currents are very powerful and cover a large area. This contrast in water temperature and opposing direction of flow creates a great deal of turbulence both at and below the water's surface.

This results in an ever changing underwater landscape. It may result in the deposit of enough sand in a given area that a temporary island forms one day, but through the reverse force of erosion, vanishes the next. The danger to smaller faster vessels in such a situation however is not so much what is visible *at* the surface but more so what is just *below* the surface and virtually undetectable. The *Ruby's* maneuverability was superior to that of larger ships and thus she could change course quickly and avoid most uncharted and even very small land masses that appeared at the surface during daylight hours. But like any other vessel she would be unable to avoid running aground if the land mass was just below the surface and visible only at a very short distance.

So with this knowledge in mind the *Ruby's* experienced captain chose wisely to stay at a safe distance off shore of the North Carolina barrier islands especially at night. However, during daylight hours he opted to move back closer in toward the barrier islands, thus cutting some distance and time off the voyage to Charleston, South Carolina. This was a distinct advantage over the larger coasters. In most cases their captains chose to be safe rather than sorry, and therefore maintained a constant distance off the treacherous coastline. Of course there were those who faltered due to arrogance, ignorance, or simply sheer incompetence at the helm. Those unfortunates would often perish along with their crew.

The *Ruby's* captain knew how dangerous the area could be. His chosen method of adjustment was a pattern of abrupt changes in direction. It was similar to the zig zag tack maneuver which Elijah had learned under Owahou on the *Virginia Gray*. When the command was ordered on the *Gray*, however, there was always a headwind which necessitated the maneuver. But on the *Ruby* there was no headwind that day. So when the *Ruby* abruptly changed course once again in a zig zag pattern for no apparent reason, Elijah took note but did not question it. Still he was perplexed and even more so at daybreak the next morning.

As the first rays of morning light glimmered off the green waters of the Atlantic and Labrador Current, the *Ruby* once again changed course abruptly and headed west southwest away from the rising sun and toward land. Once again Elijah's inquisitive mind was rolling but he restrained himself and kept quiet. Just before noon his restraint paid off. As the sun shined brightly overhead he could barely see a strip of land off in the west southwest direction. He also noticed that during the entire morning a crew member had been positioned in the crows nest high above deck on watch. Elijah's curiosity was peaking and he was about to give in and inquire when he heard the sailor in the crows nest above him yell loudly.

"Sandbar off the near starboard bow.........less than a half a mile!"

The captain was on deck and immediately reacted with a series of commands which in just seconds turned the *Ruby* in a south southeast direction. Elijah understood that a sandbar was a submerged island just below the surface of the water. But to his amazement he never knew a sandbar could be that far away from land. By his estimate the *Ruby* had to be at least 12-14 miles off shore. He was curious but too busy to speak as he was very focused on following the orders of the captain in exact detail. He sensed the urgency in the captain's voice and surmised the situation to be serious.

Just as the excitement seemed to be diminishing the silence was broken once again as the crows nest sailor screamed at the top of his voice "Sandbar dead ahead and starboard bow.....falling off 10 degrees portbow! Imminent!"

Once again the captain reacted with loud and rapid voice commands. This time there was the unmistakable sound of panic in his voice. The command called for a course due East. Elijah wasn't sure what the word "imminent" meant but the tone and emphasis of the crewman's voice suggested danger. And when he saw the captain joining in and grabbing and pulling lines himself he began to understand. The warning meant that the *Ruby* was perilously close to the sandbar and in immediate danger. Once all lines were taut and secured, the *Ruby* began to turn into the wind but still slightly at an angle sufficient to catch some of it in her sail. Any more of a turn would have put her in irons, with no propulsion and forward motion capability.

The captain quickly called up to the nest for a new bearing relative to the sandbar. "Where in hell is it now boy?"

The sailor replied in a loud but shaky voice, "Hits centered 4 degrees port bow..... closin inside a quarter mile sir!"

Elijah saw the blood drain from the captain's face. The captain could no longer disguise his fear. His body froze in a rigid posture and he stared straight ahead in the direction of the sandbar. For a few moments there was absolute silence as the captain stood speechless. One of the senior crew members recognized the paralysis of panic as the captain appeared almost catatonic.

The senior crew member's blue eyes glared wildly as he turned up to the nest and hollered, "Last bearing."

But the sailor in the crows nest also seemed panicked as well and when he apparently could not respond the self appointed seaman in charge screamed "Git yer Arse down on deck now sailor! Before the main cracks and...."

His lips moved but with no sound as his words were consumed by a deafening roar that seemed to be coming from beneath the ship. At the same time Elijah felt the *Ruby's* forward progress all but cease. He lost his footing as his body was thrown sideways and against a hogshead next to the rail. He landed on his back on was laying on deck looking straight up into the bright sun. Off to the right of the overhead sun he saw his fellow crewman's arms and legs wrapped tightly around the main mast just below the crows nest. The position of the main mast relative to the sun told Elijah that the *Ruby* was listing badly to her side. He grabbed a line thinking that he would attempt to secure himself to one of the masts. He tried to call out to a fellow crewman but strangely there was no audible sound coming from his voice. He then began to understand.

A very loud and deep grinding sound filled the air. It was punctuated by a background of creeks and groans of boarding under extreme stress.

It seemed that the vessel would come to a complete stop at any second. It was obvious even to the least experienced of the crew that the *Ruby's* hull was scraping over the outer reaches of the submerged sandbar. Just as her forward motion ceased she then lurched forward aided by a small wind gust and the action of a wave. This same stop and start sequence repeated itself several times. Then she finally came to a complete stop.

The only sound for a brief period was that of the waves crashing against the port side of the *Ruby*. At first no one spoke, as the reality of potential tragedy began to settle on the young hearts aboard the imperiled vessel. The fine sleek solidly constructed *Blue Ruby* had run aground........but miles off shore....and with no other ship in sight. Each one of the crew suddenly (if not a believer before) found a burning desire to beseech their god in prayer. The words came in silence but from their soul's depths they sought help from the ultimate power. They felt helpless and with good reason. They *were* helpless. There was nothing any of them could do. It was completely out of their hands.

It is in life threatening situations such as that of the *Ruby's* crew that men learn about themselves. Dire circumstances render them helpless before their Creator. It was the first such experience for most of the young crew. In rare moments where men are forced to face their own physical demise the barrier of ego is replaced by a consuming presence of humility. Those who survive may benefit from such an experience in a positive way however. It is in this spiritual cleansing and rebirth that boys would often become real men. They recognize their relative insignificance within the awesome power of nature. And yet they still embrace their inextricable spiritual link to the One that created it, their Creator. Elijah had already grown through such experiences.

Even in what for most was an encounter with sheer terror, Elijah remained relatively calm. It was not due to any superior knowledge of seamanship or skill. It was more about how he had processed his previous experiences in similar circumstances. He had already learned humility over and over during his life. He had already learned how to open his soul and listen. And as a consequence of these past experiences he believed that he had been chosen for a divine task that had not yet come about. He believed that he would survive the ordeal upon the *Blue Ruby* even if others did not. It was less a conscious thought process and more of an overall feeling. It was cognition of the awesome omnipresence that surrounded him and the understanding of his spiritual connection and integration within it. He did not even think about tragedy or death. He just simply waited for the *Almighty* to right the *Ruby* and move her off the sandbar. And Elijah's *Great God Almighty* …....................did just that.

A succession of powerful waves had struck the bow with such force, that for most it felt like the *Ruby* would capsize. But instead, the lifting of the bow eventually just moved her off the sandbar and back into the sea where she moved forward seemingly of her own accord. The captain and crew were in shock at the sudden but welcome turn of events and remained silent for awhile after the *Ruby* was afloat once again. They were brought back to reality when the very low level sound of someone's voice pierced the quiet. It was Elijah. He was giggling. It slowly turned into laughter. The captain at first glared at his new crew member with disgust. But within seconds the laughter became contagious and soon the entire crew were smiling and laughing along almost in unison. And just seconds later the captain joined in as well. One might assume that it was comic relief. And indeed it was…... at least partially. But it was also an involuntary response as a gesture of thanks to the Creator for the outcome of the serendipitous series of events that would soon become nothing more than another tale of adventure on the sea.

As the laughter died down the captain barked out a few commands in order to re-establish control and the recognition of hierarchy aboard ship. It was almost an afterthought, as the *Ruby* was already headed in a due east direction away from land…...at least for the moment. As things returned to normal on the *Ruby,* Elijah's curiosity emerged once again, and he began to ask questions about the area and the obvious uniqueness of its sandbars. He was briefly educated by the senior crew member on the geography relative to the two major currents and their impact on the land and water in the surrounding area. He was surprised to hear of the frequency of ship wrecks in the area and of the tragic loss of life as a result. It was information that was viewed with a high priority as Elijah listened intently and stored it safely in his memory. He was confident that he would sail near the area again and he wanted to be prepared as best he could in the future.

With no apparent damage to the hull of the vessel the *Blue Ruby* was once again underway and at full sail. Her course however was redirected to steer very clear of the treacherous North Carolina barrier islands. They maintained a south southeast sail for another day until they were off the southern most point of the North Carolina coastline. It was at that point that the captain began steering the *Ruby* back in a west southwest direction. Their new course had them heading almost directly toward Charleston Harbor in South Carolina.

CHARLESTON HARBOR

After the ordeal on the sandbar off the North Carolina Outer Banks, the *Blue Ruby* made excellent time in her approach to Charleston's busy Harbor. Her arrival was ahead of schedule and early enough in the day to gain the services of a preferred local pilot who had a reputation for being competent and fair. He lived up to expectation as he brought the sleek coaster safely into dock about three hours before sunset. When he was paid he commented on the *Ruby's* ease of handling. From the point of view of a busy harbor pilot it was a very welcome characteristic.

With several hours of daylight left at the final destination port, normal procedure would have been to unload cargo designated for Charleston merchants and subsequently begin loading the outbound cargo before sundown. Thus the captain ordered the unloading of all remaining cargo immediately. To the crew's surprise however he refused to load any new cargo until the next morning. He wanted to lighten the *Ruby's* weight in order to allow her hull to sit as high out of the water as possible during the last hour of sunlight. He had already sent word to a local shipbuilder and repair carpenter to come and give his vessel a full inspection for any damage that the coaster may have sustained in her temporary grounding on the sandbar.

The captain even ordered the whole crew excepting himself and his first mate to go ashore and stay the night if they wished, so long as they were back at sunrise the next morning…….and sober. He also ordered them to take as much of their own personal items as possible in order to further reduce the weight of the *Ruby*. He wanted every possible inch of the ship inspected closely. He was responsible for the fine vessel and also had an attachment to her. Command of such a capable and beautiful ship as the *Blue Ruby* was a coveted position. He wanted to protect both her and his position.

Just as the last crewman left the *Ruby* the ship carpenter arrived. He instructed the captain and mate to loosen the lines to the docking posts and to use their oars to push the *Ruby* about 14 feet away from the dock itself. He got into a small rowboat between the *Ruby* and the dock and began his inspection at the port bow moving along the hull toward the stern. He then moved around the stern, inspecting the hull from the starboard up to the bow. He reported no obvious damage from the exterior that he could see. But in order to proclaim the vessel as generally seaworthy he would also have to inspect the hold and especially the keel and ribbing.

He then boarded the vessel and headed down into the hold. He advised the captain to be on the lookout for any stowaways and especially runaway slaves. He said there had been several runaways reported just in the previous few days. He explained that the *Ruby* would be a target for any runaway slave attempting to flee north by sea since she was not destined for any other Southern ports on her return to the Northeast. The captain vociferously expressed his appreciation for the warning. He advised the local carpenter that he would maintain a watch all night and report anything out of the ordinary to the local authorities. However, as a northerner and one who was sympathetic to the plight of southern slaves, the captain redirected the carpenter to the inspection and away from what he deemed an uncomfortable topic regarding runaways and stowaways.

The inspection was finally concluded and the report was good for the *Ruby*. She had sustained no structural damage during the grounding on the sandbar. The carpenter presented his bill for the inspection and was paid. As he reached the dock he turned back toward the captain and once more admonished him of the local runaway slave situation. Elijah was still sitting on the dock and overheard the brief conversation. He also noticed that when the carpenter began to walk away, the captain turned to the first mate and rolled his eyes in disgust. He turned toward Elijah with a welcome smile and motioned him to come aboard. But just as he arose to board the *Ruby* a young man came running over to the captain and placed an envelope in his hand. Without a word exchanged between them the young man turned and disappeared behind an old warehouse. The captain once again motioned for Elijah to follow him aboard the *Ruby*.

He excused the mate and told him that Elijah would be staying on board to maintain security for the first evening shift. He ordered the mate to return however by midnight so that he could relieve Elijah of the post. He then invited Elijah in to his private quarters. They sat for a moment in awkward silence. The captain pulled a bottle of dark rum out of a cabinet and poured himself a drink. To Elijah's surprise the captain acknowledged that his newest crew member did not drink alcohol. Elijah did not speak however. He was singularly focused on why he was in Charleston and did not want to reveal anything at that moment that was not absolutely necessary.

The captain said "I know quite a bit about you son. Way more than you think. We don't have much time left to speak now and it is very important that you listen to me carefully. I know that you are courageous and a man of good moral character. I know why you were sent here and where you came from and who you apprenticed under. I have your papers of transfer to your new ship. One of their crew has been absent from the vessel since they docked here early this morning. He will not be returning. So they will be eager to have an available cabin boy and crew member with my recommendation. They are shipping out just after sunrise tomorrow. The original departure was scheduled for today but there was some cargo that was held back on purpose by the shipper to be loaded *only* tomorrow morning. It ensured their presence in port tonight which is as you now know a necessity. Otherwise you would not have been available to join the crew. She is headed south to Savannah. It will give you the opportunity to visit that port and study its characteristics and people."

The captain paused to sip his rum and to allow Elijah a moment to recompose as he understood the shock value of his words on the unsuspecting young man. Elijah was quietly amazed at what he had just heard and wanted to ask many questions, but to his credit exerted extraordinary self discipline and remained tight lipped. He had no idea that the captain was aware of his agreement with the Bermans.

The captain then continued. "When we finish our talk here you should go up on deck and sit where you are very visible to any passers by until about an hour after dark. Then report to your new ship. I will take watch in your place until my mate returns. Your new ship is the three masted coaster anchored at the end of the dock nearest the sound."

Pausing to allow Elijah a moment to absorb it all, he then continued saying, "After you have served on this new coaster for a period of 3-4 months you will be re-assigned to other coasters but only for periods of no longer than 4-6 months at a time. When you complete this period of further training and investigation you will then begin to carry out your assignment from the Bermans. Do you have any questions?"

Elijah was somewhat stunned but nevertheless still focused on the task before him and replied in the most polite terms. "No sir. I don't have any questions sir. Uh...well...I mean uh... yessir I do.... but me thinks it best to go on about me business here sir and uh...thank ye very much for ye help. May God Almighty bless ye sir."

The captain looked the young man in the eye and nodded his approval. They both rose from their sitting positions. The captain smiled as the two shook hands. Elijah then turned to go up on deck for his hour of watch. The captain followed to the point where he could see Elijah standing next to the rail.

"Good luck to you son. May God be with you."

Elijah turned and said "Thank ye sir. I'll sure be in need of heem for awhile."

GROWING BEFORE THE MAST

For the two years after his departure from the *Blue Ruby* Elijah continued developing his skills as both a cabin boy and as a sailor. During that time he visited every major port city from Boston to Savannah and many of the smaller ones as well. Had he been assigned to just one ship that sailed as a transatlantic vessel for that same period of time he would have very likely achieved the class of ordinary seaman. But part of fulfilling the commitment that he made to the Bermans required him to work on not just one, but several different coasters. And with every new ship there would be a period of adjustment to yet another captain and another crew. He would have to prove himself worthy of their respect in each individual case. And it seemed that no sooner had he reached that point, that he would then be re-assigned to another ship. The frequent changes in his work environment proved very frustrating for a young man who had repeatedly demonstrated both the ambition and work ethic requisite to improving one's lot in life. There were many times that he regretted accepting the mission and at least two instances where he came very close to quitting and returning to Mist Harbor. But he somehow found the will to persevere and stick to his word.

Part of the preparation for his mission was to learn as much as possible about the people, customs and the surrounding geography of the southern ports along the East Coast. He was also expected to make contact with at least one member of the abolitionist group in every port he visited in the South. It was these folks who facilitated his communication with the Bermans for the most part. But during the four overnight stops in Philadelphia he was able to visit them and enjoy a good meal and indulge in all the comforts of home. The visits with them always drew the three closer and their encouraging words renewed Elijah's energy and commitment to their goals. By the end of the two years the Bermans had become almost like surrogate grandparents to him.

It was during his fourth visit with the Bermans that he was told that he was ready to move into the real action phase of his mission. It had been two years since their first meeting and both Sol and Mrs. Berman expressed their pleasure and pride at seeing his growth as a competent sailor and more importantly as a young man of high moral character. They repeatedly expressed their gratitude for what he had endured over the period of time that he served before the mast on the various coasters. They also emphasized the critical value of the information that he had gathered and provided to them during that period. As promised they gave him the documents that released him of any further obligation. This in effect granted him the legal right to walk away from any future action at that point had he chosen to. But he had a clear moral obligation to fulfill and the close relationship he had with the Bermans was more than enough motivation for Elijah to insure that he would indeed do just that.

So after a restful and rejuvenating seven days with the Bermans, Elijah met his new captain and crew. It was with an air of optimism and excitement that he first boarded the elegant *Sunflower* on a hot humid August morning in Philadelphia Harbor. She was the most beautiful vessel he had ever seen. The *Sunflower's* reddish brown mahogany wheel and railings stood out clearly against her pure white sails which were still wrapped tightly on their booms. The early morning sun revealed a prominent oak grain running through her thick triple masts. Her lines were perfectly coiled on her shiny deck and appeared virtually unused. From stem to stern every aspect of the *Sunflower* suggested nothing spared in her design, construction or maintenance.

Instead of the first mate it was Captain Richard Stile who welcomed his new crew member on board the pristine *Sunflower*. And to Elijah's pleasant surprise the captain personally led him on a full tour of his ship. Before assigning Elijah his position and duties, Captain Stile provided a full history of the *Sunflower* and its owners, builders and current crew including himself. It was an unprecedented introduction for a new crew member to say the least. He asked Elijah if he had any questions and then patiently answered each one in detail. There was something in Captain Stile's voice and smile that Elijah, in his discerning way, deemed to be both honorable and sincere. The professional demeanor and patience in which he spoke with Elijah was indeed impressive. But there was more to it than that. Perhaps it was the ease at which he established and maintained direct eye contact when speaking to his newest crew member. Elijah wasn't sure exactly what it was, but he felt confident that Richard Stile was truly a good man with a kind heart. He surmised that the special treatment he received that day was somehow connected to his association with the Bermans and their righteous mission. And Captain Richard Stile seemed to be the type of man that would be involved with such an effort.

But still Elijah was disappointed to learn that his duties on the *Sunflower* would be primarily that of cabin boy and sailor upon demand. At first he felt it was degrading to be relegated once again back to the lowly position of cabin boy. Yes, the lad from Mist Harbor had grown somewhat in his emotional maturity over the last two years but he was still a young man and driven on occasion by ego. Elijah had expected to possibly share the duties of cabin boy with another crew member of equal experience. But he also hoped to function as a sailor for at least half his time under Captain Stile. After a day at sea, however, he refocused on his *real* mission and remembered how important it was. Perhaps in his renewed sense of responsibility he saw how insignificant the duties at sea were when compared to his higher calling as a God fearing and righteous man. He also remembered Sol's advice for him to lay low and do nothing to draw attention. The less folks knew about Elijah and his secret agenda, the better. He remembered Sol's exact words.

"Elijah. It is very important that during your mission you live in the shadows. Listen and observe. Listen more than you think you need to.....and especially before you speak. Watch with your eyes open..... but do not stare. Remember son, it is the bird that struts with wings spread and that sings the loudest that becomes the easiest prey."

As the *Sunflower* turned due south under a strong tailwind her sails filled and Elijah said a silent prayer of thanks for his release from debt. He also asked for continued guidance and discipline and for the courage he would need to carry out the task that was just days ahead. And there would be no more trial runs. This time it was for real. He had questioned the decision of the Bermans two years before in delaying his direct participation in the mission at that time. But more recently he had begun to appreciate the wisdom of their plan. He was infinitely more prepared in his seventeenth year of life than when he walked into Sol's shop as a young naïve boy from the ghettos of Mist Harbor two years earlier. But as the *Sunflower* sailed out of the port of Philadelphia his senses seemed to heighten. And although the reality of the increased risk to his well being was duly noted in his mind, it seemed to prefer the space between his throat and his belly to settle. It manifested as an ever increasing tightness as the *Sunflower* moved further and further south.

When the *Sunflower* glided smoothly into a bustling Baltimore Harbor he was visibly edgy. And by the time it docked in Norfolk he had become filled with anxiety. Then when it finally dropped anchor in Charleston Harbor at dusk on an oppressively warm humid evening, his anxiety had evolved into all out fear. And when he reported to his new ship the next morning his voice betrayed his self discipline in the form of an obvious tremble. It was all he could do just to speak. Fortunately however his boyish appearance, even for seventeen, played a disarming role in his first encounter with the ship's first mate. The mate assumed that Elijah was several years younger than his real age and thus less experienced than he actually was. So he was not surprised to see signs of fear in the young man.

The first mate feigned a look of concern but then laughed out loud saying, "Ye Sermons ain't ye?"

Elijah replied "Yes…yes..sir. That ud be me sir."

"Well git below boy and git at yer work. The capn's a waitin fer ye. Ye be fine once we get ta rollin with the seas of the Gulf Stream and the Noreasterly winds at yer face. Ye got Scotch Arish in ye, right boy? Ye belong uponst the water."

"Yesir" replied Elijah.

Somewhat relieved and as ever thankful to his Great God Almighty to clear his first obstacle, he quickly turned away and headed down toward the captain's quarters. The contact with the first mate seemed to break the tension for Elijah. The knot in his stomach disappeared and he began to feel more confident. By the time he reached the captain's quarters he felt almost normal again. However, he was completely unprepared for his next encounter. When he actually saw the captain he almost burst into laughter. He was even shorter than Elijah but his girth seemed to equal his height. He was so heavy that it was an effort for him to simply pivot his body a quarter turn when Elijah entered the room. When his weight shifted the floor boards creaked and groaned from the stress. He was dressed in a shiny gold jacket with matching pants that looked as if they would split at the seams with a slight bend of the waist. His breathing was labored and it sounded to Elijah more like snoring. It was hard to tell where his chin ended and his upper chest began. There was no visible proof of a neck or collar bone on his body. He was truly one of the strangest looking men that Elijah had ever encountered...... and especially as the captain of a coaster.

And unfortunately for Elijah, the captain's demeanor was even worse than his appearance. When Elijah introduced himself the captain just growled and stared expressionless while peering at him over his tiny wire rim spectacles. He never uttered an intelligible word in the two to three minutes that they were in the presence of each other. He just continued growling with an occasional syllable thrown in for good measure. Elijah was simply incredulous. He just stood motionless and quiet and waited patiently for any direction at all. He strained his ears and mind to understand any of the sounds. And other than a few curse words it was futile. He was thankful when finally the first mate interrupted them.

The mate told the captain he needed Elijah up on deck to help lash some extra hogsheads securely on deck as there was no more space in the hold for additional cargo. Apparently expecting no response from the captain, he took Elijah by the left forearm even before he was finished speaking. Without another word he led the shocked young cabin boy toward the steps leading up onto the deck.

Elijah was incredulous at what had just taken place in the captain's quarters. He turned and glanced over his right shoulder back at where the captain still stood motionless. Once more their eyes met. There was something in the rotund captain's look that was unnerving to Elijah. He sensed the presence of evil in the man. And although still youthful, Elijah was nevertheless very perceptive in his ability to judge character and kindness...... or the absence thereof in a man's heart. The assessment of his new captain's personality as one filled with bitterness and evil would later be proven accurate. And the next time their eyes would meet in such a manner........ there would be hell to pay.

PART II

THE WEST AFRICANS
EMBATO

EMBATO

"I learned that courage was not the absence of fear, but the triumph over it. The brave man is not he who does not feel afraid, but he who conquers that fear. "
Nelson Mandela

"Embato moy ar deuk bi!" Embato protects the village.

A significant portion of his life had been spent in preparation for his first step into manhood. Finally the big day arrived. He would be acknowledged as an adult and accepted into the brotherhood that was responsible for protecting the village of Gambeya. It was a responsibility but also a coveted honor. One granted only upon successful completion of intense training over much of his childhood and early adolescence. From ages 7-10 years he studied with the elders learning of his people's history, spirituality, culture, language, and medicine. And from 11-14 he was trained in hunting, fishing, survival, fighting skills, and battle strategy. Embato Ngawai was the first of his Ongaway Clan to ever achieve the revered position of Protector by his 14th birthday. It was a time of great optimism for the entire village and particularly so for Embato's family and clan.

The medicine chief, Guyoime, formally presented Embato to the elders for his final challenge of the day. The young man stood bravely as the flesh surrounding both his triceps were pierced with a thin solid ivory point by two fellow protectors. The entry points were in the back of the upper arm and exit points toward the front and outer side. The Ivory stays in the flesh but protrudes at both ends. In order to keep the Ivory in place during the healing process a thin twine of bark is soaked and then tied several times onto both ends. The resin from the bark acts as both a disinfectant and as a temporary glue which holds for about four weeks. During the wound healing the flesh grows tightly around the ivory thus permanently securing the ancient symbol of courage and sacrifice. It is a symbol that can strike fear in the hearts of enemies. There is, however, significant pain during the healing period.

As the ceremony began Chief Guyoime proclaimed Embato to be an exceptional student and warrior with special gifts from Borombi (Creator). During the long oratory there was a moment when Embato thought he would pass out from pain and exhaustion. His prayers to Borombi, however, sustained him and he was able to endure. But still, it was a great relief when he witnessed the chief elder extinguish the sacred fire. The ceremony was finally over! Before placing the ceremonial torch back in its protected position, however, the elder signalled the start of the celebration by kindling the festival fire.

The celebration began with traditional song and dance followed by a feast. But the events surrounding the sacred rite of passage left Embato with little energy for celebration. The adrenalin flowing through his body since early morning had helped to subdue the physical pain and see him through the day. But as the harvest moon rose into the clear night sky of Senegambia, he began to tire. Soon afterward he thanked the elders and all those in attendance and quietly slipped away to the prayer hut. On that night it was reserved especially for him. Although he was spiritually strengthened, he was exhausted after the three day fast and solo vigil that preceded the ceremony. As he whispered one last humble prayer of thanks to Borombi he fell quickly into a deep sleep. In the dream world he was one with the spirits of Kimbo and other warrior ancestors. And they acknowledged his achievement and surrounded him with their protection.

The next morning Embato could barely move his arms due to the soreness from the piercing. But he still had to demonstrate his ability to withstand physical pain, an integral part of being a protector. Although in agony, he stepped out of the kipjo and into his new life with a smile. He walked directly into the bright sun of an early fall morning which revealed the details of his handsome face and lean body. The other protectors waited for him to join their sacred circle which they had formed a few feet from the prayer hut. They knew his pain from their own initiation experiences but were forbidden to express any empathy. It would be viewed as an insult to Embato's manhood.

Before leading the morning prayer, his first act as a village protector, Embato was required to break into the sacred circle in order to become part of it. It was more symbolism than action but nevertheless did require some modified degree of physical force and thus some significant pain. By breaking the sacred circle he was temporarily weakening it and demonstrating his ability to overcome physical pain. Conversely by joining and healing the sacred circle he once again made it whole and actually increased its strength beyond what it had been prior to the break. This simple act symbolized two of the most important characteristics of the brotherhood: strength and unity.

While still maintaining the circle, each protector simultaneously turned toward the East to face the early morning sun. Embato prayed first, giving thanks for all of nature's life sustaining elements. He concluded by seeking guidance from the ancestral spirits and asking Borombi for protection for all his people. Each protector also made a brief supplication to Borombi but with a personalized slant of their own creation. As each member prayed, the group turned slightly in a counterclockwise motion so as to eventually acknowledge all directions and thus the entire universe. Spiritually empowered, they were ready to take on their daily responsibilities.

Upon completion of the prayers the group of fourteen protectors broke up into four subgroups; two groups of four each and two groups of three each. The two groups of four each were generally the oldest but always the most competent of the protectors. One of the elder groups of four was responsible for patrolling and protecting the village while the other hunted local game and fowl. Both groups started from a point opposite each other and moved counterclockwise in a circular direction at a specified speed based on the position of the sun. This pattern of movement enabled them to stay at safe distances from each other during the day. The smaller, younger and less experienced groups of three each also alternated every other day mimicking the actions of their elders but doing so in a much smaller circle and closer to the village.

Embato was initially assigned to the younger patrolling warrior group of three each. He was already superior in strength, speed and skill to that group's leader but humbly followed him. It would have been disrespectful to assume a leadership role on his first day as a protector. He also needed time to heal before any serious physical exertion requiring the use of his arms. This would also be an opportunity to strengthen his bond with the others and learn from them. Everyone seemed to like him and he felt the same toward them. He was eager to learn and always asked for the gift of new knowledge in his prayer.

Most of the villagers and protectors acknowledged that Embato was a very special young man. He had indeed been given many talents and physical attributes by Borombi. But this was only part of what made him special. He recognized the value of his gifts within the context of their potential contribution to the survival of his people. His father had explained to him several years earlier that the gifts were given by Borombi *only* for the benefit of the people and not as a source of personal admiration for himself. He remembered his father's exact words.

"Embato, if you use the gifts for personal gain then Borombi will take them from you. You must always think of our people first and act in their best interest."

His father was wise and had put it into simple words that a young boy could understand.

And Embato understood the concept of communal responsibility relative to his unique gifts even at the age of ten. The acceptance of the gifts as a *responsibility* instead of a personal asset was what separated Embato from the others who were also gifted. That understanding was what motivated him to be vigilant and studious. It also led him down a path of humility instead of conceit. It was this unique combination of personal characteristics that led Embato to a position of respect with his people.

After several days Embato's arms began to heal and he was told to join one of the elder groups in patrolling the outer circle boundary. This group was always at greater risk than the others and thus was made up of the elite among the protectors. Each one possessed superior strength, speed and skill to that of the members of the elder hunting group. With the exception of Embato, their age range was from mid twenties to late thirties.

Jimba Suweata, the eldest at 42, was the leader of the protectors of Gambeya. He welcomed Embato with some concern regarding his young age but also with enthusiasm and expectation regarding his future. He was always supportive and willing to invest time in Embato's development. Over time Jimba would begin to see Embato as his future successor. Koli 24 and Somil 28 followed Jimba's lead with their acceptance and support of Embato. They also recognized the potential in the young man as a valued protector and possibly a great leader. The two of them were humble and wanted only what was best for their people without regard to personal reward. They provided excellent role models for Embato. It counter balanced the effects of the fourth member of the elite group.

The remaining member of the elite patrol group, Zokia, was gifted with greater physical attributes than the others but was insecure and prone to jealousy. He was resentful of Embato's rapid development and rise in communal popularity. Because Zokia had not learned the lesson of humility as a boy his progress toward a leadership role had not developed as some elders had expected. This became a source of frustration for him.

Zokia, at 33, was approaching the traditional peak years of value and leadership as a protector in his culture. He saw himself clearly as the successor to Jimba. More importantly, his recent actions began to expose his attitude and an element of selfishness. Koli and Somil both noticed it and quietly discussed it between themselves. Jimba also began to detect a change in Zokia's attitude toward the group and more specifically so toward Embato. Embato, having no previous peer level interaction with Zokia, was unaware of any changes in him. He did however notice a difference in how he was treated by Zokia than by the other protectors. Zokia never took time to explain any changes in field tactics to Embato and on several occasions had severely criticized him in the presence of other protectors.

Displaying the appropriate level of respect for Zokia as an elder protector, Embato complained to no one but slowly began to direct all his inquiry and attention to Koli, Somil, and Jimba. After several months Zokia began to take offense to the lack of attention from Embato and complained to Jimba of the young protector's lack of proper respect. When Jimba suggested that Zokia approach Embato as a peer instead of a subordinate Zokia reacted with shock and anger. Jimba had no choice but to be direct and blunt in his response.

"Zokia, if you are truly secure in your manhood and as a protector, then you should not feel threatened by Embato or anyone else. Just work with him and teach him like Somil and Koli have done successfully. We must all work together to protect our women and children. That is our mission. We cannot sacrifice that goal in favor of one individual's needs. Perhaps you should return to the village prayer hut and pray to Borombi for spiritual guidance in this matter. You are free of patrol responsibilities for the remainder of the day."

Zokia was furious. In an overt act of defiance and disrespect he turned his back on Jimba without the customary lowering of the eyes and subsequent bowed head and he stormed back to the village. The tense conversation would prove to be a turning point for Zokia. He felt betrayed by Jimba and vowed to himself that he would get even.

Just before sundown the hunting and warrior groups returned to the village. Jimba designated Somil, Koli, Embato and Darkai, another young protector, to stay several hundred yards outside the village as the evening guards. Embato's position was downwind of the village center and he could smell the aroma of the rich spices which were used in preparation of the final meal of the day. He even caught occasional glimpses of the village fires through the dense savannah grasses and foliage of the trees that surrounded Gambeya.

He fantasied being back in the security of his parents love, feeling the warmth of the cooking fire, and filling his belly with a good tasty stew. But the life of a protector was not one of self indulgence. It was one more often of great personal sacrifice and endurance. Pushing aside his hunger and exhaustion, he thought of how honored he felt to have been chosen for such responsibility. He was indeed happy that after many months of training he was finally able to contribute to the security and perpetuation of his people.

Embato settled into his assigned evening guard duty and utilized his well developed senses of hearing and sight. He listened for sounds that might not fit into the normal Senegambian night. He had also become adept at detecting very subtle changes in shades that could indicate movement. He was conditioned to utilize the lowest levels of ambient light such as that of a cloud obscured moon. He could tell by the bend of a tree limb whether it was supporting a four legged or a human adult. He knew the smell of the lion from that of the cheetah, the jaguar, or even a human intruder. He knew how to make his own body scent disappear. He had already rubbed down his entire body with the oil of a powerful indigenous herb. The residue from the leaf was effective as a natural deodorizer. Even though still youthful he was prepared for his responsibility and began to feel more secure as a protector.

About three hours before sunrise Jimba sent Ibrim, one of the elders and a former protector himself, to relieve Embato of guard duty. This would give Embato a chance to eat and catch a couple of hours of sleep before the prayer circle at sunrise.

Jimba later told Embato to meet with Guyoime, chief medicine elder, before rejoining the group on the outer patrol circle. Embato quickly consumed his helping of the morning meal, a combination of several grains toasted and densely fused together with mild spices and water to a paste consistency. He then approached Guyoime's hut. Guyoime was just concluding his morning spiritual meditation. He had his back turned to Embato with his eyes closed but yet was aware of Embato's presence. He told Embato to enter the hut and sit next to him.

"Do you embrace the life of the protector Embato?"

Before Embato could answer, Guyoime continued, "Do you ever have moments of doubt, fear, or loneliness?"

Embato was torn between blurting out the truth but at the same time not wanting to disappoint the respected chief medicine elder. Embato's image of the model protector did not always coincide with some of his sensitivities and fears. He was afraid that the truth might cast doubts on his continued development as a protector and perhaps leader; that he might bring dishonor on his family should Guyoime diminish or terminate his role. His breathing was shallow but noticeably faster and he was experiencing serious inner conflict as he formulated his response. His heart was pounding so loud within his body that he thought Gyuoime would hear it.

Suddenly Embato recalled his final challenge ceremony and how at his weakest moment he felt that he would pass out. He remembered that his renewed strength had arrived only after praying for help from Borombi. Yes! Of course that was what he needed at this moment. As soon as the request for guidance had formed as a prayer the answer came back to him from the Creator. Borombi helped Embato to recall when his father told him that the truth and the creator were inseparable. Borombi, the Creator, could not exist in one's life without truth and without truth one was not in unity with Borombi. Without Borombi, one's abilities would be greatly diminished. The simple truth *was* the answer!

"Yes, honorable Guyoime. I am afraid sometimes."

Guyoime sat silent with no expression for a brief period. Even though Embato knew that he had done the right thing he was fearful that his responsibility as a protector may have come to an abrupt end. After several agonizing moments Guyoime spoke.

"Fear can be destructive to anyone, including a protector. It can cause one to temporarily lose all strength, to turn away from their responsibility, to completely fail..........but such loss and failure only occurs if one lies to himself and others about his fears. We all must first recognize fear. Then we must admit that it is ours. And finally we must confront it. Once we have done so, then...and only then can we begin to overcome it."

"You must understand, Embato, that everyone and every creature experiences fear. Even the great lion has fear. It is part of life. What actions one takes as a response to fear is what separates the courageous from the coward. The protector must always place his fear second to that of his responsibility to his people and to his Creator. His well being is never his first thought. Embato you must pray to Borombi and the spirits for courage; for the ability to place the well being and security of our people over that of your own."

After a few more moments of silence Guyoime continued. "The village elders are pleased with your rapid development as a protector. We have commanded Jimba to prepare you for leadership. We all believe that you have been selected by Borombi for this ultimate responsibility. You see, Embato, I knew before you did, that you would speak the truth today, even though you were fearful of losing your role as protector. Your beliefs and values were instilled by your honorable parents. Their actions were dictated by Borombi. They were also fearful of losing you when you became a protector, but they learned to overcome that fear in the same manner that you have. You both recognized the power of truth and that Borombi and truth are inseparable."

Guyoime paused in silence for a moment as if listening to another voice and then continued. "Embato it is also very important to understand that as the universe unfolds Borombi may alter your path and choose other roles for you in other places. It is of the greatest importance that you listen to Borombi and follow his plan.....even when it may cause you personal pain and loss. Your life's mission on earth is to help the people.......*all* people."

Embato was stunned. He was barely 16 at that point. Could he have misunderstood Guyoime. In less than two minutes time he had gone from what he thought to be the loss of his protector role to that of becoming the eventual successor to Jimba. But strangely enough he began to feel at ease with Guyoime's message and accepted it. The great warrior spirits surrounded him with love and support. He felt the security of their presence. Guyiome respectfully acknowledged the presence of the warrior spirits and then excused Embato.

As Embato walked toward the outer circle his body seemed to move with a fluidity and ease that he had never experienced before. Rather than a surge of physical power it just seemed more like an absence of resistance. Then all of a sudden, it hit him. This must be what his father use to refer to as "the great balance".

Yes, of course! His father had explained that when one's physical being merges in balance with one's spiritual being that all obstacles in life are diminished. Embato had let go of the concern for self and had simply expressed what was truly in his heart to Guyoime. By doing so he had removed a barrier between himself and Borombi. He had opened a major spiritual portal; one which he would use throughout his life. He simply grasped the awesome power of living in truth with Borombi and all people.

Embato understood that his expanding role placed an even greater responsibility upon him than before. But he also knew that he was not alone in that role. Thus it was with a renewed sense of confidence and security that he rejoined the protector group on the outer circle. Everyone but Zokia welcomed him back with a smile and a kind word. Zokia ignored Embato but it no longer was of concern to him.

He understood that all actions, including Zokia's, were just part of Borombi's unfolding universe.

During the following year Embato continued learning field tactics, improving his battle skills, and developing his physical senses. He was also taking on more responsibility as a leader in training. Somil and Koli recognized his development and understood its value to their people. They had become best of friends with Embato despite the age differential. Their leader, Jimba, continued as Embato's mentor and became like a second father to him. The elite brotherhood was acting in unison and in the best interests of the Gambeyan people. There remained one exception however.

After learning of Embato's appointment to leader in training Zokia complained incessantly. He first approached Jimba once again but the chief protector's response was no different than before. Zokia then appealed directly to the elders but few had ears for his negative message. His volatile behavior only reinforced the elder's earlier decision in favor of Embato as the leader in training.

Only days later Zokia joined the other patrol group so as to avoid routine contact with Embato. He refused to speak to or even acknowledge Embato from that point on. The conflict created by Zokia was of little consequence to Embato however. Embato could not afford to be distracted from his mission as his people needed him. But he was no longer the same naïve youngster as the day he had joined the group. He had duly noted that Zokia was a selfish person and that he was not one to be trusted.

During the following year Embato grew stronger, taller and emotionally more mature. Just before his 18th birthday he stood almost 6 feet tall and weighed nearly 180 lbs. He was unusually thick for a Gambeyan and very muscular. His heart and mind matched his physical maturation. He had all the attributes that any family would like in a mate for their daughter. And most all of the village daughters concurred.

The young women of the village had not escaped *his* eye either. But there was only one that was very special to him. Briami was 15 and well proportioned with high cheekbones that framed her beautiful dark eyes. Her body was lean but curved and was suited well for multiple childbirths. He had fallen madly in love with Briami and had already asked her parents permission to jump the broom with her. He had offered them seven fresh carcasses of fowl thus demonstrating his sincerity of intention to marry her. If they accepted his offer then the date would be set for approximately six months later. He hoped they would be joined as man and wife prior to his period of eligibility to succeed Jimba which was just after his 18th birthday.

All seemed to be well in Embato's world and with that of the Gambeyan people. The hunting and gathering had been exceptional for several years in succession. Such favorable conditions reduced conflict with other tribes and resulted in minimal loss of life from battle during that time. The only real concern was that of the murder and recent kidnapping of some members of a village to the southwest of Gambeya on the banks of the Senegal and Gambi Rivers.

There were reports of men with white skin, and long straight hair who traveled on large vessels. The Gambeyans called the men "tubab". Their weapons were full of magic and evil as they emitted terrifying thunder and fire and sent what appeared to be round river pebbles great distance with much velocity. The round pebbles could cause severe harm and had reportedly caused the deaths of several strong warriors from coastal villages. Embato had already seen some of this in a dream. He knew the dream was a clear warning from the spirits. He had advised his fellow villagers not to venture to the rivers in spring for their hunt and fishing. But once Zokia got wind of Embato's warning he immediately attempted to discredit the idea.

Zokia immediately volunteered to lead a patrol group to the Gambia River to protect the hunting and fishing expedition and he personally guaranteed each member's safe return. Had the elders not seen through his false bravado they may have appointed him leader of the patrol and placed the protectors and their village at unnecessary risk. But many were aware of the Gambia Basin's recent history and danger.

The elders convened to discuss Zokia's proposal. They deliberated four days on whether or not to even send the group to the Gambia at all. It was a real dilemma for them. Some felt that their village may not survive a full year without some of the Gambia River Basin's bounty of fish which was usually acquired in late spring and early summer. Those same members supported the escort patrol group idea put forth by Zokia. Others, including Guyoime expressed deep concern for the safe return of the expedition. On the fourth day they finally reached consensus on a compromise of the two opposing ideas.

The group would indeed go to the Gambia this spring and Zokia would lead a protector patrol group to accompany them. However, Guyoime and several other elders held that the danger revealed in Embato's dream vision was very real. They demanded that Embato also lead a protector patrol group with the expedition to the river. They argued that the two protector groups together would be formidable and would increase the chances of safe return of the group and the food. The elders agreed but pulled Jimba, Somil and several of the younger protectors out of the expedition patrols. They were to stay in Gambeya to maintain security for the women, children and elders. Jimba, had always led any expedition which was considered high risk. Thus his absence on the expedition was an expression of confidence in both Embato and Zokia.

The elders announced that the Gambia River expedition would leave in seven days. The fisherman and the protectors began their preparation. Embato and Zokia met with Jimba and discussed alternative strategies for defense and retreat if necessary. Jimba directed Embato's group to lead and protect from the front position until they cleared the lands of their rival tribes, the Ungawah and Mobutai. Embato and Zokia would then reverse their positions for the second half of the trip. Zokia protested and argued that he knew the geography better and had more field experience on river expeditions. Jimba hoped to get through the planning session without conflict but it was clear the time had come for the simple truth. Jimba spoke softly but with authority.

"Zokia, you are an experienced and proven warrior with great strength, speed and agility. But you do not listen to Borombi. Thus you are not anointed for leadership as is Embato. Your judgment is not clear in times of conflict. You frequently make decisions based on your own personal well being and not on that which is best for Gambeya and your protector brothers. Therefore you will either, submit to my command and follow my instructions or stay behind to assist in the protection of the village."

Zokia was clearly embarrassed and angered by Jimba's statement and responded in a very loud, disrespectful tone. "Li du deeg du yoon! This is not fair! I will speak directly to the elders and they will support me. Your favored young friend should be the one to stay at home and play games with the small ones like the child that he is".

Speaking directly to Embato, Zokia turned abruptly to face him and with a condescending grin said "Embato, perhaps you can hide from danger amongst the young women whose pleasure you seek."

The entire group was stunned at such blunt language. Several moments of uncomfortable silence passed. The terrible insult angered Embato. Yet he maintained respectful posture with his head bowed slightly down but in the direction of Zokia. Zokia, then in an action clearly meant to provoke attack, stepped to within inches of Embato's face.

With a deliberate delivery and a very gutteral tone Zokia said "Tell me Embato............ do you still require the sustenance of your mother's breast?"

Embato and Zokia were so close now that they could smell each other's breath. Both of their chests expanded simultaneously in an outward direction consistent with the Gambeyan display of pre conflict posture. Jimba, sensing imminent violence stepped toward them both. He had full confidence in both Embato's ability to defend himself and to remain calm under pressure. But he also recognized the extreme personal nature of the insult. He knew that Zokia's words had violated a deep sacred place in Embato; a place reserved only for truth .

The severity of the insult required a response from Embato. It was dictated by protector code. Embato had no choice but to conform to tradition. It was, however, his choice as to what type of action to take. As Jimba moved closer to them Embato slowly raised his head to a level where his eyes met directly with Zokia's. Embato felt full empowerment of the spirits. He was calm and steady and after a few tense moments his breathing slowed almost to a bare minimum. Jimba, sensing a disarming confidence in Embato decided to stay back and allow the drama to unfold.

From everyone's viewpoint it seemed that Embato had initiated the stare down posture. The stare down was a useful tool utilized in some cultures as a warning signal and sometimes a substitute for physical violence during individual disagreements. If not interrupted by the leader, or by further physical aggression on the part of one of the participants, it could last up to an hour. This case however was different. It was not a normal stare down. There was a level of intensity in Embato's eyes that was almost surreal. Embato's calm demeanor had unnerved Zokia.

Zokia began to feel uneasy and less confident very quickly. He grew increasingly weak of body and mind and was sure that something unnatural was happening to him. Beads of sweat appeared on his forehead and his breathing was visibly faster than before the conflict. He understood that he had committed a grave error in going too far with his insult.

Zokia believed in a creator but was more secular than most in his everyday life and thus gave little credence to the concept of a spirit world. But he had no other plausible explanation for this instant diminution in his strength. Perhaps he *had* offended the spirits. Nevertheless he had no recollection of ever having such an experience like that before. For fear of losing face however he could not back down. Zokia realized that he had placed himself unnecessarily in a real dilemma. After only a few more moments he weakened further and he could feel an involuntary twitching in his extremities which further eroded his confidence. His was near panic.

In contrast Embato was no longer emotional but almost serene. He had become one with the spirits and Borombi long ago and he lived with the confidence of one who is so blessed. He knew that he only had to ask for their help and they would be with him in time of need. He knew that at some point in the future he *would* indeed have to fight in the defense of both self and community. But he was confident that this moment of conflict with Zokia was not one of those instances.

Embato and the protectors saw the obvious signs of fear in Zokia and Zokia was aware of that. The humiliation of it was crushing to his fragile ego. And Embato knew there was no need for further embarrassment. Speaking in a calm but steady voice he addressed Zokia directly.

"Zokia, I respectfully ask that you never speak of my mother again.......... or of anyone that I care for."

Embato paused long enough to be assured that Zokia's eyes blinked several times in rapid succession thereby indicating agreement. Seconds later he began to slowly lower his head in a selfless and unnecessary act of respect in order to allow Zokia to save face and to bring a peaceful end to the conflict........at least for the moment. Embato acted unselfishly in order to restore unity and strength to the group and prevent further degradation of Jimba's and Zokia's relationship. He knew there would likely be other future conflicts with Zokia. But for now his people needed the protectors to act at full strength in order to secure their lives and culture. He could not allow disagreements or his ego to subvert that sacred mission. He had given Zokia a way out and Zokia was smart enough to seize the opportunity. Having been allowed a modicum of respect, he nodded in agreement and walked back toward the village alone. Jimba then directed everyone to split into their respective subgroups and continue their daily routine for the day. They would meet later to finalize the plans for their expedition to the Gambia River.

After their late afternoon meeting the group headed back to the village. Embato was in an exceptionally positive spirit. He and the other protectors who were assigned to go to the Gambia River were excused from night watch. At last he was free to spend some time with his beloved Briami. He spotted her assisting with the central cooking fire. She smiled sweetly in his direction. His heart fluttered and he smiled back at her. He had restrained himself in front of others in spite of his urge to grab her and hold her tightly in his strong arms. Before he could properly address her she spoke first.

"Hello Embato. Hello Somil. I hope your day was blessed with goodness from Borombi."

Somil, acknowledged her with a nod of the head. After a quiet and somewhat socially awkward moment Somil giggled sheepishly and politely excused himself so the two lovers could speak in private.

Embato smiled from ear to ear as he said "It was a good day to be alive Briami. I was in the presence of the great warrior spirits and even now Borombi has blessed me with your presence".

There was another brief moment of silence as they gazed into each other's eyes. For the moment it was as if no one else existed but the two of them. They were both riding that unique wave of emotion that accompanies true romantic love only in its embryonic stage. Moving closer Briami whispered into Embato's ear.

"Oh Embato! I must tell you my heart is filled with joy. I overheard my father tell my mother today that he had decided to accept your offer. He will consent to our marriage!"

Embato was shocked and momentarily speechless.

Briami cautioned "But I am not supposed to know. So Embato you must go to him now and humbly ask for an answer to your proposal."

Having comprehended nothing Briami said after hearing of her father's consent, he was intoxicated with joy. He lost all sense of proper public etiquette and lifted her in his arms and swung her wildly in a circular motion.

Looking skyward Embato said "Thank you Borombi. You have blessed me with much happiness!"

Concerned that others might have witnessed the sudden outburst Briami sternly said "Put me down immediately.....if someone sees us and tells my father he might be offended and refuse your offer."

The threat of losing Briami was indeed a sobering thought. Embato quickly released Briami and resumed appropriate posture. He abruptly but politely said "Good evening Briami".

He had addressed Briami in a very formal tone just in case there were others listening. He immediately set out for her parents hut for what he hoped would be an evening of celebration with members of both their families. The earlier conflict with Zokia and any concern regarding the upcoming expedition were erased from his mind. He was truly happy and relaxed. It was a rare moment of personal indulgence which he allowed himself to fully experience.

Embato was standing in front of Abdoulaye's hut before he had formulated how he would initiate the conversation about his beloved Briami. The young Protector waited respectfully several feet from the opening until he would be acknowledged. AbdouLaye came out and stood as Embato maintained the proper bowed head position of respect toward an elder. His large frame actually blocked a portion of the bright orange setting sun behind him. AbdouLaye greeted him informally which Embato interpreted correctly as a sign of acceptance.

"Embato, there has been another offer for Briami. It is one which in our traditional ways is viewed with greater value than your offer. It included both that of fowl *and* beast."

Embato's heart sank. Could it be that Briami had misunderstood her father's comments earlier? Perhaps he *had* decided to accept an offer…. but maybe not Embato's. AbdouLaye was a perceptive and wise man. Quickly discerning the disappointment in Embato's facial expression and with no intent to cause him undue emotional pain he continued.

"Your offer was of fowl only Embato".

The young Gambeyan Protector was psychologically disciplined and mature beyond his years and rarely lapsed into denial of even the most painful experiences. So he began in earnest to prepare himself for great personal loss and suffering. He silently asked for strength and courage from Borombi.

Interrupting Embato's thoughts AbdouLaye said "Like my grandfathers before me, I have always followed Gambeyan tradition with respect and loyalty. Surely you understand that our adherence to tradition is critical in how we define ourselves as a people and in preserving our culture."

Embato appreciated the unusual deference paid to him by AbdouLaye in taking the time to explain the reasoning for his decision. It was an unprecedented act of respect in Gambeyan culture. There was no requirement upon elders to do so, and Embato certainly had no expectation that AbdouLaye would offer any explanation to him in the matter of his daughter's future. But still Embato was experiencing incredible emotional anguish as his heart was breaking. He began to feel an enormous loss of control. Immediately he closed his eyes and prayed to Borombi with the deepest sincerity he could bring forth. In total humility he asked only for the strength to get through this moment of despair.

Continuing AbdouLaye said, "As you know Embato we have many traditions and many sacred beliefs. In rare instances their intersection may seem to bring about confusion and inner conflict. When this occurs it is necessary to seek spiritual guidance and to search deep within ourselves to find the answer. We must get to the very purest part of our soul….. that part where we seek refuge during crisis….where we release all false pretense and are stripped naked to our core....where we are one with Borombi. It is our ultimate truth....our *only* real home."

Out of necessary respect Embato remained attentive but was confused as to why the need for such depth in the explanation. Most fathers would have simply exercised their authority in such matters and stated the case, yeah or nay. Embato knew, however that AbdouLaye's words were true and he found them to be comforting during a moment of personal pain. Even though eager for AbdouLaye to simply conclude he remained attentive and in submissive posture.

In a more emphatic tone AbdouLaye said "The only justification for a departure from strict tradition is the revelation of divine truth. I speak of that which I prayed for and found today...... with guidance from our spiritual leader Guyoime. This truth does represent a departure in one of our traditions, but I know that it is right and of divine origin. Embato........ it is no longer my responsibility to choose my daughter's mate. That burden has been lifted from me. The spirits have spoken through Guyoime and have mandated that you, Embato, are the anointed one for Briami. No one, not even a loving and responsible father is permitted to interfere with the will of Borombi and the spirits. Briami is meant for you and you for her. The two of you will be one. It is final my son."

Prepared for heartbreaking disappointment, it took a moment for the message to register properly in his mind. Could this be real? Did he misunderstand AbdouLaye? He was speechless. He was adjusting to having been pulled back and forth between two emotional extremes: happiness and despair.

Just as Embato fully embraced AbdouLaye's final words he saw Guyoime emerge from inside the hut. Guyoime had had been listening in on the conversation but did not interfere with the right of AbdouLaye to inform Embato of the decision. As he stepped into view his graying coiled hair gave the appearance of a halo. The sun's direct rays were illuminating it with a bright glow. From Embato's viewpoint the halo was confirmation as to the wisdom and power which the spirits had vested in Guyoime.

Guyoime confirmed AbdouLaye's words. "It *is* final. You and Briami *will* be joined as one by Borombi."

Pointing in the direction associated with new knowledge, the East, he continued, "Briami has been escorted to the hut of fertility and she awaits you there. Go now and join her. Pray thanks to Borombi for the gift of a beautiful woman and ask for the ability to make strong healthy children."

Embato understood these words clearly. In Gambeyan culture perpetuation of the people was paramount to almost everything else in life. Childbirth was the obvious method of accomplishing the objective. The marital vows, the ceremony and the subsequent celebration were merely a formality and secondary to getting on with the real task at hand. Although there would be a future celebration of the marriage it would coincide with the celebrations of other marriages or events of importance to the community at large. Producing a new life in Gambeya was considered the single most important contribution one could make. So it was with a dual purpose that Embato understood and acted on Guyoime's command. While obviously excited about making love with his choice of available females he was also eager to complete his role as a valuable "productive" member of the village.

Embato expressed his appreciation to AbdouLaye and Guyoime for their wisdom and decision as they joined hands and formed a small circle. They jointly acknowledged Borombi and the spirits and thanked them for all that was. They excused Embato and he turned east and ran to his bride to be. For several weeks to follow the fertility hut would be his shelter for joy, romance and love........but it would never be his home. His *true home* was in his soul. It was just as Abdoulaye had described it minutes before. Home was that special place of goodness and truth where Borombi lived within him. His true home would be with him always...... wherever he was.

The afternoon sun had just disappeared behind the savannah grasses to the west initiating the natural world's symphony of dusk. Embato's trained ear honed in on the antiphonal songs of the winged ones as they offered both their thanks to the sun and their beseechment to the night. It was both he and Briami's favorite part of the day. He was eager to get to her so they could enjoy the last few magical moments of the passing of day into night.

Briami had anticipated his arrival with excitement as well but also with a bit of anxiety. She crawled through the opening of the hut and looked up just as Embato arrived. Their eyes met with an intensity of passion that lives only in young lovers. They knew they would finally be together as one with the blessing of the elders and the spirits. It was the first opportunity they had to display affection in privacy. She closed her eyes as their lips met and the tender kiss sent a slight quiver down her spine, settling in the tips of her toes. The melding of two loving souls into the wholeness of one had begun. They had become so emotionally connected that they could read each other's most intimate thoughts even before speaking them. Their act of physical union would be the first step in the natural order of progression from that of lover to family.

Briami interrupted the embrace and whispered into his ear, "I love you Embato and I want to be yours now......but we must go inside the hut... please."

They both crouched to enter the privacy of the sacred shelter. Once inside they dropped the leather cover to obscure the entrance from sight or sound. Lying down on the mattress of thatched grasses, their eyes met once again.

"I am sorry I caused you shame outside Briami. I was so happy to see you that I lost control for a moment. The meeting with your father......."

Briami placed her forefinger over his lips and kissing it she said "We can talk about it another day. This is our time to love and be happy and......."

Embato moved her finger and kissed her with sensitivity beyond his youthful inexperience. Her beautiful femininity consumed him bringing forth his manhood in its fullness. Their fantasies had been filled with thoughts of physical and emotional pleasure but the actual experience was proving to be even more than they invisioned. It was intensely physical and metaphysical at the same time. For a brief period Borombi had granted them complete insulation from anything beyond themselves. At that moment it was as if nothing else existed in their world but their oneness and their love for each other.

They immersed themselves in each other as they indulged in the uniqueness of man and woman becoming one. Their union was sanctioned and choreographed by the spirits through thousands of years of natural evolution. And Embato released an expression of love and passion within Briami's body that encased both the seed of his own immortality and the miracle of new life. It was purely received and securely nestled deep in the natural protection of Briami's warmth just the way Borombi had intended. Their union would bring forth the regeneration of life and, as nature had intended, ensure its continuity.

As the evening grew into night they continued talking and sharing in the pleasure of each other. Just before dawn they stepped outside to view the natural wonders of the West African night sky. It was a crystal clear evening and the crescent moon appeared just above the Western horizon as bright stars seemed to be visible in every direction. They prayed together giving abundant thanks to Borombi for their oneness. Briami continued as she beseeched the spirits of fertility to bless them with offspring.

After a moment of quiet Embato looked into Briami's eyes and said "I love you Briami. And I love our new child with all my heart."

Briami smiled and replied "I hope your wish comes to pass Embato but why are you so confident that your seed has already become fertile in me?"

Answering in a very serious tone he said "I have had several visions from the dream world in just the last few days. In one of them I was told that your body would accept my seed and that our son would begin growing in you. We will be blessed with a strong healthy boy. Briami, you must promise me now that you will always do what is necessary to protect him and see that he grows into a strong and humble servant to Borombi and to our people no matter what *our* future holds."

But before she could reply Embato suggested they go back inside the hut and sleep.

Once inside the hut Briami said "Embato you speak as if I might have to raise our child by myself. You will be his father and protector and we will both live to see and love our grandchildren."

"Briami, there are many dangers in my mission and responsibilities as a protector. What if…"

Briami interrupted him saying "Please do not speak of this ever again Embato. All of Gambeya knows that you are blessed with special gifts from Borombi and protected by the warrior spirits. You will always be here with me and our son. Embato you will always be in my heart. We are one."

Embato paused for a moment and said "Yes Briami, we *are* one and we will *always* be in each other's hearts.….but you must understand that we do not control our pathways in life. The directions we travel are controlled by the spirits. I just want your word that you will do what is necessary for our son to be properly cared for."

Briami wanted to press the issue further but decided to wait. There would be other opportunities to talk. In a submissive tone Briami said "Yes Embato, I will always do what is necessary to keep our son safe and happy. He will be taught the truth and he will grow just as you have. He will understand and carry out his responsibility as his father before him."

Briami then curled up in the warmth of Embato's strong body. It had been a wonderful day and evening but she was exhausted. Totally unaware of how future events would change their lives she quietly entered the dream world.

Embato, on the other hand, did not enjoy the luxury of immediate sleep. Unlike Briami, he did not share the same blissful ignorance of the future. The spirits had warned him of events to come during his dream visions. He was forbidden by Borombi to speak of them to anyone except Guyoime however. The spirits had warned that changes would profoundly alter both their lives forever.......and sooner rather than later. It was yet another burden of responsibility on one who had been anointed for special service by Borombi.

Both of the two young lovers were allowed to sleep well into the next day and were exempted of any communal obligations. It was a benefit afforded to first night mates in the fertility hut. After a leisurely walk to the stream for fresh water they returned hand in hand to the hut where they made love once again. After a midday meal they emerged from the fertility hut and took a walk just outside the perimeter of the village. Jimba, Somil, and Koli wre returning from outer circle patrol. Jimba acknowledged Briami and requested to speak with Embato privately. Briami respectfully agreed and walked in the direction of her parents hut. She wanted to greet them and thank AbdouLaye for his approval of her marriage to Embato.

Embato had learned from Jimba that the Gambia River expedition had been delayed for twenty one days. Had the expedition left according to the original timetable Embato and Briami would have been together for only about four days. Jimba explained how there had been more reports of the Tubab kidnapping locals near the river. The elders thought it wise to delay the trip. They also mandated that further battle training and more sophisticated contingency plans be completed. Everyone agreed with the logic...............except Zokia. He was adamant in his opposition to the new timing. Embato was not surprised. He had been warned by the spirits that Zokia had a hidden agenda regarding the expedition. It would bring about danger to Embato and require action of self sacrifice on his part.

Over the next three weeks Briami and Embato grew spiritually closer and deeper in love. She discussed their new family's future together and spoke of her desire for more than just one child. Embato found it painful to consider their future plans together. He focused on short term goals such as the naming of their son. After a brief discussion they settled on Ibrahim Sakool. They used the letter I for Ibrahim from her ancestral grandmother's name, Isianna. They used the letter S from Embato's ancestral grandfather's name, Saulisar. It was a historical custom unique to Saulisar's lineage.

Saulisar had actually been born in Ethiopia. He was the son of a Jewish mother and a Muslim father. He tragically lost his parents in war and subsequently was sold into slavery and was transported to West Africa. After several years he escaped and fled to Senegambia. He was found near death in the bush but eventually was adopted by a young Gambeyan couple who had not been blessed with fertility. Borombi had answered their prayers for a child but in a way that they had not expected. Nevertheless they welcomed and loved Saulisar as their own. Although he would be raised as a Muslim he retained some memories of Jewish tradition. As a father he quietly introduced the Jewish custom (borrowed from Ashkenazim European Jewry) of naming a newborn with the first letter of an honored and deceased relative's name. Embato had explained to Briami that it was necessary to carry the unique tradition forward in order to honor his grandfather properly. Her love for Embato had opened her heart *and her mind* to the new tradition as well as some other unusual methods that followed.

Embato and Briami spent every evening together especially at dusk. He would identify different four leggeds, winged ones, and crawlers by their sounds. They also studied the positioning of the various stars and planets. Each night he would teach her something new. He tested her new knowledge one night. The exchange was enjoyable for them both but for him it became his future connection to his son. It was a necessity. He knew that her responsibilities to Ibrahim would be much greater than that of only the mother. She recognized some of the unorthodox methods he required of her but she trusted his judgment implicitly.

Their experience in marriage was beyond happiness. It was pure joy for them both.

Their three weeks flew by. It was the final day before departure for the expedition. After morning patrol that day Jimba told all the expedition protectors to spend the time with their families and in prayer to Borombi. Embato visited his parents and siblings. It was very emotional for all but especially so for him and his father. His father had reached a high spiritual awareness in his life and had ears for the spirits. In his farewell to Embato he opened his heart with words of encouragement.

"My son, I am so proud of you. You are truly a blessing in our lives and for our people. My pain in seeing you leave to face danger is great."

A single tear rolled gently down over his prominent nose and dropped out of sight. "I find it tolerable only because you and I will speak to each other through the spirits from time to time. We will see each other again my son."

Embato fought back the tears inside him. He did not want to contribute to his father's pain. With conflicting emotions they embraced and smiled into each other's eyes one last time. Embato then turned toward Guyiome's hut and prayed fervently for emotional strength and courage. He would need it.

After a brief prayer with Guyoime he rushed to be with his beloved Briami. They had tried to live an entire lifetime in three short weeks. They were grateful and happy for their experience together, but they were saddened by the necessary separation soon to occur. They made love and prayed as one for long periods of time during their last few hours together. It was cleansing and empowering to them. They knew that they both had to be strong for each other. Briami mentioned that she had not felt well in the morning for the last couple of days. She had spoken the words with a sheepish grin and a soft giggle. She was simply confirming what he already knew. She was pregnant with their new son, Ibrahim.

They held each other as they watched the sun set and then the moon rise. It was perhaps their last opportunity to absorb the magic of their favorite moment of the day. Embato pointed out the North Star which glowed exceptionally bright.

"This special star of the north will connect us to each other and to our son. Every evening I will look at this star and know its light shines on you and Ibrahim also. I will see you and Ibrahim when I look at it in the heavens.....and you and Ibrahim will see me in it as well. No matter what paths the spirits have chosen for us we will always be connected as one through the bright star of the north. Borombi has provided it for us."

Gazing deeply into each others eyes no further words were necessary. They retired to the fertility hut where they made love for the last time. He held her next to him and caressed her belly in his large strong hands. They entered the dream world together as one.

Embato was awake and out before dawn. He met at the village center for the morning payer circle of all the protectors. The elders and villagers joined them because it was a special day. They beseeched the spirits for special protection for all whom were going on the Gambia River expedition. As the sacred ceremony concluded Jimba approached Embato. He went over the final plans for the trip and warned him to watch Zokia closely.

"Follow the plan unless the spirits direct you to alter it. Avoid unnecessary contact with Zokia where possible. If you must speak with him then always have Koli or at least one other protector present. Embato, you must always remember the primary mission. It is to secure and bring food and skins back to the village. You are aware that the success of it is critical to the survival of our people."

Embato nodded in agreement. Jimba continued.

"The life and well being of any *individual* is secondary to that of accomplishing our goal. No one is exempted from this rule. Take Borombi and the spirits with you my son and may they bless your journey."

Embato thanked Jimba for his guidance and leadership. He then led his group and the entire expedition out of the village and across the savannah in a southerly direction. As the group moved rapidly forward their family members watched until their beloved brave men finally disappeared below the horizon altogether. A profound sadness consumed Briami for a moment. But then she remembered that as long as she had her new son she would have a part of Embato with her no matter what happened during the expedition. She lovingly caressed her belly where the precious new life was forming.

EXPEDITION TO THE GAMBIA

Embato's group continued leading the expedition for the first half of the trip as planned. Zokia's group guarded the rear. All the members of Embato's group held him in high regard as a leader. They were confident in his ability and decision making and were to a man much more content than if they had been assigned to Zokia's group. Their confidence was well placed as there were no incidents on the first day and they covered significant distance.

On the second day they traveled around the fringe area of a rival tribe. Again there were no problems but their pace slowed as they had to be more careful and deliberate in their movement. It was an area of moderate danger and required additional caution and stealth. The spirits had blessed their journey. Borombi was with them.

By the third day they were back on schedule and heading into Mobutai territory. It was anticipated to be the area of greatest danger second only to that of the Gambia River Basin itself. Compounding the situation was its local elevation. It was only several feet above sea level and thus subject to much moisture and heat with little wind. It was the home of many annoying insects that the Gambeyans were not accustomed to dealing with. As a precaution the group had cleansed their bodies the night before with the smoke of the cooking fire and rubbed their skin down with the essence of crushed leaves from an indigenous plant from their village area known to discourage annoying insects.

As they began traversing the area however, the biting and stinging insects seemed to be immune to what had in the past been an effective remedy. The swarm became unbearable. Some expedition members began to seek refuge in the bush which slowed their progress. Others began to slap the insects from their bodies making sounds that might draw attention to their position. They had to somehow get past the area faster. Instead of taking the longer and safer route around the periphery Embato led them on a run through an open area that would save them several miles and valuable time. Unfortunately it would also increase their exposure to the danger of encountering the Mobutai.

After only several minutes Zokia realized that he and his group would be exposed and less protected in the rear and he was furious. He left his post and sprinted to the front to catch up to Embato. Unwisely he called out in a very loud voice demanding a return to the original plan of travel. Embato couldn't believe it. There they were in a field of open space at least two miles across and already potentially exposed to the eye of the enemy.........and why would Zokia foolishly call attention to their presence? Embato turned quickly and grabbed Zokia by the throat and squeezed hard with his large powerful hand so that Zokia could not speak or even breathe.

Emphatically he said "That was very foolish Zokia! Do not raise your voice again! You have alerted the Mobutai of our presence and possibly compromised our mission. If you do anything else to place any of us or the mission in jeopardy I will not hesitate to kill you. Do you understand me?"

This was a different Embato than Zokia had dealt with in past encounters. Embato was singularly focused on completing the mission at whatever the cost may be to *any* individual, including him. The survival of his people depended on it. He was determined to follow the plan that Jimba *and* Borombi had laid out for him, and Zokia got the message loud and clear. Although still enraged and certainly embarrassed, he quietly nodded in compliance and retreated to the rear without further incident. He would bide his time, however, and seize the opportunity for revenge later.

Every expedition member had either witnessed the dramatic event or heard about it within minutes. If there was previously any doubt about who was in charge of this entire expedition, Embato had just eradicated it. He announced that he would remain in the lead position for the remainder of the trip to the Gambia in contrast to the earlier plan. He also gave the command to run at full speed until they cleared the field. There was total and immediate compliance. Almost all of them were winded and thirsty when they finally reached the dense bush cover. So the command was given to slow to a trot so that they could begin to recover but keep moving forward.

Embato was still very concerned of potential conflict with the Mobutai. He had spotted one of their warriors on the opposite side of the clearing during their passing and he knew that the Mobutai had to have seen them. He was surprised that there was no pursuit by them. Yes, there would be time for water, but only when they were out of Mobutai territory. Embato made that clear to all. There was no argument.

Just before nightfall they had successfully cleared Mobutai territory with no further sightings of them. The expedition group was thankfully less than a day from the northern edge of the Gambia River floodplain. Embato had led his men through the two regions of greatest risk. They were also a day ahead of schedule. He was exhausted but thankful to the spirits for their progress thus far. He asked Koli to assume command while he went to a nearby stream to cleanse his body and to pray by himself. Dusk was approaching and he wanted desperately to locate the North Star in privacy and connect with Briami in spirit.

He spoke through the spirits of his love and loyalty to his beloved Briami and to his people. He knew that she to would see the same starlight and think of him. He prayed that the spirits would reveal his message to her.

After his evening prayer and beseechment were completed he returned to the group. He assigned night guard duties at 3 hour intervals so that everyone would get some rest and would be essentially fresh for their push to the Gambia the following morning.

As the first morning light washed over his face Embato began to recall a dream vision he had just experienced during sleep. In it he saw himself in battle with the Tubab and Mobutai warriors whom were fighting side by side. He was separated from his fellow protectors except for his loyal friend Koli. The odds were overwhelmingly against their survival. He identified an escape route but the spirits caused its disappearance. In the distance he could see Zokia walking back toward Gambeya. As he focused in on Zokia he appeared to be smiling. The vision was a bit confusing to him but he interpreted it as a warning of danger to himself and Koli. He sought out Koli and described the vision to him. Koli respected the spirits and took the warning seriously. They both agreed to stay within voice range of each other for the remainder of the mission.

The expedition members approached their destination with renewed spirit and energy. They were confident in their young leader in spite of the danger they might encounter. Even though there clearly was risk along the Gambia River the Gambeyans knew the area very well. The Tubab would be reluctant to follow them too deeply into the bush or jungle. The Gambeyans also felt confident of their fighting skills in hand to hand combat. They were yet unexposed to the advanced weaponry of the Tubab however. In a perfect scenario they would spend seven days fishing and hunting and return safely to Gambeya with great stores of food and hides without conflict. The group was very optimistic as they neared the Gambia that afternoon.

They approached the basin upstream where the river was too narrow for the great boats of the Tubab to travel. Their plan would be to move cautiously closer to the mouth of the Gambia each day. The Gambia's mouth was also the estuarial ecosystem which was the most biologically productive portion of the river. The fish harvest would be richer and easier to claim there but the risk of encountering the Tubab would be greater. But for the first night the fishermen would set their nets at their arrival point in the Gambia's narrow upstream portion near their camp-site. Since there were only about four to five hours of daylight left the hunters quickly fanned out into small parties of three in their search for game. They wanted to maximize their time spent while in the risky environment.

At days end the group gathered for prayers near an oxbow lake that had once been part of of the Gambia's channel. It was protected from view of the river and therefore safe for overnight camp. Even Zokia joined in with thanks for their good fortune thus far. Both Embato and Koli raised their eyebrows in skepticism but followed with their own expression of thanks and beseechment for a successful mission on behalf of all their people.

The protectors split off into their own group where Embato confirmed the next day's plan and assigned night guard duty. After an exhausting four days as leader he was ready for a much deserved full night's rest. His sore muscles relaxed when his body made contact with the soft layered river grasses that was his bedding for the night. As he settled into a comfortable position he focused on that familiar bright star of the north. He saw Briami and Ibrahim in his mind's eye and smiled at them. And he entered the dream world...... where they smiled back at him.

The sense of optimism in base camp was palpable on the morning of day five. Even the meager portions of dried fruits and cold grains could not dampen their enthusiasm. There would be no hot food until they were once again safely out of both the Gambia Basin and Mobutai territory. The rising smoke of a fire could easily give their location away, compromising their safety. It was only one of several personal sacrifices they would endure as they were all of one mind with Embato. They were proud to follow his model of sacrifice for the welfare of their people.

Embato gathered the protectors into the sacred circle for their prayers but Zokia was late. Embato sent Koli to search for him but he was no where to be found. Embato was concerned but could not delay the patrol's departure. The day's hunting and fishing plans were already in motion. Koli led the protection effort for the hunting group and Embato replaced Zokia as lead protector for the fishermen. Koli's group was to venture no more than two miles north of the Gambia where the fishermen would be.

The hunting and fishing parties were successful and preparing to return to base camp by midday. Koli escorted the hunting group back to base camp where they would begin to skin and dry the meat. Two protectors were assigned to stay with them. Koli chose Mbaye and Bubucar, his best fighters, to go with him to rendezvous with Embato's group near the Gambia. They previously agreed to meet at the sun's three quarter position in the safe cover of the oxbow lake. Koli became concerned when his group arrived at the lake and Embato's group had not.

Koli led his group to the river bank to look for them. Just before reaching the Gambia he was relieved to see a protector and two of the fisherman walking toward him. Their catch had been almost twice that of an average day from year's past. The extra weight had delayed the group's departure. Embato and the other protectors had to help the fishermen transport it up the steep slippery trail. Since they were unable to transport the entire catch on one trip they would have to return for the remainder.

Embato was surprised but relieved to see Zokia waiting for them at base camp. Embato calmly but authoritatively asked where he had been all day. He nervously explained that he had experienced severe stomach pain during the night which prevented him from sleeping. About two hours before sunrise he had gone deep into the bush to relieve himself. When he attempted to return to camp he became dizzy, disoriented and lost. About midday he felt better and found his way back to camp. By the time he returned both protector patrols had left so he stayed to protect base camp. Embato and Koli both glanced at each other and shrugged with skepticism.

In a formal tone Embato said "You and Koli and I will discuss this matter privately after we return with the remainder of the catch from the

Gambia. But we must leave immediately so that we can get back to base camp before sundown."

Zokia in uncharacteristic submission said "Yes you are right Embato. I will go with you and help."

Neither Embato nor Koli believed Zokia's story. They agreed that no well trained, disciplined protector would foolishly put himself in such a situation. If Zokia was really ill and had to go into the bush at night he would inform one of the guards as to his whereabouts. In fact Zokia could not have left camp without being seen...........*unless he did not want to be seen.* Clearly he used his stealth training to sneak away on purpose! They agreed there was a problem but that they should manage it after returning to base camp with the remainder of the fish.

The warning from Embato's dream coupled with Zokia's suspicious behavior left Embato with a heightened awareness for anything out of the ordinary. With that in mind he selectted Koli, Mbaye, Bubucar, and three of the stronger fishermen to accompany him back to the Gambia. He was concerned about having Zokia along but felt that at least he could keep an eye on him that way. He certainly could not leave him in charge of base camp without Koli there. So he appointed an expe-rienced and trusted protector, Nana, as lead protector until his return from the Gambia.

Nana was intelligent, strong and had long been a loyal protector and had Embato's full confidence. Nana was also observant and intuitive regard-ing the developing situation with Zokia. Like the other loyal protectors, Nana understood the importance and priorities of the mission. Embato instructed him to break camp and lead the expedition back toward Gambeya by sundown if Embato's group had not returned. If questioned he was to explain that it was a direct command from Embato and that the large bounty of game and fish already in base camp would meet the needs of their people. Nana would also be responsible for inform-ing Jimba and the elders of the expedition's events and particularly of Zokia's behavior. Historically in the event of loss of any expedition member there would be a mandatory inquiry conducted by the elders. Embato knew Nana was aware of this rule and would be prepared to report all events in detail.

Embato led his group toward the Gambia in a steady run. He had positioned Zokia between Mbaye and Bubucar followed by the three fishermen and with Koli at rear guard. The fast pace allowed them to cut the normal time to the Gambia almost in half.

He slowed to a walk and stopped about two hundred yards short of the bank so they could all catch their breath before loading the fish and heading back to camp. It would also give him and Koli an opportunity to scout the area briefly before entering the water's edge where they would be most vulnerable to an enemy. He gave the all clear sign by extending both arms above his head with the left palm turned in to his body and the right palm turned outward.

Koli stayed hidden from view and positioned himself on high ground where he could continue observing the immediate area. Everyone else formed an assembly line which started on the steep bank and extended into the water where the nets were placed. The afternoon current was too strong for the three fishermen so Embato, Zokia and Mbaye had to pull the nets themselves. It would require exceptional upper body strength since the current robbed their legs of the ability to support any of the weight.

Embato grasped the twisted vine netting and grunted loudly as he lifted it out of the water above the current's resistance. His biceps, triceps, and powerful chest muscles flexed and the veins surrounding them bulged on the surface of his dark skin. Beads of water droplets clung to his coarse black hair and glistened in the late afternoon sun. He was the embodiment of near physical perfection. He was part of the superior results of the evolutionary selection process; Borombi's system that engineered their bodies to function efficiently in a harsh natural environment. The Gambeyan Protectors were nature's chosen ones. They were simply the best of the best.

Zokia struggled but finally got the full net of fish into Mbaye's hands. Mbaye in turn was able to maneuver it onto the river bank where Bubucar took it up the steep trail and into the hands of a waiting fishermen. They repeated this same process until all the nets containing the valuable protein source were on land. They rested for only a minute or two before Embato said they must move on.

The group had less than an hour of daylight remaining and the heavy catch would slow their pace considerably. Embato was also concerned that they had been exposed on the river for too long. And even though Koli had reported nothing out of the ordinary, Embato could not assume they had not been seen. He had also noticed Zokia nervously looking up the trail while they were in the water. Perhaps Zokia was legitimately concerned for the same reasons as Embato and the others. But still his strange behavior possibly suggested otherwise. Which ever the case.... it was time to depart the Gambia River basin and the inherent potential danger it held for members of Embato's expedition.

Koli led the group up the trail and in the direction of base camp. He held his spear in his left hand and one end of a net in the other. Directly behind him was a fisherman who held the other end of the net in one hand and the end of the next net in the other. Everyone in the chain continued in this same formation except for Embato who also held the end of the last net in one hand and his spear in the other. Mbaye, Zokia and Bubucar had weapons hanging from their backsides as both their hands held nets. Finally they were on their way to base camp, a more secure location. They held in their possession the food source that would help guarantee the survival of their people for another year. Embato was somewhat relieved as they approached the hidden oxbow lake.

The group had moved through their most vulnerable period without incident. Any experienced attacker would have surely struck them while in the water and at their weakest point of defense. Embato began to wonder if he had judged Zokia too quickly. He surmised that the warning in his dream must have been meant for another time and place. For the first time that day he was confident of their safe return to Gambeya.

He began to look forward to that night's spiritual communication with Briami and Ibrahim in the light of the North Star. He pictured himself lying comfortably on the grass matting while gazing up into the Senegambian night sky and falling off into the..........

His thoughts were abruptly interrupted by a series of terrifying sounds that were akin to thunder. The booming noises came from behind the group and left Embato and several others temporarily deaf. No one except Koli recognized the sound. Before turning back to survey its origin, Embato saw Yambou, the fishermen closest to him, lunge forward and fall to the ground. He appeared completely motionless as if struck down by the yellow fire that on rare occasions had bolted down from the clouds. But there were no clouds. The entire sky was crystal clear and absent of anything but blue.

Just as Embato and Mbaye began to recover from their initial shock they both focused more clearly on the horror that lay just forward of their position. Yambou lay face down on a net full of fish that had opened causing its contents to spill and cover the width of the trail. A bright sliver of sun from the west had found its way through the dense bush and settled across the middle portion of Yambou's upper back. It revealed a large hole where his right shoulder blade should have been. The space was large enough to have held Embato's fist in it. Blood was escaping from it in spurts with every pulse of his still beating heart. Bits of the missing shoulder flesh contrasted vividly in pink and red against the solid white bellies of the fish that surrounded his body. The scene, though surreal through the eyes of Embato, was shocking and grotesque. He had witnessed severe injuries and even death on occasion but never anything so powerfully violent.

Embato's first thought was from the heart. He wanted desperately to help Yambou but his training and discipline kicked in. In order to protect the mission he must first identify both the source and direction of the threat. He released the net and drew his spear back in the pre-release position while quickly turning toward his rear. As he did so he glimpsed an object passing just over his head with great speed. It was

Koli's spear! It had traveled almost seventy feet from the lead position and with pinpoint accuracy found its intended target. The sharp point struck its victim in the sternum at a slight angle veering directly through his heart and partially exiting his upper left back. Embato immediately recognized him as the same Mobutai warrior they had seen across the large open field just several days before. As the Mobutai warrior was hit he instantly released the grip on his weapon which appeared to Embato to be a shiny cylinder on one end and a thick piece of wood on the other. The Mobutai's legs gave way and his eyes bulged as he dropped to his knees. The weight of his body snapped Koli's deadly spear shaft in half as the Mobutai fell forward to the ground.

Koli had engaged in battle with enemies who had used the same weaponry once before near the Gambia. He to had been caught off guard by the sudden loud noise and violence, but he did not suffer the same length of shock paralysis that they did. His reaction time was faster and his thinking clearer and more decisive. He did not have the luxury of time or even the support of Embato and Mbaye at first. In that moment he *was* the leader. For a few terrifyingly lonely moments all their lives were in his hands alone. Even if they heard his commands they would not have responded quickly enough however.

Koli did not wait to see the Mobutai warrior drop and die. He was already moving in order to dodge sharp spear points and scanning for another shiny weapon. He knew of its accuracy, ability to inflict severe damage, and ability to be used repeatedly, unlike his spear. And there was always more than one. But where was it? After loading his leather sling with a round stone he instinctively raised it above his head and began swinging it in a circular motion. He had completed two of the four circles when his trained eye caught a bright reflection from the setting sun off to his right. He stepped toward it with his left foot and immediately released the stone at its optimum point of centrifugal force. And as the speeding stone made contact with the bearded Tubab's temple his weapon fired. It had been aimed directly at one of the two standing fishermen. Had Koli's stone been released an instant later, the fishermen would have probably suffered the same fate as Yambou. The shiny weapon had fired an object which splintered a tree trunk not more than a foot to the left of the fortunate fisherman. Borombi was with Koli as the warrior spirits summoned his courage and skill.

The second booming noise had much less impact than did the first. It actually startled the others from their initial shock and jolted them into action. Embato counted four more Mobutai and at least seven of the strange looking Tubab. He saw only two more shiny weapons both of which were in the hands of the Tubab. The four Mobutai were yelling to each other and pointing toward Embato. As the four began to run in his direction he had already taken aim at the tall thin one who seemed to be giving the directions. By the time he released the spear they were less than thirty feet from him. He threw it with all the strength he possessed and his accuracy matched that of Koli. The point struck the tall Mobutai in the abdomen with such force that it ripped an opening four inches long in his gut and passed through his back carrying with it several inches of lower intestine. He immediately fell to his side while trying to hold the remainder of his intestines and stomach inside his shredded torso. He transitioned within seconds of the initial injury.

The sudden loss of their leader caused confusion between the Mobutai which slowed their momentum. Embato noticed that they were holding some type of large thick nets and that two of them were moving laterally to encircle him. Having no remaining weapon other than his body he turned forward to retrieve the spear from Yambo's lifeless body. His eyes delivered yet another painful message to his shocked psyche. Mbaye was crouched on the ground in front of him bleeding profusely from his upper left chest.

Mbaye had sustained a debilitating injury to his left arm and shoulder during the battle but still had use of his right. He struggled to stand after falling to the ground from being hit. Dazed and a bit disoriented he was able to lean against a nearby tree and prop himself upright. Quickly regaining focus he pulled his spear upward and rested it briefly on his right shoulder in order to gain a proper hold. The Tubab were advancing closer but his vision was blurred from the rapid loss of blood. He prayed loudly to Borombi screaming in a high pitch.

"Please Borombi…. give me final strength and clarity for my people!"

Grimacing in agony he gripped his spear just behind his right ear. As the Tubab moved closer his eyes began to focus enough to see the outline of one of them. Just then Embato ducked as he ran past Mbaye.

Calling to his dying friend he said "The two with shiny weapons are twenty paces in front and four to your left."

In an instant Borombi answered Mbaye's prayer and rewarded his courage and unselfish devotion to his people. The bright sunlight illuminated the man as he moved out of the shade and into view. Mbaye was able to determine that the advancing figure's white skin color stood out in contrast to his dark beard and long reddish hair. This was indeed Mbaye's enemy. He pulled the spear back and in the same seamless flowing motion thrust it forward with his last remaining bit of strength. It struck the stocky red haired Tubab in the throat just below his adam's apple severing his windpipe and carotid artery. It had almost beheaded him. The Tubab's shiny weapon fell to the ground beside his convulsing body. At the same instant Mbaye felt a burning pain in his chest even before he heard the loud boom released by one of the shiny weapons. He fell forward from the violent impact. His last visual image in the earthly world was that of his loyal and brave brother, Bubucar.

Bubucar held the last remaining weapon still in the possession of the Gambeyans. He spotted one of the Tubab holding the other shiny weapon. In a calm, disciplined manner the lanky but powerful Gambeyan positioned his spear just above and behind his right cheek and began the initial motion of attack. His long lean bicep coiled into a tight round mass as he abruptly terminated the backward motion and began the forward thrust. Just as he released the deadly weapon however he was stunned by a violent blow to the back of his head and neck.

It caused the spear to veer off to the right falling short of its intended target. Bubucar's scull had been crushed. He fell limp beside his long-time friend and fellow protector, Mbaye. Due to the massive damage to his cerebellum, Bubucar's brain had ceased functioning thereby merci-fully sparing him of any additional pain. Together he and Mbaye joined the world of the warrior spirits. His attacker stood over him while still holding a spiked wooden club in his grip. It dripped with the blood of one who just seconds before had courageously fulfilled all expectation of his role as a protector.

As Embato reached for Yambo's fishing spear he saw Koli emerging from the bush where he had taken cover long enough to reload his sling. He very quickly swung and released another round stone that passed within inches of Embato's head. Embato turned just in time to see a Tubab falling barely ten feet behind him. He was still holding the shiny fire spitting weapon. The stone had only stunned the gray haired middle aged Tubab after glancing off his lower jaw. It did, however, give Embato a moment to think clearly and decisively. He yelled to the surviving fish-ermen, Muumbar and Jamibi, to run as fast as they could back to base camp and warn Nana so the expedition group could escape safely back to Gambeya.

The two humble fishermen hesitated as their eyes conveyed conflict. They desperately wanted to stay and fight with their brothers. Even though they were not designated as protectors they were brave Gambeyans and would have proudly sacrificed their own lives in the battle. But Embato could not allow it. Leaving no doubt as to his sincerity and feigning anger, Embato spoke decisively.

"Go now! If you stay there will be no one to warn them and then our whole village will be at risk."

They immediately obeyed the young leader whom they had grown to love and respect. With a slight quiver in his voice Jamibi yelled "Yes Embato, ...Borombi is with you brother!"

With no further delay they sprinted up the trail and disappeared into the dense bush. Embato immediately redirected his attention toward Koli. He ordered him to follow the fishermen and insure their safe arrival at base camp. Koli let one last stone fly and successfully disabled one of the Mobutai warriors. He then turned up the trail without any last words to his good friend and faithfully carried out his directive. Embato was relieved. He was confident that his decisions and commands would result in the expedition's safe departure for Gambeya. He was equally confident that he had just sealed his own fate to that of whatever the Mobutai and the Tubab wished it to be.

Embato turned back toward the Gambia just in time to see Bubucar fall next to the lifeless body of Mbaye. Of all the bizarre and violent events that he had been witness to that day, this was by far the most shocking. The loss of both Mbaye and Bubucar in the same instant would have been devastating in and of itself. But it was the incredulous circumstance surrounding the tragedy that initiated Embato's momentary paralysis.

From the instant Embato saw Bubucar fall, the action around him seemed to occur in slow motion. For a moment it was as if he were no longer an active participant but observing the scene from a distant point. The senselessness of what he had seen was overwhelming. His survival instinct eventually reconciled the disconnection from reality however. It only took direct eye contact with a demon.

Embato had not trusted him for years and theorized that he may be up to no good. But clearly he had underestimated the depth of sickness and evil that had permeated the man's soul. The warning from the spirits in his recent vision had unfortunately been exceeded by more than he could have possibly imagined. The Tubab and the Mobutai had indeed fought side by side just as he had foreseen it. But he never anticipated that one of his own fellow protectors could simply discard all that was sacred and meaningful. Embato had just witnessed the brutal murder of Bubucar, one of his fellow protectors, at the hands of another protector.......Zokia!

Zokia committed a fatal error when he turned in Embato's direction and allowed their eyes to meet. Emerging from near paralytic shock, Embato moved towards retribution. His motivation was neither spiritual nor unselfish. His actions were no longer predicated on a strategy of what was best for the mission. For the first time in his life he was consumed by hate and a burning desire for revenge and justice for his beloved brothers. His whole focus was on Zokia as if the two of them were alone with each other. The fact that he was surrounded by the Tubab and the Mobutai was irrelevant. The only image of any consequence to him was that of Zokia standing over the dead bodies of two of the most descent and unselfish human beings he had ever known….two brave men who would have given their lives for the very person who without provocation had caused their violent deaths.

Embato's sole purpose at that moment was to inflict as much physical pain as possible on Zokia before killing him. It morphed into a blur of emotion and physical violence. He had no recollection of knocking Zokia senseless or slamming his body to the ground and choking the life from him. Zokia deserved to die more than once. But suddenly the movement in Embato's legs and arms was diminished. He was tangled in a mesh of thick netting which had been twisted around his entire body by the Mobutai warriors. In his rage of exacting revenge on Zokia he lost focus of his surroundings and became unaware of his own capture. The boom of the shiny weapon only a few feet away, however, restored his awareness. He turned just in time to see a Mobutai warrior fall dead next to him. He had a gaping wound at the base of his neck which had been inflicted by the gray haired Tubab. The Washa then pointed the weapon at Embato.

Embato was close enough that he could smell the strange odor of the weapon. The gray haired Tubab began yelling at the Mobutai and motioning for them to back away from Embato. They pointed to their comrade lying on the ground and began to argue with the gray hair until another Tubab raised his weapon in their direction. Still complaining loudly but in fear of the great weapon of the Tubab they backed away. The gray hair moved closer to Embato while still holding the weapon. Embato saw the faint wisps of smoke rising from its opening and disappearing upward into the hot humid air. He began to pray aloud to Borombi and to the receiving spirits in preparation for death. He had lived a virtuous life and had done everything asked of him. Surely Koli, Nana and the expedition group were departing for Gambeya with the game and fish from the previous day which would sustain his people. Although saddened by the loss of many good friends that day he was very proud of their valiant effort and the success of the expedition. He could enter the spirit world in peace. His last thoughts were of Briami and Ibrahim as he absorbed a devastatingly painful blow to his forehead. Still semiconscious he mumbled a final prayer to Borombi and the warrior spirits beseeching them for a merciful death. He saw the image of the great warrior spirit, Kimbo standing before him, as he faded into a peaceful space which was absent of concern or pain.

RETURN TO GAMBEYA

Nana lead the expedition without further incident back to Gambeya and reported all the pertinent facts to the elders. After several days of deliberation the elders then reported their findings to the village at large. There was much supposition among the families and friends as to the possible survival of those whom had not returned with the group. There was also talk of a rescue mission but the idea wasn't given serious consideration by the elders. The village simply could not afford any additional loss of life. All the surviving protectors were needed to safeguard the immediate area surrounding Gambeya. The threat to their people had grown with recent reports of inland incursions by the Tubab and the Mobutai.

Officially the elders proclaimed those whom were missing to have entered the spirit world. They were acknowledged each day in ceremony and prayers for a period of three moons and once per year thereafter at the celebration of harvest. Even though there was no actual proof of death it was custom under such conditions to assume it. This policy allowed loved ones to quickly move forward with their lives. It was in the best interest of the community and worked efficiently for the survival of their people. The luxury of a long grieving period was supplanted by the reality of acquiring the necessities of life.

Briami gave birth to a healthy boy who was of course named Ibrahim. She could have opted to use a name that started with the letter E to honor Embato's memory but chose to follow the decision that she and her beloved had made together. She felt strongly that Embato was still alive but never spoke publicly about the controversial topic. She kept him alive in her heart for herself and in her memory for Ibrahim. She could feel Embato's spiritual presence every evening at dusk when she took Ibrahim outside to watch and listen as day turned to night. On the clear nights she would gaze up into the sky in search of their North Star and point it out to Ibrahim and then speak to him about his father.

Ibrahim grew to know his father through his mother's eyes. He also listened intently to the experiences shared by Jimba as he described Embato's many selfless acts of courage. Ibrahim took great pride in being the son of such a revered warrior and humanitarian. During his childhood he and his mother never missed meeting Embato each time their star made an appearance.

Briami continued the tradition even after her marriage to Nana. The matter was never discussed between the two but Nana understood. Nana had loved Embato in a different way but nearly as deeply as Briami had loved him. And she knew that Embato loved Nana as well. They truly believed that Embato would have wanted someone like Nana to love and protect his precious Briami and to be a good father to his son. They were right.

HELL ON THE GAMBIA

The mouth of the Gambia River opened into the Atlantic Ocean about one hundred and seventy miles Southwest of Gambeya village. In deep water about one half mile off shore laid a great boat of the Tubab. It was quite a spectacle and was intimidating to anyone seeing it for the first time. It came into full view as the boat men negotiated the last curve of the Gambia just at the point where it opened widely and met the great water. To their right and about one quarter mile inland of the Gambia was another imposing structure. It appeared to be made from trunks of the oldest trees in the forest. The tree parts had been stripped of their bark and were somehow fastened together. It was completely encircled by a protective palisade which was also made from the trees and stood about twenty five to thirty feet high. There was a ten foot section of the palisade which could be moved forward and backward that created a temporary opening to enter or exit the structure itself.

A group of African men had just exited the great structure and were heading in the direction of their boat. The group was guarded in the front by a Mobutai warrior. He occasionally threatened to poke one of the men with his spear. All the men seemed to be walking in short choppy steps and in rhythm with each other. Their arms were pulled behind their backs and their heads bowed forward with eyes to the ground. They never looked up. In the rear of the group were two Tubab who were both holding the shiny weapons. They were speaking to each other in a language that only they and the Mobutai warrior could understand.

When they came closer the cadence of the African group's movements created an unfamiliar sound. As they approached the river's edge it grew louder. It was coming from a rope like object which appeared to be made from the same substance as the shiny weapons. The object was wrapped around each man's lower legs and feet and was connected to each man in succession. They were restrained from individual movement by the hard shiny bindings. The four captives in the boat were watching the unfolding scene with increasing anxiety. They could only wonder if they themselves would not soon be bound together in the same manner as their African brothers.

The Mobutai warrior approached the boat and motioned for everyone to get out and go ashore. The four captives had their hands bound behind them with vine and were being guarded by a Tubab from the stern. The two paddle men assisted the captives out of the boat and onto land. Once the boat was empty then the Mobutai warrior motioned for the bound group to get into it. When they were settled, the Washa in the stern motioned to the paddle men to paddle forward toward the great boat in deep water.

The Mobutai warrior spoke in what seemed to be a dialect of Wolof. One of the four captives understood him and told the other three to sit on the ground until the small boat, with the bound group, reached the great boat. The four watched patiently as the former bound group was transferred from the small vessel to the great boat. Satisfied with what took place, the two Tubab then spoke harshly to the Mobutai and pointed back toward the large structure. The Mobutai motioned for the four captives to stand and follow him toward the fortified structure. The two Tubab followed closely behind with their shiny weapons raised in the direction of the four captives. In fear of their lives the captives moved submissively forward following closely behind the Mobutai. They passed through the opening in the palisade which was immediately closed and secured behind them.

Inside the great fortress they found themselves in a spacious area that was open to the sky and sun from above. It was different than it had appeared from outside. A series of smaller contiguous structures enclosed the rectangular space forming a sort of courtyard. Each was about five feet high by about eight feet wide and together formed an interior perimeter around the entire open space area. There was a Tubab guard positioned at every other unit. Each guard was equipped with a shiny weapon. The only opening in the perimeter of smaller structures was a very narrow one which the four captives had just passed through to get inside. The design allowed for fresh air and sunlight for its occupants for at least part of each day. It helped maintain their physical health at least for the short term. And the short term was really the only concern of those in charge.

The primary goal of the unusual design of the structure however was twofold. Firstly its form was intended to *appear* impregnable from the outside and completely inescapable from the inside. Secondly it was designed to actually *function* just as it appeared. Its sole purpose was temporary but nevertheless absolute confinement and security. The appearance simply contributed to the primary goal as a deterrent. It was a necessary expense to those who stood to profit from the African slave trade, even if the occupants were only there for as little as one to four days.

The intimidating appearance of the structure was the first step in a focused effort to break the will and spirit of its newly imprisoned inhabitants. A second more brutal deterrent was the public floggings which took place on a daily basis. A different prisoner was chosen arbitrarily each day and accused of planning an escape. The punishment was intended to cause extreme pain and scarring but without permanent structural damage to the body. The desired goal was to terrorize and deter those imprisoned from even thinking of escape. The non lethal and non crippling methods used to inflict punishment were limited in severity so as to preserve the market value of the human being as a slave.

Since the four new captives were not present for the morning inspection they would be ineligible for the auction block until the next day. This was a guarantee of confinement for at least one night under terribly inhumane conditions. They were not allowed to speak and were placed with seven others in a unit of less than eighty square feet.

They were given a few scraps of food and only one bowl of water to share. The cramped space and sounds from those being tortured made it virtually impossible to sleep. And only minutes after a series of terrifying screams they saw a body being dragged across the open area by two Mobutai and one of the Tubab guards. The experience magnified the life threatening reality of their situation and effectively eradicated any thoughts of escape.....at least for most of them.

The next morning they were awakened at sunrise by the guards. Their water bowl was replenished but they were offered no food. Soon they were led into the center of the open area next to a wooden platform where they were doused with water in order to rinse their bodies. Then the four captives were separated from the others into one group and told to step onto the platform and face the sun.

The platform stood about a foot off the ground and was large enough for all four to stand with about four feet between them. The bindings around their feet and legs were removed but the ones securing their hands and arms remained intact. They stood there for several minutes while two Tubab came and stood next to them. The captive's purplish black skin glistened in the morning sun contrasting with that of the ashy white Tubab. In almost any other circumstance the African warriors' powerful muscular bodies would have been intimidating to the Tubab who thus far appeared generally to be smaller in size.

But the simple possession of superior weaponry had changed the laws of nature and thus tipped the balance of power in favor of the strange new men that the indigenous Africans called the Tubab. Prior to their capture, all four warriors had successfully defended themselves and their loved ones with their fighting skills and their strength and courage. Of course they possessed weapons and fought hard in order to optimize their effectiveness. But all the weaponry on the continent was essentially the same......until the introduction of the new shiny cylinders of death.

Therefore the physical attributes which had served the African warriors so well in the past were no longer the determinant battle asset. In fact in an ironic twist of fate their strength and endurance had become a liability. It was in fact the very reason for their capture, imprisonment, and eventual enslavement. Their personal physical assets were still very valuable, but not available for their own discretionary use. It was the intent of their captors' to *harvest* these assets and to use them commercially for their own personal gain. The immoral plan of such arrogant, ruthless people would be executed on a grand scale and with little or no regard for consequence to the captive or his/her family.

After a visual inspection the Tubab motioned for the captives to open their mouths wide. They then forced their fingers inside in order to feel the Africans teeth and gums. This caused one of them to gag and choke. As he coughed he accidentally bit the fore finger of the chubby inspector. The inspector screamed and the Tubab guards guffawed in belly laughter. The old Tubab's face turned crimson and he was furious with the guards, but redirected his anger and retribution to the defenseless captive. The inspector abruptly turned to one of the Mobutai guards and poked his fat finger in his chest. In a high pitched voice he demanded punishment for the still coughing captive. The Mobutai drew his whip and struck the captive across the back. The force and pain of the blow dropped the pathetic victim to his knees. Fearing for his life the wounded captive stood back up and tried desperately to suppress his natural cough mechanism by holding his breath until the response subsided. Assured that his proper authority and respect was restored, the chubby old man initiated the final steps of the inspection.

The inspectors then proceeded to examine the four captives' bodies in detail and recorded the size of their arms, chests, and thighs. They were even disrobed of their meager loin cloths and checked for reproductive genitalia. The process was degrading and dehumanizing for anyone, but it was particularly so for those whom had been proud warriors just days before. It was another step in the attempt to destroy the humanity, strength, courage, and spirit of people who personified those very attributes.

After the inspection was completed, the four new captives were returned to their unit and their feet and legs bound once again. They then watched as four more groups were displayed on the platform and also poked, prodded, measured, and humiliated. Two of the groups included women and children. Unlike the men's groups both the feet and hands of the women were unbound. It soon became apparent that their hands were set free in order to pleasure the chief inspector. All the women in both groups were repeatedly fondled including one little girl who had not even reached puberty.

The chubby chief inspector expressed a particular fondness for the little girl. She and her mother wrapped themselves tightly together fearing separation. The guards had to finally knock the mother unconscious in order to separate the two. As the mother fell, the little girl still clung to her limp body. When the guards pulled her away the scratches on her lower back and thighs from her clinging daughter's fingernails were visible. The hideous old chief inspector had the little girl removed and taken outside the great structure.

Hatred for the Tubab grew deeply in the hearts of the four warriors. Each to a man would have proudly exchanged places with the women in order to save them from the barbaric behavior they had just been forced to observe. But the captives' collective will remained strong. As a group they beseeched their creator to grant them the opportunity to punish the evil Tubab whom they believed intended to abuse the little girl.

The four captives were again led out into the central area and assigned an identification number. After a second but abbreviated inspection, the Tubab sat in front of the platform while holding papers in one hand and small leather pouches in the other. Each captive was brought up onto the platform individually followed by much negotiation between the Tubab and the inspectors. After the talk ceased, one of the Tubab would hand over one or more of their leather pouches to an inspector in trade for the African captive. The first three were sold and taken by a Tubab along with their guards.

When the last of the four men stood on the platform the talk was longer and more intense than with the others. He was younger and significantly larger than the other four. The same Tubab who purchased the other three handed over *four* pouches in a trade for him alone. He secured the services of a Mobutai to assist in guarding and in communication with his prized acquisition.

The four captives were led toward the entrance to the great structure with Tubab guards both in the front and rear of the group and a Mobutai to the side. The captives could only shuffle along slowly as their hands and feet were still bound. They retraced their steps from the previous day through the narrow entrance way and down the palisade path. They were glad to leave the hellishness of the great structure but were fearful of what lay ahead.

The largest of the four could not get the little girl out of his mind and began to pray for her protection just as the Mobutai spoke directly to him. He was surprised that he was able to understand most of what the Mobutai had said. He gleaned from the brief words that he would be taken back to the boat on the Gambia and transported to the great vessel in the deep water. He was warned that if he tried to escape he would be killed. Once in the small boat his feet would be unbound but his hands would remain restrained.

As they neared the river they heard the scream of a child off to their left from behind a group of tall bushes. They saw the little girl attempting to crawl toward them from behind some bushes. She was naked from the waist down and her left leg was in the grasp of the old chubby inspector. There was a Tubab guard near by but with his back turned away from the scene and obviously trying to ignore the act. The group pretended to ignore it as well but the largest of them could not. After shuffling several more feet he turned to the Mobutai.

"We are very close to the boat, and I have to release behind the bush now! I will not be able to hold it until we get to the great vessel! Please loosen the bindings around my feet so that I can spread my legs and not soil my covering and body. If not, your Tubab will be angry."

The Mobutai was suspicious but nevertheless delivered the message to the lead Tubab. Even though suspicious, the Tubab saw the logic in the captive's warning of possibly soiling the boat and garment and agreed to let him "attend his nature". He told the Mobutai he would proceed with the other three to the boat and instructed him to meet there with the captive.

The remaining Tubab guard and Mobutai accompanied the captive to a secluded area about fifty feet off the main trail. The Mobutai loosened the binding on the captive's feet while the Tubab turned his back and moved further away to spare himself the unpleasant scene. As the captive squatted the Mobutai turned his head away. They could still hear the screams of the little girl as the captive spoke to the Mobutai once again.

"You are a Mobutai warrior who is bound by code to protect the women and children. Yet you have given your soul to evil and for what? Do you not hear the little one's heart and body being desecrated? Why do you allow this? By ignoring something this bad your soul will be lost forever. Allow me to stop it. You can kill me after I kill the old evil Tubab".

The captive had attacked the Mobutai's manhood successfully. His words were true and they both knew it. The Mobutai had his justification for cooperating with the Tubab in the slave trade. But the evil actions being carried out by the old Tubab was beyond anything he had seen. Surprisingly he quickly replied to the captive in a muted tone.

"Yes, you are right. I am not proud of my actions with the Tubab but they hold my family hostage. They have agreed to release them once I have delivered an agreed upon number of captives to them. But I do not trust them. They may have already sent my family on the great vessel. I do not know where they are."

The captive said, "Then you still have the heart and spirit of the warrior and if you do what is right then the creator will watch over your family for you".

With no time for deliberation the Mobutai simply replied "Yes".

He quickly turned toward the Tubab guard and knocked him unconscious with one powerful blow of his fist to the back of the head. He then turned back toward the captive. "Go kill the old Tubab and release the little girl. Tell her to meet me down by the first curve in the river and I will take her to my village where she will be safe. Blame his death on me and tell them that I forced you to help me."

The captive did not hesitate. He ran quickly to the bushes where he had seen the little girl. When he reached them he was horrified. The old man's pants were down to his ankles and he was lying on top of the little girl. He pushed her face into the ground and was trying to enter the little girl as the captive reached them. The powerful African struck the old Tubab with a blow to the head and then twisted and jerked his neck until he felt it crack. The old man dropped lifelessly to the ground. The captive then gave the terrified little girl the instructions from the Mobutai and made her repeat them back to him. She immediately turned and ran for her life. The captive heard rapid footsteps behind him and turned to see the Mobutai running toward him.

He had just knocked the old Tubab's guard unconscious in order to make the captive's story more believable. He stopped momentarily and told the captive to go back to the small boat and tell them the story which they had agreed upon. Grabbing the captive around the ankles he said "First I must rebind your legs tightly or they will not believe you."

When he finished the leg binder he assisted the captive back to the main trail. He then turned away from the slowly shuffling captive and ran toward the Gambia to meet the little girl.

After only a few steps he turned back and said, "My name is Ambu. What is your name and that of your village? I will try to inform your people of your survival".

The captive stood a bit more erect than just before and proudly replied, "I am from the village of Gambeya. My name is Embato Ngawai." He watched as Ambu acknowledged him with a quick nod of the head and then disappeared into the bush in the direction of the curve in the Gambia.

The two warriors at another time and place might have been enemies in battle. But a strange and powerful force had emerged that threatened both of their peoples. The Tubab propensity for unnecessary violence and their apparent absence of any moral standard was simply inconceivable to both Ambu and Embato. Acts of violence in Mobutai and Gambeyan cultures were generally carried out only in defense of either their people's lives or of essential resources. It was rare that violence occurred for any other purpose. And sexual abuse of small children was virtually unheard of. The exhibition of extreme and bizarre behavior on the part of some of the Tubab was alarming and thus created common ground for Ambu and Embato to act in unison. Their codes of honor were similar and once Embato had confronted Ambu with the truth it was incumbent upon him to either act or live in shame. They both responded like the noble warriors that they were.

The two Tubab guards who had been knocked out converged at the small boat within seconds of each other. Embato arrived shortly after still shuffling along slowly in his original bindings. The old inspector's guard was very upset and excitedly explained what happened back on the trail. He reported that his boss had been murdered by either Embato or the Mobutai. Both the guards were still a bit groggy, however, and became quite confused when they realized that Embato was still bound by hands and feet. The old inspector's guard, still frustrated, wanted to blame Embato and began cursing him. He pulled the butt handle of his weapon back to strike Embato but the lead Tubab stepped in between them.

"No! He's me own property now and ye cannot harm heem." Turning to his other Tubab guard in the boat he said, "If he raises his hand agin shoot heem dead. And ye there" gesturing to his other Tubab guard, "get in the boat... Now! We must make haste to the ship before there is more trouble".

Addressing the old inspector's guard again he said sternly, "Go back to the fort and tell the agent that the Mobutai killed the old man. The crusty old bastard had it comin anyhow! He was an immoral sinner. I to have had me share of the African slave women but never have I defiled an innocent child. The rotten bastard got his just desserts as God above intended. Now, be gone with ye!"

He motioned for Embato to get into the boat with him. He then commanded his guards to loosen the bindings on Embato's feet and to assist him to a secure kneeling position just aft of the bow. The paddle men quickly shoved off and headed out into the deep water toward the great vessel. Embato understood nothing that the lead Tubab had said but drew inferences from his gestures and tone of voice. He concluded that for some reason the lead Tubab was interested in protecting him.

As the boat cut through the increasingly rough water Embato was relieved to see the great structure disappearing in the distance behind them. He hoped to never see such a place again. And he envisioned a new alliance of the Mobutai warriors and the Gambeyan protectors who together would soon burn the structure to the ground.

As the small boat moved into the open water the great boat emerged into full view. They were still a quarter mile away and yet the vessel appeared huge in Embato's eyes. He was amazed that something that large and heavy could float on the water. He thought that the Tubab must be supported by truly powerful spirits. The shiny cylinders of death and the great boat were proof enough for him. As they moved closer in broadside to the vessel he could see three tall poles extending vertically from the hull. Each had two or three smaller poles connected to them and extending horizontally ten to fifteen feet outward. He saw a Tubab standing near the top of the highest pole and leaning against what appeared to be a large basket. The man was frantically waving to the small boat and pointed in their direction as he yelled down to someone below him. The lead Tubab in the small boat looked toward their stern to see what he was pointing to. He saw three small boats heading in their direction and less than a quarter mile away. Alarmed by their presence, he immediately motioned for the paddle men to go faster.

The paddle men responded and within two minutes the small boat was abreast the great vessel. The lead Tubab yelled to several of those already on board the vessel. All of a sudden Embato saw three large white coverings appear and then be hoisted up the vertical poles by their bindings. The four captives and the Tubab climed up a rope ladder and boarded the great vessel. The two paddle men turned their small boat around and paddled back in the direction of the Gambia.

Embato was amazed at the buzz of activity on board the great vessel and noticed that most of the workmen on board were Tubab. To his surprise, however, there were two Africans. He watched with great curiosity as the Africans climbed and pulled the bindings along with the Tubab. They were not bound or imprisoned in any manner and seemed to have free run of the vessel just as the Tubab did. For a moment his spirits were lifted. Perhaps he to would work on the great vessel. He was confident that his strength would be put to good use along with the others. But his fantasy was interrupted by an incredibly loud boom.

Only ten feet to his right he saw a plume of smoke rising from the vessel. It was coming from a strange object which was about three feet long and appeared like the shiny cylinders but much thicker and with a larger opening. Moments after the loud blast the workmen started yelling and waving their head coverings while pointing in the direction of the three small boats. Embato turned just in time to see one of the small boats capsize, dumping its four passengers into the deep water. He did not see them rise to the surface and concluded that they had joined the spirit world. The other two small boats turned back toward land and moved swiftly in the direction of the great structure. Embato was in awe of the Tubab power.

A Mobutai appeared from below the level that Embato was standing on. He was bound about the hands and feet with the noisy, shiny bindings. He was lead to Embato by a Tubab who was holding a smaller weapon about a foot long. The Mobutai spoke to him in a slightly different dialect than Ambu's, but Embato was able to understand him.

"You are a prisoner and property of the Tubab. They own you just as they own their coverings and weapons and the great boat......just as they own me and the others. The main Tubab has traded some of his valued possessions in exchange for you. You will stay in the bindings until you are delivered to the land called America where you will be sold again to another Tubab. You will work in his fields and be given food, drink and a place to sleep. During the voyage you will stay below and be bound together with the others. You will be given food and water and brought to see the sun once per day. You will be instructed in the teachings of their spirit and god who is called Jesus and you must pray only to him. If you cause any trouble you will be whipped and deprived of sunlight and food. Tell the Tubab your name and then follow me. My African name is Oramba Onai".

The Mobutai turned and disappeared below the main level. Embato was incredulous at what he had just heard. He was also struck by Oramba's monotone voice and the absence of any inflection. Oramba faced Embato's direction during his talk but without any hint of life in his eyes. They appeared dead to Embato. He prayed silently to Borombi and *his* spirits for great courage, strength and endurance. He simply could not pray to another's god. His life was fueled by the unique spiritual nourishment that could only come from the truth he knew. How could their god be real if he allowed them to commit such horrific acts? Embato promised Borombi and the spirits that he would never forsake them.

After giving his name he was shoved by two Tubab toward the opening that would lead him to the unknown world that existed below deck. As he neared the opening he began to smell the stench of the hellish hold that was to be his home for the next fourteen weeks. He began to hear the whale of human agony from those who were suffering below. It all made him want to fight and die rather than join those in the wretched hold of despair in the great vessel..

In a near panic his mind raced through the alternate courses of action that might be available to him. Physically overcoming his captors was out of the question as their numbers and weaponry were too great. His eyes quickly panned several feet to his right. He calculated that he was only one and a half steps from the side rail and freedom from whatever awaited him below deck and beyond. Ther he could jump to where the deep water spirits dwelled. In order to insure his successful leap to physical death, however, he would have to temporarily disable the

Tubab guard. Without further thought he slowly bent his right knee and twisted his powerful torso in the same direction. The torque created when abruptly moving back to his left would allow him to thrust his left forearm into the chest of the Tubab guard with enough force to disable him momentarily. It would open access to the rail so he could jump over the side. Just as he pulled his left forearm up and coiled to his chest for the strike, a sudden vision of Guyiome appeared before him.

In the vision Guyiome was surrounded by Kimbo and several warrior spirits. All of them had their arms raised toward him with the palms of their hands facing Embato. It was not a sign of welcome, nor his time to rest. He was being told to stay. Instead of embracing the sanctuary of peace that he selfishly chose, he followed the direction of the spirits. He chose life..........and hope.

He stepped toward the entrance to the vessel's dark hold below. But just before entering, his eyes focused on one final image. It was an inscription in the Tubab' language framed against the backdrop of the clear blue West African sky. The symbols were neatly carved into a wooden panel just above the opening that led to the hold. He did not understand its meaning but he would never forget the image. The carved letters spelled out the name of the ship....... SEA RUNNER.

THE MIDDLE PASSAGE

Almost all Embato's time on the SEA RUNNER was spent in the horrific conditions of the ship's hold As uplifting to his spirit as it was to go topside everyday, it was just as deflating to return to the darkness and stench of the hold below. After two weeks at sea, its planking was covered with a mixture of seawater and body waste. With its heat, darkness, and very overcrowded conditions, it had become an incubator of disease and death. On average Embato witnessed a death of one of the African slaves every two to three days during the voyage. And he himself also became very ill for several weeks resulting in extreme loss of weight and strength.

But when he was well and strong, it was difficult to restrain him self from attacking those who were responsible for such senseless death and suffering. Any aggressive action on his part, however, would surely have resulted in the sacrifice of his own life and with no benefit to those fellow captives around him. Thus he suppressed his anger and instead focused on survival. He vowed, however, that one day he would fight again for his African people. But it would not be during the hellish voyage across the Atlantic to America. While in route he could only whisper encouragement to those whose lives had been irreparably harmed, and pray for the souls of those who had crossed into the spirit world.

During the voyage Embato's eyes and ears were telling him a story that his protector's mind was psychologically unable to reconcile. The experience was simply too aghast and foreign to anything he could have imagined. Thus the suppression of his emotions eventually forced him into a necessary state of psychological denial. It was simply the mind's last ditch effort at individual survival.

It was not in a Gambeyan Protector's nature to disengage and shy away from struggle and challenge. But experiencing the repeated rape, torture and abuse of humanity aboard the SEA RUNNER would have likely been debilitating to even the bravest of any warrior society. He had learned long ago to relegate his own intentions to those of Borombi and the spirits. And it was adherence to this very tenent that would place him involuntarily into a depth of denial sufficient to insure his own personal survival. Otherwise he would have attempted to protect, heal and save lives that in many instances simply were not savable. Instead he was led by the spirits once again to suppress his own will and to follow their plan. In doing so he would be of valuable service to humanity again one day. But in order to do that he would have to first survive the horrors of the Atlantic slave trade route which would come to be known historically as the Middle Passage.

Authors Note: *The Middle Passage and slave trade (not slavery itself) had been legislatively declared illegal by the United States Congress in 1806. All the states complied except one. The state of South Carolina initially resisted the federal action* *through its own state legislative efforts. It would publicly sanction the importation of African slaves for two more years officially. And unofficially it allowed the trade to continue by essentially turning a blind eye to it for a period of time afterward. Its busiest port, Charleston, had historically been the greatest single entry point for slave ships throughout the period of American slavery. And even after the U.S. Congress abolished the slave trade, Charleston remained the main point of entry for slave ships coming into the United States. In fact the majority of the 50,000 African slaves smuggled into the United States after the slave trade was declared illegal were brought in through the port of Charleston, South Carolina.*

AMERICA, HOME OF THE FREE AND...

At least seventy African slaves and two crewmen perished during the *Sea Runner's* voyage that season. And those African slaves who survived were headed into the inhumane conditions of slavery. But there must have been a collective sigh of relief when the slave ship entered the calm waters at the mouth of the Charleston River. At least there was the hope of fresh air and sunshine. Charleston, South Carolina was located on the Southeast coast of what Embato would later learn to be the United States of America. Embato had lost count of the number of days since he had last seen his homeland but he knew it had been more than three moons. And as he gazed through a tiny half inch slit between the deteriorated boarding of the *Sea Runner's* hull he realized that wherever he was, it was *not* West Africa. For an instant Embato allowed himself a moment of self pity, as he realized for the first time that he might never see his beloved Briami again.

As the *Sea Runner* glided slowly up the steadily narrowing river the images within Embato's field of vision started to make sense. He was shocked to see what appeared to be Africans moving about on shore. Although dressed in non African attire some even looked like the people of his homeland. They were spread out over marshlands that stretched all along the immediate coastline. Some seemed to be knee deep in the water. At first the whole scene puzzled Embato as clearly the workers were not harvesting any kind of fish in such a marsh. It appeared that they were attending to something growing in the wetlands. It would only be days however before he himself would rely on the consumption of a small grain that came from those wetlands for his very survival. The word "rice" would soon become part of his new vocabulary. He continued to observe the ever changing landscape as the vessel moved closer into the harbor.

The terrain transitioned from marshland to slightly higher ground but the appearance of those tending the fields did not. There were still African people working in the fields. Their effort was focused on waist high plants with white blossoms that covered the land as far as the eye could see. Once again he did not recognize the crop. He would soon learn however that "cotton" would be an integral part of his clothing in America. It would be years however before he would understand the critical role it played in the southern United States economy and thus his own enslavement. As the waterway continued narrowing and the *Sea Runner* glided closer to land, Embato began to hear the field workers singing.

Although he could not make out the words he was sure that he recognized the familiar sounds of a collective West African voice and rhythm. This lifted his spirits a bit because in his mind wherever there was singing there was also some happiness. He fantasized that when on land he might be allowed to join in and even teach them some of his Gambeyan village songs. A glimmer of hope began to emerge in his heart.. He instantly thanked Borombi and the spirits for what appeared to be deliverance from the bowels of a tortuous hell on the *Sea Runner*. Although he had suffered and lost much in physical strength and size, his mind and soul were focused on life once again.

As they moved closer still toward the harbor, a smaller craft pulled up along the port bow. The *Sea Runner* came to a stop and dropped anchor. Just as Embato was getting a close up view from below of the small boat he and several of the African captives were brought topside. As Embato reached the top step he was forced to shade his eyes from the bright sun. Once his eyes adjusted to the sunlight he observed an older Tubab with a gray beard climb on board. He disappeared into the Captain's quarters briefly. When he returned he took the wheel and began shouting commands to one seaman who repeated them to the others. The *Sea Runner* pulled its anchor up and slowly began to move forward following the middle of the harbor. Occasionally the old man at the wheel would shout loudly and forcefully until all was as he deemed necessary.

The *Sea Runner* finally came to a complete stop and was nestled up snugly against the outer dock planking in Charleston Harbor. A wooden walkway was lain down from the ship's deck to dock level. After several of the sailors had walked onto the dock, Embato and six other African captives were slowly led down the platform to the dock. They were no longer bound and were handed cargo to carry down the ramp.

As he shuffled his way carefully down the platform Embato began to take in the great variety of sights and sounds before him. There were wide stone paths with carts being pulled by animals he had never seen before. He saw small and large wooden structures and many people moving about. For the first time his eye caught the form of Tubab females. He noticed one in particular that had long straight flowing hair the color of the Sun. He was so intrigued by her striking image that he stared in her direction a bit too long.

A Tubab guard noticed Embato's stare and interest in the woman. In addition to a shiny weapon held in his left hand the guard was also holding a rope like object in his right. He raised the object and struck Embato across the neck and left collar bone with it. There was little blood drawn but the force of the blow resulted in a nasty welp where it had landed. Embato dropped the cargo and fell to one knee on the walkway platform from the blow and was close to falling into the harbor waters. His new captor was furious with the Tubab guard. He cursed the guard from the bow of the SEA RUNNER. Once all seven African slaves were safely on land his tirade escalated. The Tubab captor stormed down the platform and with one powerful uppercut knocked the guard off his feet and onto the dock. He then turned to the gathering crowd and warned all within earshot not to touch any of his property or their fate would be the same.

Although frightened and confused Embato began to ponder how his entry into this new place started much the same way as his forced departure from his homeland in the small boat on the Gambia. He was unsure as to what the rules of expected behavior were for him in his new surroundings. On the one hand he was readily punished by some Tubab for a given action but on the other hand he was defended by others for the same behavior. So he decided to be cautious about looking up and out at anything from that point on, unless specifically directed to do so by someone in authority. He simply looked down where there was little to see and hoped to avoid unnecessary trouble. And that downward look also included a slight slumping of his shoulders. By coincidence Embato was already conveying the necessary posture of submission that his captors required of all their slaves.

But this body posture was a difficult adjustment for Embato. The submissive slave body slump was not the same as the downward look of the eyes in Gambeyan culture that was meant to convey respect. The Gambeyan look carried with it an erect body posture that suggested a strong sense of self worth. But cognition of self worth was unacceptable as a slave in America. Any expression of self confidence or even direct eye contact would have to cease. Otherwise he was left with two options: death or escape. And since Embato had already chosen to survive, he would also choose the option fueled with hope. It was the idea that had dominated his being since the moment of his capture......his escape to freedom.

THE SMITH PLANTATION

Embato spent the next several years of his life as a field slave on a plantation about 40 miles Southwest of Charleston, SC. It was owned by Zachary Smith, a wealthy white man, who had been born into a life of privilege. Smith was a fourth generation American whose ancestors came from London, England. They were proud of their pure blue blood Caucasian ancestry and took every opportunity to express it publicly. Unlike most other planters, the Smith clan had no readily identifiable slaves that were of mixed race on their plantations. But it wasn't because

the Smith masters embraced a higher moral lifestyle than other planters in the region. They had not always ignored the opportunity to take
sexual liberties with some of their female slaves. Privilege, wealth, and
power often exempted one from accountability in matters of moral
hypocrisy. And the Smith Masters personified this model. Zachary once
jokingly described his ancestors' arrogant behavior as simply "They did
it, and hid it". In fact his own father sold off a mother and her newborn
because the infant's skin tone would have cast doubt on his reputation.
He felt that his father had little choice in the matter but disagreed with
his decision to split the family and keep the mother's husband on the
Smith. Years later Zachary's wife persuaded him to trade the man to the
same plantation that the mother and infant had gone to.

At 49 Zachary was very sure of his place in the still developing American
society. He was near the very top of the pyramid of wealth and social
elitism. He had a beautiful, kind wife and together thay had raised a
family of seven healthy children. But he had tried to hide her personal
history for fear of tainting his offspring with something less than a blue
blood pedigree.

Jo Ann Smith had come from poverty and was a descendent of Scotch
Irish indentured servants. Unlike her husband she understood the pain
and indignity suffered at the hands of those of privilege. Even after her
marriage to Zachary she still felt inferior in some ways to his siblings and
certainly to her in laws. When she mustered the courage to express such
feelings, however, she was rebuked and her opinion on the subject rendered invalid. Even though the feelings of inferiority stayed with her, Jo
Ann finally gave in to Zachary after her plea for understanding resulted
in his fit of rage and cursing. She became ever more isolated and intro-
verted as a result. She took her dilemma to her spiritual savior, Jesus
Christ. She grew closer and closer to the Holy Spirit and less and less
connected to secular humanity and particularly to men. This included
her husband of fourteen years.

Jo Ann was nineteen when she married Zachary. She was 5' 4" and was
blessed with an adorable smile and a well proportioned body. She had

somehow been able to maintain her youthful appearance even after giving birth to their seven children. And her beauty was duly noted amongst all the men of the area. She was aware of her image but remained a loyal wife and devoted mother. As a devout Christian she tried to live the example set by Jesus Christ. This life had led her to the conclusion that slavery was morally wrong and she grew to despise the institution. This was her mindset when Embato Ngawai arrived on the Smith Plantation as part of the newly purchased group of slaves.

ADJUSTING TO SLAVE LIFE

When Embato arrived at his new home on the Smith he was careful not to look up at first. But he was indeed listening, watching, and learning as much as possible about his new surroundings. He was particularly adept at noting direction and distance crossed with time. It was part of his training as a Protector in Gambeya. In his first month on the Smith he had committed to memory the exact number of steps of every route travelled by the slaves. He had memorized at what point to expect an incline or slope or any fixed obstacle in the path. In order to simulate darkness he often closed his eyes while walking the different paths. But sometimes he closed his eyes simply to escape some of the sights of brutality that seemed to be a part of everyday life on the Smith.

Embato was assigned sleeping quarters in a small out building constructed from slab wood pieces. It was several hundred yards down wind from the main Smith home but only about seventy yards from the overseer's quarters. The slave quarters were most often without windows and sometimes the doorway was covered with only a hanging cloth or skin cover. The slabs were not flush in their construction and provided little barrier to the elements or vermin and insects.

In the hot humid South Carolina summers the mosquitoes were abundant and aggressive at dusk and during periods of wetness. He had available natural remedies back in West Africa for annoying insects, but the vegetation on the Smith was initially unknown to him for such use. He chose to wear long pants and long sleeves during his first summer in order to minimize exposure to the mosquitoes. Their relentless attack was just one aspect of slavery that made plantation life barely tolerable.

No matter how hard he worked, it seemed he could never satisfy the overseer, Albert Jennings. Jennings was paid by Smith to manage the slave labor in a way that ensured maximum productivity. Virtually all overseers utilized methods of fear and intimidation to induce the slaves to work harder. They sometimes included public displays of physical violence perpetrated on the slaves. But some overseers were worse than others. Unfortunately for the Smith slaves Jennings was amongst the worse. He committed frequent acts of mental cruelty and physical brutality. On a weekly basis Jennings would single out a slave at random and accuse him/her of stealing or planning escape. The most frequent punishment was lashings from his whip but the variety of his sadistic acts included anything from burning the skin with red hot metal to cutting off an ear lobe.

Somehow for the first few weeks Embato had escaped punishment. Perhaps his good fortune was due to his economic value as a strong, young, and reproductive male. But regardless of Embato's high value as a slave, Jennings did not like or trust him. The overseer fancied some female slaves as objects of his physical pleasure and saw Embato as a constant threat to that. He became insanely jealous of the handsome young African. Even with bowed head, Embato still projected a presence of pride and strength that marked him for eventual punishment. When Jennings observed Embato counting during a walk to the fields one day he began to think of him as a potential runaway. He had his justification....no matter Embato's value to the Smiths.

Jennings forced the group to work past sundown on Embato's seventh Saturday on the Smith. He had hoped to elicit a grumble or ideally an open defiant complaint from Embato. But it was not to be, as Embato was simply biding his time and knew better. An hour or so after sunset Jennings told the head field slave to lead everyone back to the quarters.

In the dark Jennings stumbled on a root and fell flat on his face. As he rose to his feet he felt a small trickle of blood oozing from his nose. And he immediately accused Embato of tripping him. He then ordered four other male slaves to seize Embato and tie him to the trunk of a nearby oak. Embato was spread eagled against the tree trunk with both legs and arms hugging it. He was bound tightly about both wrists and ankles and also to the trunk. He could move only his head and neck.

Jennings then forced all the slaves including the women and children to watch the whipping. He sent one male to the Smith house to get two more lanterns so there was plenty of light. When the slave returned with the lanterns Jennings began screaming obscenities and accused Embato of tripping him on the path and also of planning an escape. Escape was often cited in association with punishment (no matter what the real offense had been) so as to discourage any thoughts of it amongst the slave population.

As Jennings voice began to crescendo out of control he was literally shaking. Jennings' whippings were not indicative of the beatings that occurred on many plantations as a routine deterrent. His actions that day were motivated by a personal animosity for Embato. And he generally had a personal need to inflict physical pain on anyone that he could. Jennings had in fact become addicted to it. With only one exception, the entire male slave population of the Smith had become his whipping boys at one time or another. He had devolved into something less than a creation of God and more so of a very sick human possessed by a demonic force.

Delivering his final verbal tirade that evening took so much out of Jennings physically, that he fell to his knees weeping. For a moment there was hope amongst the slaves that Embato would be spared. But he rose to a standing position and drew the whip back as he prepared to strike Embato across his wide muscular back. Embato prepared himself for the excruciating pain that he was about to receive. He prayed to Borombi and the spirits for courage and strength.

Jennings screamed. "Here it comes ye damnable black heathen! I'm goin teach ye proper respeck fer me self and ye master this time."

Embato pressed his forehead so hard into the tree trunk that small bits of the bark dislodged and fell into his eyes and mouth. He gripped the sides of the trunk with both his hands and feet in order to brace himself for the pain of the deep gash that was about to be opened on his back. For a split second there was dead silence. Then Jennings started the motion to bring the whip forward when suddenly the silence was broken.

"Stop that right this minute!"

A voice cried out from the darkness of the hillside which led to the Smith house. For a moment Embato thought his mind was playing tricks on him. Still gripping the trunk and preparing for the pain of the whip he heard the voice again.

"Mr. Jennings! Please drop ya whip now and untie Embato from the tree trunk".

This time Embato recognized the voice as that of Mrs. Jo Ann Smith, the lady of the Smith Plantation. All those present were shocked at the bold intervention including Embato and Jennings. Embato's shock was accompanied by a commensurate degree of relief but Jennings was furious. As the voice and the light of the oil lantern got closer he began to recognize Mrs. Smith's petite silhouette. Jennings just stood there with a look of embarrassment and shock at first. As Mrs. Smith approached, however, he lost control of his temper and glared at her. It was unthinkable to him that she would erode his authority in front of the very slaves he was charged with overseeing by her husband.

He finally summoned the courage to growl out "I'm doing me job that ye husband has told me to do Ms. Lady. This black heathen, Eeeeembato here, tried to trip me and was planning on exscapin into the night so I have to whip heem accordin to me rules."

Moving closer to her and in a low almost whispering tone he said, "If'n I don't then we could have a loss of order and authority amongst the slaves Mrs. Lady".

Jo Ann looked him straight in the eye and whispered, "Just send the rest of these folks back to their quarters and then we will discuss the situation further."

She had allowed Jennings to save some face but had accomplished her primary goal which was to prevent what in her opinion was an unnecessary and brutal act of violence on an innocent human being. She knew that Embato was as much God's own child as was she.

Except for two of Jennings most trusted male slaves, the rest were disbursed and sent back to their quarters. All were very quiet, however, and were still listening to hear what would happen next. Still in a low but stern voice, Jo Ann Smith demanded that Jennings untie Embato from the oak. For several seconds there was dead silence as both she and Jennings stared at each other. For a moment Jennings actually thought of defying her and sending one of the slaves to get Mr. Smith. But swallowing his pride, he began to think that could be a mistake in the long-term. They both spoke simultaneously.

As she started saying "Did you hear...?"

Jennings said "Yes maam" in a low guttural tone and directed the other two slaves to untie and release Embato from the oak.

She and Jennings both approached Embato and she said, "Embato, did you mean to trip Mr. Jennings?"

Embato was still stunned somewhat at the sudden but welcome turn of events. At that point the young African only understood a few key words in English. He looked down so as not to be perceived as challenging either Mrs. Smith or Jennings.

He simply replied "Embato good Missy".

Jo Ann Smith repeated her question to Embato and Embato replied once again with the same response. She then surmised that Embato did not understand what she was asking him. She then turned abruptly to Jennings and in a louder voice admonished him.

"There, Mr. Jennings, you have your apology. Now I think all's well that ends well and more importantly Embato will be able to work a full day on Monday with no injuries to hold him back. Since tomorrow is Sunday I have to be up early for church services and I suggest we all pay our respects to God. Right Mr. Jennings?"

Stuttering a bit Jennings replied, "ah...Yes, Yes Mrs. Lady. We must pay homage to God Almighty".

Embato and the other two slaves headed back to their quarters and retired for the evening. It was too late for supper. All the food was eaten except for a piece of stale bread that pretty little Ada Oiah, one of Embato's female admirers, had saved for him. She gave it to him along with a gourd of water. He looked down at Ada and for the first time his coal black eyes made direct contact with hers.

He said "Tank, miss Ada".

He quickly stuffed the bread into his mouth and washed it down with the water. Ada was mesmerized by his captivating smile.

She said "You're welcome Embato. Sleep well. We can all rest tomorrow after the Christian services at the creek in the morning. Are you going to attend?"

Embato understood the word "creek" but nothing else so he politely nodded and said "Night Miss Ada".

Ada was a bit puzzled from the response but she just assumed that he had answered in the affirmative. Her conclusion was typical of her positive outlook on life. Even though enslaved, hungry and often in physical and emotional discomfort she somehow was able to smile and exude an outward appearance of contentment. She relied heavily on her faith in God and thus far it seemed to have served her well.

Embato took note of Ada's shapely young body as she walked back to her quarters. Exhausted, however, he was at that moment more interested in lying down on his cotton and straw stuffed bedding than being with Ada. He tried to relax but his mind was still racing from the impact of the events that had just taken place only minutes earlier. Again Borombi had intervened on his behalf and saved him from severe pain and injury. He still did not understand why Jennings had singled him out without cause, but he was even more perplexed as to why Mrs. Smith had intervened. Then another question arose in his mind. How did she even know of the incident in the first place? Unbeknownst to Embato his overseer, Jennings, was at that very moment pondering the exact same question.

After a few minutes Embato's mind began to slow and then relax. His body ached from the extra long day of physically demanding labor in the oppressive heat of the cotton and tobacco fields. The well defined muscles in his large lean body began to twitch involuntarily as they finally relaxed. He was dehydrated and desperately wanted a drink of water but he felt as though he had already been the cause of enough trouble and anguish for one day. So he slowly turned over onto his left side to go to sleep. But just before his eyes closed he saw a small pinpoint of light coming through a crack in the wall. As he dozed off he realized that it was the North Star.

Earlier that evening and an ocean away a young Gambeyan woman with an aching heart spent several minutes staring at that same celestial body in the West African skies. She had prayed to Borombi for protection and nurturing of the new child growing inside her and also for the well being of his brave beloved father......... wherever he may be.

SHALL WE GATHER AT THE RIVER

The smell of simmering fat and fresh baked cornbread filled the air surrounding the slave quarters on Sunday morning. As soon as Embato awoke he recognized the source of the aromas, and wasted no time in seeking it. He followed his nose toward the cooking fire and kettle of boiling fatback. He had learned during his first few days on the Smith not to be last in line at the kettle. On one of those days he got nothing to eat at all. From that point on he was in the line as soon as he awoke. Embato had also learned the power of flirting and more importantly its rewards.

He made sure to establish direct eye contact with Miss Louisa Mae Smith, the primary cook for his group. It was very clear to all that Miss Louisa was the sole arbiter of portion control. He also learned quickly that Miss Louisa was vulnerable to his smiling face. And that a polite word directed her way would likely ensure a large portion of cornbread, rice and gravy, or even a strip of pork bacon. Miss Louisa would have treated him preferentially even without the attention directed toward her. She saw something special in him and somehow knew that his survival was very important. She wasn't exactly sure why. But she just knew the Lord had his hands on that young man...... and she didn't question the Lord. She referred to those kinds of feelings as "God's Bizniss".

Just as Embato settled down to savor the moment with some good hot food and a full day of rest, Ada came into his view. She was wearing a light weight cotton dress with tiny floral prints that had been sewn together from empty feed sacks. The bottom lifted slightly in the evening breeze revealing the young woman's pretty thighs. Even though the garment was large on her and ballooned out at the bottom, it could not hide her exquisite femininity. She sat down on a rotted wooden board next to Embato.

Ada said in a soft gentle voice "Monin Embato".

His eyes met hers and a moment of silence ensued before he replied in a hoarse voice "Monin miss Ada".

He smiled at her and for a moment was lost in the beauty of her deep brown eyes. For the first time since being taken from his beautiful Briami, he looked at a woman with the natural interest any young male would have had. And Ada was every bit Briami's equal in physical beauty. She also embodied the necessary child bearing features that acted as a subtle but powerful magnet for young men. Embato knew she was available and that she liked him. So there was no reason in his mind for haste in the matter.

Ada said "Huuray up and finish yo breakfas Embato. The Christian creek services start soon."

Embato peered at her with a stern expression and said "Embato Ngawai Gambeyan....... Borombi. Miss Ada Creek."

Although he had never attended the Sunday morning creek services Ada was surprised at his response. She thought surely by now he would have given in to the expectations of the white Christians. Part of being a slave on the Smith was either becoming a Christian or pretending to be. Embato was the lone hold out on the Smith.

Ada continued her plea. "Embato you has ta learn the ways of the white folk and live jes lak they tells us to. We has ta beleeze wut dey beleeze. Ifn you don't, den you'll be beat an whupped an maybe even sole off ta anutha massa."

Embato heard the emotion in her voice and then saw the tears in her eyes. He prayed silently to Borombi for guidance and direction. And as it so often occurred, even before the thought left his mind Borombi answered.

He turned to Ada and said, "Embato go Miss Ada."

He realized that it was in his best interest to be seen at the creek on Sunday mornings. And he would pretend to join in, but would maintain his loyalty to the truth and righteousness of Borombi. He understood the reality that Ada was warning him of after Borombi had put it into perspective for him. He would do as she suggested to keep peace and survive...... and to enhance the friendship that was already developing between he and beautiful little Ada.

Embato and Ada walked together down the winding path toward the creek and arrived just before the preacher started the morning prayers and scripture reading. The crowd was observing a moment of silent meditation. Only the sounds of Mother Nature intervened. As Ada closed her eyes and bowed her head in reverence to God, Embato scanned the horizon. Borombi spoke to him through the wind that whispered through the trees and in the songs of the winged ones. Suddenly the silence was broken with the booming base voice of Preacher Jerrell Sweet Brown.

"Fo God so loved the world, that He gave His oooooonly begotten Son..........."

He always began with John 3:16 of the New Testament in the King James Version of the Holy Bible. It was the affirmation of one of the fundamental tenents of Christianity. It was the scriptural reference to the belief that Jesus Christ was the Son of God, and that He died on the cross in order to save mankind from sin.

The sermon began immediately after the scripture and prayer. Preacher Sweet Brown spoke at an increasingly feverish pace for almost two hours, captivating his audience with great oratory skills. There were pauses as he scanned the eyes of his audience in order to maintain their attention his way. He began phrases in a voice barely above a whisper and ended them with emphasis in a loud thunderous voice. Even the small children were quiet at times. They were intimidated by Preacher Brown. He was 6' 4" inches tall and was broad in the shoulder. And had a stare that could put the fear of God in most.

Sweet Brown had reached his seventieth birthday that year. He had been on the Smith for over twenty years and had earned the trust and confidence of Zachary. He was the one slave that was exempted from physical punishment on the Smith. Sweet enjoyed special privileges, including the freedom to venture off the plantation even without a permission note. He was, however still a slave and was required to work in addition to his ministerial responsibilities. But most of his work was light in nature and rarely in the field. He was the buggy driver for the Smiths amongst other "house" duties. He enjoyed a good life compared to that of most slaves in South Carolina in the early nineteenth century. And he was very protective of his position and stature. He would not tolerate any behavior that he perceived to be a threat to his special privileges.

Sweet Brown was obligated to see that all Smith slaves attended Sunday creek service and professed a belief in God and Jesus Christ. This was part of the methodology for control over the slave population. Every plantation had at least one slave that was given preferential treatment in exchange for a guarantee of order amongst the others. It was their job to induce or enforce compliance with the values of their owners. So when Embato showed up for Sunday creek service that morning it was as if a burden had been lifted from Preacher Sweet. But he still did not trust the new African. He saw something in Embato that suggested confidence and perhaps defiance. He knew he had to break Embato's spirit or there could be trouble. And Sweet Brown always avoided trouble.

At the conclusion of the service Ada took Embato's hand in hers and led him down to the front of the crowd near the creek's edge where they greeted Preacher Sweet Brown. Even though she was confident that Preacher Brown had seen them in the crowd, she wanted to make sure he knew that Embato was there.

She smiled and said, "Monin Preacha Brown. Sho was a lovely sumon you give us. God an the sweet Jesus was all round us taday."

Preacher Sweet Brown replied, "Why thank you lil Ada. Yes the Lawd blessed us taday with a nice breeze and lots of waam sunshine."

He faced Embato and stared into his eyes for what became an uncomfortable period before smiling. He said, "And young brotha Embato, I'm so glad you joined us taday. May the Lawd bless ya and keep ya and may ya grow in His mucy and love."

He shook Embato's hand vigorously and then turned to greet another admiring member of his flock. Embato was surprised at Preacha Brown's hand strength and wondered why he gripped his hand so tightly and shook it so vigorously. It was Sweet's subtle way of letting Embato know that he was in charge of *all* the slaves on the Smith. It was of no major concern to Embato however because he viewed every experience and relationship on the Smith as temporary. He knew that the Smith was not Borombi's intended home for him. And he knew that neither Sweet Brown nor anyone else would determine his future.... ..not even the seductive allure of sweet little Ada.

DREAMS OF FREEDOM

Embato and Ada's friendship did grow but he placed boundaries on it. A serious emotional attachment to anyone on the Smith did not fit into his long term plans. In his traditional Gambeyan ethic, the male would have taken on full responsibility for the safety and well being of his mate. But such a commitment on the Smith would have significantly complicated any plan to escape and possibly terminated it altogether. He had, however, felt something stirring in his heart at that first Sunday Creek service. And he knew he could easily fall in love if he allowed his emotions to go undisciplined. His heart still ached from the loss of his beautiful Briami, and Ada could have eased that pain for him considerably. But to give in to the pleasures of love and romance would have brought great risk and a threat to his dream of freedom.

Embato's dream of freedom was omnipresent. He had hidden the degree of his desire for freedom from everyone however while biding his time and learning. But he confided in an elder slave friend, Mr. Ben. Mr. Ben had advised him to carry a different posture in order to appear broken, submissive, and without self value. So even though it was against his natural inclinations, Embato began to slump even more at the shoulder. He forced his head bent even further down whenever he was within eyesight of the white folks. Over a period of weeks it had become almost second nature, and some spoke of it, but one comment came from an unlikely source.

On a particularly hot late summer day the crop work was stopped completely for a full hour so the field slaves could get water and eat the midday meal. As Embato was enjoying the shade of a large old red oak he heard Ada's voice. He turned toward the Smith mansion and saw Ada and Mrs.Smith walking along the edge of the tobacco field toward him. Before they approached he stood out of respect, and then lowered his shoulder and head downward.

Just as he did Mrs. Smith laughed and said in a low tone "Embato, please look at me when I speak to you and stand in your normal posture".

He pretended to not understand and maintained his position. Then to his shock Ada laughingly said, "Embato, you heard Missy Lady Smith. Now do as she say. And she know you understands mosa what she say."

For a moment he was caught off guard and completely confused by the exchange. He slowly looked to the side in both directions and lifted his head slightly up to scan in front of him. Once he had determined that no one was watching them he acknowledged Mrs. Smith's comments.

"Yessum, Miz Lady Smith."

She smiled and said, "Thank you Embato. Please come with me and Ada to the house."

She turned and walked back toward her white columned mansion. Ada grabbed Embato's arm and pulled until he moved with her toward the Smith home. He knew this would draw attention so he still followed, but pulled his arm away and resumed his slumping posture. His mind was racing with the possibilities of this peculiar action by Mrs. Smith. He was relieved when they finally got to the well manicured grounds that immediately surrounded the mansion. He couldn't wait to get out of view of the other field slaves and Overseer Jennings.

Although out of their view, finally, Embato was still nervous about entering the mansion. He had never even been near it before. As they passed near the stone floor of the front of the dwelling Embato gazed at the tall white columns that appeared to be supporting the roof overhang. He was imagining the effort that went into their construction when his thoughts were interrupted.

"Embato please come in and follow me", said Mrs. Smith.

He passed through the rear entrance and stepped into the spacious kitchen and was in awe of its interior size and shiny hardwood floors. He gazed at the paintings and glass pieces that were neatly displayed throughout the living and dining rooms. Ada had to keep pulling at his sleeve to get him to keep pace with Mrs. Smith. They walked through the foyer and began climbing three flights of stairs to the fourth level. It appeared to be an attic and storage type area for the most part but he noticed an anteroom. As they passed it, Ada discreetly whispered to him.

"Dat room ova deah is fo da chiren's slave nanny."

Mrs. Smith then opened a wide door which led into a very dark room where a large piece of furniture was standing. She motioned for both of them to stay quiet. She then spoke loudly. "The house help needs you to assist in moving this downstairs Embato."

As she finished the sentence she motioned for Ada and Embato to enter the room. Once inside she shut the door and once again she spoke very loudly. "Now then, let's see...... how's the best way to carry this heavy oak china closet down to the first floor?"

She then quickly placed her left hand over Embato's lips and her right hand over Ada's lips indicating that they should not speak. She pulled the two very close and began to speak rapidly and barely above a whisper. Although Ada knew about the secret meeting between the three of them beforehand she had no idea what Mrs. Smith would say.

Mrs. Smith established direct eye contact with Embato and said, "Do not speak until I am finished with what I have to say. You absolutely must trust me and give me your word on your mother's life that you will never repeat any of this to anyone, ever!"

Turning to look at Ada and then back toward Embato she said very forcefully, "Do I have your word? You must both respond or I cannot speak any further of this. Just nod up and down if so!"

Embato quickly stole a glance in Ada's direction and she did the same in his. He was confused but followed Ada's lead and nodded. They then turned their full attention back to Mrs. Smith.

Mrs. Smith then loudly said, "Yes, you are right Ada. We will have Embato in the front where he will bare most of the weight of the piece."

Confident that she was creating a proper illusion for any within earshot, she then spoke once again in a whisper. "Embato, you are supposed to be sold to a plantation owner to work in his fields in a place called Alabama. He is sending a crew to escort you and three others back there from the Smith this Saturday."

Ada although shocked began to fight back tears and interrupted saying, "But Miz Lady......"

Before she could finish Mrs. Smith quickly placed her right hand once again over Ada's entire mouth and waved her left hand back and forth frantically indicating no talking. Embato understood part of her words but maintained his discipline and listened intently for more information.

He trusted Mrs. Smith after she stopped Overseer Jennings from whipping him several years earlier. She seemed sincere about what she was saying so Embato felt confident that she was being honest. He had little choice in the matter anyway.

Satisfied there would be no more interruptions from the two, Mrs. Smith continued. "Listen very, very, carefully.... both of you. I have just enough time to tell you only what you must know for now. I will communicate further instructions through Ada for you both in the next day or so. I am an active member of a secret abolitionist group, an anti-slavery organization which operates along the East coast of the United States. I have made arrangements for your escape to freedom in the Northern states Embato. I can only do this for one of my own slaves every one to two years. Otherwise some may grow suspicious. It has been only seven months since my last operation from the Smith so this one will be very risky for me and for the two of you. If you have any doubts about this escape, then tell me now, and we will never speak of this again."

She paused just for a split second and then continued, "Well, do you want to run for your freedom or not?"

Embato heard the word "freedom" which he understood completely. They both quickly nodded and Ada in her unbridled excitement whispered, "Yez! Yesum! Yez Mam!"

This time before Mrs. Smith could speak Embato grabbed Ada's arm tightly in his powerful left hand and placed his right hand across her mouth.

Mrs. Smith then once again said loudly, "Then Embato you will meet the others here Friday evening after field work is completed and move the chest down to the dining room. Explain to him in slave talk Ada."

She then quickly whispered the final instructions to them both. "You will go to the end of the main house path near Smith Road just after sundown on Thursday evening, the day after tomorrow. I have made arrangements for someone to transport you under cover to the docks in Charleston that evening. There you will be placed secretly on a lumber cargo ship that is bound for Philadelphia. You will be hidden as a stowaway. You will be given enough water to sustain you but there is no guarantee of food so you must take some dried fruit along with you. Once your ship reaches its destination there will be someone there to receive the cargo that you will be hidden in. They will take possession of the goods and transport you to a farm house. From there you will be transported over land to Boston, Massachusetts, where you will be safe and part of an African community many of whom will be runaway slaves such as yourself Embato."

Ada was very curious as to why Mrs. Smith mentioned only Embato's name but was unable to speak even if she had chosen to at that inopportune moment. Mrs. Smith quickly concluded. "Once you are there you are never to speak of where you escaped from. You may only speak of general conditions here and you will be expected to assist those in the abolitionist group when called upon. Do you understand everything that I have told you? Just nod yes."

Continuing after the affirming nod, she said, "Then a short prayer is necessary now. Dear God, our heavenly Father, please watch over Embato and Ada and all those placing themselves at risk in this righteous endeavor that we know you approve of. Thank you for all that we have. We remain your humble servants in the name of Your Son, Jesus Christ, our Lord and Savior. Amen. Now go back to your normal duties and say nothing to anyone about any of this. And especially be careful around Preacher Brown. He is an informant to Jennings and Zachary and a traitor to his own people. Only speak to each other about this when I have given you further instructions."

With that she reached to open the door and said loudly for any nosey listeners, "So get back to work. Your overseers will be looking for you and your midday water and food break is over."

Ada and Embato tried to appear calm as they walked down the steps and out the kitchen entrance. Ada explained as much as possible of

Mrs. Smith's plan to Embato. They parted and Embato headed to the hot tobacco fields and Ada headed toward the slave quarters to assist in preparation of the evening meal. She had been excused from any further duties to Mrs. Smith for the remainder of the day.

Embato found it difficult to lower his head and slump on the walk to the fields. In fact he felt as though his feet were not even in contact with the rich dark earth. The gist of Mrs. Smith's plan was just sinking into his conscious thinking. He realized for the first time that he could be a free man again soon! The Spirits and Borombi were working their miracles on his behalf. So he forced his shoulders to slump and lowered his head but the broad grin would not leave his face. He humbly thanked Borombi and the Spirits for their most divine intervention.........and laughed out loud at the end of his short prayer.

ESCAPE FROM THE SMITH

Embato tried to go about his life in a routine way so as not to stir any suspicion. But some of the field slaves were offended when he sat alone during break and at the evening meal. And another noticed he had trouble sleeping and asked why he was nervous. He laughed and shrugged it off as nothing. But he could not fool Miss Louisa. She figured it out after he didn't ask for seconds the night before his scheduled run. She had seen the behavior of runaways before.

All during the work day on Thursday Embato drank large amounts of water. He was trying to hydrate his body for the long journey ahead of him. And Ada had stolen almost two pounds of dried fruits for their run. As Embato and the others came in from the fields he made sure to be first in line for the evening meal. He wanted to assure himself of an extra large portion and he also wanted to consume it as early as possible so he could lie down before sundown for what little rest he would get before he slipped away in the darkness. As he approached the kettle, his eyes met Miss Louisa's. She looked as if she were about to burst into tears. But she forced a big smile and heaped an extra large portion of rabbit stew on his plate that was bigger than any he had ever gotten. He started to thank her but she stopped him abruptly.

"Now git on boy. Dez otha folk wants dey food to". She then looked into his eyes and whispered "May the Lawd Jesus watch over and protect you son. You be caful out deah. Now go.... an Embato.....live free fo da res a us!"

Suddenly it hit him that somehow Miss Louisa knew. He smiled back and whispered, "Embato love Miss Louisa".

He then turned and went to his favorite spot to eat the evening meal. It was under the swaying limbs of a weeping willow. Just as he was finishing the meal he noticed Ada walking toward him on the path from the Smith Mansion. He knew right away something was wrong because Ada was not smiling.. As she came closer he noticed a tear rolling down her left cheek. It just reached the corner of her mouth when another rolled down the right side of her nose. Embato looked quickly to see who might be watching the young couple before speaking.

"What Ada?"

She did not respond right away as she fought to regain her composure. After a few moments of silence she began to whisper in a sniffling low voice. "Daze only nough room fo one on da ship........ an Miz Lady Smith say you been chosen an......an...... I gots ta stay heah on da stinkin Smith!"

A gushing of tears followed her emotional words as Ada fought to regain her composure. Even as her heart was breaking she never made a sound. But she simply could not hold back the tears. Embato understood and respected her for being able to tell him without sobbing loudly and drawing attention.

"Embato, Ada happy fo you an pray fo yo freedom. Ada be mo happy if we bof be heah on da Smith fo eva, jes long as we be tagetha. Be'n apat from Embato..... dat jes kill Ada inside now."

He held her beautiful hand in his and said, "Embato love Ada. Embato go. Borombi's plan fo Embato."

She forced a smile and with all the courage left in her replied, "Yez, Embato, Ada know. God be wit Embato. Yo dried fruits in a sack hidden jes behin da trunk of dis heah willow. Don' foget it please. It will keep Embato alive til Embato be free. Ma heart's a breakin now but Ada know dat ifn I stays any longa someone goin see an Ada don't wont nobody ta fine out bout yo runnin. So Ada go now. Ada love you Embato."

She leaned over and kissed him on the lips and turned away and quietly walked up the path toward the Smith Mansion. He never took his eyes off her beautiful image until she finally disappeared into the early evening darkness. His heart was also hurting. There was a brief moment during her passionate plea and finally her selfless words that indecision had entered his thoughts. Until that moment he was unaware that he had begun to love the beautiful and warm hearted lil Ada. But as she walked away in tears he knew it was probably the last he would ever see of her.

After finishing the big helping that Miss Louisa gave him, Embato went to the slave quarters and laid down to rest. He was careful not to get too relaxed for fear of falling asleep and missing his escape contact. Although tired from his work, his mind was racing with excitement and fear about running. He waited patiently as the twilight slowly gave in to the near pitch black of night. Just minutes later an orange harvest moon rose on the horizon. He quietly got up and walked out of the old wooden shack and in the direction of the outhouse. He thought of Miss Louisa again as he passed the few glowing embers that remained of her cooking fire. He headed in the direction of the outhouse until well outside any possible onlooker's field of vision. He then doubled back behind the slave quarters and made his way to the weeping willow and retrieved the sack of dried fruit. He stuffed it securely inside his shirt and briskly walked toward the cotton field on the western side of the plantation. It was the opposite direction of the designated meeting spot.

As Embato moved toward the edge of the forest he began tearing several small pieces of his faded blue shirt and buried one in the middle of the field. He sprinted over to the woods edge and dropped another piece. He then followed a pathway about forty feet into the dense briary woods and stuck another piece on a thorn bush about chest high. He pricked his finger on a thorn and added a few drops of blood to the ragged piece of cloth hanging on the thorn bush. He then urinated on the ground in the same area leaving yet another scent to draw the blood hounds in the opposite direction of his actual escape route. Before he left that area he vigorously rubbed pine needles and crushed mulberry leaves on the bottom of his feet in order to reduce his natural scent.

His well thought out plan was executed with precision and would yield significant benefit for him the following morning. It would send the dogs and slave hunters hours out of their way. And it would insure him ample time to stowaway and for his ship to shove off. It would be in the Gulf Stream before his trackers' would even consider that he was running by sea and not over land.

Embato then turned East and ran the same path he had just walked but in the opposite direction. He ran toward his meeting point at Smith Road. He slowed his pace as he approached the slave quarters. He gathered two handfuls of pine straw and quickly scraped the bottom of the cooking kettle with each. They were soaked with the grease drippings from dinner. As he ran toward the Smith Road he dropped several small groups of pine needles to his right and to his left. If the hounds were to pick up his scent in the morning and follow his true path then they would be thrown off every few feet by the grease smell.

Conditions were ideal for an escape. There was just enough diffused moonlight peeping through the clouds to illuminate Embato's path. He whispered a prayer of thanks to Borombi and the spirits for their help. But as his eyes refocused on the path in front of him he suddenly realized he was not alone! Barely eight feet in front of him stood an African man almost his same size. Although startled initially, Embato maintained his composure and did not advance forward. He could not make out the man's facial features but his height and size seemed familiar. He waited for the man to speak first. As the first words rolled off the man's lips Embato recognized the voice immediately.

"Mighty dak outch heah for a walk ain't it........Brotha Embato"?

Embato paused before responding. His access to freedom was threatened. He assumed a physical confrontation was virtually inevitable and with no time to waste he decided to force the issue immediately.

He spoke in a low guttural tone akin to a growl. "Go from Embato... ya die".

Embato and the man allowed several tense seconds to pass in silence. Time was a precious commodity and Embato was growing impatient. But he did not want to force a confrontation unnecessarily that could draw unwanted attention.

"So you goin kill ole Sweet Brown is ya Embato?"

There was something in his tone and inflexion that was disarming enough for Embato to refrain from action for the moment. Another few seconds passed and Sweet Brown seemed to be enjoying Embato's anguish as his smile showed in the moonlight. Then he spoke again.

"I no goin try ta stop you son. You not goin make it to freedom anyway. De white mens is goin kill ya tomorra boy. But you still goin try. You see Embato, I don't want you heah. You wus goin make trouble for da Sweet Brown ministry on da Smith. And Ole Sweet don want no trouble heah. Ole Sweet jes want live a few mo years in peace then meet da good Lawd up yonda. I do wut I'm told ta do heah. Long as I please da white folk and dey leaves me alone I don't care nuthin bout you nor nobody else. So go head on boy!"

With that he stepped to Embato's left and out of his pathway. Embato had to make a decision at that very moment whether to believe Sweet Brown's words or not. He remembered what Ms. Lady Smith had told him in her warning not to trust him. He sought guidance from Borombi. And then he felt that Sweet Brown was telling the truth. He realized that Sweet Brown could have already disrupted his plan by simply shouting for help. He began to step past Sweet but just as Embato was passing Sweet's position the minister extended his hand to him. In his palm was a small wooden cross, the symbol of Christianity.

"Heah boy. Take this wit ya now. You'll needs it."

Rather than delay his progress any longer Embato said nothing. He took the cross and immediately disappeared into the darkness in the direction of Smith Road.

As Embato approached Smith Road near the mansion drive he slowed his pace in order to survey the area before walking out into full view. He didn't want anymore surprises. Convinced all was clear and safe he walked onto the road and looked back in the direction of the gravel drive. A big grin broke out across his whole face. Sure enough there was the horse drawn wagon with a white man sitting in the driver's seat just like Ms. Lady Smith had promised. He walked slowly along the edge of the dirt road until he was abreast of the horse.

The driver then said in a low quivering voice "No names here son. Just get in the back of the wagon.....and make haste. Get under the sack cloth and cover ye self with the straw. Don't make one sound no matter what happens. The trip into Charleston Harbor will take almost the whole night and ye'll be chilly back theah. But not like tomorrow night when ye ship coasts alongside the cold Atlantic waters in the Labrador Current. Then your arse will be cold for sure. Giddiii..yup deh!"

The nameless driver nudged the horse and they were off on the first leg of Embato's run for freedom. He stole one last look from beneath his covering as his body bounced with the bumps of Smith Road. The silhouette of the tall oaks that lined the pathway up to the Smith mansion soon disappeared from view. He was relieved to be on his way and thankful to those who made the moment even a possibility. But his final thoughts and prayers before dozing off were for the enslaved Africans he had grown to love and respect on the Smith........... those that he was leaving behind.

SETTING SAIL FOR FREEDOM

After a rough but thankfully uneventful ride through most of the night they reached the outskirts of Charleston where they pulled safely out of sight and rested. About an hour later and just before sunrise they continued and entered the city. The rhythmical sound of the horse's hooves striking cobblestone echoed off the water and seemed even louder to Embato as they entered the harbor area. He could smell the change in the air from the brackish water. It smelled like the portal to freedom. But then the wagon came to an abrupt stop.

Embato's mind began racing with possibilities. Were they finally at the ship's dock? Had the driver seen something suspicious and decided to wait before moving ahead? Was his dream of freedom near or was it to be stopped dead in its tracks? The anxiety was almost unbareable. He was so close, and just wanted the sanctuary of his hideaway aboard the ship as soon as possible. Within seconds he felt the cover being pulled off him and he cautiously began brushing the straw off his body.

The driver said "Now hurry and git out the wagon and follow me."

He stepped off the wagon and they both headed in the direction of a ship docked about fifty feet away. There were several hogsheads ready to be loaded just next to the ship. Each were numbered and marked as containing pine tar. The driver lifted the top off of barrel number fourteen.

Still in a low tone of voice the driver said "This heah one is empty. Get in here son. It'll be a tight fit but it's the only way out a heah. Once you're in ye won't be out for four or five days. Here's ye pouch of drinking water. Drink it sparingly in case ye arrival up north is delayed. Ye are to do nothing now but stay quiet. God speed young man."

Embato followed directions implicitly and was able to fit into the barrel with a bit of wiggle room. The driver reattached the top securely onto the hogshead and jiggled it to make sure. Before he turned back toward the wagon he said "Remember, not a sound from ye".

Embato heard the horse's hooves once again striking the cobblestone and then fade into the distance. As he sat in the cramped space of the barrel he silently thanked Borombi for safe passage thus far, and prayed for endurance during the voyage. His prayer was interrupted by voices nearby and also by a welcome sliver of light from the rising sun. It found its way through a tiny opening between the top cover and the body of the barrel itself.

Within minutes there were sounds of activity all around him. It was a comfort to him as it would mask any sound he made, and it signaled the beginning of the end of his enslavement. His became more anxious as each barrel rolled along the cobblestones and up the plank ramp to the ship's deck. He tried to stay calm as he felt his number 14 hogshead being turned on its side. His body rolled over and over as the barrel moved toward the ramp. He heard the heavy breathing and grunting of the dock workers pushing it up the steep ramp toward the ship's deck. He felt it suddenly swivel and tip in one direction. He knew that if it rolled off the ramp and into the harbor waters he would drown almost immediately. He was petrified in fear when he heard both workers grunting, yelling, and cursing one another. After a protracted struggle, however, the workers were finally able to get it righted and eventually secured on deck. Later both workers were bent over at the knees and wheezing with each breath. They could hardly speak.

"Gaaarrrrreat blue Jesus........ what the hayel is in heah? This un seemed alots heavier....... than the others".

The other worker, while struggling to catch his breath, responded. "Aw yer jes.....yer jes....... not use to hard work..... young'un. It's the same as the others......... they jes seem heavier when ye git to the las of em".

For a moment Embato worried that their curiosity might overcome their physical exhaustion and they would actually open it and look inside. But the conversation ceased as the two recovered from their exhausting work. Their rest was interrupted by the first mate when he demanded their return to the dock for more loading. His thunderous voice could have been heard a quarter mile down the dock.

"Git yer lazy no good arses back down heah and finish ye work or I'll beat ye black n blue me self!"

His words had put the fear of God into the two workers but they were reassuring to Embato. Finally he was on board a ship that was headed to the free side of the dividing line between states which allowed slavery in the South and those which prohibited slavery in the North. As he began to relax from the tension of the last several days he fell into a deep sleep. In his dreams he saw smiling faces from both black and white folks who were standing in a farm house with their arms extended and opened toward him. He smiled back.

THE VOYAGE

When Embato awoke from a ten hour sleep he was initially disoriented and confused. He was sore and cramping in his tight space. It was dark but Embato caught an occasional glimmer of moonlight through the opening in the top of the barrel which lifted his spirit a bit. After being awake for several minutes he tried to move, but the space was too con-fining to stretch anything but his hands, feet, and neck. His limbs and torso would have to somehow endure the pain. He lost the feeling in his feet and buttocks from the pressure of sitting in the same position for so long. He was in misery and beginning to chill even though the ship was still sailing in the warm waters of the Gulf Stream.

The vessel's direct heading toward its destination was interrupted as the first mate ordered a heading due east and away from the mainland. This would be their run for the night and part of the next day, as they sailed along the latitude near the South Carolina and North Carolina border. This strategy was followed in order to position the ship safely east of the shifting underwater sandbars along the Outer Banks of the North Carolina Coast. The area was well known, even to Embato, for its dynamic currents, treacherous shoals, and constant wind shifts. The frequent shipwrecks usually resulted in loss of cargo and vessel and often the loss of life as well. He heard some of the tragic stories back on the Smith and had already sent his prayer up regarding that aspect of his freedom journey.

After an agonizing night, a glimmer of sunlight awakened Embato, and he was thankful for one less day that he would have to spend in the hellish cramped barrel. For the first time he questioned his ability to withstand the pain for the duration of the trip, however. His joints burned as if on fire, and the muscle cramps were near unbearable. It was excruciating by midday and he was struggling to keep from moaning. He was in such misery, that at times, he wished to be back on the Smith working in the hot sun of the cotton and tobacco fields.

It had been more than a full day since Embato had water or food. He knew that he had to drink soon or risk greater dehydration and suffer worse cramping. It was a dilemma however because drinking meant that he would also have to urinate. He knew that the urine would eventually irritate his skin and also create a foul smell that could possibly raise suspicion amongst the crew. However by mid afternoon he had made the decision to drink.

For several minutes he struggled just to get the water bag opening to his mouth. He was so dehydrated, that when the first drops fell onto his parched lips and tongue, it was as if it instantly evaporated. He slowly began to take sips and then mouthfuls. The precious liquid provided immediate relief as it followed a welcome pathway down his throat. A few minutes later the life sustaining fluid flooded his bloodstream and eased his cramping muscles. It was both soothing and invigorating at the same time. For a few hours his will to survive the ordeal was renewed. But sure enough his bladder became full and was aching to empty.

In his disciplined way Embato fought the urge to urinate for another two hours. It was an agonizing struggle to hold his water until nightfall. He decided to leave the barrel so he could urinate and stretch his aching body. But it could only be done under the cover of darkness. He was well aware of the risk, but maintaining his cramped position for the remainder of the trip was out of the question.

Embato attempted to regain feeling by squirming around inside the barrel for a brief period just after dark. Sensing some restoration of flexibility, he was confident of moving about quickely while exposed on deck. So he slowly began opening the barrel top. But he stopped and sat motionless when he heard footsteps nearby. The pain was excruciating and he began to think that he might pass out. Then he heard footsteps again and they were getting louder and closer. Someone was standing next to his number fourteen barrel! He was terrified and stopped breathing for fear they may hear him.

All of a sudden the top of the barrel moved! He was panicking. Would they throw him overboard to a certain death? Or would they beat, whip, and torture him and send him back to slavery? He prepared for the worst as the top of the barrel was slowly removed. He saw the fingers of a white man gripping the barrel's edge as the fresh evening air rushed in. For a moment there was silence. His mind was gripped in terror at having been discovered. The he felt a warm stream trickle down his legs, soaking his lower body. The white man spoke but Embato was already in deep prayer to Borombi.

A HELPING HAND

"Eeeeembatoooo. Are ye still alive in thar?"

For a moment Embato considered the possibility that he might be hallucinating. Yet he was quite sure that he had heard his own name spoken by someone. Still fearful and suspicious he cautiously looked upward. A young white man's bearded face rose just above the barrel top and peered into his cramped quarters. Embato and the stranger both struggled to focus in the darkness even though their eyes were only inches away from each other. Suddenly the face disappeared below the barrel's edge and simultaneously a hand appeared in its place with a piece of hard flat bread in its grasp.

"Here. Eat this. Ye will need yer strength. The wind shifted out of the southeast and thar's a gale comin. Ye goin have to come out the barrel if'n it's a full blow. Well...answer me. Ye're alive. I seen ye eyes movin."

Embato was shocked by the unexpected contact but after a few moments mustered the courage to speak. "Embato Ngawai here massa."

The young white man was a bit perplexed as to Embato's reference to the word "massa". But time was of the essence and he would question him later about it. "Eeeeembato. Git yer arse out the barrel now. We got to exchange positions with barrel number four so we can git ye lashed to the railin. Otherwise ye arse'll get washed o'erboard when the seas start up. Come on now...stand up. Me cap'n and firstmate will be lookin fer me soon. We must make haste."

Embato had difficulty standing at first. He was so weak he could barely move and his bladder was still not empty. But with the help of the young white man he was able to finally stand and together they maneuvered a few yards forward and abreast of the stern railing. "Now hold on here big feller. Don't lose ye balance and fall over. Yer deader than hector if'n ye do, cause I can't save ye arse. I'm goin bring yer number fourteen back here. I'll need ye help with number four though cause she's full of ballast river stone and heavier than hell!"

The young man rolled number fourteen back to where Embato was standing and righted it. He was confident the sound of the barrel's rumble across the deck would be absorbed into that of the wind and rough seas banging against the hull. Embato finished relieving himself about the same time the young man lashed the empty fourteen against the rail. He was finally getting feeling back in his joints and muscles and was stretching when his new friend interrupted

"Less us hurry now and move them stones out'a number four and inta fourteen so ye'll have 'nough space inside to fit. They said you was a bigg'un. And they was telling the God's truth. I can see 'twith me own eyes."

The two men rapidly transferred the river stones from four to fourteen. In just the short time it took to complete the transfer the winds had picked up considerably. It was apparent in the young man's voice that he was growing concerned. "Lets git to movin and quickly, before I'm missed below."

He could see that Embato didn't understand most of what he was saying so he motioned for Embato to help him turn the barrel over on its side. They both got behind the barrel and began pushing it forward. The sound of the empty rolling barrel concerned Embato, but his young friend was in a hurry so he did not interfere.

"Eeeembato, hurry and git back thar in number four. Ye only have another two days or so and then ye'll be in the North where ye can be free as a bird agin......jes like before they stole ye from Afreeka. I'll try to come up tomorrow evenin and let ye out agin so ye can piss and stretch ye limbs."

They both walked back to the stern and stood next to four. "OK, in ye go friend."

Embato looked the stranger in the eye and said "Thank suh. You goot. Yo name?"

Git in ye barrel now! Eeembato! They be lookin fer me soon. Thar's no names mentioned here. Too risky. Night."

Embato quickly situated himself with both feet and legs inside the barrel. He was beginning to crouch down when suddenly he heard a loud boom. At the same time he felt the ship lurch sideways with great force. The coaster had sustained a major impact from the port side and rolled starboard and emitted an eerie creaking sound. It was followed by a hard tremor that travelled from stern to bow.

The ship had been struck broadside by a huge rogue wave, a once in a blue moon phenomenon, that came without warning. When the impact of the powerful wave was absorbed it hurled the young white man, the number four barrel, and Embato across the deck. A couple of the barrels broke loose and washed overboard including fourteen. Just as both men reached the rail of the starboard side the ship began to right herself. The young white man however was dangling precariously off the side but thankfully hanging onto the rail for dear life. Another wave's impact would surely dislodge his grip and send him to a certain death. He screamed for Embato.

"Hep me, hep me….please hep me……..Eeeembato!"

Embato heard the plea through the flapping of the sails and the ship's timbers creaking as she righted. He heard the desperation and terror in the frantic plea for help and knew he had to save the man that had tried to help him just minutes before. He was aware of the risk to himself but was morally bound to make every effort to save his new friend.

Although vision was very poor in the darkness, Embato was able to make out the silhouette of the young man's head and arm just above the rail. He dragged himself, barrel and all, to the young man's position. Stretching up from the deck, he grasped the young man's left arm in his hand and held it tightly. Just as the young man lost his grip on the rail, Embato kicked his legs free of the barrel and stood upright. With both arms and legs free, he lifted the young man up over the rail and safely back onto the deck. Even though in shock, the young man was in awe of the physical strength of his rescuer. While shaking uncontrollably he was able to eek out a few words.

"Ttthhaaannk ye Jesus,........ th, th, thank ye Eeembato."

Embato quickly took charge of the situation. He knew the officers below would be up on deck any second to see what had happened and to inspect the vessel for damage. As he spoke he also motioned for his young friend to come with him. "You come."

Embato put his arm around the man and helped him toward the steps to the lower deck. His plan was to leave the man there where he would be found and taken care of. He sat him up against a barrel and turned to walk back to number four. But he stopped abruptly when he saw a flicker of light only a few feet in front of him. The light moved up a bit and forward toward him. His heart sank as he realized that he was looking at the flame of a lantern not three feet away from his body. As the light moved steadily upward he was able to make out the features of a middle aged rotund white man. For an instant Embato thought of ducking down and crawling along the deck to his safe secure barrel.

Just as he started to crouch however a booming voice yelled "What in hell's tarnation have we here! A stowaway slave is it?" Quickly noting the African's size and obvious strength he continued. "Don't ye move narey a muscle thar.....I got me pistol behind me back and'm ready to fill yer belly with hot led."

The man then moved the lantern closer and then down toward the deck. "And a *white man* traitor a hepin em! An one a me own seamen. Now ain't that a helluva note!"

Moving the lantern back up toward Embato's head he continued. "No doubt ye a runaway ain't ye boy? Whered ye run from boy? The Bell, the Smith...or the Cornwell? Don't matter none. Ye'll be back thar in a week and ye'll be sorry ye ever gave a thought to runnin. After they beat ye slam near to death ye'll be broke from runnin. And I'll be fifty gold dollars richer fer turning ye black arse in. All's well that ends well."

He then let out an irritating guffaw of laughter which caused his large belly to bounce up and down. At that moment several other seamen emerged from behind the man. Any thoughts that Embato had of overpowering the man and throwing him overboard then vanished. The devout African prayed silently to Borombi for both self protection and for the young white man who tried to help him. But he feared for both their lives.

The rotund white man suddenly realized that Embato may have seen that he was not really carrying a weapon. Aware of the threat posed by such a large man to himself and crew, he immediately ordered Embato's hands lashed together and gave the command in an authoritative tone. "Seamans O'Brian and McClain. Lash the stowaway slave's hands together. Now!"

O'Brian said in a shaky voice "Yessir....uh... Cap'n."

Growing impatient and more fearful the Captain thundered, "Before the sun rises in the East damn it! Get movin ye dumb bastards! He's a runaway and even ye dumb arses can see he's a dangerous one!"

Embato thought it best for his young white friend if he fully cooperated with the crew. He didn't wish to make matters any worse. So he lowered his head and stood motionless in complete submission to whatever the rotund man had communicated to his crew.

The captain then turned his wrath toward the young white man. He leaned forward and put the lantern only an inch or two from the young man's face where it stayed for a minute or more. The young man could actually feel the warmth of the flame on the bridge of his nose. But he sat motionless and offered no explanation or regret. Like Embato, he also was praying silently for his and Embato's lives to be spared.

Finally the captain said "What say ye First Mate Hanson.... bout yer boy heah? Did I not tell ye he was no good from the start. I seen it in his eyes. Knew'e couldn't be trusted. He's a damnable wharf rat born out'n the belly of a whore. He's mama no doubt gave up her nasty arse to any seaman with a coin in his britches pocket. And here lies the worthless results...... such as 'tis." The enraged captain paused to catch his breath but continued the tirade. "The best part of ye rolled down ye daddy's pant leg youngin. There surely was a lot a good hard screwin wasted when they got ye boy. And now ye've decided yer an abolitionist are ye? Well, since ye love em so much we'll let ye suffer yer fate with em as well."

"First mate Hanson. Lash em both strong and hard below to the keel of me ship. If'n me ship goes down in the storm let 'em go with her to the bottom'a the cold dark Atlantic. The rest of us will have a chance to survive a wreck but to hell with these two heathens. We sha'nt be bothered with the likes of em if'n we ever do run aground."

He turned back toward the young white man once again and said mockingly, "May haps yer Almighty Jesus will untie ye and throw ye both safe upon dry land."

Once again the captain bellowed out an obnoxious laugh that ended in a choking and coughing spell. After catching his breath he barked out a few more orders to the crew and headed down the steps to his bunk grumbling and cursing til he disappeared below.

First mate Hanson executed the orders and added a few of his own mainly aimed at restoring the security of all the loose items on deck. Then he turned his attention to Embato and the young white man.

"Not a word from ye now. Jes go on down them steps yonder and follow Seaman O'Brian thar til ye git to the keel. Ye'll be lashed thar til we reach port or well........whatever the Lord has in store for us all. We'll see now won't we fellers?"

O'Brian and McClain started leading the two toward the steps to the hole. O'Brian then turned to McClain and whispered, "Me thinks me Cap'n evoked the wrath of God upon us with his sacrilege. One should never mock the power of God or another man's belief in The Almighty. It jes ain't right. Only the Lord Himself knows what our fate is now."

Hanson turned to go below. He noticed that Embato had hesitated at the top step momentarily and was looking up toward the sky. Hanson looked in the same direction and noticed a very bright star peeping through a break in the cloud cover. It seemed that the tall African was singularly focused upon it.

Hanson said "What ye lookin fer boy? That ain't nothing but the North Star. Take a good look at her cuz ye may ner see er again."

Hanson then grabbed the still shaken young seaman and pulled him up off the deck and led him toward the steps which led to the ship's hold. As they approached the steps the young seaman released an audible sigh. This surprised Hanson and he turned toward his new maritime prisoner with intention to hurl another insult but stopped short when he noticed that the seaman was also gazing upward toward the sky. After standing for a moment the frightened young man had gotten his bearings and had instantly realized the significance of the relative position of the North Star to the ship.

Still shaken from the whole ordeal but with growing confidence he slowly turned in Hanson's direction and said, "Sir, according to Capn's command and ye own orders we were headin East-Northeast. During our evening sale the North Star was to our Port bow. But it ain't no more.... sir. Look yonder..... sir. See fer ye self. It's to our Starboard stern. Our rudder was messed about during the hit of the big wave. I seen it from the railing with me own eyes. As God be me witness she's adrift........She's caught up in the warm water stream and headin north northwest.........." The young seaman paused but never took his eyes off Hanson.

In unison Hanson and the others turned toward the Starboard stern and gazed upward into the night sky. For several seconds there was an eerie silence as the unwelcome reality of the situation began to sink in. When Hanson finally turned back toward his captive he was surprised to see what he thought to be a slight grin on the young man's face. And when their eyes did meet the seaman noted the obvious look of concern in Hanson's face. The arrogant smile that was in place just moments before had vanished. The corners of Hanson's mouth, although partially obscured by gray stubble, had clearly settled in a downward direction. His chest was no longer pushed up and out and his shoulders had slumped slightly forward. Without uttering a sound, Hanson had confirmed the young man's astute assessment of the ship's dilemma and thus the most probable outcome.

Embato then voluntarily began moving toward the steps to go below. He and his fellow captive both knew they would be lashed securely to the keel. They were the ship prisoners and would be confined to the bottom most section of the interior part of the vessel for the remainder of the voyage on a stormy sea. But somehow their captivity did not seem as bad to Embato's new friend as it had only minutes before. The irreparable damage to the ship's rudder caused by the huge wave had become the divine equalizer. From that moment forward there was a good possibility that no place on the ship would soon be much safer than any other.

But the young seaman was just coming to grips with the reality that Embato's escape to freedom had been unjustly altered by evil men. He stopped at the steps and stared intently into Hanson'e eyes. Hanson saw this as a challenge to his authority. He could have left his crew to carry out the order to secure the stowaway and his helper in accordance with maritime law. But his ego got in the way and he chose to glare back at the young man. He began cursing him and unwisely hurled insults of the most personal nature. And the damage was done before anyone else understood its severity and the reaction to follow.

The frustration the young man had encountered during his life had at that very moment reached a tipping point. When he looked into Hanson's face he saw everyone who had mistreated him or anyone else he had ever cared for. The evil in his world was gazing back at him with no remorse through the pale blue eyes of first mate Hanson. In the first mate he saw the personification of the devil himself.

With his fists still bound in front of him he suddenly swung them both upward and landed an uppercut under the chin of Hanson with all the force his body could create. Hanson's head and neck snapped back in one single motion as his body fell limp onto the deck. He had been knocked out cold. The other crewman were stunned at first but stepped back as Embato stepped between them and his new friend. He intended no harm to anyone but simply wished to prevent further violence.

The entire group remained motionless and watched for any movement from Hanson's body. In the darkness it was very difficult to determine if he was even breathing. Embato slowly began to step backward and down the steps toward the hold leaving his new friend no choice but to retreat as well. He turned to one of the crew and motioned for him to follow them below just as Hanson let out with a low groan. Hanson's voice fortunately broke some of the tension. At least he was not dead. Embato stopped moving but he still had to block the angry young seaman from coming back up the steps. His dark eyes met those of one of the crew.

Embato in a calm low tone said, "You suh. You come suh. No fight. Please suh. Embato no fight. Him bad spirit. Embato no fight. Goot fo heem, fo you suh, fo Embato. Please suh…massa wan fight. Embato no mo fight."

As Hanson began to regain consciousness the crewman did as Embato suggested and began to follow them below. Embato moved backward down the steps forcing his partner to do the same. But in a last gesture of defiance the diminutive young sailor had the last word. There would be no response for that last word either. His words would all but eradicate the need or desire for any further action except perhaps that of prayer. And his voice was filled with anger but also with a resolute sadness at the same time. He just simply took satisfaction in being the one who forced each one of his captors to face their unavoidable life threatening consequence. Just as Hanson became fully conscious once again, the young sailor provided the horrible truth that no one wished to be confronted with.

"She's a headin for the shoals!"

PART III

THE NATIVE AMERICANS EAST

ELIZA

ELIZA'S AWAKENING

"A long time ago the Creator came to Turtle Island
and said to the Red people, you will be the keepers of
the Mother Earth. Among you I will give the wisdom
about Nature, about the interconnectedness of all
things, about balance and about living in harmony.
You Red people will see the secrets of Nature. You
will live in hardship and the blessing of this is you
will stay close to the Creator. The day will come
when you will need to share the secrets with other
people of the earth because they will stray from their
Spiritual ways. The time to start sharing is today."
Don Coyhis, Mohican

Creator had provided adequate warning signs earlier on the trail when
He spoke clearly through the hawk's unusual posture and the peculiar
call of the crows. But the Native elder had neither eyes nor ears for their
true message that day and chose to continue his journey into town.
Emotion had clouded the elder's judgment resulting in a departure
from his characteristically cautious behavior. It had been driven askew
by the disappointment he saw in his beloved granddaughter's teary eyes

earlier that same morning. It was her response to his denial of her first request to make the near half day's journey with him and his nephew, James. Sometimes he found it almost impossible to say no to her. She could be quite persistent. And on that particular morning little Eliza had finally caught her grandfather in a moment of weakness. But the tall wirey elder deeply regretted having made the decision to bring his ten year old granddaughter into town. He realized that in doing so he had placed all three of their lives in jeopardy.

Eliza, in her innocence, just wanted to satisfy the burning curiosity she had about the town. She had never visited it in spite of the fact that she had lived her entire life a mere fourteen miles from it. At first she had become completely consumed by the variety of items in the store. But even *she* began to sense her vulnerability when the large white man, who had been staring in her direction for several minutes, approached her. She stood motionless at first as he bent over and positioned his plump cheeks within inches of her quivering lips. She first focused on the grotesque dark rot in two of his three remaining front teeth when his lips parted. And she could smell the stench of his horrid warm breath even before he spoke. Repelled by the sight and odor, she lifted her small right hand to cover her nose and simultaneously turned her head to the side. But undeterred, the man began the downward motion with his right hand in an attempt to stroke her long dark hair.

The keen interest she had expressed just seconds before in the red and yellow candies and shiny trinkets in the glass case had been erased by the intrusion. She suddenly wished to be back in the security of the piney woods near her home at Swan Lake. She felt safe there amongst her family, fellow villagers, and her winged and four legged friends.

As his grimy soiled index and middle fingers touched ever so lightly on the top of her head he let out a long sigh as he spoke. "You shore are a perty lil thang ain't ye darlin. How'd ye like to come home to the farm with Mr. Jennette and the Missy? They could give ye........"

Suddenly the man's words ceased. He was reacting to the sudden shock of a sharp pain in his right wrist and the loss of movement in his fingers. When he lifted himself up and away from little Eliza he felt an even more intense pain on the back of his neck. Before he could turn or even speak he heard a deep male voice that seemed to fit with the source of the paralyzing pain he was experiencing. But strangely enough the sound didn't come from beside or behind him. It came from across the room.

"That's enough James. Ease up slowly nephew."

There was a slight pause and then the voice continued. "Now sir if you would be kind enough to please back away from my granddaughter, my nephew is going to release your wrist and neck and there's no harm done here. Eliza, come over here with me now."

It was a voice that suggested a sense of balance in experience and reason. It represented the wisdom passed down through countless generations in a tradition of adaptation that had ensured survival in a hostile environment.......even against insurmountable odds. It conveyed pride in James' adept defensive actions on behalf of his defenseless little cousin. But it also recognized the benefit of restraint after an appropriate and measured response to an obvious threat. Tsalgena knew just how far he could push some members of what had become the dominant segment of the population surrounding the area in which he lived and where some of his ancestors had lived for hundreds...maybe thousands of years. And most of the time he was accurate in his assessment of such volatile circumstances. But the situation that morning in Alligood's Dry Goods store was not one of them. In that instance it would quickly take an unanticipated turn toward violence.

The elder leader of his small community had learned over his seventy winters to avoid confrontation with most white people if at all possible, and especially those of great wealth. In the past either he or someone he cared for had suffered some loss whenever conflict went too far with them. But when it came to Eliza's well being, everything else was secondary. He would always pick *that* battle above all others. And on that day he did what any other loving grandfather would have done. And almost all of the white folks in the store that morning empathized with his actions. The one exception, other than the offender, happened to be a local wealthy land owner who employed the filthy intruder as the slave overseer on his plantation.

It was at the planter's own direction that his overseer had approached Eliza. He secretly saw the young girl as a potential slave to be seized. But he would later use deceptive language when speaking in his defense. The planter would avoid using the term "slave". Instead he would use the word "apprentice". He would even vehemently argue later that "twas not only in the best interest of the little mulatto injun gal but twas my right to lay claim to her".

Most of those present knew his reputation. They were aware that he had already taken two young free Black males into "apprenticeship" from their parents through bribes and manipulation of the local courts. And he was confident that he could repeat the same process over and get the same results with Eliza if necessary. But not wishing to spend the money and time on the crooked judge again, he arrogantly assumed that he could simply take his newly discovered prize right on the spot that morning. He was also confident that her elderly grandfather was incapable of protecting her against his overseer. And he was confident that he could depend upon the sheriff across the road from the store to support him if it came to that. But he had failed to account for James. And in his arrogance he had also underestimated the tenacity and resolve with which Tsalgena would act on behalf of his beloved granddaughter.

Tsalgena grew more concerned when James still had not released his powerful grip on the offender. The young Native heard his uncle's words but he was furious. He was concerned the man, once released, would draw his pistol or knife and harm Eliza or his uncle. The tension increased with every passing second, and soon all the shoppers fled the store. Once again Tsalgena repeated his original direction to James but his nephew refused to comply. James responded by telling Tsalgena to take Eliza and leave and *then* he would relinquish his seizure of the man. The young man then motioned for Eliza, who had been too frightened to move at all, to join her grandfather. She immediately ran into his open arms. Tsalgena then backed up toward the front door with Eliza while still watching the planter in his peripheral vision. He opened the front door and with Eliza behind him moved halfway through it but stopped as he straddled the doorway.

In a demanding tone he said "Eliza is safe now James. Let him go…or there will be more trouble than we need…….. Nephew! Now!"

Finally James began to loosen his grip as he took a half step toward the door. He let go of the man's wrist and neck and turned to move closer to the door but still watched him over his left shoulder. After shaking his right hand to restore the blood flow, the large white man reached beneath his tattered green jacket and pulled it back revealing a large black pistol. He began moving his hand toward it, but James moved rapidly back toward him with his long knife already in hand and held at eye level. By the time the man drew the gun James had his left arm wrapped tightly around the man's neck resulting in a firm choke hold. His other hand held the razor sharp edge of his prized bone handled knife just above the man's right ear. Once again the large man was helpless.

With no one else to interfere the planter then pulled out his gun and took aim toward James and the overseer. James quickly spun around with his captive so as to position the man between himself and the planter. The overseer however in a surprise move suddenly dropped to one knee causing a portion of James upper body to lunge forward and be dangerously exposed to the planter's weapon. Tsalgena heard the trigger of the planter's gun cock. He immediately pushed Eliza into the arms of an attractive young white woman standing on the outside steps who had witnessed the entire event from its start. He then lunged to move forward into the store but was bumped to the side by a large powerful white man. The courageous elder fell headfirst against the rough weathered edge of the door facing. He felt the flesh over his left eye split open just as he heard the loud pop of the planter's gun discharging. He saw the flash on the wall and as he lifted himself up he began to detect the unmistakable sulphuric odor of ignited gunpowder.

He regained his balance and in one fluid motion lunged through the doorway, drawing his hunting knife in his right hand and a four inch stone point in his left. He then raised his left arm up and across his chest with the point, and lowered the knife to his side coiling it back to strike. He saw the planter standing with the gun at his side while the thin wisps of gray smoke still swirled upward from its barrel. The evil man's chest and throat were exposed. Before Tsalgena moved he could already see in his mind's eye his knife thrusting through the man's gut and then pushing vertically up into his lungs and heart. The stone point at the same time would come forward in a backhand movement across his chest slicing the man's throat and carotid artery. But just as his body weight shifted to initiate the skilled fighting maneuver, the large white man that had bumped him out of the way stepped in front of him. Tsalgena stopped dead in his tracks. The large man had already seized the planter's gun, and then holding his own weapon up, took immediate charge of the situation.

"Now both ya'll drop ye damn knives right now! Ye hear me! Now!"

Tsalgena immediately dropped his knife on the floor and placed the point back in his pouch. He turned and expected to see both James and the overseer on the floor in a pool of blood. But surprisingly neither was injured and they were in the same position as he had last seen them before the gun fired. He then saw a hole on the back wall of the store only inches from his nephew's head. Realizing that no one was injured he then repeated the large white man's order to his nephew.

"Drop your knife on the floor nephew. Do as Deputy Spencer said and release the man."

Finally James obeyed his uncle and dropped the knife and then released the man. He then looked to Tsalgena as if awaiting further instructions. It was then that he noticed the blood rolling down his uncle's face from just over his eye. He started to move toward him but Tsalgena held his hand up motioning him to stay where he was. Tsalgena appreciated his concern but needed a moment to further assess the situation. He was just piecing everything together himself. He then realized that it must have been Tim Spencer that knocked him into the door jam. He looked toward the deputy and was asking what had happened when the planter interrupted.

"Deputy! What in hell far's goin on heah? Ye don't owe that old injun any explanation. They started all this. These heah savages was attackin my ovaseah just as ye can see. I had the right to blow em both to kingdom-come and had ye not mettled in my affayaahs I woulda sent em both to hell wheah they belong."

When the deputy politely tried to speak the planter screamed, "Wheahs yo boss at? I'll have ye job by sundown. Ye shouldn't even listen to nuthin they got to say. This whole damn thang heah is an outrage. Ye wait til I see the sheriff and have my say with judge Harper."

Spencer responded in a confident tone saying "Mr. Jennette. Please suh jus take yo man, and I believe it'd be best for all, if ya go *yo* way suh and let these folks go *theah* way. Lets all cool off a little and if theres any more action to be taken suh, then the Sheriff will pay you a visit in the moanin. We'll git all this heah stuff straightened out latah. Allright suh? Uh jus one mo thang suh. I'll be holdin yo guns suh for now and I'll see to it that ya get em back in the moanin. Now thank ye suh."

Tsalgena was as shocked as the planter and the overseer were. Fair treatment in such circumstances had never surfaced as even a remote possibility in his mind. He expected that he and James would have been thrown in jail at least for the night. He was deeply appreciative to Deputy Spencer for his fairness but still surprised at the result of his intervention. For the first time since the whole unfortunate incident began, the wise old elder gave silent thanks to the Creator. He asked forgiveness for not listening earlier that morning to the obvious signs of warning. And he would later explain that very important aspect of the experience to James and Eliza for their own spiritual growth and future well being.

The planter continued his vehement protest and loud cursing as he headed for the door. But without the use of weapons he was powerless to change anything. So with his overseer at his side and his damaged ego in tow he stormed out of the store and down the road. However, the deputy and Tsalgena both knew they had not seen nor heard the last of him on the matter. Both men understood the urgency for Tsalgena and his family to get back to their Swan Lake area village as soon as possible. Tsalgena and any others observing Deputy Spencer's actions that day understood that there would very likely be consequences for his good deed. Spencer had only been fair but under the circumstances it was clearly an act of courage and morality on his part. The arrogant powerful planter had the resources necessary to exact retribution on the deputy, Tsalgena, and his family if within reach. But once Tsalgena, James, and Eliza were back safely in their swampy remote home area, it would be a much greater challenge and probably not worth the effort for the powerful landowner. And Deputy Spencer knew that. Nevertheless the simple act of having upheld the law and protecting the innocent without prejudice had exposed him to great personal risk.

Tsalgena gazed into Deputy Spencer's youthful blue eyes and he saw innocence and naivety. He felt a sense of responsibility to the man and his family. And he wished to express his gratitude. "We are all very grateful to you. And although you did the right thing I don't understand why. And I am now concerned for your safety deputy."

The deputy smiled and said "Miz Taylor come and got me and tole me what wus goin on ova heah. She told me the whole story. Tsalgena you shoulda come and got me and I would'a handled everything. But you and yourn need to be gittin on back up in them woods and the swamp before that rotten bastard and his low down ovaseah gets up a posse and comes a lookin fer ya. Tsalgena, I've always known ya to be a good man. And ya ain't ner lookin fer no trouble. But ye'r a injun and lotta folks opinion is ye still ain't got the same rights as the rest of us. Ya understand don't ye Tsalgena? Now ya'll need to git the hell on outta heah like I said. I can't protect ya'll all night heah."

Tsalgena motioned to James and they both quickly left the store. Once outside he found little Eliza still shaken but nestled safely in the arms of the young white woman. He thanked the nice woman and apologized to her and all those nearby for the frightening disturbance. He also looked in Mrs. Taylor's direction and nodded in respect. He knew it best for all however that he didn't thank her publicly for her intervention on his behalf with Deputy Spencer. He understood the risk to a well intentioned white person who would be seen as being too kind to Africans or Natives in that place at that time. But her risk was very small when compared to that of a stubborn old Native elder who had chosen to live publicly in the traditions of his ancestors along the path of the Good Red Road. And nothing would deter him from passing that knowledge and way of life on to his precious little Eliza.

THE NEW WORLD?

The so called "new world" was not new at all to those who were already living in it. It was their land......the homeland of North America's indigenous people........ those who would be called American Indians or Native Americans. The indigenous people who greeted the English speaking Europeans upon their arrival in the sixteenth century were the descendents of the continent's original inhabitants. Some of the members of those Native American tribes that inhabited the Coast and Coastal Plain areas of eastern North Carolina were also the ancestors of Eliza Harva Hudson.

The land that Eliza and her *native* ancestors lived on was revered as spiritually sacred. In fact the land was not even viewed as an "it". The land was part of a larger relationship that existed between the people and the One who had made it available to them, their Creator. It was seen spiritually as the Mother........ Mother Earth. She (Mother Earth), along with Father Sky and Sun, provided the peoples' physical resources that sustained them during life. When their physical lives ended, their bodies were returned to Her and absorbed into Her soil. Thus they became a tangible part of Her once again. This cycle was repeated over scores of generations and often in the same general location. Therefore virtually all Native lands could have been viewed as sacred. And Eliza's view was consistent with that. Her people had been there for a very long time.

Some believe that Eliza's North American pre-decedents were on the continent for fifty thousand years before the first sighting of the European intruders from across the Atlantic. Thus from the Native perspective the absurd claims of discovery and possession by Europeans was confusing and perhaps even quite comical.......at least initially. It would, however, prove to be the basis for centuries of violent conflict between the two groups. European greed, religious arrogance, and blatant racism became the fuel for what would become the Red Holocaust on North American soil. For some Native American nations the European concept of the new world and the conflict surrounding it would tragically result in genocide and their complete extinction. For other Natives it would stop just short of extinction, but still bring about the loss of most of their homelands, language, culture and religion. But ironically for many Europeans the "new world" would be a lure of potential wealth, freedom and hope.

THE EUROPEAN INVASION

The North American continent represented opportunity for virtually every class within the societal hierarchy of England. But for England's royalty, its wealthy, and its religious leadership, the continent held the potential for perpetuating wealth and power. It was the means for sustaining their lavish lifestyles and their dominance over the masses. So it was truly ironic that Europe's poor and religiously oppressed saw North America as a possible *haven* that would rid them of the ills of that very same system. Although they were excluded from the first few groups of settlers, they would soon follow in mass once the Gentry had established their claims and system of rule in the new English colonies.

The first attempt at colonization by the English was done so using those at the upper tier of the middle class. Those selected were well established craftsmen or small business owners who saw opportunity to advance their wealth and class. However, the risk for the original 116 brave souls that formed the first English speaking colony on Roanoke Island in 1585 turned out to be very real. When their leader, John White, returned from London with supplies the colonists had disappeared. And their story became known as The Lost Colony and remains the oldest unsolved mystery in American history. One of the most popular theories to the mystery suggests that the surviving colonists intermarried and were absorbed into local Native tribes, some of whom could have been Eliza's ancestors.

About twenty years later a permanent English colony, Jamestown, was established and named after King James who succeeded Elizabeth on the throne. Soon after its establishment, many members of Europe's poor and oppressed immigrated to North America. They were by design, however, largely excluded from any significant benefit by the three power groups of England. Many were indentured servants and others simply were viewed as an expendable human resource. In fact most were initially abused much as they had been in Europe. They were treated no better than Eliza's Native American ancestors or the African slaves that would be taken against their will from their homelands and forced into centuries of slavery in America. All three of these groups would be manipulated and abused in order to accomplish the goals of the wealthy and powerful in *their* new world.

The ultimate goal of England and its colonial leadership was to subdue, and if necessary, eradicate Eliza's ancestors and their indigenous brethren so as to claim their lands and resources. "Saving" native souls through forced religious conversion and "civilizing them to proper European ways" was simply a cover as a means to an end. Thus England's elite would, in their greed and blind arrogance, completely ignore the inherent human rights of those whose preceding generations had occupied the so called *new world* for literally thousands of years. Eliza's Eastern Native American ancestors were simply viewed as obstacles that would slow European progress and occupation of America. And slow it they did!

ELIZA'S ANCESTRY

Eliza's Native ancestry was mixed with several different blood lines, as was the case with most surviving Natives who chose to stay in the immediate vicinity of where the first contact between English speaking Europeans and Natives took place. It included a mosaic of both Algonquin and Iroquoian speaking peoples. This Native mix would have included remnants of Hatterask, Secotan, and also those more aligned with the Skaru:re (Tuscarora), the Machapungo (Mattamuskeet). But her own personal identity was first and foremost as a descendent of both the Skaru:re, the Tuscarora and the Algonquin coastal peoples, particularly the Hatterask.

Perhaps it was the Tuscarora's reputation for such courageous and sustained resistance to the European invasion that motivated her and many others to so proudly lay claim to that particular heritage as their primary Native identity. The Tuscarora were known as Mangoaks, "fierce warriors" to many of the Algonquin speaking tribes of the area. And the name was well deserved. The Tuscarora had indeed been the last powerful Native force near the area where Eliza was born and raised. They not only dominated the other tribes but had also dramatically slowed the westward expansion of the European colonists in the region. With their respectful place in Native American history secure, the Tuscarora would continue being held in very high regard by anyone of Native ancestry within the area of their domain for generations to come. And this was especially true for the Southern Tuscarora.

Eliza's Tuscarora ancestors, like virtually all other Native Americans, had lived with a strong sense of balance with their natural environment. They took only what they needed, and no more. And for several centuries Eliza's Algonquin coastal and Tuscarora peoples had hunted, fished, gathered, and traded along the coast and interior coastal plain of North Carolina. The primary area the North Carolina Tuscarora controlled was bounded by the Roanoke River to the North and by the Neuse River to the South. The Pamptico (Pamlico) River flowed between the two and ran roughly parallel to them. It served as a dividing line between the Northern and Southern bands of the Tuscarora. In spite of increasing English colonial pressure, the Tuscarora continued to control most of this area until the early seventeen hundreds.

Eliza's Tuscarora ancestors spoke a language that was Iriquoan and had some similarity to that of their Native brothers to the west, the Tsalagi

(Cherokee), but with some shared words from both the Algonquin and Siouan languages. This may have been the result of absorbing members of some smaller Native nations whose primary populations had been previously decimated by European colonial aggression or by disease. Their language and dialect continued evolving. And this was dramatically so for those who were living amongst or connected to the emerging European dominant community of the immediate area of her birth. And by the time of Eliza's childhood, not all, but most of those folks were speaking English as their first language.

Although knowledgeable in agriculture the Tuscarora did not depend upon it for survival to the same degree as the European colonists or some of the other southeastern Natives. In contrast they were less sedentary and required a very large area for hunting in order to acquire the necessities of life. This lifestyle difference, however, would prove to be a contributing factor in the ultimate demise of the Tuscarora as a powerful Native nation in Eastern North Carolina.

TUSCARORA TROUBLES

The Tuscarora's ability to roam freely was gradually curtailed due to the westward expansion of the intruding European colonists. And resentment grew as some of the Tuscarora territorial lands were taken by means of violence or through deceit by some of the more unscrupulous colonists. This was particularly so in the Southern Tuscarora territory where the colonists settled in greater numbers than in the northern half. These conditions placed Eliza's Tuscarora ancestors and the colonists on an inevitable path of future conflict.

The loss of their hunting lands was exacerbated by the fact that at the same time the European demand for deer skins was increasing. The deer skins were used to trade for some European made items that the Natives had grown dependent upon, such as metal knives, tools, guns and some clothing. Recognizing the growing Native dependency on European goods, the colonists applied their European market economy and effectively inflated the value based on demand. Consequently many Natives ran up debts with some colonists beyond their ability to ever pay-off. Colonial traders then used this as justification to begin kidnapping the children of the Tuscarora debtors and subsequently selling them into slavery to satisfy their parents' debt. These actions were viewed as violations against the entire community and thus required a response.

Eliza's Southern Tuscarora ancestors met and cited the most intolerable offenses: desecration and theft of their sacred ancestral lands; and enslavement of their children, the Nation's very future. They had no choice but to defend themselves. But before they could take any planned strategic action they suffered yet another loss that would severely compromise their defensive capability.

During all the conflict and turmoil brought on by the presence of the colonists the relations between the two separate bands of Tuscarora had deteriorated slightly. The Pamptico River where Eliza spent much of her life had once been a boundary of benign trade differences. But the differences evolved into bigger issues due to the increasing Native dependence on colonial trade items. Because of this dependence the colonists manipulated the political and military situation in their favor in a most profound way.

During this time period the European colonists were clearly inferior in numbers to the collective of area tribes when fighting as one unit. Therefore going to war with the entire Native population would have most assuredly resulted in their defeat. So the colonial leadership would apply the principle of divide and conquer toward the Natives. The same strategy had served the interests of the rich and powerful over the masses in much of Europe for centuries. And it had already worked well with some other Native groups in North America. In fact it would prove to be an effective strategy when applied not only to Native Americans but also for centuries to come with African slaves *and* poor whites.

Colonial leadership's strategy was simple. They threatened to cease trade with the Northern Tuscarora if they aligned with their Southern brothers in war against them. There were other factors as well but the trade threat strategy paid off. The Northern Tuscarora placed such great value in their lucrative position in brokering trade in the area that it obscured their judgement. In a very shortsighted decision they agreed to stay neutral in any conflict between the colonists and their Southern brothers.

Had the Northern Tuscarora understood the long term ramifications of their decision not to defend their southern brothers, they clearly would have chosen a different path. But they had no clue as to the seemingly unending throngs of Europeans that would eventually overrun their sacred lands. It was simply a matter of employing whatever immediate strategy they could in order to cut their losses and survive to perhaps fight the colonists another day. But it indeed severely compromised the ability of their Southern brethren to survive a protracted conflict under the leadership of the European aggressors.

THE TUSCARORA WAR

In spite of the profound loss of support from their Northern brothers, however, the Southern Tuscarora saw no alternative but war with the colonists. Chief Hancock led his Southern Tuscarora warriors in their first attack on several eastern North Carolina settlements in the fall of 1711. With their backs against the wall the Natives fought with great tenacity. Their fighting skills were clearly superior to those of their more agrarian European foes and the results of the initial conflict bore this out. The colonists were soundly defeated in a humiliating loss. After suffering major casualties and setbacks the colonists were desperate to end the hostilities. So through a series of false promises put forth during negotiations they were able to bring about a temporary cessation of violence. But they simply used the truce period to regroup and fortify their military resources in preparation for more fighting later.

An account of these events is described by Theda Perdue, Ph.D., in her scholarly work, Native Carolinians, The Indians of North Carolina.

"Local whites retaliated, and finally in January, 1712, South Carolina sent a company of Yamasee, other Indians, and whites under the command of Colonel John Barnwell to subdue the Southern Tuscarora. Barnwell's forces captured Fort Narhantes, a Tuscarora stronghold, after a bitter battle. The invading soldiers failed to take Fort Hancock, but the Indians nevertheless agreed to a truce. During a subsequent conference, however, Barnwell's troops killed 50 Tuscarora men and seized about 200 women and children as slaves. This act of treachery led to renewed hostilities, which raged throughout the summer. The desperate Carolina colonists promised Tom Blount of the Northern Tuscarora control over the entire tribe in exchange for his collaboration. Blunt accepted the offer and captured Hancock, whom the colonists executed. In the spring of 1713 Colonel James Moore of South Carolina attacked Fort Neoheroka and killed or captured more than 900 Tuscarora in the successful assault. The surviving Southern Tuscarora were forced onto a reservation near Lake Mattamuskeet........."

MATTAMUSKEET

The Mattamuskeet Reservation that some of Eliza's Southern Tuscarora survivors were confined to was already home to the remaining local indigenous population itself. But as European immigrants continued flooding the area it started to become a sort of Native inter-tribal melting pot. At some point between first contact and the Tuscarora War some surviving members of Eliza's Algonquin coastal ancestors would have likely been adopted in with those already living on the Mattamuskeet Reservation.

Some of her Algonquin coastal peoples had originally inhabited parts of the barrier islands, the Outer Banks, that separated the Atlantic Ocean and the Pamptico Sound. And the Mattamuskeet Reservation was located just a few miles from the Pamptico Sound. Based on this close proximity and the need for trade there would likely have been interaction and probably some intermarriage between Natives on the barrier islands and the Mattamuskeet even before contact with the Europeans.

And any such interaction existing *before* first contact would have surely increased *afterward*.

As the European population steadily increased it created additional pressure on the Mattamuskeet Reservation. This would have motivated some of the remaining Algonquin coastals and others to seek safe haven elsewhere once again. Thus the reservation likely became a sort of Native bloodline distribution center for other parts of the state as well. Many of those reservation descendents would eventually be sprinkled like fertile seeds over a large part of Eastern and Southern North Carolina where they would have either formed or joined parts of other Native peoples. Some of their descendants may have emerged over two centuries later amongst Native groups again displaying the proud name Tuscarora in as many as three different bands in southern North Carolina. And still others may have become part of the Lumbee Nation.

This relocation would have further diminished the presence of any descendants of Algonquin coastal nations in the area. Perhaps this contributed to the thinking of historians who used the words "extinction" or "disappearance" in discussion of Eliza's Hatterask/Croatoan ancestral nation. The historians cite key reasons as: intermarriage with whites; death from disease or conflict; and possibly relocation along with the original English colonists of Roanoke Island. And there is little doubt that all three factors played a role in the diminution of the Hatterask/Croatoan peoples as one identifiable Native *nation*. But in no way..... absolutely no way does that guarantee the extinction of all the *individuals* with ancestral bloodlines from that nation!

They never disappeared! They did what every other Native group that was under the pressure of insurmountable odds of survival did! They sought refuge in other places and/or with other peoples including whites and Africans. And some employed an adept, but historically generally undocumented underground survival strategy for their cultural preservation. In order to survive near their ancestral lands they would remain underground until it would be safe to surface once again.......

even if it wouldn't be until the *late twentieth century!* It was one of four available options that Eliza had to choose from.

PASSING? ASSIMILATION? OR CREATIVE COEXISTANCE?

After European colonists gained the upper hand in Eastern N C, Native people were forced to fight, flea, or adapt their lifestyles in order to survive. Living openly and fully as a Traditional Native within the larger dominant community was not one of their choices. Attempting to do so would have brought some degree of mistreatment at best, and at worst it could mean loss of property, freedom, and even life. So it should come as no great revelation that some of those who could *pass* for white, in fact selected that choice as the one with greatest odds for survival. And many others selected complete *assimilation* as their best chance for survival. Those who had selected the option to stand in defiance and *fight,* paid with their lives or freedom. But there were those, including Eliza, who chose the remaining option; the *underground* method that allowed survival *and* preservation of culture.

Those stubborn souls incorporated necessary elements of appearing to live in the ways of the larger community but with an intelligent twist. It would include some elements of Traditional Native American culture, religion and values but seldom if ever anything that crossed the line of tolerance from the larger community. The expression of these values was sometimes muted, but it, nevertheless, was an inner act of defiance and was accomplished in creative ways. It was an ingenuous adaptation.

The hostile environment for Natives that Eliza was born into in 1815 would require one's ability to sometimes disguise their defiance. She chose a hybrid lifestyle that incorporated subtle acts of defiance but only *masked* as capitulation. She would indeed by necessity bite her tongue on occasion. And most assuredly she would not be allowed to openly proclaim and/or promote her Native culture outside the safe zone of her immediate community. But as an adult she would find hidden ways to embrace and express her Native identity that would go undetected by those outside her community. It was a phenomenon that sadly was still part of her grandson Thomas' life as late as the mid twentieth century in Eastern North Carolina.

Interspersed in some Native methods of hunting, fishing and agriculture were occasional gestures to spirit or ceremony. They would have likely gone undetected by anyone ignorant to the spiritual side of Native culture, as most of the larger community would have been. Also language and dialect would be an underground method of conveying connection to the Native world. This method of subtle, safe, but very real connection to spirit and/or ancestors would be passed on by Eliza to her offspring and they would in turn do the same for their successive generations.

An example of this manifested in agriculture and involved the simple act of planting sunflowers. Eliza's grandfather always planted sunflowers at the end of his vegetable garden. The sunflowers yielded edible seeds, but in the traditional Native point of view the sunflower represented far more than a functional food source. In Native thinking everything has a spirit. But the sunflower's spirit was *especially* sacred because it behaved differently than many other plants.

Sunflower plants turned to face the rising sun in the east every morning and then followed its path during the day until it set in the west. This was a special connection between the spirit of Father Sky and Sun and the spirit of the sunflower. Together in their daily dance, both Father Sun and the sunflower plant were acknowledging the Creator of all that is. For this reason it provided protection for the other food crops.

From the European perspective, however, the plant was of low value compared to some other crops. It did not represent the best use of available fertile soil and thus discouraged. But it was considered a minor nuisance and therefore tolerated. For traditional Natives like Eliza, however, planting, nurturing and observing the sunflower was a non threatening action which preserved the connection to her past and honored her ancestors.

Eliza also utilized speech as a marker indicating one's identity as a traditional Native. This might be expressed as a minor voice inflexion or slight deviation in pronunciation of a particular word. She used the name of the body of water where she and her ancestors lived in this way. The Europeans called it the *Pamlico* River. The original Algonquian word was "Pamptico". Feigning ignorance of the English version she pronounced the word phonetically as Pampico, a hybrid version, which combined both the Algonquian and English pronunciations. When coupled with direct eye contact, the message would be clear to another Native, but not offensive to outsiders. It was an astute application of coded language that she knew could be passed down without negative consequence. And it would indeed emerge in her grandson, Thomas' vernacular as late as 1980!

The pressure to conform to the ways of the larger community would steadily increase as Eliza grew older. And she would have to continually adapt her subtle underground methods. However, to those "with ears" for the subtleties, her message would remain steadfast and with clear intent:

"I am a mixed blood Indian and proud of my ancestry. But I am forced to live within the dominion of those who will not tolerate me as such, and so I *appear* for the most part to live in their ways. I do this in order to survive and to live near the sacred places of my ancestors. But I have not forsaken my people, my culture, or my Creator. I occasionally speak and act in code so that my children and my children's children and successive generations will know the truth; so that when the Creator and the Ancestral Spirits, the Manito Aki, speaks to them they will understand. They will know why they are inseparable from their Mother Earth in spirit and in physical life. They will understand their love for her and their unique commitment to protect her. They will eventually understand why their thoughts, values, and ultimately their actions will often be different from others. They will understand that their love of the Creator will sustain them as they endure the suffering and social isolation that living in truth always brings. They will understand why they are compelled by the Creator to......... *walk the red road*".

MATTAMUSKEET: MULTICULTURAL REFUGE

By the time of Eliza's birth, many of the surviving Tuscarora had fled the area. Even the remaining members of the Northern band finally gave in to the pressure of an ever increasing European immigrant population. They abandoned their last remaining lands in the area in 1803 and migrated north to the area of their original homeland. In New York they re-joined a very powerful alliance of six separate Native nations known as the Haudenosaunee , the Iroquois Confederacy. They still maintained their separate identity as Tuscarora but gained a much needed measure of security in the great numbers offered in the alliance. However, some of those who chose to remain in Eastern North Carolina were confined to the Mattamuskeet Reservation.

The Mattamuskeet took in survivors of previously decimated regional tribes such as the Machapunga, Chowanoc, Hatterask and others. No longer a theat to colonial expansion, they were essentially ignored as long as they stayed in their place. And their place was generally on the reservation or in desolate swampland that others rarely ventured into or cared little about. But labor needs in the area often placed Natives, Africans, and poor whites in the same"boat", both literally and figuratively. And this aspect inadvertently contributed to the multicultural makeup of Eliza's homeland and ancestral reservation.

Both Native Americans and Africans were utilized in the maritime industry along side poor whites on the East Coast of North America during the period of American slavery. Some sailed under indenture, slavery, or as free men for hire. They held positions as stewards, watermen, seamen, mates, pilots and in rare instances as captains. And some manned whaling ships from New England and were members of tribes of that area such as the Wampanog or Narragansett. Their ships often followed the Labrador Current to its intersection with the Gulf Stream just off Hatterask Island, NC where shipwrecks were a common occurrence. And any Native survivor of a shipwreck in that area would have been taken in on the closest Native reservation. And that was the Mattamuskeet, near where Eliza grew up. And it remained a haven for

Native survivors until its dissolution in the late eighteenth century only a few years before her birth.

The Mattamuskeet Reservation was originally designated as a geographic location "reserved" for the Mattamuskeet Nation. But over time it had opened its arms to so many homeless Natives that it became home to a diverse and continually evolving mix of people. And because of that tradition of caring for those without family or a people, it became more than just a location.

When Eliza and her people identified themselves as Mattamuskeet it was as much a reference to culture and mindset as it was to her mixed bloodline or geographic origin. The word "Mattamuskeet" began to signify a specific way of life and a value system instead of a *place*. Over the years her ancestors lost their reservation and nation status, but their collective spirit continued to live as part of the same area grew into a refuge for *anyone* in need; Native or non Native. And it was this very "Mattamuskeet" mindset that would eventually create profound changes in Eliza's life. But it was the combination of it, her Hatterask soul, and her tough Skura:re/Tuscarora will that would determine who she would become as a human being.

ELIZA'S TRADITIONAL INDIGENOUS LIFE IN HYDE COUNTY

Eliza's childhood was shaped largely by where she grew up. Most of her life was spent on the mainland in Hyde County, North Carolina, a very low land area barely above sea level. It was bordered on the west by the Pungo River and on the south and east by the Pamptico Sound and on the north by the headwaters of the Alligator River and surrounding marshy wetlands. About thirty miles east across the Pamptico Sound lay the Island of Hatterask, an object of great fascination to her during early childhood.

Her people successfully practiced sustainable agriculture based on knowledge acquired through much experimentation from generation to generation. Eliza learned with Tsalgena how to maximize crop production without totally depleting the soil of its nutrients. They added local oyster shell pieces to the soil which helped balance acidity levels and boost fertility. And they planted bean hills at the base of the corn plant where the bean vine could attach and run up the corn stalk to seek the optimum amount of sunlight that it needed. Her tall corn stalks would block much of the sun light during the hottest summer periods and thus inhibit weed growth at its base and also provide cover for the squash that hugged the soil. The broad low level leaves on the squash plants covered the soil helping to maintain moisture for all three. (It was later discovered that corn used nitrogen from the soil while beans actually put nitrogen back into the soil.) Tsalgena called the corn, beans and squash "the three sisters", because they all flourished when planted together. Such knowledge would prove to be critical in the survival of those who would be dependent upon Eliza later in life.

Because of their agricultural efficiency and the abundance of seafood and game there was ample time for spirituality, ceremony and play which allowed for a balanced life. It was the collective nature of Eliza's traditional people to be satisfied with the essentials of life. This value, however, was inconsistent with the work ethic that seemed to be at the core of thinking within the larger community that surrounded them. But what the larger community may have deemed laziness, or lack of work ethic, was to Eliza's people a very valuable and in fact *necessary* life renewing experience of re-creation.

Traditional Natives viewed the larger community as obcessed with material gain and thus consummed in the amount of work required to satisfy that need. Conforming to the larger community's excessive work ethic would have diminished the Native's immersion in Creator and His Creation, a core principle in their culure and spirituality. Tsalgena instilled this principle in Eliza early in her life. As an adult, however, she would sometimes be in situations where her public behavior would by necessity conform to that of the larger community. But within the privacy of her mind, she would adhere to Traditional Native

Spirituality, the belief system that would provide strength during her childhood.

Eliza's play was mixed in with her love and respect for the natural world. She was especially fond of the winged ones and marveled at the variety in her area. Her favorite on the mainland was the chachaquises (woodpecker). She was amazed that one that small could generate such a loud sound. However, she particularly enjoyed watching the different plovers, gulls and other species of water fowl that were plentiful on Hatterask Island.

HATTERASK... ELIZA'S SACRED PLAYGROUND

The natural beauty of Hatterask was breathtaking but the land less than ideal for agriculture. In fact the word "Hatterask" in Algonquin means "place where nothing will grow". There were, however, patches of maritime forests on the island along with smaller scrub cedar like trees, vines, and sea grasses. While this was adequate in sustaining a modest deer population, the locale did not provide adequate resources for a steady supply of grains, corn, beans, squash, potatoes, etc. So when Eliza's people visited Hatterask they relied heavily on the island's protein rich seafood which was available in substantial quantities.

Eliza's ancestors who were indigenous to both Hatterask and the mainland had learned to harvest the best that both had to offer based on seasonal variation. And their gravitation to available resources was a significant factor in what drove the migration back and forth between the two locations. In the warmer months of late spring, summer, and early fall some would live on the islands. In addition to its abundance of seafood, it also provided a steady cool breeze that was helpful in minimizing the annoying effect of the mosquitos that flourished in the area during hotter months. And like her people, Eliza also appreciated the tasty seafood, but her fascination with Hatterask was with more than the physical sustenance of life it offered.

Eliza pleaded with Mary and Tsalgena every spring to allow her to go with the group that visited the North Carolina barrier islands in summer. But her first visit wasn't until the age of nine in 1824. Their sail due east across the Pamptico Sound took the entire day as they encountered a stiff headwind during the last few miles and were forced to sail on a tack north and south. Eliza was puzzled when the vessel continued to sail parallel to the shore line, first one way then the other, instead of heading straight to land.

She looked into her grandfather's weathered face and said "Why can't we just go straight grandpa?"

He had anticipated the question. "Well, this way we get to see more of the sound and the gulls that you love so much....... And besides it's the only way to move forward when you have a headwind blowin straight into your bow."

She was confused but just shook her head up and down politely as if his explanation made perfect sense to her. This brought a smile to Tsalgena's face and he struggled not to laugh out loud. Eliza was truly the apple of his eye.

As the vessel finally reached the opening of the Woccocon (Ocracoke) Inlet Eliza's eyes grew as big as silver dollars. She was in awe as she caught her first glimpse of the Great Water. Almost trancelike she gazed at the endless frothy white caps rolling between the rising breakers one after another. The warm water of the Gulf Stream had pushed its way northwesterly and hugged the shore that day. It bathed the entire area in a blue that had existed only in Eliza's fantasy until that very moment. The sand dunes towered high above the beach and appeared almost pure white in contrast to the backdrop of an azure blue sky. She watched the slender sea grasses dance atop the dunes' crest bending over in submission to the strength of the steady ocean winds. The sights were thrilling beyond her expectations. And she would always remember that first impression of Hatterask vividly in her mind's eye.

Even at the tender age of nine she realized that she had experienced something so awesome and beautiful that words could only diminish its meaning. She could find none that adequately described it. It was later in her life, however, that she would recognize the full impact of that first magical experience at Hatterask. For Eliza, it would be the physical confirmation of perhaps the most critical of traditional Native values. The magic of Hatterask initiated her understanding of the true meaning of the principle of the inseparable relationship between Kew'as, the omnipotent Creator, and His Creation.

The experience with Eliza on Hatterask that summer had been unique for Tsalgena as well. Seeing the reaction of his beloved granddaughter to the awe and beauty of his maternal spiritual homeland filled his heart with joy. It brought back memories of his childhood on Hatterask during the mid eighteenth century. He understood like few others what Eliza felt. It was part of a unique bond shared between them.

In a dream before her birth Tsalgena learned that Eliza would embrace the Traditional Native Spirit and have the gift to communicate with the natural world, especially with her winged friends. The message came as no great surprise to Tsalgena. It was a hereditary characteristic that apparently manifested in every other generation without regard to gender. He had been blessed with the gift as well but had never spoken of it to Eliza. His maternal grandmother had the gift before him but it had not been limited to just the winged ones. She had grown up on Hatterask and was as much a part of its magical elegance as Father Sky and Sun. He was eager to see if her spirit would manifest in Eliza.

Eliza and Tsalgena's time together on Hatterask that summer seemed to fly by. She relished every moment of her last day there. It was late summer and her family was needed back on the mainland to help with the harvest of the food crops and the uppowoc (tobacco). That afternoon she and Tsalgena went out for a walk after salting down the manchauemec (crocker fish). Tracing the footprints of their ancestors, they walked the Buxton Ridge trails that overlooked Pamptico Sound and led to the desolate sandy beaches of the island's ocean side. They stopped there and gathered a few wampum shells and while looking out on the sea prayed together. Later they turned back west and once again were in view of the Pamptico Sound. The afternoon sun eased slowly down below the tree tops of Buxton Ridge and disappeared into the serenity of the Pamptico where it would rest for the evening. They strolled back along the ridge trails and watched dusk slowly obscure the horizon that just moments before had separated sky and water. And as the faint early evening glow of the western sky gave way to darkness, the nocturnal magic of Hatterask emerged. It was a cloudless night sky filled with thousands of bright stars.

Tsalgena pointed to the east and said to Eliza "Look out over the great water little one. Do you see the light that never changes location? Look just along the horizon where the great water meets Father Sky during the day?"

Replying excitedly she said "Yes grandpa! It is a beautiful bright star. But why is it so close to the great water....... and why does it bob up and down?"

With a loving smile and a subdued laugh he said "It is the new light-ship of Diamond Shoal. It is like the lighthouse at Cape Point but it is out in the great water. It does not move because it is anchored in the same place both day and night. It tells ships of sail where it is safe for them to travel while near the banks so they will not run aground and break apart. You will not be able to see it in the light of day. It hides like the stars."

Just at that moment the wind shifted out of the east and brought with it a chill off the ocean. As they turned away from the beach and headed toward the ridge Eliza placed her tiny fingers into the warmth and security of Tsalgena's hand. Tsalgena looked down onto her smiling face and couldn't have been more content. She was his special gift from the Creator. He knew now that the ancestral spirits of Hatterask had recognized and embraced her........ and she them. And she knew how fortunate she was to have a grandfather who was so wise, strong, and kind.

When Eliza got up the next morning she ran down to the beach and sure enough the light on the lightship had disappeared just like Tsalgena said it would. It became an object of true fascination for her. She hoped to see it again on her next visit. It offered an added element of security because it was helping to prevent the tragic loss of life. The lightship had no doubt been responsible for saving many vessels and had become part of the seascape viewable from her favorite playground. She was already anticipating her next visit to the island that had quickly became her favorite place on Mother Earth.

COMING HOME

In the late spring of 1829 when Eliza was fourteen she and Mary both accompanied Tsalgena to Hatterask Island for another annual pilgrimage. It was only Eliza's third trip to the "place where nothing will grow" but this time she felt as though she was coming home. For much of the summer on the island they were blessed with good weather and many clear nights. Eliza and Tsalgena appreciated the beauty of the night sky and together studied the positions of the most prominent stars.

As the summer months raced by, both mother and daughter also grew closer. Their relationship was evolving as Eliza was no longer the dependent young child she had once been. Although still petite in physical stature, Eliza was rapidly maturing emotionally and psychologically. Mary recognized the transformation and began to view her as a young woman.

Mary and Eliza spent lots of time together mending the nets, salting the fish, and gathering wood for the fire. And on some mornings after breakfast they took walks in the forest and along the shore together filling their apron pockets with herbs and shells. Most of the longer slender fragments were saved for Tsalgena's points. But Eliza and Mary saved the flattened purple and white wampum shells for making jewelry. Over the course of the summer they created several beautiful wampum necklaces and bracelets as gifts for extended family members. It was an expression of gratitude to those who stayed behind on the mainland thus enabling their family to spend summers on Hatterask together. Their lives were good.

The close knit family was immersed in each other's love and in the love of their Creator. They were content in their relationship with Mother Earth and shared an especially sacred attachment to Hatterask. For Eliza it was her sanctuary from any threat on the mainland and her true spiritual home. For some unfortunate others, however, the waters surrounding it could be a place of absolute terror and death.

Hatterask remained an area of potential danger to ocean going vessels and Eliza continued to struggle with this conflict. How could the incredibly beautiful place that gave her peace and happiness also be such a dangerous and sometimes deadly place for others? Perhaps it was this inner conflict that endeared her to a floating structure positioned twelve miles out in the sea that she had never even seen before, except for its bright light in the evening.

The Diamond Shoal Lightship had become a positive symbol that bridged the conflicting extremes in Eliza's experienc on Hatterask. It served as a counterbalance to her fear of shipwrecks near the island. But unfortunately Eliza's sense of security with the lighthship would vanish with its destruction during a violent late summer storm in 1827. It had met its demise just days after she returned to the mainland at the conclusion of her second summer visit. The land based Cape Point lighthouse had survived the storm. But positioned on land, it was not as effective in warning approaching ships as the Diamond Shoal Lightship had been several miles out in the sea. Thus the frequency of shipwrecks increased.

Tsalgena had explained to Eliza, as best he could, the duality of good and bad in all of life, and especially with shipwrecks. But she was unable to reconcile her conflict of conscience regarding the claiming of salvage from the wrecks by locals. She was troubled by the act of receiving anything as a direct result of another person's loss. It was especially troublesome to her if the tragic event resulted in the loss of life.

Eliza was, however, very proud of her grandfather's past heroic efforts during the tragic shipwrecks on Hatterask. He always did his best in attempting to save the lives of those that he could reach in the surf. Even in his seventies he had jumped into the surf near Buxton Beach in a lifesaving effort. His heroism resulted in the rescue of a mother and small child who had been passengers on an ill fated sailing ship.

Even with the island's frequency of shipwreck tragedies there was no government or community sponsored lifesaving organization in the first half of the nineteenth century. Whenever lives were saved it was done so simply out of humanitarian concern by very courageous individuals who happened to be in the area at the time. And Tsalgena epitomized that ethic. His ancestors had created that very model of selflessness and courage for him to follow. Thus for Tsalgena, there was historical precedent.......an expectation of doing as they would have done if present during a shipwreck.

The ancestral obligation did not stop at just *saving* one's life however. Traditional Native Americans were compelled by spiritual belief to offer *permanent refuge* to unfortunates who were without family or means of survival. It was widely believed among many Native cultures that the act of taking in orphans, or anyone in dire need, would guarantee the surrogate parent passage into the Spirit World. This action by *Native* people in the early nineteenth century may have yielded some unintended practical benefits as well to the adopting family.

An additional helping hand was always a plus in a semi-agrarian society. However, if the adopting family was Red or Black, and the adopted individual happened to be a Caucasian, then there was a more complex but profound benefit. Bringing the Caucasian in as a family member would have likely been seen by the larger community as an attempt at assimilation. And that may have reduced the risk of racially motivated mistreatment. Tsalgena welcomed the added security for his family but saw it as an unintended consequence of his actions. He was simply adhering to a core belief in his Traditional Native American Spirituality.

If some were less prone to render Red people harm because of Native adoption of a Caucasian then so be it. Tsalgena's attitude on the subject was characteristically forthright and simple. During an elder council meeting he revealed that he had been given a vision by the spirits that he would soon be "taking in" those in need of family and protection. And that at least one would be a white man. He explained his point of view on the matter.

"My decision to take into my home those who are alone, hungry, or with no means is done so because it is the right thing to do. I follow the tradition practiced by my ancestors which was given to them by the Creator as part of The Original Instructions. It is one of the highest moral acts a human being can commit on this earth. If others choose to see it differently based on their own beliefs then that is their choice. If their view of my reasoning makes them less likely to hurt us in some way then that is a good thing for both of us. They can think what they want, so long as they just leave me and my family alone."

Contrary to what some within the larger community believed, the presence of a dependent Caucasian in a Native family would have little if any effect on traditional values or principles held by those family members. In fact it was far more likely that the dependent individual(s) would adopt the values and behavior of those whom had restored and nurtured his/her life. Naturally the adopted one(s) would have been grateful to their adopted parents and held them in high esteem. And certainly with the passage of time the relationship would likely become one of mutual loyalty and caring for one another as in any family.

This factor when combined with the longstanding Native tradition of benevolent adoption would figure prominently in the fate of two strangers. These future Hatterask Island shipwreck survivors would be without means of support or family. Fortunately Tsalgena had been forewarned and was prepared to act. And it would indeed be in the near future that he would face that decision. But it would not be in the summer of 1829.

BACK ON THE MAINLAND

Once again the family returned to the mainland in early fall and prepared for what they hoped would be a mild winter. Each night when Eliza settled into her warm featherbed mattress, her mind's eye would envision the smoothly sculpted white sand dunes of her summer haven. By the early spring of 1830 she was already negotiating to ensure her return to her favorite island once again.

At first Tsalgena and Mary were amused at Eliza's obcession with the topic. But by mid April her incessant promotion of the idea had begun to annoy them. Eliza was unaware they had made a commitment several weeks earlier to see that all three of them would make the pilgrimage to Hatterask together every year. They had discussed the idea with the elders and all agreed that it was the Creator's will for Eliza to spend every summer of her young life on Hatterask Island. The small community was committed to making whatever sacrifices necessary in order to bring the plan to fruition. So on a bright sunny morning in late April Tsalgena interrupted another one of Eliza's concerted efforts at persuading him to take her to Hatterask that year.

"Eliza, my beloved grandchild, you must be quiet and listen to me for a moment."

Eliza prepared herself for temporary setback and was already thinking of her next strategic counter move when Tsalgena invaded her thoughts. "Your mother and I have arranged for all three of us to go to Hatterask for the full season. Now you must stop your constant begging and start preparing. We leave for the banks in seven days."

Thrilled beyond words she grabbed her grandfather around the neck and squeezed him tightly. Suppressing her exuberance she said in her most formal tone, "Thank you grandfather. I am very sorry for my bothersome lollygagg of Hatterask. I will go right away and help pick the berries and then I will help with the planting of the beans, squash and corn." As she turned away she was grinning from ear to ear.

Tsalgena said to her, "Little one.......it is the will of the Creator and of our ancestral spirits. That is why it is to be for........ *this* season".

Although he was confident that the summer pilgrimage to Hatterask would always include the three of them, he did not speak of it to Eliza. His heart was filled with great joy when he saw her eyes light up upon learning that she could come along on the annual journey. He wanted to see it again every year for as long as he would live.

Their stay on Hatterask in the summer of 1830, Eliza's fifteenth year, was peaceful as there were no rescue efforts required of them. Whatever wrecks that may have occurred on the banks that summer were not in close enough proximity to their campsite to require their assistance. Thus much of her time during their stay was spent with Tsalgena on the edge of the Atlantic surf and also on the calmer waters of the Pamptico Sound. She continued expanding her knowledge of the different varieties of fish and shellfish.

Tsalagena allowed Eliza to be actively involved in catching the fish. Although it was not the traditional female role, his action would be immune to any serious criticism by other traditionalists in the community. They understood that moderate deviation from tradition was sometimes requisite to the survival of their people. And they trusted Tsalgena to make the appropriate judgement.

Tsalgena's decision wasn't just about the fish however. It was part of a bigger plan. Tradition dictated that Tsalgena pass on his vast knowledge to his off spring before passing over to the other side. And the ideal traditional standard would have been to do that with a son or grandson. But the Native world had been turned upside down for more than two hundred years since first contact with the English speaking Europeans. And their survival required constant adaptation and the application of common sense in situations such as the passing on of critical knowledge. Therefore Eliza would be the recipient of his wisdom and it would be incumbent upon her to do the same with her offspring in the future. Her role relative to gender was secondary to her role as a knowledgeable

Native survivor. And her insatiable need to know invaded virtually every aspect of Native life.

WHITE CAP

It was yet another season of fun and learning for Eliza as she identified several new types of wildlife and plant life on the island. Without question her favorite memory of the summer of 1830, however, was when she first sighted the elusive Red Wolf. The four legged friend appeared to her on a ridge that over looked the sound. She saw him on four separate occasions that summer. She knew it was the same animal each time because he had an unusual white triangular shaped marking just above his eyes that ran down the back of his head. She called him White Cap.

White Cap never came very close to their campsite and was always alone. The sighting would turn out to be an aberration of the norm. Conventional wisdom at the time was that the Red Wolf population was indigenous to the mainland of Hyde County and points north but not to Hatterask Island itself. Tsalgena explained to Eliza that White Cap's appearance was a special expression of acknowledgement to her from the Creator because of her love and caring for Mother Earth. At first she was a bit skeptical of her grandfather's point of view but as the summer grew on she began to understand the uniqueness of her experience with White Cap. In the end she fully accepted Tsalgena's observation of the matter as truth.

Her last sighting of White Cap that season occurred the evening before the family departed for the mainland. This time she knew that he had seen her. As their eyes met, his ears folded back and his front legs stretched out in front of his body toward her, almost in a canine play like position. He then raised to a four legged standing position and faced the Atlantic surf where he stood motionless for several minutes. He turned back toward Eliza and reestablished eye contact with her. And then he once again faced the ocean and watched as the waves rolled steadily in toward the white sandy beach. Lowering his body to the ground, he again rested on all fours, and stared intently out onto the sea.

White Cap was still in the same position several minutes later as the sun began to slip beneath the slick cam western waters of the Pamptico. His image gradually disappeared from Eliza's view as darkness consumed the surrounding land and seascape. She was perplexed by White Cap's unusual behavior but encouraged at his level of comfort with her presence in such close proximity. It was unusual behavior for a wolf to be sure.

The evening breeze swept over her with a slight chill hinting at the imminent change of season. Her petite body responded with a slight quiver just as she heard Mary's voice calling for her. She turned in the direction of the sound and saw the reddish orange flames of the campsite fire tapering upward as they trailed small billows of gray to white smoke. In the background she took in the magic of the starlit Hatterask sky. Reflecting back on the day, she was not sure what the significance of her encounter with White Cap was but she felt that it was special. She quietly beseeched the Creator for clarification and humbly asked to be reunited with White Cap once again next summer.

On the trip back to her Hyde County home the next day she could not stop thinking of White Cap. She began to recall details of her experiences on the mainland with Red Wolves. In the rare instances that she observed them she did not recall any similar behavior to that of White Cap. The moment that they detected her presence they immediately fled in the opposite direction. They had learned to fear humans.

White Cap on the other hand seemed to have no fear of her at all. Eliza began to understand just how fortunate she was to have been selected by the Creator to have the encounter with White Cap. Although his behavior was not threatening it was clearly unusual. After contemplating the meaning of the experience for awhile she recalled Tsalgena's words regarding the aspect of the Creator's acknowledgement. Eliza theorized that White Cap must be of both the earthly and spirit worlds. His physical form was clearly of Mother Earth but his spirit was beyond that of any other Red Wolf. Yes, of course, he walked along both paths.

TO AND FRO ON PAMPTICO SOUND

Their vessel eased through the marsh grasses of the shallows as they approached their main land home. Eliza could see some of her friends and relatives waiting on the shore. She searched for the gifts of purple and white shell jewelry that she and Mary had made. It was customary to provide gifts for those who unselfishly stayed on the mainland in summer. It would be good to see them again and thoughts of the reunion with loved ones gave her a warm feeling inside. But that evening as she gazed back toward the serene waters of the Pamptico Sound she focused her eyes in the direction of her beloved Hatterask. She thought about her new friend, White Cap. She was already anticipating her next sighting of him.

Each stay on Hatterask enriched Eliza's life in a myriad of ways which included her developing relationship with White Cap. She would also continue expanding her knowledge of the area's geography and wildlife as well as her ancestral history. It would all be part of her spiritual growth and understanding of the interconnection of all life with that of the Creator.

And each year Tsalgena refused to make a firm commitment guaranteeing the threesome's journey together to the island until just days before departure. He could not deny himself the heart warming indulgence of seeing the excitement that he brought into Eliza's life with so few words. After the second time he did it Eliza was no longer surprised but delighted just the same. The whole exchange of coy looks and verbal hints between the two had become an annual ritual. She began to understand how important it was to her grandfather and enjoyed playing along with the idea. She would always react with a look of excitement and offer up a big smile and hug for Tsalgena as she feigned surprise. He was beginning to show the inevitable deleterious signs of aging and she would have done anything to help abate his symptoms. Even his joint pain seemed to momentarily disappear when they danced through their annual right of spring. It would become one of her most poignant memories and her favorite story to tell from her youth.

In the spring of 1833 Tsalgena once again led his family on their annual pilgrimage to Hatterask. The three were of one kindred spirit when it came to their love of the island. And yet each had their own separate personal area of interest that allowed them time and space to interact alone with Mother Earth and their Creator. Tsalgena even at his advanced age was an avid fisherman and was enjoying the benefits of an exceptional fishing season. Mary enjoyed collecting some of her largest and most beautiful wampum shells ever. And by mid-summer she had already completed several unique necklaces. And Eliza began to focus more and more on her developing relationship with White Cap. At eighteen years of age she and White Cap were entering the fourth year of their friendship. Although still petite in physical stature Eliza was now a full grown young woman. And she had grown more confident and secure, and this included her ability to handle herself in the presence of White Cap.

She did not view him as a pet, however, and wisely chose to respect his wildness. She saw him as an equal being to herself with perhaps even greater spiritual powers. She noticed that he seemed to be spending more time looking out on the sea as the summer wore on. On several occasions during his stare she heard him even whimper aloud. His movements seemed to be a bit more deliberate and his posture more erect. His ears seemed to be almost constantly extended fully upright as if hearing some unusual sound undetectable to humans. But still Eliza was unable to connect anything of consequence to White Cap's unusual behavior. She began to consider the possibility that he might be ill and perhaps aware of his impending death. She prayed daily for his health and well being.

WHITE CAP'S WARNING

In early September the family was preparing for their return trip back to the mainland. Two days before their scheduled departure they gathered around the campfire for the evening meal. The tranquility of the evening was suddenly interrupted by a shrill high pitched howl which seemed to be originating from the direction of the ocean. It occurred four times and each lasted several seconds. They all recognized it as the familiar sound of the mainland Red Wolf that would occur primarily just prior to mating season in the spring. But it was early fall, and although sound travels very well over water, it could not possibly be heard on Hatterask all the way from the mainland even if it *were* Spring.

Eliza knew that it had to be White Cap and she immediately began walking toward the sound. Tsalgena warned her against leaving the fire and wandering in the dark alone. And although Eliza was an adult she still had great respect for her grandfather's wisdom about such things. After considering his warning she quietly sat back down. After their meal they retired for the night.

They awoke the next morning to a thick cloud cover accompanied by very warm humid air. Tsalgena said that there was a "blow a comin" as the wind had shifted over night and the gusts were stronger than they had been all season. He informed his loved ones that their trip home scheduled for the next day would be delayed due to the radical change in the weather. He was particularly concerned with respect to the abrupt wind shift out of the southeast. Eliza had already noticed the changes in the elements as well but weather was not the focus of her attention that morning.

Eliza was still very concerned about White Cap. She was so worried that she rushed through her morning meal of stewed clams and then quickly excused herself to gather wood for the evening fire. But instead Eliza immediately headed for the ridge where she had most frequently encountered White Cap. After she disappeared into the small brush Tsalgena left camp to follow her. He could read Eliza's emotions well and generally could predict her response to a given situation. He had seen the fear in her eyes the previous evening and understood the importance of her relationship with White Cap.

Once Eliza entered the bush area and satisfied she was no longer visible from the campsite, she began to run. She stopped to catch her breath at the sand dunes and scanned the top of the ridge for her four legged friend. She was relieved after spotting White Cap on the ridge where he was engaged in a trance like gaze out over the Atlantic. His presence on the ridge at that time of day was cause enough for alarm as he had previously only appeared in late afternoon just before dusk. Because of her increased level of concern Eliza dispensed with her typical conservative approach to White Cap.

She screamed his name twice in succession with as much sound as her little body could deliver. "White Cap! White Cap!"

He looked deferentially in her direction but quickly refocused his attention in the direction of the turbulent sea. Eliza moved rapidly in his direction but he seemed completely ambivalent to her approach. As she moved up toward the top of the ridge she realized that she was physically closer to him than she had ever been before. She had no fear, however, as her only concern at the time was for *his* well being. She was within about seven paces of him when he abruptly stood and stared even more intently toward the crashing waves. Suddenly he bellowed out a shrill howl that sliced cleanly through the sounds of the unusually rough surf and strong winds. Eliza could not imagine what the source of his bizarre behavior might be.

She moved several paces closer to White Cap's position. As she neared the dune ridge she thought she heard a faint sound that wasn't a part of the natural elements all around her. She considered the possibility that the strong winds could be playing tricks with her ears. The roaring winds were already at gale force and it was all Eliza could do to continue standing upright. The sands began to whip harshly against her exposed skin and into her eyes. Forcing herself to ignore the stinging pain she continued pushing forward and up the last few paces. She finally reached the crest of the ridge adjacent White Cap's position but she was careful not to interfere with his field of vision. Instinctively she cupped her hands and pressed them firmly against her forehead. They protected her eyes and upper cheeks from the blowing sand but also obscured her vision. She cautiously parted her fore and middle fingers creating an aperture which framed her first brief glimpse of the raging sea. The head wind had become so strong that she turned back to the side every few seconds just to breathe easier.

Eliza was frightened and exhilarated at the same time. She respected all that Mother Earth would bring forth. But that moment was very different than anything she had ever experienced before. It was a raw display of nature's unbridled awesome power. It was humbling and she stood in awe of the Creator. She felt very small.

Facing due east and directly into the howling wind she was able to view the constant motion of a very stormy Atlantic. She had never seen the waves reach such towering heights. They seemed to be about the same level as the roof of their cabin on the mainland. The gigantic rolling swells and deep troughs were frightening even from her vantage point high on the ridge. They were beginning to crest four hundred feet off shore and within just a few seconds came crashing violently onto the beach with a deafening roar. The bubbly white patches of sea froth created by the breakers' immense size and strength had blown all the way up the ridge and were skipping their way across the flattened sea grasses. Several curls of the foam landed on White Cap's snout but he was oblivious to it. He had not moved since Eliza reached the ridge and continued to stare out onto the sea. Without flinching he endured the fierce winds and swirling sands. He seemed to be singularly focused on something in the sea.

Eliza strained to identify the object of his attention but saw nothing other than the huge rolling waves. Then she heard the unusual sound again. This time it was louder and more defined. She quickly turned her back away from the ocean and faced the Pamptico in a futile attempt to avoid what would soon become the unavoidable. She sought sanctuary from the reality of the events which were happening before her. She wished so badly that it was all a conjuring from within her own imagination or perhaps just the extreme elements playing with her senses. But somewhere within her she knew otherwise.

She turned back into the roaring winds once again to look out over the still heaving surf. The false security of her denial suddenly vanished.

There it was again. It was the unmistakable sound of terror on the sea. It was the peel of a ship's bell. The sound had somehow fought its way through the roar of the wind and the thunder of the pounding waves and had rudely invaded Eliza's resistant consciousness. It was the tolling of distress and impending disaster. For those terrorized souls aboard the helpless vessel it was a frantic plea for help. For some it would be a final and desperate expression of hope.

Eliza had not seen it yet but she knew it would soon rise above the horizon on one of the large swells and into her view. She immediately prayed for the souls of the unfortunates on board and could only imagine the panic they must be feeling. Suddenly something appeared on the sea but only for an instant. In between two huge swells Eliza was able to make out the tattered remains of a mainsail rippling briskly in the stiff wind. It was still partially attached to its mast pole which amazingly was still in tact.

Only seconds passed before she was able to get another sighting. Again it rode high upon the crest of a large swell and was for the first time in full view from shore. What her ears had suggested, her eyes now confirmed. It was indeed a ship in great peril. Of the three masts, only the main was still standing. The foremast had sheared off just several feet above deck level. There was a small section of the third mast hanging by its rigging off the port stern. Just as the vessel disappeared once again into a deep trough Eliza heard a voice from below the ridge. She turned and was surprised to see Tsalgena climbing up toward her.

In a very scolding tone Tsalgena said, "Little One, why are you so close to the angry water? You were supposed to stay near the camp while gathering wood for the fire!"

He tried to pretend as though he was angry at her but Eliza knew that the real emotion in his voice was only genuine concern. He saw the tears welling in her eyes. As he reached the top of the ridge he extended both of his long muscular arms out to her. She fell into the security of his grasp and they hugged each other tightly. Glancing to his right

Tsalgena observed White Cap standing several paces away and staring out onto the ocean. Tsalgena then understood why Eliza was where she was in spite of the threatening conditions. He appreciated her devotion to the unusual four legged but at the moment his thoughts and actions remained clearly more about Eliza's welfare than of concern for White Cap.

Tsalgena thought it strange that a wild creature whose nature was primarily nocturnal chose to be out in the day and in close proximity to humans. At first he suspected the Red Wolf could be diseased and confused. And most assuredly White Cap *had* behaved differently than any Red Wolf that Tsalgena had ever encountered. But after a few more moments of observation he also concluded that White Cap was not ill at all. On the contrary he seemed to be quite focused and in control. Tsalgena began to conclude what Eliza had already known for sometime. White Cap must have been given special powers that could have come only from the manito aki, the spirit world. His thoughts were suddenly interrupted by a familiar but uniquely ominous sound.

The ringing of the ship's bell found Tsalgena's ear. He recognized it right away. It initially struck fear and disappointment in his heart almost as much as it had in Eliza's. But the decades of difference in their experiences, particularly in life threatening circumstances, had conditioned him to respond in an almost involuntary manner. During his life on Hatterask he had answered the distressing call of several ships' bells. Each experience had been different in some ways but always incredibly challenging. In every instance there had been a moment during the rescue effort when he thought that he would lose his own life. Yet somehow he had summoned the courage, strength, skill and physical endurance to save at least one life in every incident and survive.

Tsalgena understood his responsibility in such times of danger. It was all a part of the circle of life. The Creator had placed him there at that very moment for a purpose. He did not ponder the why of it. He just did as his father had done before him. He did what was expected of him as dictated both by island tradition and by the Creator within him that dominated the essence of his humanity.

He and Eliza simultaneously turned their faces into the powerful winds that had accompanied the large swells. They both looked out onto the sea and squinting from the stinging grains of swirling sand began to scan the horizon for the imperiled vessel. Eliza knew where to look and quickly pointed out the position where she had last observed it. As one large swell moved forward the still erect main mast of the schooner appeared just behind it. Another huge swell lifted the ship high into view and then slammed its hull violently into the trough below. Tsalgena knew that the ships backbone, its keel, could not withstand much more impact. He estimated the beleaguered vessel to be about a thousand feet off shore as it was just beyond the first breakers. It would be only a matter of minutes before the vessel would break apart in the extremely rough seas. Time was of the essence.

THE RESCUE

Tsalgena somehow remained calm even though surrounded by the threatening powerful winds and the sight and sound of the huge brealing waves. He had already formulated a lifesaving plan for those aboard the stricken vessel. He knew what had to be done and he was prepared to courageously do his part. Looking down the dune toward Eliza he yelled loudly, "Run to the camp and bring back the strongest and longest hemp lines that you can find. Tell your mother to bring blankets and the small anchor. And hurry little one. We have very little time. I will make brief ceremony and prayer to the Creator and then go to where the water and land meet. Tell Mary to meet me there and you stay on the ridge. Mary will know what to do when you both return. Trust her judgment and do not question her actions no matter what. Now hurry!"

Eliza then sprinted back down the ridge and soon disappeared amongst the scrub brush and trees. Her mind was racing with different possibilities. And her concern for those aboard the doomed ship suddenly was secondary to the unwelcome reality that her own grandfather's life would be in jeopardy in a matter of just several minutes. She made her own prayers for the safety of Tsalgena and for those aboard the ship as she ran.

As she approached the edge of the camp she began screaming loudly for her mother. Fortunately Mary was still in camp just having begun to lash many of their belongings together in preparation for the sustained winds that were already upon them. Hearing the fear in Eliza's voice she immediately dropped everything and ran towards her frightened daughter. Eliza quickly explained the situation and relayed Tsalgena's instructions. Mary threw four blankets around her neck and shoulders and draped the anchor and its line over them. As per Tsalgena's instructions Eliza gathered the coils of heavy hemp line and threw them over her shoulders. She gave Mary one of the two coiled lines and quickly grabbed the anchor from her. Mary did not resist. She had witnessed the maturation and confidence in her daughter's actions over the summer and had begun to place a great deal of trust in her judgment.

Though slightly smaller than her mother Eliza had more physical strength and endurance and was much faster on foot. Eliza also knew that if the lines and anchor did not get to Tsalgena in time that the blankets would be useless. She began walking as fast as possible toward the sea with the heavy load. Eliza looked back over her left shoulder and spoke to her mother in a blunt voice. "Ma, follow me! Stay on the ridge when you reach site of the sea and dig the anchor into the sand as deeply as you can. Then throw the other line down onto the beach to me."

For the first time in her life she was about to defy her grandfather's instructions. But she was simply reacting to a specific threat. And although she was confident in her decision she prayed to the Creator for clarity and strength. "Oh Creator, my God: If I have made a wrong decision then please reveal it to me before I reach the ridge. If not then please give me the strength and endurance to help in the rescue of those poor souls aboard ship........and please, please...........surround my grandfather

with your love and protection; provide him with strength he will need.....
and please.........spare my grandfather's life. Aho!......Amen!"

Back on the ridge Tsalgena prayed to the Creator and simultaneously
made a quick tobacco offering to all of Creation including the sea. In
his most reverent and solemn tone his ceremonial words were: "I pray
oh Kewas for strength and endurance greater than that diminished by
my years, and for the well being of the souls aboard the stricken ship. Be
with me Grandfather and all the ancestors. Aho."

Just prior to the beginning of his prayer and offering he rubbed his
body down with the essence of a small handful of herbs as an act of
purification. In less urgent conditions the purification ceremony was
more often carried out by fanning the smoke of the burning herbs all
over the body with a feather or feather fan. But the method(s) of physical purification were always secondary in importance to the words and
intention of prayer and beseechment to the Creator.

Having completed his spiritual obligation he then stripped down to his
underwear and turned into the direction of the sea. This was always
his most difficult moment. No matter how many times he voluntarily
entered a raging sea in order to help those at risk, the experience never
seemed to get easier for him. In fact with each event it had become more
difficult to take that first step into danger. Thus in every rescue effort
there was an increasing degree of courage required. This was largely
due to his growing awareness of the complex, extreme dangers he faced
in the effort. In every instance thus far, however, he had somehow overcome the body's natural defense mechanism to act in self preservation.

In order to override that instinctive resistance and physically step into
the raging surf Tsalgena would be forced to consciously subjugate the
value of his own life to that of others, therby embracing the strong possibility of his own death. If he allowed his natural instinct of self survival
to first enter into the equation then there would essentially be no *real*
rescue effort. Throwing a line to a helpless victim from the safety of
knee deep water, as some chose to do, would clearly be viewed as an act

of caring. But it was not the kind of heroic act of courage and self sacrifice that Tsalgena knew was incumbent upon him.

Even at his advanced age the elder's valuable experiences had rendered him still more effective than most on Hatterask at sea rescue. But he had learned early in life that any natural talent or any acquired ability that was granted by Creator was always done so conditionally. The condition was that the God given ability was to be used to benefit others before self. His ability was purely a responsibility. So it was with that understanding that he was once again able to courageously place himself in jeopardy.

At the core of Tsalgena's strategy was an approach consistent with his belief system regarding the relationship he enjoyed with Mother Earth. He worked *with* her natural elements and forces instead of trying to fight *against* them. He was aware of the religious viewpoint that referenced man's supreme dominion over earth. But in contrast, his belief was one of a harmonious relationship between man and the natural forces of Mother Earth. And since Creator and Creation were inseparable, he felt that man's dominion over Mother Earth was tantamount to having dominion over Creator. Tsalgena believed that the omnipotent Creator and His creation was just that......omnipotent. Therefore Creator/Creation was dominant over man. Thus his rescue effort was an act of submission and respect to the Creator *and* His creation, as opposed to an attempt to overcome any aspect of its awesome power.

Tsalgena's plan involved a series of trial runs. He would enter the surf and venture out about fifteen to twenty feet and then return to his original starting position. He did this at several different points along the surf in order to determine the presence and strength of the existing currents, undertow, and rip tides. He would mark their location relative to a stationary single point of reference on land. Once he had established a mental map of the individual danger zones and their varying strength or directional flow then he could try to avoid the opposing force. If he was careful enough to maintain an accurate estimate of his position in the surf relative to the different flow zones, then he could actually use them to his benefit in some instances. He could essentially *ride* a powerful current to a given point. Even under optimum conditions, however, every rescue effort had required all his attention, skill, expertise, and physical stamina. And the extreme conditions, on the day that would come to be known amongst his people as the day of White Cap's vigil, were anything but optimal.

Just as Tsalgena stepped to the edge of the surf Eliza reached the ridge crest. As he began to rapidly study the different eddies and wave break points he once again caught full view of the ship. It was much closer to shore than before and by his estimation very near the sandbar. There was little time left before she would be slammed into the bar and break apart. He was preparing to enter the surf when he looked back in the direction of the ridge and saw Eliza bending over on all fours and motionless.

Eliza was near exhaustion from carrying the very heavy anchor and hemp lines. The proud grandfather watched as she raised the heavy rusted anchor high above her head and thrusted the bottom portion into the sand with a force that seemed beyond the capability of someone her size. A subtle smile lifted the downward contour of his lips as he watched her secure the hemp line to it with a fine double hitch. He felt very blessed by the Creator to have had a granddaughter whom had listened and learned from him so well. If today was to be the last day of his life on Mother Earth then he could die with the satisfaction of knowing that the best aspects of his spirit and soul would live on in both Eliza and Mary. It was a good day to die.

He called up to her, "Hurry little one, it is time."

Eliza desperately wanted to rest but she glanced over and saw White Cap staring directly into her eyes. She understood his look. "Yes White Cap. I know that I have to go and help grandfather".

No sooner had she finished the sentence when she heard Mary's voice calling to her, "Eliza, where is grandpa?"

Eliza raised her arm and pointed down onto the beach. She slowly stood up and turned to her mother to tell her to bury the anchor deeper but Mary spoke first. "Eliza go to him. I know what to do. You are strong and can help him. Secure him with the hemp line and be prepared to pull when he signals but do not go into the water past your ankles. I will hold the anchor and line tightly when he is pulled out to sea. You must pull with all your strength....but *only* when he is moving toward shore. You can do it Eliza. You are strong."

Finally catching her breath Eliza replied, "Yes mama, I know. We must both alternate or we will reach exhaustion too early and will be of no use to grandpa."

Mary then threw the other hemp line up to Eliza and she ran it down to Tsalgena's position. When Tsalgena saw Eliza running toward him he was confused at first. He then saw Mary emerge on the ridge crest and begin to bury the anchor deeper in the sand. He continued watching as she properly secured her body against it with the hemp line wrapped tight around her waist. As Eliza approached his position near the edge of the angry water Tsalgena wanted to scold her but there was no time left to argue the point. He simply accepted Eliza's self appointed elevated role of responsibility..... *and* her additional risk. Eliza handed him the line and he secured it tightly around his waist. He gave Eliza a nod of his head in approval as he turned and ran a few steps down the shoreline. He then abruptly turned into the surf and for a moment disappeared beneath a turbulent surface of frothy white.

Tsalgena resurfaced several feet further out but soon disappeared once more. When he next resurfaced he waved one arm which was the signal for Eliza to pull the line in to shore. Tsalgena swam in the direction of the shoreline as Eliza expedited his forward movement by pulling on the line. The system was functioning as planned. When Tsalgena reached shore he smiled at Eliza. "You did good little one. The ancestors are proud of you.....and so am I. But it only gets more difficult from here on."

He took a moment to catch his breath and then in a more stern and emphatic voice he continued. "Listen carefully Eliza. Under no conditions…. and I mean absolutely none….are you to enter the Great angry Water. If the Creator decides it is my time to enter the spirit world then so be it. If I do not have your absolute agreement and promise on this point, then we will leave this place now, and those poor souls will have to find their own way somehow."

He knew that her heart would not allow her to abandon the victims aboard the ship and also that she had never broken a promise. Eliza responded with a smile. Tsalgena looked up at Mary. He put his hand over his heart and then extended it in her direction. She acknowledged his expression of love by mimicking the gesture back in his direction. He could not see the flood of tears streaming down Mary's face. Eliza reached up and kissed Tsalgena on the base of his hand and tasted the salt from the droplets that rolled down his forearm.

Their emotional exchange was suddenly interrupted by a cracking sound so loud that it cut through the deafening roar of the seas and winds. It reminded Eliza of the sounds they had heard during the Winter of Snapping Trees back on the mainland when Eliza was a small child. The freak ice storm had lasted for a day and a half. The ice had become so heavy that it had split oak trees that were four feet in diameter.

Tsalgena, Eliza and Mary turned and gazed in unison toward the sea. They remained silent as there was no need to speak. The loud crack had spoken in the most descriptive of terms telling them in detail what they needed to know. The ship had begun to split apart almost dead center amidship.

By the time Eliza and Tsalgena looked out and located the vessel the bow and stern were already separated. The bow portion moved rapidly toward shore for a few seconds but then took an abrupt nosedive. Most of it was submerged but a portion of the keel remained above the surface. To their horror they could see two people hanging from the top end by their hands.

Tsalgena was shocked by what he had just seen. He had no understanding of how the two could have positioned themselves to be holding onto the cracked keel of a ship in rough seas. When the next swell appeared they saw the last rail of the stern portion disappear beneath the surface. Sadly it took four helpless sailors who had been holding on for dear life with it. Tsalgena immediately ran back into the surf. He quickly turned and said, "There is no more time. I cannot study the paths of the other currents. I must swim directly to the two who are still alive now or there will be no chance for their survival."

Eliza pleaded, "Please be careful grandfather!"

When Tsalgena disappeared beneath the surface Eliza began to count silently to herself. He did not resurface again until almost a full count of eight. She too had held her breath unknowingly the entire time he was submerged. He surprisingly had made good progress on a direct line toward the two helpless victims who were still hanging from the broken keel. Tsalgena was trying desperately to get through the heavy breakers and to the larger but less turbulent waves. He reached about one hundred feet out when a super large swell began to break just in front of him. His only chance to prevent serious injury or even death was to somehow get beneath the break. He swam directly into the huge wave's path as fast as his old but fit body would move. And he was within just a few feet when it began its break. Suddenly he was staring directly into a moving massive wall of water that towered over him by more than three times his height. And to make matters worse he was at the very point at which its maximum release of energy would take place.

Thoughts began to race through the elderly Native's mind but he immediately realized that he was powerless to act. And in the split second before full impact he flashed back to other moments in which he had faced death. It was then that thousands of years of evolutionary conditioning kicked in...... just as the Creator had designed it to do. There was no longer any freedom of choice in the matter....nor any further responsibility. He was neither hero nor coward. At that moment he just was.

All his systems shut down in preparation for the worse and his only remaining conscious thought was of the beginning phrase of the death chant. For him the chant was as much a part of his ancestral conditioned response as was any other of his involuntary actions. But before the thought could even begin to materialize into an utterance he had absorbed the initial impact of the super huge breaker.

Just seconds before, he had born a self imposed responsibility for the lives of the two shipwreck victims. But the power of the raging sea had profoundly altered the entire situation. The Creator had relieved him of *all* responsibilities. He had without conscious effort submitted completely to the dominant forces of his beloved Mother Earth and She accepted his submission. The sustained force of the wave's impact created a deafening sound and then it surrounded him in complete darkness. The elder slipped into a dream state somewhere between consciousness and unconsciousness. And then there was only silence.........and peace.

Eliza had spotted the huge swell even before Tsalgena had seen it and was shocked as it completely dwarfed her grandfather's body. She then had to watch the release of its awesome power as it crested and then broke directly above him. She saw him disappear in the massive turbulence. With legitimate reason she feared the worse but nevertheless still prayed aloud for Tsalgena's safety. As the remnants of the huge breaker reached the shoreline Eliza was forced to retreat about forty feet from her original position and yet was knee deep in the foaming water. As it began to recede she scanned the surface of the sea but saw no sign of her grandfather. Thus far she had followed with discipline her grandfather's instructions. She had suppressed her urge to pull on the safety line and had maintained her position as best she could just as she was told. She kept replaying his words over in her mind. "Under no conditions............. are you to enter the great angry water."

She glanced briefly toward Mary and White Cap's direction. Mary maintained a tight hold on the line and had in her own disciplined manner not moved from the buried anchor. White Cap on the other hand had stood once again and was staring as intently as ever out upon the huge swells. Eliza quickly turned her focus back to the surf and could only watch as the huge swells were relentless in their attack upon all in their path. She grabbed the line tightly and leaned back parallel with the sandy beach and began pulling the line with all her strength. There was stiff resistance but until she saw signs of her grandfather's survival she would continue to pull the line in.

Tsalgena had been under water for almost a full minute. The force of the crashing water had driven him all the way to the bottom and in the tumult his head had slammed onto the abrasive sand. He had lost consciousness and the vision in his left eye had been impaired by the impact. But as he began to regain consciousness, he saw light through his right eye and instinctively propelled himself toward it. He was still, however, unsure if he was dreaming or had crossed over into the spirit world.

Tsalgena had survived a direct hit by what was possibly the largest wave to ever strike Hatterask Island during his lifetime. Upon surfacing he regained full awareness and instantly turned to look for the two people that he had started out to help. But then he realized that he was being pulled toward the shoreline. After a quick visual scan he was able to make out the figure on shore that he knew had to be Eliza. He immediately formed a circle above his head with both arms, the signal to release the tension on the line. Within a few seconds Eliza saw him and released the tension and the line began to meander its way out into the surf.

Eliza and Mary were both relieved to see Tsalgena emerge into view. But they understood that he was still in grave danger and still determined as ever to save the two remaining victims. And following his example they instantly resumed their duties with the discipline that Tsalgena would have expected of them. They adhered to the same ancestral covenant as their respected elder.

Tsalgena was safely beyond the point at which the monstrous waves were breaking and once again scanned the horizon for the two survivors. As he rode upon the crest of a swell he saw the two people clinging to the thick oak keel which was still vertical to the water line. They were only separated from him by the trough of one swell. He could see that they both appeared to be young men perhaps within a few years of Eliza's age. Given his relative position to the men, he suddenly realized that he must be floating directly above the submerged bow of the ship. Aware of the danger he quickly began to swim on a diagonal out to sea but also away from the young men.

The young men were confused by his erratic maneuver and attempted to get his attention by yelling over the sounds of the wind and seas. Tsalgena could not hear them, but even if he had he would not have wasted his precious energy by turning in their direction unnecessarily. Confident that he had cleared the danger of any sharp projectiles from the wreckage of the submerged bow, he then turned back and began to swim the additional twenty feet to reach the men. As another swell pushed him higher he was shocked to see that the two men were not holding on to the keel at all. They were actually *lashed* to it by both hands! He then understood why they had been able to hold their grip on the keel during the rough ride. He also recognized a new problem however. In the rough seas it would be near impossible for him to loosen the wet knots that apparently were holding the two men fast to the keel.

Tsalgena's thoughts of a revised plan were interrupted when another loud crack shot through the air. He watched as the upper portion of the keel broke loose from the submerged wreckage. It was both a blessing and a curse. The dilemma of extracting them from the stationary bow portion of the wreckage was no longer a problem. However the section of keel that they were lashed to was tapered in its length and would float, but not completely horizontal to the surface of the water. The two ends of the keel remnant would alternate positions with the wave movement. While one man's end was out of the water the other man's end would be under the water. For the first time Tsalgena began to have doubts as to a successful outcome of the rescue effort for both men.

With the next swell Tsalgena reached the two men and their unstable keel support. He immediately checked the lashings and quickly confirmed his original assessment. The three of them would have to somehow get to shore with the young men still securely lashed to the heavy loose keel section. Tsalgena gave the signal for Eliza to begin pulling and immediately grabbed onto a cross bar that was still firmly in tact with the keel. Surprisingly they made significant progress toward the shoreline. The real test was about to come, however, as they entered the breaker zone.

The breaker zone was always the deadliest part of any rescue effort. And two dominant factors were working against the odds of their survival. The unique circumstance of being lashed hard to an odd shaped, unstable keel remnant placed the two in great peril. This factor combined with facing the ever changing currents and unpredictable breaker patterns common in Hatterask waters would dramatically reduce the chances of survival of all three men. The possible scenarios were simply unpredictable and too complex to plan for. They would just have to take their chances and make adjustments as best they could within the dynamic forces of the Atlantic surf. All Mary and Eliza could do at that moment was pray and assist if the opportunity materialized.

Eliza and Mary understood that the most life threatening part of the rescue was about to take place. They had watched with a strange combination of pride and fear for almost fifteen minutes as Tsalgena had, for the most part, successfully executed his rescue plan. Although they had both noticed some decremental changes in Tsalgena's physical strength and agility, neither had ever consciously thought of him as being physically old........... until that day. And by the time the three men reached the breakers Tsalgena appeared to be exhausted. He never even looked toward shore to give any further signal. This caused Eliza to rethink the instructions that her grandfather had given to her in such an adamant tone just minutes before.

For the first time she began to consider the possibility of her entry into the raging surf. She knew that she could not sit and watch her grandfather slip into absolute and unrecoverable exhaustion. Within seconds of a brief prayer for guidance she resolved that the question was no longer *if* but *when* she would enter the powerful seas. She looked up the ridge to Mary and signaled her to come down. Mary had anticipated the move and was already standing. She quickly checked the security of the buried anchor and then began running toward Eliza. Eliza turned her attention back to the sea that still held Tsalgena and the two young men captive. Gripping the line tightly she frantically scanned the breaker zone for any sign of them but there was none.

Approaching the edge of the first breaker zone, Tsalgena began to feel very week and was struggling to maintain a grip on the keel remnant. The young man quickly untied the line from around his body and tossed the end of it to one of the two men. He grabbed the end of it and motioned for the other young man to grab it with him. They both grabbed the line and held onto it with a firm grip. It was their first direct connection to possible safety on dry land.

They saw the small young woman standing on the beach holding the life line and assumed that Tsalgena would swim safely back to shore to relieve her. They were surprised however to see him still gripping the keel remnant with his left hand and forearm. Tsalgena while lying on his back then rotated his right shoulder and extended his arm behind his head in the water. He cupped his hand and with a powerful stroke pulled his hand and arm through the water back in the direction of the two young men. The forward motion toward shore of all three men created by the propulsion of Tsalgena's skilled strokes was slow but effective. They were very fortunate to have actually ridden atop the first breaker and even made significant headway in the process. However, the head of the smaller of the two men had submerged beneath the water's surface along with the tapered thinner end of the keel remnant for several seconds during the wave break. When he bobbed back up to the surface he coughed up a mouthful of salt water and began to panic.

Tsalgena knew that the young man could only survive one or two more of those sustained submersions. He also calculated that there was at least one more submersion in store for the young man no matter what. He knew that the only way to save both their lives involved putting his own life in even greater jeopardy. Without further deliberation his alternate plan of action began. Between breakers he quickly swam under the two young men in order to get behind them. As he did he felt a sharp and sustained pain along the right side of his upper torso and then along the length of his right thigh. He knew that he had been severely gashed by the splintered edge of a broken framing crossbar that was submerged. As he emerged once again above the surface he noticed a crimson tinge to the swirling waters immediately surrounding his body.

Exhausted, the elder respectfully asked his Creator to grant him just a few more moments of consciousness. Just as he completed the prayer he heard the rumbling of the large swell behind him. As it began to break he pressed both hands against the thickest portion of the keel remnant. As the full force of the breaker began to fall over the three he kicked his legs out behind him in full extension and simultaneously pushed the keel remnant up and forward with all the force he could muster from his upper body. His heroic effort provided just enough forward motion for the two young men and their keel remnant to ride safely above and along the crest of the wave for several seconds before being temporarily submerged in the frothy aftermath. The large breaker had moved them over forty feet closer to shore. They were close enough to see the dark brown pupils of Eliza's bulging eyes.

Eliza was watching the whole process intently and as the breaker flattened out she instinctively began to pull hard on the line. As its full length eventually rose above the surface of the water she realized that the two young men were holding on to the end of the line that should have been with Tsalgena. Where was Tsalgena? For a moment she considered the possibility that Tsalgena was holding onto one of the framing crossbars of the keel remnant. But soon she realized that the crossbars could no longer be intact because the two young men were still lashed to the keel remnant and only chest deep in the surf. The crossbars curved shape would have placed them quite visibly several feet above the young men had they still been attached. It appeared that the two young men were floating toward her and would in deed survive the ordeal............ but *without* the one who had acted so unselfishly in order to save both their lives.

Eliza quickly slipped off her frock and ran into the surf. As she reached the point in the great angry water where she was waist deep she yanked hard on the line pulling it toward shore. She quickly moved laterally to her right adeptly avoiding the massive keel remnant as it passed by her. She never released her grip on the line and started to scream at the two young men. "Let it go. You can stand now."

As he released his grip on the line the smaller of the two young men looked directly at Eliza and for the first time their eyes met. Before he even spoke, however, Eliza read the message of gratitude and sincerity within them. He was still gagging and coughing from the salt water he had swallowed during the last breaker. But he somehow found the strength to speak between gasping for breath. "Thank ye miss. May the Great God Almighty bless ye............and the old feller to."

She heard him but was already looping the line and knotting it securely around her waist. She turned her full attention to the huge intimidating breakers and courageously began to move toward them. Just before entering the turbulent water she glanced back over her left shoulder in the direction of the beach. She saw the larger of the two men standing in the shallow surf. He had somehow extricated himself from the keel remnant. Although distraught and panicked by the disappearance of Tsalgena she took some momentary solace in the fact that two lives had been saved because of her family's combined efforts. She quickly turned back toward the breakers just in time to see a twelve foot wave cresting no more than fourteen feet in front of her. She dove under it and disappeared in a mass of foam, sand, and water. She had learned to swim as a child and had strengthened her ability to move in the strong currents off Hatterask as an adult.

By standing upright the large man had been able to exert enough force on the line that it finally slipped over the end of the splintered keel. This freed the movement of his body but not the full range of motion of his arms. With his hands still bound together he began to move toward Mary. At about that same moment Mary loosened the line and then looked out onto the surf. She saw the man looking directly at her while poking his chest excitedly with both forefingers. He was breathing too hard to speak. Once he knew he had her attention he then swiveled his torso toward the sea and pointed with both hands toward the breakers. He repeated the emphatic gestures once again.

Suddenly Mary understood. The large man intended to go back into the breaker zone to help Eliza and Tsalgena. But Mary intervened and motioned for him to come to her. Ignoring her for the moment he then turned toward the still raging sea and was able to locate Eliza. While maintaining focus on her position he backed up onto the beach until he reached Mary. She handed him the line to hold while she retrieved a small oyster shucking blade from her apron pocket. She furiously began cutting into the lashings that bound his hands together. After a couple of minutes she was able to cut through the tough hemp thus freeing the man's hands.

Maintaining tension on the line they both walked rapidly toward his young friend. When they reached him the larger man took the blade from Mary. He then dropped to his knees and cut through his friend's lashing in just a few seconds. Finally the terrified young man was free of the keel wreckage. It had saved his life when the ship first broke apart but ironically due to its instability had almost taken his life in the breakers.

When the large man looked back up at Mary he saw the panic in her eyes. She had already lost sight of Eliza in the large swells. At that point the only way to find her for sure was to hold the line tightly as he would pass through the breakers and ultimately into the rolling swells. He turned and ran toward the breaker zone lifting his legs high over the surging water until he was almost chest deep. Diving beneath the surface he avoided the direct impact of the first of the breakers. He then looped the line and knotted it neatly around his waist just as Eliza had done. All his actions, like those of Tsalgena and Eliza were done without hesitation or thought of self.

The two young men were already indebted to the brave elder who had acted with such courage to save them. They were amazed at the physical strength and endurance displayed by one who was at such an advanced age but they knew he was in trouble at that point. The larger of the two men began to swim further out into the breakers. His swimming skills were not as efficient as Tsalgena's but as a powerfully built young man his strength and endurance were clearly superior.

He quickly made it through the breakers. As he rose higher with one of the swells he saw Eliza in the trough below him and several feet to his left. As he dipped into the trough she floated high upon the crest of another swell and then disappeared once again behind it. Given the extreme conditions she appeared remarkably calm and in control of her tiny body. Assuming her to be relatively safe for the moment he began to focus his efforts on locating Tsalgena. It had been at least three to four minutes since he last saw Tsalgena just behind their position on the keel remnant. Several swells passed as he continued scanning the surface for any sign of the brave elder. He prayed for divine intervention on Tsalgena's behalf as four more swells passed. The situation was bleak.

As the large man rode another swell he saw Eliza once again. She was swimming parallel to the beach and to his right but then momentarily disappeared behind another swell. As he floated once again high above her he saw something several feet to her right. It was Tsalgena! But the old man's arms were not moving and only his face was above the surface. The young man swam as fast as he could in their direction. In less than a minute he and Eliza converged on Tsalgena's position. When they reached him he was very pale and his eyes were closed but his mouth was slightly open and he appeared to be taking quick shallow breaths. He quickly grabbed Tsalgena's long hair in his fist and made for the shore line with the old man in tow. After several strokes he paused to catch his breath. While kicking his legs to stay above water he loosened the line from his body and raised it into Eliza's field of view. She grabbed the line in her hands and dove beneath the surface.

As Eliza struggled to wrap the line around Tsalgena's waist she was horrified at what she discovered. There was a gash along Tsalgena's rib cage that appeared to be an inch deep and several inches long. She was concerned that his ribs may be broken. After four exhausting and frustrating attempts she was finally able to secure the line around Tsalgena's waist. Emerging once again above the surface of the water she signaled the young man to head for the breaker zone.

Already near exhaustion the two began to make slow but steady progress toward the shoreline with Tsalgena in tow. But the raging sea was constantly changing flow direction and rapidly consumed what little energy they had remaining. The young man had to stop more frequently to rest as they inched closer to the breaker zone. He alternated between his left and right arms with every few strokes. By the time they reached the first large breaker Eliza was struggling just to maintain her own buoyancy and was no longer able to assist the young man in his effort to save the brave elder.

Tsalgena was in and out of consciousness. The young man signaled Eliza to go ahead through the breakers ahead of them. He knew she was reaching exhaustion and that he soon would be in no condition to help her. He was also concerned that the lines may get tangled around their limbs in the turbulent surf and restrict their movements in such a way that they may be unable to stay above the surface. Eliza offered no resistance but forced her weary arms to propel her body slowly toward the safety of the shore.

The young man was so concerned for her safety that he seriously considered giving up on Tsalgena and concentrating his full effort on saving the young woman. He felt that Tsalgena would have understood and in all likelihood would have directed him to do so had he been lucid enough to communicate. Like Tsalgena, he understood the common ground shared between all living beings regarding the subjugation of self in favor of the preservation of their offspring. He would have without hesitation given his life for that of his descendants.

But he was determined to save them both! So he prayed for a few moments and once again rested his upper body while using only his legs to stay afloat. He was able to regain some desperately needed strength for the challenge that was only seconds away. As his thoughts and prayers merged into a single stream of consciousness he began to feel calm. Then an emerging wave of strength and confidence began to flow through his mind and body. Aware of its source he silently thanked his Creator. With renewed vigor he strengthened his grip on the fine long flowing strands of gray and black hair that had become Tsalgena's life line. And with the elder securely in tow once again, he began to propel his body forward toward the safety of land.

By the time the young man reached the breakers with Tsalgena, little Eliza was already being hurled through the last deluge of turbulence that she would have to endure that day, and not a second too soon. She was exhausted and desperately struggling to keep her mouth and nose above the water's surface. Watching intently from shore, it became obvious to both the smaller young man and Mary that little Eliza was no longer able to move in the water at all. Once they recognized her absolute loss of control and her close proximity to shore they concluded that her survival was literally within their grip. Eliza was going under anyway so they had nothing to lose by attempting to pull her into an area where she could be reached by one of them. Mary was beginning to feel faint from the near thirty minutes of constant physical and emotional stress. She fell to one knee and dropped one hand from the line.

Physically and emotionally exhausted, Mary reluctantly released her grasp on the only tangible life line to her beloved Eliza. She placed the sole responsibility of Eliza's life in the hands of a young man that she had known for only minutes............and in the hands of their Creator. She whispered a brief prayer for the lives of both her only child and of the courageous young man as well. She watched hopefully as the brave young man ran toward the relentless turbulent seas.

The small young man strained to pull on Eliza's life line against the power of the Atlantic undertow and held his ground during several breakers. He thankfully had been able to move her closer to safety but she was still unable to stand in the surf. The young man was panic stricken when her head began to submerge. He pulled on the line with every ounce of strength that his diminutive but muscular body could muster. It was now or never for Eliza. She was helpless. The young man was sure that the grace of God was the only thing standing between her and certain death. With one last surge of energy he pulled and was able to reel in about four feet of the line. Without warning, the tension on the line ceased and he suddenly fell backwards into the knee deep chilly water. For an instant he was bewildered but shortly grasped the terrible truth. The line somehow had come loose from Eliza's body or had been severed by something in the water.

The young man immediately jumped to his feet and sprinted toward Eliza's position. He was not much of a swimmer but had learned to stay afloat as a child when he fell into a small pond. So when he sprang into action on Hatterask that stormy day, and voluntarily placed himself in harm's way, he clearly was not thinking of his own safety. He was singularly focused on the safety of one person. His one and only concern was the pretty young woman whose life was in peril. His action was predicated on values and emotions imbedded deep within him even before his conscious reasoning could have entered the process. Perhaps he felt obliged to respond in kind for his own life having been saved just minutes before. Perhaps it was instant romantic chemistry, love at first sight. Or perhaps it was an opportunity for the young man to make his seemingly insignificant life meaningful. But whatever *it* was.........*it*... was real. In his view Eliza's life was infinitely more valuable than his own. His single action in that brief period of time was a dramatic commitment of caring and unselfishness. It would highlight the profound essence of his humanity..... for Eliza..........and for himself.

Although short he was very fast afoot. In the blink of an eye he was chest deep in the water. With his next step, however, he was unexpectedly over his head and subsequently swallowed a mouthful of surf soup. A surge of panic gripped him but he summoned the courage to move forward into even deeper water. Gagging and coughing he threw up much of the seawater but never once took his eyes off Eliza. She was almost within his reach at that point. He began flailing his arms in a frantic effort to move forward to her. As the next wave broke and flattened out in their direction, the moderate impact pushed her close enough that he was able to grab her right arm. The wave wash once again receded and he was able to touch bottom on his tip toes.

The frightened but brave young man dug into the moving sand with one foot in attempt to stabilize his body. He held onto Eliza tightly as the powerful undertow began to pull her back out. Finally his most optimum opportunity to save her arrived in the brief interlude between the last undertow and the next wave break. He was able to stand up briefly with both feet, and with no undertow to contend with, he began stepping backwards toward the beach pulling Eliza along with him. After several steps he flipped her over onto her back and with his right hand under the back of her limp neck he lifted her head out of the waist deep water. She had only been under for a short period, but he had been unable to detect any signs of movement in her body.

He pleaded frantically to his omnipotent God for her recovery. Her eyes were closed but as her nose and mouth cleared the surface of the water she coughed and spit out several mouthfuls of the briny mix. He was relieved to see the pupils of her deep dark eyes as they opened wide. She was a bit startled and confused, however, and did not immediately recognize her rescuer. He released her head once she was able to stand but maintained a secure grip around her tiny waist and arm.

The two finally struggled through the rough surf and were able to eventually make their way arm in arm out of danger. As they neared Mary's position in the knee deep water they both collapsed. Mary ran toward them and together the three struggled onto dry sandy beach where Eliza collapsed once again. Mary fell to her knees next to Eliza and hugged her tightly as tears began to moisten the middle aged woman's weathered reddish brown cheeks. After several seconds passed she extended her hand to the young man who was still kneeling beside them in an attempt to recover from the physically taxing ordeal. As their eyes met, Mary placed her hand in his and in a quiet quivering voice expressed her appreciation for his heroic efforts.

"Thank you son."

She then gently pulled him toward her and Eliza. The three of them embraced in a moment filled with the purest of emotions brought on by a unique life changing experience which they had just shared together. He began to feel a great wave of emotion and fought hard to hold back the tears but lost the battle quickly. He was thankful that neither of the two women could see the glistening evidence of what he considered to be an unmanly weakness in himself.

The two women and the young man had never laid eyes on each other until just minutes before. But in that moment of elation there was a level of comfort with each other that was almost family like. Maybe it was the raw spiritual energy of all three having been touched by the miracle of divine intervention. Or maybe the aura of Hatterask had already begun to work its special magic. Or perhaps it was the intersection of both. Clearly the young man and woman were immersed in the euphoria of surviving a truly life threatening ordeal.

But for the young man there was another dimension of the experience taking place. For him it was more personal. It was beyond the energy and exhilaration that one experiences during an adrenalin rush. The feeling was more about comfort, security and peace .... and of belonging. He didn't understand why. But for the first time in his life he felt like he was in a place that could best be described by the simple word "home." The young man was already family.... even before Mary and Eliza knew his name.

As Eliza began to recover she anxiously looked back out toward the water and said, "Where..... is grandpa..... and your friend?"

Still breathing very hard the young man turned toward the sea and scanned the large rolling swells for any sign of them and shouted, "There.... over there!"

From a crouched position he pointed straight out onto the sea directly in front of them. Eliza was still too weak to stand but looked over her left shoulder. She could not see them and turned back toward the beach just as she spewed up a stream of greenish sea water that she had swallowed only minutes before. She could no longer sit up and feeling very weak fell face first onto the sand. Mary quickly supported Eliza's head in an upright position with the palm of her left hand. It was her intent to prevent any further swallowing for fear of her daughter choking to death on her own fluids. The young man then crawled over to where the line was coiled. He picked it up and in a rather clumsy manner slowly began to tie it around his waist. He felt like he would pass out at any moment but forced his limbs to move. He slowly stood and began to stumble once again back toward the pounding surf. Mary quickly grabbed the other end of the line with her free right hand and in a circular rotation of her wrist slowly wrapped it into a secure grip between her thumb and palm.

Mary admired the young man's courage but knew that he was near complete exhaustion. She was doubtful at that point that he was in any position to be of help to Tsalgena or his friend. But she chose not to interfere in his decision. She would simply continue praying for all three of the men and hope for the best. She was determined however to do everything in her power to keep him alive. After all, he had placed his own life in jeopardy and by doing so had saved Eliza's life. So she held fast to the other end of his line. And if he did lose his life to the stormy sea, then at least she could eventually pull his body back to shore for the respectful burial that he deserved.

Mary never lost hope for the survival of all, but reality had taught her to approach everything with a slant to the practical side of life. She had suffered too much loss and endured too much pain in her life to respond with an expectation of unrealistic positive results. Her philosophy was to expect little and always prepare for the worse. If the outcome were to be positive then all was well that ends well. If it was to be negative then there was no real element of shock involved and one could quickly pick up the pieces and move on with survival. Her great aunt Deneen had once described her as very even keeled and most dependable. Mary was often quiet and reserved but where her family was concerned she was as solid as a rock. Her concern for the young man's well being was no different at that moment than that for her own father, Tsalgena. She whispered a brief prayer for the lives of Tsalgena and both of the young men as she watched her new friend enter the water yet another time.

"May the Creator give you all strength and life", she said. "Be careful...... son", she yelled to the young man.

The smaller young man was too tired to turn and acknowledge her. He was focused simply on doing what was necessary and morally right at that moment. And that was to simply stand, keep breathing, and move forward back into the hellish peril that he had just minutes before escaped. Doing right meant doing exactly what his friend would have done for him in that very same situation. And he was obliged by his own simple code of humanity to voluntarily plunge into a very threatening sea to help an old man who had already saved the young man's life that day.

Neither Mary nor Eliza would have thought any less of the young man had he just collapsed on the beach and left his friend and the old man in the hands of the Creator. He was smaller in stature than both and not nearly as strong and was clearly exhausted. But his body's self survival mechanisms had been overridden by something more powerful. When he saved Eliza's life and understood what he had done he was instantly rewarded with a renewal of self worth. And for that moment it became the sole source of his being and motivation. And he understood why. It was simply the act of sacrifice and of giving that had added value to his life. So he offered up the only thing he had that day.....his life. It was in no way a death wish. He had more reason than ever to live after looking into the pretty young woman's beautiful dark eyes and having been embraced by her and her mother in genuine acceptance and appreciation. He could, however on the other hand, and if necessary, die as a man of contentment. At least once in his lifetime he had become the fortunate recipient of real love and respect. And even in the midst of such threatening conditions he realized that there was nothing that could rise to a level of greater importance in his life than that.

The shock of the cold water and the sheer power of the raging Atlantic Ocean surrounding his body jolted him with a slight surge of energy. With the next breaker he felt his feet lose contact with the sandy bottom and once again the disconcerting sensation of his own body's buoyancy along with the subsequent loss of control. He could barely see his friend and the old man through the froth but calculated that they were just on the edge of the breakers maybe fifty to sixty feet out from his position. Occasionally his friend's entire head would emerge from beneath the water but then once again submerge for a long period. Each time his friend disappeared beneath the surface he noticed that the old man's head would rise above the water. The young man began to notice a pattern to the action of the two men submerging and rising. It suddenly made sense.

In order to save the old man, his friend was forced to go underwater and from beneath Tsalgena's limp body, push him up above the water line. This maneuver did allow Tsalgena a brief opportunity to breathe. However, most of the energy being spent by his friend was resulting in vertical as opposed to forward motion. Consequently there was very little progress toward shore. Even if his larger and stronger friend had the energy reserves to make the long journey forward it would take them at least a half hour at that rate to get past the breakers and into standing water depth. And clearly the larger man was tiring.

The weary young man would have to move quickly through the breakers toward Tsalgena and his friend. Once he reached them he and his larger friend could both support the old man's body with one arm while propelling their own bodies forward with the other arm. It would be treacherous for all three but it was the only chance of survival for Tsalgena and his friend. It became apparent to him that his heroic friend would die before giving up on saving the elder from drowning.

The smaller young man clumsily moved forward into the relentless breakers. His progress was slow but in spite of the odds against him he somehow finally reached the two men. He could see that the old man was very pale and only semi conscious and his friend was beginning to choke on sea water. He reached them just in time to avoid certain tragedy. He grabbed his friend by the arm and pulled it away from the old man's head and replaced the supportive position with his own arms. He immediately was forced under water himself but successfully kept the old man above water. After several seconds he emerged and his friend had somewhat recovered enough to once again help support the old man. The smaller young man moved to the right side of Tsalgena and placed his left hand under his head and with his right arm began to stroke as best he could in order to help propel the threesome forward. His larger friend did the same on the old man's opposite side and mirror imaged the young man's actions. Although both men were exhausted they amazingly were able to move the threesome forward with some synchronicity in their motions.

They survived the first large breaker as a unit but the second one was larger and significantly more powerful. It forced them apart from each other and all three were submerged for several seconds. When both the two young men emerged the old man was nowhere in sight. They literally had about seven seconds to find him before absorbing the impact of the next breaker. Treading water as best they could they both searched frantically.

Just before the next breaker the larger man went under to search beneath the surface for Tsalgena. As the imposing wall of water began to break over him the smaller young man caught a glimpse of something only inches to his side that looked like a darkened Man of War or Jelly Fish. Just as the full impact of the breaker hit, however, he realized that it must have been the old man's flowing dark hair. Just before being tossed around by the wave's powerful rush of turbulence he reached out and grabbed it. He wasn't sure at first but as he emerged above the water he knew that he once again had the old man in grasp. He struggled but with his last bit of energy he pushed Tsalgena's head above the water and once again was forced below the surface. It was at that point that he could fight no longer. He decided that it was time to give up and submit peacefully to the ocean that had been the object of his fascination for almost his entire life.

He was cramping horribly in both arms and legs and began throwing up the liquid that he had swallowed earlier. As he coughed he swallowed even more of the salty water and the cycle repeated itself. He began to think that he had done himself proud and that his God above would be happy with his efforts and would receive him with love. He began to beseech Him in silent prayer for the souls of his friend, the old man, and himself. His final prayer was for the pretty young woman and her mother who had given him perhaps the greatest gift in his life. He was saddened as he calmly released his grip on the old man's body. He had held his breath for as long as he could and he felt that his lungs would burst. He was tired and ready to get it all over with and began to pray for a quick painless end.

Just as the involuntary response to breathe forced the small young man's mouth open his head and upper torso were suddenly and inexplicably propelled out of the water and into the open air. At the same time his body was jerked several feet toward shore by a sudden pulling force. For him the whole process became a blur and he initially thought that he might be hallucinating while dying. But when his forward momentum slowed and he began to submerge again he realized that he really was still alive.

Completely confused and disoriented by the totality of his experience that day he turned to look for any sign of his friend and the old man. Just seven or eight feet behind him he saw his powerful friend stroking with his right arm and pulling the old man behind him by the hair with his left. He concluded that his loyal friend had somehow miraculously held onto Tsalgena and simultaneously pushed him up and out of the water.

The larger young man seemed to have renewed strength and energy and a look of determination in his eyes that was absent just minutes before. Before the smaller young man could speak or acknowledge his friend with a simple wave of his arm he was suddenly jerked forward once again for another several feet. Then he was pushed further forward by the wave wash from a breaker behind him. As the wave wash began to recede he was jerked forward yet for a third time. His forward motion was such that he was once again able to touch bottom. Just as he did he saw the pretty young woman and her mother standing on the beach both pulling the hemp line. In his mentally confused and exhausted state he had completely forgotten that he had tied the line around his waist when he left the beach several minutes before. The collective force of the pull created by the two women had been equal to that of an adult male. With renewed energy the small young man raised both his arms above the water and waved to them.

Mary and Eliza kept the line tight in order to prevent the undertow from pulling him back out to sea but stopped short of forcing any further forward momentum. They pulled the slack in the line in as he began to move upright into waist deep and then knee deep surf. He turned expecting to see his friend still towing the old man but was stunned to see his friend standing in waist deep water with the old man draped over his shoulder. He could hardly believe his own eyes. It was nothing short of a divine miracle. All of them were going to survive! But his elation began to fade when he noticed the crimson streams flowing from the old man's chest and leg.

Once assured that the three men were no longer in need of the life line Mary and Eliza began running toward them. As they got closer they were shocked by the sight of the bright red blood oozing from Tsalgena's leg and torso. The women ran into the surf and reached up to assist the larger man but he continued plodding forward, shaking his head side to side and waved them off with his hand. They continued gazing at the gashes on Tsalgena's body as the group moved up the beach to higher ground. Mary began to apply pressure to as much of the wound site as possible with her hands as they walked. Upon reaching the base of the ridge their progress slowed.

The large young man, although very strong, was taking shorter steps as the angle of the incline increased and his breathing was growing louder and heavier. The veins in his calf and thigh muscles began to bulge as he struggled up the steep sandy ridge. As he reached the crest he dropped to his knees with Tsalgena still draped over his shoulder. Mary quickly grabbed two blankets. She spread one flat out in front of the large young man and the other she and Eliza wrapped tightly around Tsalgena's body.

The two women then both pressed firmly against Tsalgena's open wounds in an attempt to stop or at least slow the bleeding. Mary instructed the smaller young man to help them move Tsalgena on to the other blanket. They carefully transferred Tsalgena onto the blanket which became a makeshift travois or stretcher. Eliza and the larger man grabbed the two front corners of the blanket and Mary and the smaller man grabbed the rear corners and in a well coordinated effort they moved in the direction of their camp. As they moved down the sound side of the ridge Eliza glanced back to see White Cap watching their every movement. Looking him directly in the eyes she silently asked Creator to yield some of White Cap's unique spiritual power to the healing of her heroic grandfather.

As they neared their camp Tsalgena's breathing was so shallow that it was undetectable by sight alone. He was extremely pale and the two young men feared the worse. Mary and Eliza were also concerned but they knew Tsalgena was very fit and strong for his age and they remained hopeful. The group stopped for a few seconds to rest and Mary and Eliza applied pressure to the wound sites once again. The bleeding had slowed to a point where they thought that they might be able to stop it altogether if he remained stationary for a brief period. This would also give the two men who had been baring the brunt of the load a chance to rest. After several minutes they were satisfied that the bleeding had stopped and they once again headed in the direction of camp.

Once they reached camp Mary removed the wrap from Tsalgena's wounds and cleaned them thoroughly with fresh water. She also applied an herbal ointment which was effective against infection and as a healing agent. She then boiled several strips of white cotton cloth, and after cooling, wrapped them as a bandage on the wounds. She and Eliza took turns applying light pressure to the wound for several minutes afterward. They covered Tsalgena with two blankets and wrapped their bodies around his to insulate his body's warmth. He was very cold and his body had begun to mildly convulse after several minutes of severe shiver.

However, their concern for Tsalgena gave way to their own exhaustion as the group fell fast asleep in early afternoon.

Only a couple of hours later Mary was awakened by a Plover's incessant pecking at bits of cornbread fritter that remained on the bottom of her iron skillet from the morning meal. But Eliza and the two young men continued sleeping soundly. Mary lovingly covered the three with the last dry blankets that she had. She then knelt next to her father and thanked the Creator for sparing the lives of her family and of the two young men. She respectfully asked the Creator to spare her of ever having to suffer through such an experience again. Her silent prayers were interrupted by the sound of an extended deep grown coming from Tsalgena. It indicated that although he was still in great pain, his breathing was a bit stronger. She was thankful for the encouraging sign of hope for his recovery.

TSALGENA'S FIGHT FOR LIFE

After the exhausting ordeal everyone slept soundly through the remainder of the afternoon and night. The next morning Mary awoke to the reassuring sounds of the seagull's high pitched shrieks. The first glimmer of daylight was just filtering through the trees of the dense maritime forest. A single star slowly disappeared as Father Sun gradually bathed the whole landscape in its welcome warmth and brilliance. Slowly the subdued grays and tans of twilight gave way to nature's pallet of bright colors. The fullness of the Creator's work unfolded in its visual splendor, soon followed by the familiar sounds of island life. Each day was a new beginning, and an opportunity to experience all that Creator would bring their way. This was the prism through which Tsalgena had taught Mary and Eliza to view each day's sunrise........in spite of life's adversity.

It was within this context that Mary awoke and immediately gave thanks for a clear sky and dry earth and for the lives of Tsalgena, Eliza, the two young men, and herself. She gently nudged Eliza and softly spoke her name. "Eliza. Eliza, wake up dear. Father Sun beckons..........and we must get started with the meal preparation."

Eliza's eyes opened and she replied, "How is grandpa?"

"He groaned in pain throughout the first half of the night but has been sleeping peacefully for the last few hours. His breathing is a bit stronger but he needs hot clam soup in order to regain some of his strength. Please wake the two young men and send one to gather additional firewood and take one to the sound side and dig for clams….and hurry. If your grandfather is well enough we must be ready to cross the Pamptico back home to the mainland in a few days. That is of course providing that the seas have calmed from yesterday's blow.

Eliza rolled over and began to sit up. Every part of her body was sore and stiff from the beating she had taken yesterday in the rough surf. Slowly she crawled out from beneath the warm blanket. She reached over and tapped the smaller young man on the shoulder.

"Morning."

He opened one eye and for an instant thought he might be dreaming.

"How are you feeling", Eliza continued.

The young man began to observe his surroundings and began to recall some of the events of the previous day but was still a bit confused. He was seeking confirmation of exactly where he was after the surreal trauma of the previous day. After a painful stretch and yawn he began to gather his thoughts and then in a half joking way he responded to the beautiful young woman.

"You wouldn't be an angel now would ye miss?"

She giggled and replied, "No, I'm not an angel."

His eyes squinted from the bright morning sun as a smile spread across his chapped bearded face. It hadn't been a dream after all. He had landed miraculously on a strange beautiful island with literally nothing but the clothes on his body and with no means of support. But he couldn't have been happier. He had cheated death and in the process had discovered a deeper self worth. And perhaps best of all he was staring directly into the eyes of purity and goodness. She wasn't an angel but she was indeed *angelic* in both appearance and demeanor.

Rising and turning away Eliza said, "Let's go, we must hurry to the Sound side and dig clams for the morning meal. Please wake your friend and ask him to gather wood for the fire."

The smaller young man found the seemingly simple task of standing upright to be quite a struggle. He also was very sore and worn out from the previous day's ordeal. He first tried stretching his limbs out but recoiled in pain. Then after considerable effort he was finally able to stand. He slowly shuffled over to where his friend was just beginning to stir. As he approached his friend the larger man suddenly sprang from beneath the blanket and although wincing from the soreness in his body jumped several yards back. He also was still exhausted and a bit disoriented. But Eliza's warm smile was welcoming and after a few seconds seemed to put him at ease.

Addressing him she said "Please..... gather wood for the fire."

His smaller friend said, "He knows only a few words of the King's English missy and he jes don't trust strangers. He has been abused by lots of folks. and I'm bout the only one he trusts. He shore ain't affeared a me cuz I ain't no match for heem in size nor strength and........"

There was a slight pause. He was momentarily unsure as to the wisdom of continuing the explanation of his friend's behavior. But his instincts regarding the caring people whom had saved the lives of both he and his friend and whom had also given them temporary sanctuary eventually overcame his caution.

Mary interrupted his thoughts and said, "And young man, what is the other reason?"

He took a deep breath and silently asked for God's protection of him and his friend as he said, "He was a stowaway aboard ship. He is a runaway slave. And….I uh…..I helped him stay hidden until we ran aground. He was hiding in an empty hogshead that was marked as cargo. I secretly watched over him until we were to dock in Philadelphia. When I heard the blow a comin I went up on deck to help him. That's when we were struck by a real big wave and all hell broke loose! Uh…..I mean…uh. I'm very sorry for slippin with me tongue missy and misses. That's how us sailors talk on the seas."

At first Mary seemed a bit offended but then she remembered that it was quite normal for sailors to use fowl language. And it was not as if he had taken the Creator's name in vain. So she nodded for him to continue and ignored Eliza's snickering. The young man then continued his story.

"Well…. taint no need a me goin on and on bout all this with all the details. But after the wave struck we was found by the captain and ordered lashed to the keel of the ship. I knew the ship was headed for trouble and figured we'd all probably go down. When she broke apart in the rough seas yesturdy I made me peace with me Lord Jesus. I thought me life was done but then God sent us a good strong man and two fair angels. I'm truly thankful that The Great God Almighty seen fit to deliver us to you good folks and……."

Tears began to well up in the young man's eyes. Mary and Eliza exchanged glances. Mary knew what Eliza was thinking and broke the silence.

"You are both good and righteous young men. You did the right thing for your friend on the ship. And you did the right thing in the eyes of the Creator yesterday when you risked your own life to save my father and daughter and each other. In our people's ways you are now part of our family. You and your friend are as my sons".

She hugged the young man and reached her hand out to the larger young man. He slowly moved in their direction and eventually held her tiny hand in his. He then put his arm around his young friend's shoulder.

He did not fully understand their words but their actions and tone of voice had effectively communicated their concern and good intentions toward him.

Eliza joined them momentarily in an expression of caring and recognition of family connection. She then broke the quiet sanctity of the moment, however. "We are all connected by the Creator as family now. And our grandfather needs our help in the way of sustenance. Please, can we all quickly go about our task."

The smaller young man made sure through a combination of words and gestures that his friend understood his responsibility. Mary went back to the meal preparation and the larger young man began gathering wood for the fire. Eliza and the smaller young man started walking in the direction of the Pamptico Sound to dig clams. Tsalgena began to stir slightly but remained asleep. Eliza turned toward her mother and started laughing almost hysterically. This brought a smile to everyone's face but also a bit of wonderment as to the source of the humor.

Mary finally said with a slight giggle, "Eliza, what is so funny?"

After a couple of deep breaths Eliza regained her composure. Looking first at the smaller young man and then at his friend she said, "We are all family now but we don't even know your names."

Mary, Eliza and the smaller young man chuckled and then his friend, still somewhat confused, joined in more as a polite accommodation.

The smaller young man said, "Me name is Elijah Sermons.........and my friend is called Eeembato Ngawai".

PART IV

THE

FAMILY

CHALLENGE ON THE MAINLAND

"American Indians share a history rich in diversity, integrity, culture, and tradition. It is also rich in tragedy, deceit, and genocide. As the world learns of these atrocities and cries out for justice for *all* people everywhere, no human being should ever have to fear for his or her life because of their political or religious beliefs. We are in this together, my friends, the rich, the poor, the red, white, black, brown and yellow. We share responsibility for Mother Earth and those who live and breathe upon her. Never forget that."
Leonard Peltier

Even after the emotional and physical stress of the shipwreck and rescue effort all except Tsalgena were in good health. And they were thankful and optimistic in spite of their elder's debilitated physical condition. The tough old Native however began to show signs of recovery earlier than anyone expected. By mid afternoon he was able to sip some of Mary's nourishing briny clam soup. The bleeding had stopped but his flesh wounds were still very tender. And his rib and leg bone injuries were serious enough to severely restrict movement. Just before dusk, however, he asked to have his head propped up against a log. He wanted to see the last glow of the big orange sun as it appeared to gradually submerge beneath the ever darkening surface of the western Pamptico Sound. It was his way of affirming his will to live. Eliza had anticipated his wishes and voluntarily tossed a pinch of tobacco in the direction of the west. She considered it an honor to carryout part of her grandfather's daily ritual on his behalf. Her simple act elicited a subtle but encouraging smile from the elder.

As the group settled down for the night Mary told Tsalgena that she and Eliza had decided that they would have to delay their trip back to the mainland for a few more days. They were surprised when he did not offer argument to the contrary. But the experienced sailor knew how rough the waters of the Pamptico could be. His wounds needed to heal more in order to handle the constant motion that would undoubtedly be a part of the trip back to the mainland. They were confident that Tsalgena's cousin, Andrew, would most likely delay his voyage to Hatterask for at least three or four days after the storm anyway. Everything seemed to be working out for the best after all. The delayed departure for the mainland would give them all a chance to rest and to experience the beauty and tranquility of Eliza's magical summer homeland.

Over the next four days they all worked cooperatively under Mary's direction and got to know each other better. While going about their daily tasks and preparing for their trip to the mainland they began to share personal experiences from their past and even some of their hopes and dreams for the future. Given their different backgrounds there was some difficulty in communicating however. English was the first language for Eliza and Elijah, and to a lesser extent even for Mary and Tsalgena. But there were still misunderstandings due to some of Elijah's Scotch Irish brogue and Mary and Tsalgena's mix of Algonquin and English dialect. And Eliza was able to help bridge some of their particular language gap. But communication with Embato was a much greater challenge for all of them.

They recognized none of Embato's native Senegambian language and what little English he spoke was in a very thick accent. But Embato was very motivated to adapt as he clearly understood the unique risks that lay in wait for him on the mainland of a slave state in 1833. He began to expand his English vocabulary rather quickly with some help from Eliza. Out of respect for their African friend the others also tried to learn a few words of his native tongue as well. But it was more of a symbolic gesture than one of practicality.

Concealing a runaway slave in Hyde County would be challenging enough in itself without the added complication of communication issues. There were no other survivors from the ship wreck and there was no one else anywhere near their campsite on Hatterask. So there was no immediate threat to Embato's safety in the short term on the island. But the group had to prepare for the increased risks as they neared the mainland. There were plantations near their home where fields of tobacco and cotton were being worked almost exclusively with African slave labor.

During periods of its history North Carolina had allowed white indentured servitude or the use of Native American slaves but by the 1830s the institution of slavery in the Tar Heel state was almost all African. And although the transatlantic slave trade was no longer legal, slavery itself remained at the core of the economy of the southern United States. And powerful plantation owners could seize and claim any person of African ancestry who could not produce documents proving he/she was free. So the new family had to create a strategy that could successfully hide Embato from public view. Otherwise the efforts put forth and the risk incurred by all in the anti-slavery freedom chain from Owahou, to the Bermans, to the captain of the Blue Ruby, to Elijah, and so on, would have been all for naught. Not to mention of course the profound loss of personal freedom to Embato himself. Thus each embraced the moral imperative of providing a safe home for Embato, and if necessary, an alternative pathway to freedom for him.

During their remaining time on Hatterask they formulated a plan to initially hide Embato upon their return to the mainland. The plan also laid out a couple of possible escape routes north for him in the near future should that be his choice. Embato began to understand the basics of the plan and at one point asserted his own intention clearly enough to be eventually understood. The group finally surmised that Philadelphia was not Embato's choice as a destination of freedom. It had been his only alternative for escape from the Smith Plantation so of course he acted on it when the opportunity arose. But he was adamant in his effort to explain where it was that *he* desired to go. They assumed that he wanted to return to Senegambia. But the situation had changed during the time since his capture and enslavement. He knew that Briami would have accepted a new mate and father for their child as was the custom in Gambeya. And there was no guarantee that his parents were even still alive. So he had chosen an alternative destination that was much closer to the southeastern United States and probably more accessible. But of even greater importance to Embato, it was one that would very likely welcome him with open arms.

Embato had mentioned the name of a place that no one recognized but they were able to rule out Gambeya and Senegambia. But try as they may, there seemed to be little or no progress in recognition of the place. Embato kept repeating the word over and over. Frustration was beginning to take its toll on all as Embato and Elijah became angry with each other at one point. But then Eliza repeated the word as she had heard it from Embato.

Very slowly she said "I ee tee?"

Excitedly Embato yelled "Yes! Embato go Ayiti. Afreekan free."

All of a sudden it made perfect sense to the two women. They had heard mention of the place several times in conversation with Tsalgena and his brother. Tsalgena had told the story of one of their Native ancestors who had been captured during the Tuscarora war and sold off into slavery in Ayiti.

AYITI

Ayiti was the original indigenous Native name of the country that would later be called Haiti. Embato was very proud that it was the only country in the western hemisphere to have had an African slave rebellion resulting in a military and political success. The uprising took place after a long history of perhaps the most brutal treatment of any slave population in the entire world. The bloody revolution battles continued for about twelve years before the colonizer, France, finally gave up. Many were shocked to see a world military power be conquered in battle at the hands of an ill equipped army of African slaves. And the international significance of the loss was exacerbated by the futile decision of the infamous Napoleon Bonaparte to send in an additional 58,000 French troops during the last two years of the conflict.

In terms of its population Ayiti had become a smaller Caribbean version of West Africa. In fact many of Ayiti's African slaves had come from or had ancestral ties to Embato's homeland, Senegambia. So when Embato became aware of Ayiti's freedom for African slaves it became his destination of choice.

While on the Smith, Embato had listened intently to Henri Lafrance's stories of his life as a slave in Ayiti. Lafrance had been traded to Zachary Smith's father in 1789 (just before the slave rebellion) from a planter in Ayiti. And it gave the elder slave great pleasure to educate his Smith brethren about the success of their African Diaspora elsewhere. And Henri knew that he had planted a seed of real hope in the young African man from Gambeya. Although Henri's chance for physical freedom had long sense passed, a part of his spirit would escape along with his young friend Embato. Knowing that he had helped keep hope alive in the proud Gambeyan Protector would be of great solace to Henri in his few remaining years.

Embato still yearned to see his family and village in Gambeya. But his unfortunate experiences in America *and Africa* had framed Ayiti as a safer place than either. He knew the French were humiliated in their defeat and that any further intervention in Ayiti was very unlikely. And France's failure became a symbolic warning to the rest of the world's colonialist's nations to stay away as well. Thus the young Caribbean country led by freedom loving Africans had become the new destination of hope for runaway slaves.

Ayiti was *Embato's* choice, and thankfully, he had finally been able to communicate that to his new friends on Hatterask.

A HATTERASK ROMANCE

Mary conducted a brief adoption ceremony for their two new family members the day before departure from Hatterask. Just before it, however, Elijah had requested a private talk with Mary. He explained that although he welcomed their love and kindness he did not want to be Eliza's brother. At first Mary seemed confused. When she asked why, Elijah was not forthcoming with an answer. She could tell that he was uneasy with the topic and she reached for his hand and held it. She whispered a prayer for clarity and understanding and paused for a moment. And later Elijah found the courage to speak. He said that he had feelings for Eliza that were not of a brotherly nature. He had fallen in love with her almost at first sight and wanted her as his woman.

When Mary realized Elijah's dilemma a warm smile broke out on her face followed by a polite giggle. She patiently explained the Native perspective on adoption relative to his particular situation. She told him that indeed Elijah would become a member of the family and in effect the son of Mary and the grandson of Tsalgena.........but still of no blood relation. So his intentions did not violate the Native clan way and thus did not preclude him from marriage to Eliza at some point in the future. In fact had he married Eliza first, then the relationship between he and Mary and he and Tsalgena would have still been the same. Mary was actually relieved that Elijah had been forthcoming with his true feelings and thankful that he understood the situation. She was not concerned about Elijah's intention toward Eliza at all. Because she knew something that he did not. She had seen the look in Eliza's eyes when she interacted with the handsome young man from Northern Ireland. She knew the feeling was mutual between them.

Eliza thought she had successfully hidden her true feelings about Elijah. But Mary knew her daughter very well. She would have detected the most subtle change in her precious child's behavior. And there was a definite sparkle in Eliza's eye when she looked at Elijah that had not been there before his arrival.

It was normal for Mary to recognize the familiar signs of a blooming romance in a young woman. Although middle aged she had once walked along Eliza's youthful path. The whole idea warmed her heart. And from what she had observed of Elijah thus far left her with no reason to object. She had seen the humility and the raw goodness in the young man. And she believed that the union of the two had already been sanctioned by the Creator and orchestrated by the spirits. She also knew that her wise old father was aware of it as well.

Even through his pain Tsalgena had noticed the change in Eliza. He and Mary were amused and had exchanged glances with each other during the yougsters' flirtatious behavior. Eliza was indeed the apple of her grandfather's eye and always would be. But Tsalgena would gladly trade some loss of her attention and affection in exchange for the relief and security of knowing that she would be in the care of a courageous, humble and loving young man. Eliza's and Elijah's compatibility was obvious to Tsalgena and Mary. Both of the two youngsters loved and respected their natural surroundings and their Creator. And Elijah was in need of and deserved a good family. It seemed to both Mary and Tsalgena that all was working out in the divine way the Creator intended it to.

The two young men's lives had been saved. Tsalgena's life had been spared and he began the recovery process. Eliza and Elijah were well into what seemed a match made in heaven and Mary had two new sons. The situation on mainland Hyde County would be almost idyllic for the newly formed family except for one remaining challenge: That of providing Embato's continued safety and his ultimate escape to freedom.

JUST BETWEEN FRIENDS

As Tsalgena's family and close friends on the mainland diminished in number they grew together as a community and understood the necessity of collective strength. They were all poor by economic standards and quite diverse racially as their membership came from a mixture of Native, European and African ancestries. Some would have been considered half breeds and others simply social outcasts by many members of the larger community in the area.

Whenever those in Tsalgena's community who may have appeared to have some African features were questioned by outsiders they always claimed mixed blood Native and European ancestry. The technique of "passing" undoubtedly saved those of color who may have otherwise been targeted for slavery. For this reason most of the group stayed literally in their community. The only ones who had any semblance of routine contact with free white society were Tsalgena, his brother Alden, his cousin Arvel, and his nephew, James. The women ventured outside their small domain infrequently and only when accompanied by at least two or three males. They were generally safe as long as they stayed near home. The children were however a different case entirely.

The non white children were generally forbidden to venture outside the confines of their Swan Lake enclave. It was a time well documented with incidents of kidnapping of African and Native youngsters for placement in "apprenticeships". The concept of apprenticeship was a devious mechanism used by slave holders to seize free African or Native children on the premise of teaching them a trade or skill. It was often used to disguise what in fact was forced child slavery.

Most of the surrounding community were tolerant of the occasional contact in the small towns with the three or four Native men and for the most part did not harras them or their families. And most (excluding slave holders) cared little of their existence. The swampy area surrounding Swan Lake that Tsalgena's people occupied was for the most part of no interest to the wealthy planters. It was rough country most of which was not suited for commercial agriculture and the accessibility in and out was difficult for those unaccustomed to the area. But both these factors were a blessing to Tsalgena's people in that it afforded them some necessary isolation and thus security.

Most of the Hyde County folks viewed Tsalgena's people as very different from themselves. And some, in their arrogance, even characterized them as savages who were incapable of ever being "civilized". Those folks were also veary fearful of Tsalgena's followers. Therefore those within the mainstream community had little or no interest in venturing into the isolated area that was home to Tsalgena. Any rare visitation was usually done by armed groups often led by an officer of the law. And it was most often related only to the search for a runaway slave. No civilian individual or even a small group would dare go into the area by themselves. But even when the law *did* come around….. Tsalgena's community was prepared. They all knew the signs presented to them by their winged friends when someone approached from the outside. But still they added another precautionary measure of protection. They always had a lookout person posted near the land side of the borders of their enclave. A community bell would be immediately sounded as a warning when outsiders approached. The women and children would be hidden safely from view and in some instances would retreat deeper into the swamp until the threat had subsided.

So the remote home territory occupied by Tsalgenas's friends and family was somewhat of a protected area even for Embato. But everyone knew that at some point in the future he would be discovered if he stayed. That eventuality could bring much trouble to the community. And they all understood the consequences. But even with that reality hanging over their heads each individual would have enthusiastically supported Embato's decision to stay if he so chose. It was easy for them to empathize with his situation. They all had an ancestral connection to some form of victimization by a few powerful members of the larger community whether through slavery, indenture, rape, theft, land loss, etc. And some had been targets of the actual abuse themselves including Tsalgena. But this had helped to drive them together. They were bound in unity by both their love for each other and by their collective mistrust of those who had a history of bringing unjust pain and suffering into their lives. And Embato became a part of that circle the moment he landed on the inner banks of mainland Eastern North Carolina. The simple act of adoption on Hatterask had secured his position in Tsalgena's clan. For as long as Embato chose to stay with them their fate would be inextricably linked to his. That would prove to be a heavy psychological burden for the former Protector from Gambeya however. And it would be only a short time after joining Tsalgena's community that one event in particular erased any illusion to the contrary for him.

TROUBLE ON THE TRAIL

It was a mild and sunny October day. Embato and Elijah had been busy shucking corn for most of the morning. Then after the mid day meal they were spreading some crushed oyster shells and picking late squash in a portion of the high ground designated for agriculture. They were passing the time talking near the tall sunflowers that Tsalgena planted at the end of his rows. Elijah was explaining to his brother what Eliza had told him about the placement of the sunflower plants and why they were of a high spiritual significance to many southeastern Native Americans. He said that the sunflowers would turn to face the rising sun in the East every morning and then follow the sun's path throughout the day until it set in the West. In the Native way of thinking this made the sunflower a spiritual plant as it clearly had a special relationship with Father Sky and Sun.

Elijah raised his index finger that was still darkened with the rich black soil of the Swan Lake area and pointed toward the top of the sunflowers. "See over yonder Eeembato. Thar tis, plainer 'n day. The plants is a facin the sun. An I watched em all morn. An shore as hell they done exackly wut Eliza said they'd do. They follered the sun all day."

Embato looked up and the sunflower plants were indeed facing the sun just as Elijah said. He smiled and began to laugh. And then Elijah joined in the laughter. It was a moment of happiness shared between two good friends who were growing in their brotherhood. In the time since they were taken in and adopted by Tsalgena and Mary they had settled into a new life that seemed tranquil and balanced with family, spirituality, work and play. Their community and immediate surroundings had provided a degree of insulation from the harsh realities in their past that for the moment seemed quite distant to them. But they languished in a false sense of security.

The sound of the communal warning bell suddenly interrupted Embato and Elijah's laughter with its call for alarm. It tolled loudly and reminded them both of the harsh reality that existed in their time and place. Yet again they were forced to deal with the peculiar conditions in which they lived. They both jumped up and grabbed the baskets that were filled with the blessings of the fall harvest and ran as fast as their tired legs would carry them in the direction of the communal longhouse. Only a few yards before reaching it they saw Tsalgena as he stepped from the darkened entrance into the bright afternoon sunshine. They both recognized the look of concern in their adopted grandfather's eyes as they dropped the baskets next to the steps leading up to the longhouse entrance. Without hesitation the elder spoke confidently but with a clear sense of urgency.

"You must go with the women and children Embato. Arvel will guide you into the swamp thickets where you will be safe until the threat is over. You and they are to wait there and stay quiet until Andrew comes for you. If.....but *only* if..... you hear the howl of their hounds then Arvel will take you to the headwaters of the Alligator River where you will stay hidden until either Andrew or I can get to you to take you safely away over water. Just do whatever Arvel tells you. The spirits are with you grandson. Now go!"

Tsalgena then turned to Arvel and handed him a brown cotton bag and said "Here Arvel, take this. If they bring the hounds then crush these dried hot peppers and spread them on your trail behind you for as long as they last. You know what else to do."

Arvel took the bag in his left hand and gripping his pistol in his right gave Tsalgena a quick nod. He then motioned for Embato to follow him. They both turned northwest and headed for the swamp thickets. The women and children were already gathered and awaiting them at the edge of the community. Tsalgena waited for them to safely disappear into the woods and then he turned his attention to Elijah.

"Come with me grandson. You and James and I will meet the intruders at the head of the main trail. Bring one of the baskets and give it to James. I will bring the other one."

As they walked past the cabins Tsalgena explained the different contingency plans just in case there was any trouble. Tsalgena looked at the doorway of each cabin they passed by and gave a nod of the head. Elijah observed the adult male from each family standing in the shadows just behind the doorway and each held their long barrel gun up in acknowledgement as he and Tsalgena passed. A well built brown skinned young man was standing in the doorway in the last cabin before the head of the trail. He walked out toward them and just before joining the two tucked a sheathed hunting knife in his waist behind his back. Complying with Tsalgena's earlier instructions, Elijah handed his basket off to the young man, Tsalgena's nephew, James. Tsalgena positioned Elijah in between he and James and they proceeded toward the trail but slowed their pace.

Tsalgena cautioned James sternly saying "Just stay quiet James. Your physical countenance will speak for you. Pray for patience nephew."

Turning to his grandson he said "They will separate us by directing their first question to me. But they will have no ears for my words. Then they will begin to speak to you. Their ears will be yours. They will stare at James in disgust but will not show him the respect of speaking directly to him. To a man they all fear him. Together the three of us will provide the balance of strength, goodness and wisdom that the spirits chose for our people's protection and safety today. Trust in the Creator Elijah. Allow Him to speak through you today and all will be well. Now pray for guidance and give Him your tongue."

Tsalgena's direction to pray was good advice but Elijah was way ahead on that aspect. He had been praying off and on ever since he heard the bell ring the second time. But it had taken on a greater sense of urgency once he saw the armed men standing in each doorway. He called on God Almighty, Jesus, and even the spirit of his grandma. He was frightened enough to know that if ever there was a time to call on everyone and everything sacred.... this was it. His stomach was in a knot. It was only seconds after Tsalgena had finished speaking that he saw a group of white men coming up the trail. All but two of the nine were prominently displaying their guns. The armed men stopped about seventy yards away from Tsalgena's position. Then one of the unarmed men continued walking toward them. He was dressed in all black including a hat that had a wide circular brim with a round bowl shaped top. He had a long dark beard with some gray streaks that became apparent as he stopped within about three feet of their position.

Smiling in Tsalgena's direction he said "Afternoon Tsalgena. I trust that the Lord has been watchin ova ya and yo good folk."

Tsalgena was expressionless but replied in a pleasant voice "Afternoon Preacha Jacob. This un is my grandson Elijah Sermons. Uh, and you know James."

The man nodded politely toward James and extending his hand toward Elijah said, "It's a pleasure to make your acquaintance Elijah. I know you must be a blessing to yo grandfatha."

After shaking hands and without giving Elijah a chance to respond he said "Tsalgena I need to speak with you in private for a moment. Can we step over here unda this loblolly pine?"

Tsalgena did as the man requested but replied in a voice loud enough for James and Elijah to hear him say "What's on your mind Jacob?"

Still in a rather loud voice the preacher said, "Well suh. The sheriff ova yonda and.......his....uh..his men wanted to have a look around heah a bit. They are lookin fo a nigra slave runaway. He's a young fella bout seventeen or so. Skinny thing really. He ran from the McGill yesteddy. And Sheriff Ronald, well.....he would be much obliged if he could bring his men through heah and take a look.....uh...with his hound. But its jus one ole hound dog ya see. The pack is a few miles back trackin towards the Pamlico Sound."

He paused for a moment and said in a very low tone just above a whisper "Tsalgena...jus between me and you now... I know you ain't hidin the runaway heah.... Cuz...uh... I know wheah he's really at. But ya know I got to pretend like I'm suspicious. They know I know you and that's why tha Sheriff sent me up heah firsz cuz he figured I could talk you into it. So jus let em come on in and let that ole hound tell em that the runaway ain't been no where neah heah and they be on theah way and out yo place and uh....all's well that ends well...right Tsalgena?"

Elijah and James heard enough to get the gist of the conversation but Elijah was still a bit confused. Nevertheless he braced himself as Preacher Jacob motioned for the others to join him. And before Elijah could take several good deep breaths four of the men were face to face with him. Two of the others were standing a few feet from James and stared intently in his direction. James was not intimidated however and maintained direct eye contact with the larger of the two men as they stood watch over him. The other two men began to walk through the community with the hound who kept his nose to the ground most of the time. The other man stood with Jacob and asked Tsalgena about the basket of squash and pumpkins. Tsalgena and James handed the baskets of fresh vegetables to him. Tsalgena began to speak but the man ignored him and abruptly walked away and joined the sheriff and the other three men standing near Elijah.

The sheriff without introducing himself addressed Elijah just as Tsalgena said he would. "What's yo name son? And wheah bouts you from?"

Elijah answered with a confidence that surprised even him. "Me name's Elijah Sermons sir. I come from Ulster on the northeast coast of Arelan sir. An I'm pleased ta meet ye sir."

The rotund sheriff paused for a moment and then blurted out "Well I be son va bitch. That's where my grandpappy came from. Came in up Nawth and then worked his way south through the Pennsylvania foothills. And then he moved on down through the Appalachians but got tired a fightin them damn Cherokee injuns. So he moved on down this haeh way, wheah he settled heah in Hyde County...... Swan Quarter. Well Lijeh...I know a good white Scotch Arshman such as yo self ain't goin lie to anotha one...right son?"

"No sir. Me grandma...may God Almighty bless her soul...taught me to always tell the truth sir."

"Well Lijeh. Have you seen a young runaway slave roun heah in the last day a two son?'

Elijah replied, "Well sir. What'd he look like?"

For a few moments the sheriff just quietly stared at Elijah with his cool grayish blue eyes. He was incredulous at the young man's response. Turning toward two of his men he removed his tan felt hat revealing an almost completely bald head. He scratched it slowly from back to front twice. Elijah began to think he may have made a terrible mistake in his response. And that ill feeling grew when the sheriff stared at him once again. The sheriff then began to methodically place the hat back on his head with the front brim covering his eyes at first. His left hand held the front lip of the brim in place while his right hand slowly pulled the back rim down over the back of his head, eventually righting the hat to its original position. But as the front brim had lifted above the Sheriff's eyes, Elijah was quite surprised to observe what appeared to be a slight smile. By the time the hat was in its final position the smile had developed into an all out grin. The sheriff all of a sudden turned two the other four men and began laughing loudly. At first they seemed to be caught off guard and just stared at their leader with a look of bewilderment. But after a few seconds one of them started laughing along with the sheriff. Then the other three immediately joined in. Finally regaining some of his composure the sheriff turned back toward Elijah and still laughing spoke in broken phrases.

"Did you say….. What'd he look like?"

Laughing again the sheriff once more sputtered out "What'd he look like?

The sheriff turned toward Jacob and Tsalgena and said "Did ya'll hear that?"

He then abruptly turned back to Elijah and got so close that the brim of his hat bent downward as it pushed up against Elijah's forehead. In his peripheral vision Elijah saw James simultaneously move his right hand up his side and toward his back and turn towards him and the sheriff. The two men standing next to James lifted their weapons and stepped in between James and Elijah. There was complete silence and no one moved for a moment. Elijah was gripped in terror and remained at a loss for words. But he prayed silently. And as he began to fear the worst for he and his family the silence was broken. The sheriff's whole body started shaking as he once again broke into laughter.

"What in hell did ya think he looked lak boy? He looked lak a damn nigra slave, boy."

He bent over at the waist in uncontrollable laughter. And the other four men joined in the laughter once again. As the sheriff stood up his huge belly bounced up and down and he once again went into uncontrollable laughter. As the laughter died down the two men with the hound came around the corner of the same cabin that James had come from with looks of frustration on their faces.

The main with the lead on the hound said "Sorry Sheriff but ole Pete heah ain't found nothit suh. Ole Pete's the best I got Sheriff. If Pete says he ain't been heah then he ain't been heah. An that's a fact suh."

With that, the two trackers and the hound started back toward the trail. The sheriff gathered his other five men along with the two that were watching James. With no words or warning the entire group in unison turned away from Elijah, James, Tsalgena and Jacob and headed back toward the trail. The sheriff never acknowledged Tsalgena or James just as the elder had predicted. He did however turn back over his right shoulder and tipped his hat back toward Elijah and guffawed once again. Elijah caught the last few words he muttered through his laughter.

"Whatd he look like? Damn boy...now that theah's a damn goodun."

Preacher Jacob looked at Tsalgena and with a smile said "Well old friend. All's well that ends well. Evening Tsalgena." Turning towards the trail but looking back over his shoulder in the direction of James and Elijah, Jacob politely said "Evening fellas."

And just that quickly it was all over. The sheriff and his men disappeared in the distance and Tsalgena and James turned and without a word to Elijah began walking toward the longhouse together. But Elijah stood motionless for several minutes longer. He was still trying to absorb the meaning of the bizarre events that had just taken place. He gradually began to make sense of at least some of it. And finally he was able to see the humor in his question as to what the runaway slave looked like. But for some reason he just did not feel like laughing about it. He was truly thankful for a non violent result. But he remained confused as to why Tsalgena and James abruptly walked off together and without a word to him. He could find no plausible explanation for their uncharacteristic deferential treatment of him. And he was left with an uneasy feeling about it.

Later that evening he once again pondered the strange events of the day. He began to settle on some answers that were of a more profound and deeper nature than he had expected however. And later he realized that there were parts of it that he would have preferred to remain ignorant about. In fact he found himself wishing that he could simply forget the entire event altogether. A division had emerged between him and Tsalgena for the first time in their relationship. And other than simply allowing the passage of time there was little or nothing he could do to bridge that gap. The circumstances that caused it to exist were manmade, and yet ironically in opposition to the most Divine nature in man. He began to understand the relevance of Tsalgena's earlier predictions of the behavior of the sheriff and the other eight men, all of whom happened to be white. They would treat Tsalgena and James with either total disrespect or as if they simply did not exist. And in contrast he remembered Tsalgena's prediction as to how those same men would treat him so differently.

For the first time he understood that no matter how empathetic he was toward his African brother or his Native grandfather that he could never truly understand what it felt like to be mistreated by the white folks solely based on an attitude of racial superiority. He had been mistreated during much of his life for many different reasons. And clearly he felt the emotional pain and had suffered the damages and carried the vestiges as a result. But according to the rest of the white world he was still white. And to many white people it would never matter what he thought or how he lived or what his religion or values were. As long as he appeared to be racially white to them, they would in most cases treat him differently than they would his own adopted loving family members who happened to be of another race. And there was virtually nothing he could ever do to change that fact. He could not control how others saw him and thus treated him. It was a feeling of helplessness. And it deeply saddened him.

Elijah didn't have the formalized education to express the totality of his feelings in an intellectually coherent manner. And it would have been challenging for most to do so given the complexities of the issue. But he did know right from wrong. God had given him a good heart and a good conscience with an ability to feel things very deeply. And there is no doubt that he felt every aspect of it. And thus in his way he recognized, *and* to some extent suffered, parts of the unique human tragedy caused by the blatant racism that permeated much of life in America during his lifetime.

After dinner that evening Tsalgena came over to Elijah and placed his weathered wrinkled hand on Elijah's shoulder and said "You did good today grandson. You listened well and followed my guidance. You gave your tongue to the Creator and He disabled the evil and hatred in those men through you."

Tsalgena paused for a moment and then continued "Elijah. Creator makes us all a little different on the outside. But on the inside we're all just about the same...well, at least when we start out. I will never know how it is to look like you. You will never know how it is to look like me. But here, our survival requires us sometimes to use what we appear to be on the outside, for the betterment of all. That is what you did today. And for a moment it does separate us. And that may be painful for us both. But it is a short term personal sacrifice that we have to endure for the good of us all. Tomorrow is a new day grandson. Tomorrow we are all the same people again. Like Preacher Jacob said, 'All's well that ends well'. Get a good nights rest Elijah. The sunflowers will be expecting you at their side first thing in the morning. Night grandson."

Tsalgena's words were soothing. And they did make Elijah feel better than he had earlier that afternoon. But the young Scotch Irishman from the ghettoes of coastal Northern Ireland learned yet another lesson as to how the ills of society could adversely affect community, family, relationships, and individuals. It would be the same illness that would eventually drive his adopted brother, Embato, to leave him and their new family. And as they lay in their beds that night neither could speak of the sad reality that was sure to follow the threatening events that occured just hours before. But for the first time they both realized that their paths would have to diverge. The events of that day were only the symptoms of a much bigger human tragedy that was rooted in the evil institution of slavery. But for Embato the threatening events were a call to action. He could no longer allow his presence to place those, whom he had grown to love and respect, in harms way.

AN EPIPHANY

As late summer transitioned into fall on the mainland of Hyde County, temperatures cooled and the daylight hours grew shorter. The harvest period was always busy for Tsalgena's community. And in the first season with their new family it was extremely so for Elijah and Embato. Although their elder patriarch had recovered from his flesh wounds he still walked with a limp and the range of motion in his upper body was significantly diminished from what it had been prior to the rescue on Hatterask. So in addition to their own chores, Elijah and Embato had taken on the bulk of the physical labor that Tsalgena had been responsible for in the past. Nevertheless Tsalgena pitched in where possible and he did show some continuing improvement.

The elder was blessed to have his two new grandsons and thanked the Creator for them. They both worked long and hard but it was clear to Tsalgena that Embato was clearly Elijah's superior when it came to physical strength, endurance and productivity. Yet Embato never acknowledged any comments regarding his own ability. He went out of his way to always include Elijah when discussing their work. He admired his young friend's work ethic and respected his effort in trying to match his output. The two quickly grew closer. The bond that had been forged between them when they were discovered at sea and later during the ordeal of the shipwreck was an inseparable one. They had become brothers.

They had bunked together since their arrival on the mainland. This afforded ample opportunity for long talks every evening......excepting a few evenings when Elijah would mysteriously disappear for an hour or so. But when together the two brothers opened their hearts and talked about their childhood, their families, former friends, and of their homelands. And each night Elijah would try to talk to Embato about his religion. It was inherent in his belief as a Christian that he try to win others over to his Savior, Jesus Christ. But as the conversation reached that point it would only be seconds before he would hear his brother snoring. It was Embato's polite way of ignoring the subject. He did not want to discuss such things because he did not want to disappoint his younger brother but at the same time was very devout in his own spiritual beliefs. He had no intention of capitulating to Elijah on the issue.

But one night Elijah started the discussion on religion earlier than normal as they were heading back to the cabin. Embato finally was cornered. (And Elijah *could* talk. Tsalgena once jokingly told Mary that Elijah could probably talk a wolf off a fresh deer carcass.) So Embato knew that he either had to respond or risk missing supper. Embato listened for anything that he could see as common ground between them in terms of religious belief. And when Elijah finally said something he could relate to and agree on, the African was delighted.

Elijah said "Eeeembato, me thinks the god ye pray to is the same one I pray to. The Great God Almighty made the heavens and the earth. And He made man and woman. So if he is the One that done all that then He's all powerful. And there just can't be but One. Maybe ye jes got his name wrong. But tain't no matter. He still hears ye jes like He hears me and jes like He hears Eliza and all the rest of em."

Embato did not hesitate as he immediately replied "May be Elijah. Embato juz know dat Borombi good, strong. He lead Embato good. Yo god good, strong. Maybe they same. Embato wan food now. Come. We go."

The two walked side by side toward Mary's cabin. They had somehow found enough common ground and mutual respect for each other's beliefs that finally there was a spiritual equilibrium of sorts between them. Elijah was satisfied that his brother loved his Creator and that

315

their Creator was one in the same. He never brought the subject up again. And for Embato that was a welcome relief.

For the first time in years Embato felt fully alive. He was once again an integral part of a caring descent community of people. He worked hard because it was *his choice* to do so. He felt indebted to the people that had taken him in and at their risk. They were deserving of his best efforts. He marveled at the contrast in how he was treated amongst Tsalgena's people when compared to his treatment on the Smith. And yet many of Tsalgena's people appeared to be of the same race as the Smith family. He was not sure that he could make sense of it all but he somehow knew that it was as Borombi had intended. So initially he just accepted it and was thankful for it.

As Embato grew more attached to his new people he began to see clearly that differences in appearance and language were superficial in terms of a man's worth. He saw that these people truly cared for him. None of them looked like him or spoke like him and it simply did not matter. They saw him for the man he really was inside. And that....and only that...is what mattered to them. That simple realization led him to a moment of epiphany.

It was then that Embato began to finally understand why Borombi had led him on such a tumultuous journey. His life lesson was to understand that there were good and bad people in all races and cultures. In a strange way he felt himself begin to let go of some of the vestiges of the pain and suffering he had endured at the hands of the bad tubab. Incredibly it seemed that he was able to even consider forgiving them. He thought that perhaps he would one day even be able to help his brothers in Ayiti experience that same feeling. He was thankful for Borombi's teachings.

Had the laws of the land and the rules of behavior outside their small sliver of America been the same as it was inside, then Embato may never have left Tsalgenas's community. But sadly for him and his people they were not. It would be another thirty three years before the American

Civil War would result in the abolition of legalized slavery. And he knew the time was drawing close for his departure. It was already mid November and there was a chilly nip in the air. It was also the time for harvest ceremony of thanks. And he wanted to remain with his adopted family long enough to be a part of the celebration and thanks to the Creator. And there was one other ceremony that he wanted to be a part of before his departure as well.

THE BONDING CEREMONY

There would be more work later in the preparation for the cold winter moons but in mid fall there was a time set aside for prayer and celebration and a few well deserved days of rest. It was also a time for those who wished to be bonded together (married) to declare their intentions for one another and to do so publicly in ceremony. It was well known in the community that Eliza and Elijah were in love. Therefore, it was of no surprise when Tsalgena proclaimed that Eliza would be bonded to Elijah during the fall harvest ceremony of thanks. But even as a formality it was still a source of pride for an elder to make the announcement. It was only one of many blessings that Tsalgena was thankful for.

He and the community had been blessed with fair weather and a good harvest from the fields, the sea, and the forest. And on the first day of the harvest celebration the entire morning was designated for prayer. It would be followed by an afternoon feast featuring local game and seafood and a colorful array of fresh vegetables. One of the children's favorites, fresh apple cider, would be served along with the traditional winauk (sassafras) tea. The preferred seasonal beverage of the adults however was their persimmon beer. And everyone would indulge in the seasonal sweet fruits, nuts, and Mary's delicious pumpkin pie.

On the first day of the celebration the air was crisp but there was an abundance of bright sunshine. So they agreed to move their tables outside the communal longhouse near a large old oak tree. They wished to be as close to their beloved Mother Earth as possible while bathing in the warmth of Father Sun. The celebration continued under a deep blue sky that was partially obscured by a canopy of tall oonossa (pine trees). Their lower limbs drooped around the tables as if the Creator's arms were surrounding them with His love and protection. The limbs were covered with boughs of pine needles and dotted with brown cones that held the seeds of their perpetuity. A gentle lake breeze parted the arms of the oonossa. The opening was just wide enough to channel in a beam of bright sun that fully illuminated the right side of Tsalgena's long slender body. He was facing South......the direction of healing.

Tsalgena made the tobacco offering acknowledging the Creator and all of His Creation. He spoke a few words of thanks as he held the talking feather, a gift from one of the nearby nesting Bald Eagles. He then passed the dark brown feather with white tip around to everyone allowing each person a chance to speak uninterrupted by others. When the feather came back to him he asked for special blessings for Eliza and Elijah in their union. He then turned toward his other new grandson Embato. His facial expression changed dramatically from one of joy into one of solemnity.

The words came very hard, but tradition obliged him to inform and he forced his tongue. As he spoke the words, even he had no ears for them. But he was still the elder Chief of what remained of his local band. It was his responsibility to make public the content of any decision reached by any council or individual that would impact the community. He had no choice in the matter. Tears welled in his eyes, but in his way the brave elder invoked self discipline and was able to suppress them.......momentarily. But as the first few words were spoken his lower lip betrayed his attempt to hide his emotion. At first it was just a slight vibration that only he was aware of. But as he forced more of the words out it progressed into a quiver. He hesitated. A small single teardrop formed and gently rolled sideways just before falling from his right lower eyelid. It darkened the exposed tip of a dry oak leaf that lay partially under the toe of the elder's black and red beaded moccasin. It wasn't alone very long though. He did his best but his heart was too swollen with sadness. The tears flowed across the weathered brown skin of Tsalgena's face. The experience seemed to give him some emotional relief. And then he remembered.

In an instant his mind's eye relived the entire sequence of events that day on Hatterask Island when they had both saved each others lives. There was a period of silence and then the quiver ceased and the tears slowed. With new resolve he spoke with sincerity.

"Our new beloved grandson....our brother....our friend.... is leaving us when the next sun rises in the east for a place where he will truly be free. It is where Creator wills him to be."

Tsalgena moved closer to Embato and with his left hand began waving his feather fan toward a large clam shell filled with burning cedar and tobacco. The motion of the fan caused the swirling gray smoke to wash first over Embato's head and then his entire body. Tsalgena prayed for protection and safety of Embato and then for strength, wisdom and endurance during his journey. He then invited several elders to come forth and pray over and smudge the young man in the same way. They beseeched the spirits to guide him along a safe and happy path. When they finished there was a moment of silence intended for each individual in the community to make their own prayers for Embato. Tsalgena then broke the silence.

"Aho.....Amen".

He then turned toward the entire group and in a solemn voice said "Those who are travelling with Embato already know who they are and the nature of their responsibilities. Once our relative has left us then his name is not to be spoken aloud except in the whisper of one's own private prayer until grandmother moon grows full and then shrinks again to her current position. And now Embato wishes to speak briefly before you. Please give him your ears and allow his words to seek refuge in your open hearts. After he is finished speaking then everyone will have the opportunity to greet him personally in the People's way. When the last person is finished then we will all smile once again with my grandson and beseech the spirits to join us in the celebration of the union of his sister, Eliza, and his brother, Elijah. When the last words of the bonding ceremony are spoken then we drum and sing and dance our prayers in the sacred circle. We dance to bless and honor the sacred bonding of Eliza and Elijah as one."

Tsalgena then once again acknowledged Creator and continued his prayers. "Creator, we thank you for the old ones and for the saplings and for the moccasin trail in between. Aho…Amen."

Tsalgena took a deep breath and let out an audible sigh as he moved closer to Embato. It was a relief to get the words out. His grandson's impending departure would be a time of both sorrow *and* elation. The community was sad at the obvious loss of a valued and beloved family member. But they were also happy that their loved one would be free and eventually be where he felt that Creator willed him to be. Their approach to loss was exemplary of the way of most indigenous cultures.

Once the impact of a decision or event was absorbed, Tsalgena's people acknowledged the loss but did not dwell in depression. Of course they would still hurt occassionally, but they embraced the reality and celebrated what good there was in it, and moved forward. It was the same cultural ethic practiced in Gambeya on a continent half a world away and by Elijah's ancestors in the lowlands of Scotland. They acknowledged loss, and memorialized it in their ceremonies and rituals. But they quickly moved on and focused on the well being of the community. It was with that traditional principle in mind that Tsalgena acknowledged Embato's departure, but then proceeded with the business of the perpetuity of his people by initiating the bonding ceremony.

After Embato spoke and was greeted by the elders and members of the community, an elder Holy Man, Winga, began preparations for the bonding ceremony. Just before sundown he smudged the entire sacred circle with the smoke of cedar and tobacco. He then created a smaller circle inside the sacred circle, near the East Gate, by laying down some fresh cut pine boughs and white sand from Hatterask. Eliza and Elijah were then smudged individually and then together. Winga prayed in a low voice beseeching Creator and the spirits on behalf of the couple. He humbly asked for their protection and the resources necessary to sustain their lives. And finally he beseeched Creator to direct the spirits of fertility to bless them with many beautiful healthy children.

When Winga finished the beseechment he draped a blanket around Eliza and Elijah as they knelt in the small circle. He also bound Elijah's right hand to Eliza's left and gave them a large purple and white clam shell filled with a few spoonfuls of water from the Pamptico to drink together. Finally he pulled the blanket over their bodies covering the entire area of the small circle. They were told to take a moment to exchange their vows in privacy and say to each other whatever their hearts were holding inside. When they finished their vows they stood and faced the East. Then they removed the blanket and assisted each other in untying the hemp from their hands. Elijah then took a ballast stone and crushed the clam shell. At that point Winga turned toward those gathered near the sacred circle and announced that Elijah and Eliza were bonded as one under the love and protection of Creator. As they approached the opening at the East Gate they turned and acknowledged spirit in the West and then kissed. They were one.

Tsalgena, Mary, Embato and the elders lined up to offer their well wishes followed by the other community members. The drummers played and sang and those in regalia danced their prayers in the sacred circle. The feasting and celebration went into the early evening as Father Sun slipped behind the thick pine forest that surrounded their swampy homeland. The fire burned bright and hot, still taming the chilly evening air even as the crowd dwindled. Tsalgena motioned to Winga and several of the men to follow him into the communal longhouse where Embato and Elijah awaited them. Tsalgena gave Elijah a look of disapproval and motioned for him to leave addressing him in a stern tone.

"Go now to Eliza. She will be expecting you. You agreed to abide by our customs and......."

Before he could say more Winga interrupted and asked Tsalgena to speak with him privately in the corner of the room. "Tsalgena, I have spoken to Elijah, Eliza and Embato and have blessed this change in our custom due to the very special circumstance of Embato's departure. You must know of course my friend that I consulted the clan mother and women's council after prayer to Creator for guidance on this before making such a decision. Please believe me Tsalgena, it is the right one. Eliza and Elijah will be separated for tonight so that your two grandsons can spend their last night together. As you know they have a very special brotherhood. You of all people should understand. They both saved each others lives. Yes, Tsalgena, this is a departure from our tradition. But it *is* what Creator has willed. You must trust your old friend Winga."

He placed his large right hand on Tsalgena's left shoulder and with a disarming smile said "You will understand by the time you close your eyes for sleep tonight. Please trust me my friend. All will be well. Aho!"

Tsalgena grumbled a few disapproving words under his breath but then proceeded with the meeting. He methodically laid out the full plan one final time in detail. Embato, Elijah, and Tsalgena would leave an hour before sunrise on foot. They would quietly make their way along the trails through the swamps of Northeastern Hyde County around Swan Lake and to the headwaters of the Alligator River. They would meet Andrew at a hidden point where he would be waiting with the boat. At sunrise they would begin to sail north up the Alligator River and across the Albemarle Sound and camp overnight near the mouth of the Pasquotank River. On the second morning they would continue up the Pasquotank and put in as it narrowed before reaching the Dismal Swamp Canal. There they would camp for the night but Andrew would sail back to Hyde County and return to meet them at the same location in four days. On the third day out they would once again follow the trails on foot through the swamps of Northeastern North Carolina and into Southeastern Virginia. They would rendezvous with a wagon about 20 miles south of the port of Norfolk, Virginia. The driver was a local Methodist minister and a secret member of the Underground Railroad.

Reverend Jacob Reynolds had been a friend of Tsalgena's community for some time. Jacob would take the three into the port where the Atlantic Ocean and the Chesapeake Bay meet near Norfolk Harbor. That is where a ship would be docked that would be outbound for Port Au Prince, Ayiti, Embato's destination. Once the ship would be docked in Ayiti and under anchor, it would be considered on Ayiti soil and thus subject to the laws of that country. Embato could essentially walk off the ship unimpeded as slavery there was strictly prohibited. The ship's captain and crew could do nothing for fear of retribution from the locals.

It was a well thought out plan and if carried out with caution and care would be one of moderate risk at least until they would reach the port of Norfolk. And fortunately Jacob Reynolds in addition to being a devout Christian and a deeply spiritual man could be very devious when it came to creative plans of escape and deception. He also had a network of friends that were as devout to the abolitionist cause as he was and they were eager to assist. Some of them lived near Norfolk and agreed to serve as lookouts at various points in the journey. Others would create a distraction near the ship if need be.

Jake also had members of his church who, while considering themselves Christian, somehow still justified there positions as slaveholders. He was adept at manipulating their guilt into help for his church. From time to time he borrowed the services of a slave to assist him in deliveries or to accompany him on trips. To assist in Embato's escape he had secured the services of Felix Gibbs a local field slave on the Gibbs Plantation.

The plan was to have Embato wait under cover in the bottom of a large box on the wagon while Tsalgena stood watch. Felix and Jacob were to load the first several cargo items from Jacob's wagon onto the ship. The last box had a false bottom that was large enough for a man to lie down in. It was also stocked with rations of food and water for about 7-10 days and with a change of clothes. It was to be the last box loaded by Felix and because of its weight would require Jacob's and Tsalgena's assistance. Embato would be hidden in the bottom of the box. He would be safe aboard ship in the large box which would be stored in the back of the hold and out of sight of the crew for the entire voyage. It was a scheme of genius, but like all successful slave runs, was in need of a bit of divine intervention to insure its successful execution.

So before he ended the meeting in the longhouse that night Tsalgena asked Winga to perform one final smudging for all present and to beseech Creator and the spirits for protection during their journey. Tsalgena concluded by admonishing everyone to say nothing about the plan. Although he trusted his community he thought it best that only those involved know the details. He didn't want to place anyone in a position to have to lie to local authorities in order to protect themselves and community. He established direct eye contact with everyone as he repeated the basic expectations of each person. But there was one set of eyes and ears that he was unaware of. And they had seen and heard everything from *outside* the room.

FAREWELL

Before turning in for the evening Elijah and Embato sat under the moonlit sky and shared some personal experiences with each other that they had kept to themselves until that moment. During the conversation Elijah learned why the North Star had been so important to Embato. They agreed they would occassionally look at it with memories of each other in the future just as Embato had done with Briami. Elijah gave his brother and best friend a small oak wood carving of a Bald Eagle that he had been working on since they had been on the mainland.

He said, "It ain't much but its small enough that ye can take it with ye in yer pocket. I made it small of a purpose cause I knew..........I knew that one day ye'd have to go and ye might have to stay in a hogshead or sumpum agin and ye wouldn't a had no room for nothit big."

They both laughed. It was easier than crying. They could stop laughing. But they would have had a lot more trouble stopping the tears.

Embato pulled a wooden cross from his pocket and put it in his little brother's hand.

"Elijah. Dis fo you. A preacha man give to me when Embato slave fo da Smith. Me understand now bout his god. Jeezus good. He yo god to. You keep. It help you remember Embato."

"Thank ye Eeembato. Yer a good man. I'm sure n hell goin miss ye round here. I love me new wife and I thank me God Almighty and Jesus fer her and me family but thars gonna be a empty hole here fer a long time after the morn. Well I guess we had better git at least a few hours of shut eye. We got ourselves quite a journey ahead a us."

"Yes Elijah. Good night."

Neither of the young men slept well. They were full of both excitement and trepidation about their journey and the risks surrounding it. They tossed and turned throughout the night and it seemed like only an hour or two when they heard Tsalgena walking toward their sleeping quarters. By the time he opened their door and whispered to them they were already out of bed and half dressed. In another minute or two they were out of the cabin and heading toward the trails. But Tsalgena checked with them to make sure they had all their essential items for the trip before they reached the edge of the woods. With a very solemn tone of voice he admonished them both.

"There is to be no foolin around on the trails. Keep quiet. No talk til we get into the deep waters in the middle of the Alligator. Watch your stepping."

The message was understood. The reality of the risk to all of them had settled in on both of the young men. The sun had been up only for about an hour when they reached the point where Andrew was waiting with the boat near the headwaters of the Alligator River. They made sure that they were all covered including their faces as they climbed aboard their boat, the *Viola*, which was hidden well in a small tributary. Tsalgena advised Embato to lay low until they got away from the mainland and into the Albemarle Sound. As long as no other vessels approached too closely then it would be safe for him to sit up once they were in open water. He did not have to hide for very long however. The winds were with them and by early afternoon they were well into the Albemarle and sailing rapidly in a due North direction.

Under an increasingly cloudy sky Andrew turned northwest into the mouth of the Pasquotank River as a sliver of afternoon sun peaked through the pines to their west. They continued under sail a few more miles up the Pasquotank and put in where they camped for the night. The next morning they were under sail once again by sunrise, but their progress was slowed by a headwind out of the northeast. The stiff breeze required them to tack back and forth across the Pasquotank for most of the day. To make matters worse the winds died completely just before reaching the bustling port town of Elizabeth City, North Carolina. At that point Elijah and Andrew paddled against the current until they were near exhaustion. Tsalgena and Embato relieved them just before sunset as they neared the drop off point near the Great Dismal Swamp Canal. Andrew kept an eye forward off the bow and Elijah watched aft from the stern in case any other vessels approached while Embato was paddling in full view. Thankfully they reached their drop off point without incident however. They maneuvered the *Viola* into a marsh where they could not be seen from the busy confluence of the river and canal.

Even though it was dark Andrew shoved off into the cool murky headwaters of the Pasquotank. He could not stay with them overnight because even in a remote area the boat might still draw attention if someone happened by. He looked Embato in the eye and gave him a wink and a nod as he drifted slowly back out into the current to head south. He had already spoken to Elijah to confirm their original plans to meet Tsalgena and Elijah back at the same location in 4 days. So Andrew simply drifted down stream a few hundred yards and dropped anchor in a small creek and slept in the *Viola* overnight.

Elijah questioned Tsalgena as to why they had not continued up the canal since it was faster than travelling on foot. Over a small warm campfire Tsalgena explained. He spoke quietly to his grandsons about the history and significance of the Great Dismal Swamp Canal. He said that they would stay close to the canal while on foot during the next stage of their journey in the morning. But they would have to stay out of sight of the canal as it was a well travelled waterway and full of Planter folks.

The Dismal Swamp Canal opened in 1805 connecting the rivers and sounds of northeastern North Carolina directly to the port of Norfolk. It was a shorter route than the poor roads the regional planters and lumber mills used before. The canal was particularly busy in late Fall as suppliers were trying to get as much shipped as possible before the threat of freezing over and shutdown. And with lots of traffic came lots of people. And they would pass much closer to each other than when out in the open waters of a sound or river. So avoiding the canal was clearly in the best interest of anyone attempting to hide a runaway slave.

They understood Tsalgena's explanation and were once again in awe of the elder's wisdom. They finished their meal, prayed together, and then turned in as they would be heading out at sunrise on foot over difficult swampy terrain and likely at a brisk pace. Their plan was to meet Preacher Jacob about sundown the following evening just across the state border in Virginia.

It was a grueling hike through the swamp and dense brush but Tsalgena led the entire way. He still walked with a slight limp from his earlier injury but he maintained a blistering pace. He was on a mission of righteousness and its success depended upon stealth *and* precise timing. He would not rest easy until Embato was safely on board the ship that would finally deliver him to real freedom.

They had actually progressed according to plan in the early part of the day but had to alter their route twice in the afternoon due to unexpected over wash of the trail. The changes put them behind schedule and Tsalgena said that they would have to increase their pace. He had not accounted for the recent heavy rains when he originally estimated the time it would take to reach the road where Jacob would be waiting in Virginia. It was imperative that both groups converged at the meeting spot within minutes of each other.

Any increased exposure for Jacob and Felix could have easily placed all of them in greater jeopardy. Even though Felix had a pass for North Carolina, he would be in Virginia. Virginians may be reluctant to take the word of a preacher they did not know. And suspicion of slaves as runaways was heightened when near a seaport like Norfolk. It was well known that if a runaway could successfully stowaway on a ship their chances of reaching freedom safely were dramatically better than attempting to run over ground. The travel time was usually shorter and certainly the exposure to risk (once safely hidden aboard ship) was significantly diminished. Thus the closer they got to Norfolk the more important it was for all to be at the agreed upon location at the same time thus limiting their exposure.

So at sunrise the next day the group turned in a northeasterly direction toward the meeting point and Tsalgena actually broke into a trot. Elijah and Embato looked at each other with concern for him. He was strong and in good health for his age but Tsalgena was asking his body to do something it was no longer conditioned for. But he had no choice. The failure to anticipate changes in conditions along the trail was his mistake. It had cost them time and possibly unnecessary risk. Increasing the pace was the only available corrective action at that point. He would have to accept the added stress to his body and beseech the spirits for extraordinary help.

In only minutes the Elder's breathing became labored and soon it was accompanied by a wheezing sound every time he exhaled. But he gave no credence to Embato's plea for him to slow down. When Embato faked being exhausted with loud breathing it only angered Tsalgena and he sternly told Elijah and Embato to stay quiet and keep moving. Embato grew more concerned and at one point thought of just giving up the journey and returning to Hyde County. But he respected his grandfather's strong will and approach to personal accountability. He knew that Tsalgena would not agree to turn back even if it killed him. Embato prayed for Borombi's help for all three of them.

The spirits were with them and just before sundown they reached their destination. They all fell down on the dry grasses adjacent the road gasping desperately to catch their breath. After they rested for a few minutes Embato and Elijah looked at each other and began to smile. In another couple of minutes Tsalgena looked up and caught their gaze. He began to smile as well.

Elijah gasped and with a grin said "GrandPa Tsalgena. First thing was.... I was afeared that ye would pass over back yonder on the trail."

Pausing to catch his breath he continued. "But then after awhile I commenced to breathin so hard me self that.......I was more afeared that it twould be me instead a ye. Jes for a minute I could a swore I hearn them swamp demons a singin fer me......but then I figured out later that twas only them screechin Red Wing Blackbirds."

They all fell once again flat on their backs but this time with uncontrollable laughter. It was a welcome moment of relief from the stress they had just endured. For the first time since they left Hyde County they felt very confident that they were actually going to successfully execute their plan. Embato's reality of freedom was closer than ever but first they had to connect with Jacob and Felix.

With no sign of the wagon they laid low in the brush adjacent the road and waited. Within only a few minutes however they heard the creaking sounds of wagon wheels and the heavy breathing of a mare. They stayed perfectly quiet and then they heard the sweet and welcome sound of Reverend Jacob Reynolds voice.

"Whoa up deh. Anybody about heah?"

Tsalgena knew Jacob's voice well but waited for a second call from the pastor before answering. He then peeped around the edge of a pine sapling and looked to make sure it was only Felix and Jacob. He was relieved to first see Felix and then the familiar wide brim black hat with rounded top that Jacob never left home without.

"Yep Jacob. We're coming."

Elijah and Embato scurried toward the wagon and were about to hop into the back when Jacob stopped them. "Hold on a minute fellers. Uh... Tsalgena I think there's something I should tell you before you climb on board my wagon. There's a problem."

Tsalgena sighed along with Embato and Elijah and in a bit of an irritated voice said "Well, what is it Preacher?"

"Well Tsalgena. I didn't find out about this til yesterday evening when we stopped to spend the night about forty miles back.....and it was too late to turn back. She just....well she hid herself and......"

His words were suddenly interrupted by a muffled voice from beneath the wagon cover in the back. As the cover slowly peeled back, the silhouette of a petite female appeared. Even in the low light of dusk Tsalgena's old eyes recognized the figure instantly.

"I'm sorry grandfather but I had to come see Embato off and I wanted to be with Elijah.......Uh...and you of course. Please don't be angry. You know that I can stay up with you on the swamp trails and....."

Elijah squeezed her hand and shook his head indicating she had said enough. Eliza then smiled sheepishly at her grandfather. Inside his heart melted but he could not allow her to see his true feelings. He frowned at her at first and then growled. He turned away from the group and began to curse under his breath but loud enough that Elijah and Embato understood him and then they began to giggle. And then Felix turned to look at them and he joined in. After a moment even

Reverend Jacob lost control and began to laugh as well. But as Tsalgena turned back in their direction they forced themselves to regain composure. They understood how soft his heart was for his precious little Eliza but they also understood his expectation of respect for his elder status.

He climbed up on the wagon seat and said "Allright. Let's get going. There's nothing we can do now."

He motioned for Felix to get in the back with the others and told them all to stay hidden under the cover in between the cargo boxes. He used a stern voice but when he turned back in Jacob's direction he smiled. Jacob smiled back. He knew Tsalgena well. Tsalgena understood why Eliza did what she did. He was surprised that she had not approached him at the Celebration of Thanks and argued to accompany them then. He counted himself fortunate back then but obviously prematurely. He silently thanked the Creator for delivering them safely to their final stage in their journey to Norfolk Harbor.

SAFE HARBOR... IN NORFOLK

Jacob and Tsalgena shared the reigns of the wagon during their overnight travel so each could rest a bit. Their progress was slowed by the darkness but they reached Norfolk two hours before sunrise. They continued through the main street area where many of the businesses were located and then turned toward the docks. But instead of stopping near the ship, Jacob turned down a side street and stopped behind a small dry goods store about a block and a half from the dock. Jacob explained that the owner and his wife lived in three rooms above their store on the third floor where they had an unobstructed view of Embato's ship from their front window.

Jacob asked everyone to remain quiet and stay in the wagon until he could assure the store owners that all was well. He saw a light in the window and knew they would come. They were expecting him and heard the wagon as it pulled up. A short stout man dressed in a white long sleeve cuffed shirt and black pants opened the front door and allowed him to come in. After a moment Jacob came out and told everyone to quietly and quickly enter the store but to not speak yet. Jacob politely introduced everyone but initially only with first names. Irving and Sarah relocated to Norfolk from the Northeast about twelve years earlier and had owned the store for the same period.

Tsalgena's group was offered hot tea and sweet cakes which they enjoyed, except for Embato, who was too nervous to eat. He had less than an hour before he would once again crawl into a very tight space aboard yet another ship for freedom. And like before, he would have good caring people assisting him at their own risk. As much as he hated to leave his adopted family he wanted to get safely aboard the ship as soon as possible. He knew that once his box was secured in the hold of that ship, that he was all but free, and that his family would no longer be in danger because of him. He and his ship would soon be bound for the newly formed country of Ayiti where the reality of freedom awaited him.

Irving, Tsalgena, Embato, Jacob and Felix went into the bedroom to meet privately to go over the final details. Jacob spelled out exactly how the box was to be carried on board. Felix would be at one end and Tsalgena and Jacob on the other. They also discussed contingency plans in case they were caught. If so then Jacob would take full responsibility, claiming that neither Tsalgena nor Felix knew the contents of the box. And Elijah and Eliza would remain in Irving and Sarah's home until either Tsalgena or Jacob returned for them. If neither were free to do so then Irving would keep them properly hidden until arrangements could be made to get them safely back home. They were about to leave for the ship when the bedroom door opened.

Elijah stood in the doorway and stared silently at his grandfather. But Tsalgena had expected the intrusion. Before Elijah could speak Tsalgena stood and quickly addressed him. He explained why Elijah was not allowed to accompany them aboard ship to help load the box. Irving had informed Tsalgena and Jacob earlier that news of the shipwreck off Hatterask Island had reached the Norfolk docks. And though it had been months ago, there were some folks that believed that the cabin boy/sailor may have survived. His was the only body not accounted for since Embato's presence aboard as a stoway was unknown. And since he was a brand new crew member the shadow of suspicion surrounded him. News had also reached Norfolk that a runaway slave was in the Charleston area the same day the ship departed for the Northeast. Some saw it as coincidence but others had not. Thus it was best for Elijah to lay low and out of sight.

Tsalgena put his arm around Elijah and said "Remember now Elijah. You are no longer responsible just for yourself. You are the protector of Eliza. She must now come first in your life."

Elijah nodded and turned to walk back into the front room. Although disappointed he understood. And Tsalgena's words *were* helpful. The wise elder had framed his argument with a sense of responsibility and commensurate respect for Elijah. Elijah took pride in being Eliza's husband and looked forward to when he would be the father of their children. But at that moment he had to prepare himself to be strong as he said his final goodbye to the brother whose life Elijah had played a pivotal role in rescuing from slavery; the one who had courageously returned the favor in saving Elijah's life and the life of Tsalgena. He kept telling himself that it was a time for happiness. Embato would be free. His brother would finally be treated like any other human being instead of like chattel or a beast of burden. After a few moments he began to understand the real impact of those thoughts. He decided that even though Embato's departure was a loss to him that it *was* indeed a time for happiness for his brother, and that he *would* be strong.

Embato was the last to emerge from the bedroom. He stood proudly and faced each person individually. He thanked Irving and Sarah for their help and for protecting his brother and sister. He thanked Jacob and

Felix and then shook Tsalgena's hand for the last time. They embraced and looked each other in the eye for several seconds and smiled. Embato turned to his little sister whom he loved just as the one he had left behind in Gambeya. They hugged tightly and Eliza began to cry. She felt honored as he lovingly wiped away some of her tears on his shirt sleeve. He then turned to his brother.

"Embato thank Borombi fo family. But much fo Elijah. You save Embato. You give life fo Embato. Embato love Elijah. My broda. You no foget star. Embato go now. Soon Embato free."

They shook hands and hugged each other, but neither shed a tear. They summoned the strength to put their own emotions aside for each other. It was no different than it had ever been between them. They had depended upon each other ever since their meeting aboard that ill fated ship in the Gulf Stream. But it was finally time for them both to go their own way. The peculiar institution of slavery had predetermined the ultimate outcome of their encounter even before they met, resulting in the sorrowful ending of their relationship. They were living proof that even the strongest of human bonds were still subject to the destructive forces of an insensitive dominant society and of the hypocritical laws of their government.

Tsalgena, Felix, and Embato followed Jacob down the steps to the front door. Jacob cracked the door open and peaked up and then down the street. He stepped out and looked around thoroughly in all directions once again. Satisfied of no threat he motioned for the rest to come out. He quickly jumped into the wagon and opened the box, removed the cover to the false bottom, and assisted Embato inside it. Just before Embato tucked his head inside he looked up to the front window and saw Elijah and Eliza gazing down. Their eyes met his and he waved goodbye one last time. With a heart full of hope he prayed that the next pair of eyes he saw would be those of an African dock worker in Port Au Prince, Ayiti.

BACK HOME... IN HYDE COUNTY

The plan to place Embato securely on the ship bound for Ayiti was carried out flawlessly. Everyone accepted their risk and considered their participation an honor in helping Embato. Jacob, Felix and Tsalgena joined the others back at Irving and Sarah's home above the store for hot tea and biscuits. Jacob offered a prayer in thanks for a successful beginning to Embato's journey to freedom and for their safe return to Hyde County. It was a time of mixed emotions for Eliza, Elijah and Tsalgena. They were hopeful for their loved one's freedom but also saddened by his absence. Eliza and Elijah began to speak of their loss but Tsalgena abruptly cut the conversation off. He explained that their presence at Irving and Sarah's home was a possible source of trouble should they be seen. He thanked them for their hospitality and help and motioned for everyone to leave.

On the way out Elijah noticed a small ceramic item attached to their door frame. Realizing what it was, he turned toward them and smiled. They looked up at the sacred object and then smiled at each other and nodded in agreement. They both looked into Elijah's eyes and grinned.

Irving laughed and said "By the way young Elijah. The Bermans of Philadelphia send you their well wishes. Sol is my brother."

He pointed to the sign above the front door of the store. It read "Berman's Dry Goods". Elijah was a bit shocked but very happy to have encountered a relative of his friends. He found it gratifying that the Bermans knew their efforts were not in vain and that he had fulfilled his agreement with them. It made him proud. He slowly turned and in a very confident voice bid them farewell.

Irving said "And mazel tov to you Eliza and to you Elijah on your marriage."

"Well thank ye Mr. Berman. Ye both have ye selves a good Sabbath tonight."

The group then crawled into the wagon and Jacob once again led a short prayer invoking the name of Jesus Christ, his spiritual savior. He turned to Felix and offered a special prayer for him, that one day he to would find freedom. He looked at Tsalgena and sighed.

"Well old friend. All's well that ends well. We did it with the help of God and Jesus.........and uh..... the help of the spirits."

Tsalgena smiled and then yawned long and loud. He was very tired but satisfied with the fruits of their efforts. He looked over his shoulder to check on his two newly weds but Eliza and Elijah were nestled in each others arms and already under the wagon cover. He smiled and leaned back in the seat and said his own prayer of thanks to Creator.

"Hieyah! Giddiup deah!"

Jacob gave the command accompanied by a gentle slap on the mare's buttocks with the whip and they were off. They made good time and reached the drop off point for Tsalgena, Eliza and Elijah about mid morning of the following day. It was much further south than the original pick up location had been. The new location was in northeastern North Carolina and only a two hour walk to the meeting point with Andrew. It was no surprise to anyone when they reached the headwaters of the Pasquotank River at noon and saw Andrew waiting for them there. He was as dependable as anyone Tsalgena had ever known. Tsalgena nodded to Andrew and he understood that all went well. The two weren't much for words with each other. They just sort of had an understanding about things that required little conversation.

They shoved off and sailed down river until sundown when they pulled up to shore and camped overnight on the western banks of the Pasquotank estuary. They were so exhausted from the stress of the last several days that they were fast asleep before Andrew could even cook his clam stew.

The next morning greeted them with a stiff breeze from the northeast and they were well on their way at sunrise. Instead of backtracking due South across the Albemarle Sound and down the Alligator River, Tsalgena directed Andrew to head East toward the Outer Banks. As they approached Roanoke Island, Andrew turned right and headed due south into the Croatan Sound. Tsalgena pointed out several locations along their route but seemed most interested in the towns of Manteo and Wanchese which appeared to their East. He said they were named after two important coastal Algonquin speaking Natives that were some of the first to interact with the Europeans. Soon after however a light rain began to fall so they sought shelter in the marsh banks where they slept in the boat overnight. The *Viola's* sails provided cover from a light but steady, chilly mist.

The next morning the clouds had moved off to the east and the group sailed into the northwestern waters of the Pamptico Sound at sunrise. Elijah and Eliza were mesmerized by the white sand dunes set against the deep blue horizon along the northern Outer Banks. By noon they disappeared from view as the Viola was approaching the widest portion of the Pamptico Sound. Off in the distance to their East they could still see a long stretch of white sandy beaches. It was their summer home, Hatterask Island. Eliza asked to stop but Tsalgena held his ground and directed Andrew to a heading of west/southwest towards mainland Hyde County. So Eliza and Elijah satisfied themselves with only a sighting of their magical place until it disappeared from view.

Instead of dropping everyone in the Long Shoal River cove Tsalgena altered their course again. Tsalgena told Andrew to take them up into Wysockan (Wysocking) Bay as close to the ancient shell mound as possible. This surprised Eliza as the new drop off point placed them a full day's walk back to their home. But without hesitation Andrew followed his old friend's command. Once they entered the calmer waters of Wysockan Bay, they lowered the sail, then he and Tsalgena paddled the vessel through the marsh grass. At first the grass appeared too high to pass through. But Tsalgena knew better. They were at peak high tide which provided just enough depth for the *Viola* to glide further into the marsh than even Andrew thought. And the mound was visible from the point at which they stepped onto solid land.

The shell mounds along coastal North Carolina were created by Native Americans. They were the result of the accumulation of discarded shells which had once been the protective home for clams and oysters. Since shellfish was a dependable source of high quality protein food for the Natives, each successive generation became more proficient at harvesting them. So over a span of many generations the volume of consumption was considerable, hence the prominent mounds. And the shell mound located at what the locals called Mount Pleasant was an especially sacred place for Tsalgena.

As a young boy he spent time at the site with his grandfather where they harvested and consumed the tasty shellfish. Because of the ease and steady quantities of harvest his people viewed these fruits of the sea as a special gift from Creator. This was in stark contrast to the amount of effort required to produce land based food crops. The Native perspective viewed this as Creator expressing special love for His people. And Tsalgena wanted to make sure that this understanding would be passed on to future generations. And that could happen only if Eliza and Elijah understood the ancestral and spiritual relevance of the shell mound.

Just before sundown the three prayed together and then dug for clams and mussels. They may have had better luck digging in the early morning but the essence and symbolism of the experience was of greater importance to Tsalgena than the harvest itself. They offered some of their meal to the spirits and specifically acknowledged Tsalgena's parents and grandparents as they tossed the shells onto the mound. He felt relieved once he had imparted his mound widom to Elijah and Eliza. And afterward the three fell asleep at the edge of the mound. The warmth it had stored from Father Sun during the day was a comfort to them and viewed as yet another special gift from Creator.

The next morning they awoke to the shrieks of the numerous gulls that seemed to be claiming the mound as their home. But curiously they hovered above it as if waiting politely for the three visitors to awake and leave. After their morning prayers and tobacco offering, Tsalgena and Elijah dug for clams while Eliza prepared the fire. After breakfast they headed on foot in a north-northeast direction for home. As they walked away from the mound Elijah turned back for one last look. The gulls had already covered the mound's surface. Their continuous shrieking reminded him of his childhood in Northern Ireland. He was satisfied that his grandma would have liked Tsalgena and Eliza, and would have approved of his membership in their family. The mound had become special to Elijah already. Tsalgena and the spirits, including Elijah's grandma, had worked their magic.

In order to reach their Swan Lake village they would have to cover about fourteen to seventeen miles. They rested just on the eastern most point of Lake Mattamuskeet and a drink of cool fresh water renewed their energy. The remainder of their route home would include the fields of several plantations. In one of the fields they saw an African man turning the soil with a mule and plough.

Tsalgena had planned to rest and pay respects to the spirit of the revered Chief Wingina in the woods near the secret burial grounds. But it was forbidden to reveal the location….. even to an African slave. Only a handful of elders knew the exact location of the sacred grounds of Wingina's final resting place. There was a legitimate concern that if found by outsiders it would be plundered for jewelry and trinkets. So he thought it best to keep moving and draw as little attention as possible. All three waved politely to the slave as they passed near him.

But instead of a casual acknowledgement, the slave dropped the reigns of the mule and started waving frantically with one arm and pointing towards a barn off in the distance with the other. He sprinted toward them. Clearly he was trying to warn them of something. Tsalgena had crossed the fields of the Mason plantation on several occassons before without incident and had assumed it to be safe passage. Nevertheless he quickly scanned the horizon for anything out of the ordinary. Near the barn he saw two well dressed white men standing next to a third in overalls. He quickly redirected Eliza and Elijah toward the tree line just in case there was trouble. He looked back in the direction of the three men and observed them moving toward him at a fast pace. Just at that moment he began to understand some of what the field slave was trying to say.

"Missa Tsalgena…..you needs to git outa heah. Massa Jennette is da new massa now. Massa Mason gone. He sold da plantation suh…and theah Massa jennette standin….right ova deah by dat barn. He say ifn any da field slaves see ya, ta come n git him raight now! Run mista Tsalgena! He want dat lil girl!

When Tsalgena heard the name "Jennette" he understood immediately why his friend reacted the way he did. Had he known Jennette owned the Mason Plantation he would have certainly avoided it. He assumed that Jennette was still angry over the incident in town after Deputy Spencer intervened and embarrassed him.

Just before Tsalgena turned to run into the woods for cover he saw the flash and a split second later heard the crack of the long gun. The projectile whizzed by him and splintered a chunk of bark off a pine only a few feet away. He yelled to Elijah and told him to take Eliza and crouch low to the ground and run into the pine woods. Elijah gripped Eliza's hand in his and never looked back. He just kept moving forward and deeper into the pines as possible. After several minutes of no gunfire they stopped. Tsalgena was a few paces behind.

"We must keep moving. The three of them won't come this deep into the pines by themselves but they will gather others and surround the tree line waiting for us to come out. There is an old trail about another half mile to our East that we can use. It will lead us back to the edge of our village. But the road is very near where we pick it up and we must get past that point before they arrive."

Tsalgena stepped his pace up and continued, "We will be safe as long as we don't stop anymore. They won't follow us into the Swan Lake swamps. Jennette only shot at us because he was within his legal rights to do it. According to the law we were trespassing. We crossed onto his property without his permission. Had I known that Jennette bought the Mason we would never have taken that route."

"Mr. Mason was a fair man….not like Jennette. He even spoke to me once or twice when I cut through his tobacco fields. I've known Will, the field slave, since he was a boy. We must pray and ask the spirits and Creator to watch over him. If Jennette saw him warn us he will get a beating. Eliza, you have to walk faster. Elijah, go in front of her. Your steps will help crush the briars for her. They don't know about the trail but they *will* be on the road soon."

In another few minutes they reached the old hidden trail and soon passed the point where it comes closest to the road. They were once again on their way toward home without having been detected. But Tsalgena continued pressing their pace as they still had about four miles to go and with less than two hours of sunlight remaining. They made good time however and were in view of Swan Lake about a half hour before sunset.

HOME

When they neared the edge of the community Tsalgena stopped and offered a pinch of tobacco and a prayer of thanks for their safe return. Continuing his prayer he turned toward Eliza and Elijah and smudged them both with the swirling smoke of burning dry cedar and tobacco. When finished he gently placed the smudge shell on the ground while it was still smoldering and began speaking to them. He assured them that jennette was afraid to pursuit them into their Swan lake village and that they were safe. He thanked them both for their devotion to the community and for their assistance in the effort to free their brother. He knew that they both were still melancholy about losing their brother's friendship. But he knew that *Elijah* would suffer in a more profound way than Eliza. So he addressed him directly.

"Elijah, you are a good man. You will be a good protector and provider to Eliza and a good father to my great grandchildren. You are also a good brother. Your love for your brother is completely normal because of the unusual circumstance in which your lives crossed.

When you met him you were alone in life. And Creator brought you and him together for your healing and growth as men. You were asked to do something very important. And you chose righteousness when you placed your self at risk in order to help a man that you did not even know. Your brother recognized the value of that courage and returned the favor in saving your life. That kind of unselfishness in both of you is the part of a man's soul that is divine. When the purity that dwells deep in a man emerges in him, it changes him. He has a stronger connection to his Creator in everyday life. He is able to love and be loved with greater depth and passion than before. He is able to forgive and forget his encounter with pain and in so doing he is healed and grows strong. Elijah you *and* your brother are both on that path of healing now. Yes grandson, we will all miss him and he will miss us. But it is the right path for you both. It is the path of hope."

Tsalgena paused and kissed Eliza and said "Good night grandchildren. Go and rest tonight. You must both be very tired."

He smiled as he walked toward his cabin. It had been sixty three winters ago but he still remembered the first night after the bonding ceremony with his Mattamuskeet wife. And in a moment of clarity based in realism he didn't expect there to be much sleep for Eliza and Elijah on their first night alone as man and wife. But that was the way Creator had intended it. And besides…he wished to see his first great grandchild sooner rather than later.

The young couple pondered his words for a moment as they watched him disappear into the twilight of early evening. The message seemed to balance Elijah's emotions and he felt happier. They then strolled past the communal longhouse and headed in the direction of their cabin. As they walked through the stand of tall pines they gazed through an opening and into a night sky that sparkled with thousands of stars. They both saw it at the same time. It was the brightest star in the heavens. In honor of their brother, whose name was not spoken, they paused and remembered him with a prayer and hoped for the best for him.

And only hours earlier and an ocean away, a beautiful young Gambeyan woman was gazing at the same star in the West African night sky. She was unable to sleep that evening. She decided to step outside her hut for a breath of cool night air and instantly identified the North Star just above her. It had been years since she had seen the love of her life........ except occasionally in the eyes and smile of her handsome young son. She had remarried and moved on with their lives in the Gambeyan custom. Still, however, she hoped for the best for the father of her son, and she to offered a prayer for Embato.

Suddenly Eliza and Elijah realized they were alone for the first time since their bonding ceremony. It was their first opportunity for privacy in several days. A sheepish grin spread across Elijah's face as he pulled his bride's petite body closer to his. Their lips met in a long passionate kiss. As they walked hand in hand toward their cabin, he realized that he was truly blessed and expressed his thanks to Jesus and his Great God Almighty above. But his prayer was shorter than usual. They entered the cabin and although both were tired and in need of rest........... they didn't go to sleep right away.

The brave young woman with indigenous roots to Hatterask and the courageous young man with ancestral ties to the Scottish Lowlands were deeply in love. And their bodies welcomed the warmth of each other on that chilly late fall evening. She held his hand in hers for a moment. Then she slowly positioned it on her abdomen. He smiled. And then his eyes opened wide as he felt the first flutter. It was followed only seconds later by a rapid and more forceful movement. He stared inquisitively into her dark brown eyes and she smiled back. And then she acknowledged his unspoken question with an affirmative nod of the head followed by a giggle. He instantly reflected on the last several months of his life while focusing on the few opportunities of intimacy they had somehow created together. He was thankful for each one......but even more so for the outcome. Their physical union had simply been a natural expression of the intense love they shared since that very first moment of eye contact on Hatterask Island. And the blessing of that union, months later, would be a beautiful baby girl named Kellister.

Eliza thought back on the unusual manner in which the two young lovers were brought together. A Hatterask Island shipwreck was the last thing she would have wanted. But in hindsight she understood the divine nature of the event and saw how Creator had answered her prayers. She had prayed for a good man to come into her life and for one who would be deserving of her and her family. She hoped for a man that would love and honor the Creator and His natural Creation; a tough man of inner strength but also one with humility and kindness. And she had asked for a man that could provide the seed that would bless her with many healthy children.

Elijah had hoped for many of the same qualities in a good woman. And he prayed that he would one day be part of a loving family and a safe community where he would fit in and be of value. And Creator chose to bless them both with all that they had asked for and more. And for a brief, but profoundly meaningful period, Creator blessed them both with Embato, and he with them. In His divine way, Creator provided the unique circumstance which brought the three together and which ultimately fostered their inter-dependence and respect for each other.

All three were deeply spiritual people who endured hardships throughout the early portion of their lives that many would not have survived. But even with the incredible odds against them, they persevered and never gave up. Their ability to survive was fueled by their abiding faith *in* and devotion *to* a loving God, their Creator. And He blessed all three of them in return for their love and devotion with the one unique human virtue that can sustain when all others have been exhausted..........hope.

ACKNOWLEDGEMENTS

I am most thankful to the Ancestors who preserved and/or contributed to the oral history or to the historical context of this work before their passing:

Thomas Martin Popperville, Cap'n Tom, Hyde Co. & Washington, NC 1885-1980

Ara Bennett Reynolds Popperville, Rockingham and Washington, NC 1885-1985

Robert Poperwil, Lowland, NC 1887-1989

Virginia Gray Popperville Quick, Hyde Co., Washington, DC, Durham, NC 1922-2008

Esdale Popperville Shepherd, Pamlico Co., Washington, NC 1920-1988

Viola Bullard Parsons, Rowland, NC 1935-2010

Carl and Joyce Bornfriend, Frisco Native American Museum, Frisco, NC, for facilitating my Journey Home

Hope Shepherd Van Dorp, NC, for remembering

Leonard T. Shepherd, NC, for your persistant research

Carol Christian West, Durham, NC, for your editing skills and encouragement

Allison Kaitlan Parsons, for your editing skills and love

Sallie Greif Parsons, for sharing Jewish life and culture and two great children

Charles Eagletail, Silver Spring, MD for living and teaching the Traditional Ways

Charles Sweet Medicine Shepherd, Fayetteville, NC for sharing Mattamuskeet history

Daniel FireHawk Abbott, Jamestown, VA and Eastern Shore, MD, for displaying, teaching, and keeping our primitive Coastal Algonquin skills alive

Marco Gibbs & Family, Englehard, NC, for sharing your knowledge of my people

Code Thiam, Silver Spring, MD for sharing Senegal and Wolof linguistics
KaeLi Spiers and staff of **Outer Banks History Center, Manteo, NC**
Linda Molloy and **James Charlet**, Chicamacomico Life-SavingStation Historic Site and Museum, Rodanthe, NC
Fells Point Maritime Museum, Baltimore, MD
Reginald F. Lewis Museum of Maryland African American History & Culture, Baltimore, MD
R.S. Spencer and membership, Hyde County Historical Society, Swan Quarter, NC
Pamela Sawyer, Hyde County Register of Deeds, Swan Quarter, NC
Dorothy Redford, Somerset Place, Slavery-Plantation Life, Creswell, NC
The Old Slave Mart Museum, Charleston, SC
Nina Poperwil Holloman, Williamston, NC
Joan Charles, Volunteers and staff of The Mariners' Museum, Newport News, VA
Irmina Ulysse, for sharing your version of Haitian Culture
Lou Anne Nesbit, for your editing input
Shaheen Akinitsisahn Richardson Day, for your creative artwork
Walter Day, for your legacy
The Virginian Pilot Microfilm & Archives Dept.
American Beacon, Archives, Norfolk, VA
North Carolina Gazette, Archives
Baltimore County Public Library, Towson, MD
Museum of the American Indian, Smithsonian, Washington, DC

CHARITIES SUPPORTED

A portion of the sale from this book will be equitably distributed to the following charities:

J/P Haitian Relief Organization (Founded by Sean Penn)

The Kichwa Santa Domingo Community of Archidona, Ecuador

Made in the USA
Middletown, DE
09 April 2016